The People of Godlbozhits

Judaic Traditions in Literature, Music, and Art
Harold Bloom and Ken Frieden, *Series Editors*

The People of
Godlbozhits

LEYB RASHKIN

Translated from the Yiddish by Jordan Finkin
With an Introduction by David Rechter

Syracuse University Press

For a listing of books published and distributed by Syracuse University Press,
visit www.SyracuseUniversityPress.syr.edu.

ISBN: 978-0-8156-3552-9 (hardcover)
978-0-8156-1092-2 (paperback)
978-0-8156-5418-6 (e-book)

Library of Congress Cataloging-in-Publication Data
Names: Rashkin, Leyb, 1903 or 1904–1939. | Finkin, Jordan D., 1976– translator. |
Rechter, David, 1958– writer of introduction. |
Title: The people of Godlbozhits / Leyb Rashkin ; translated from the Yiddish
by Jordan Finkin ; with an introduction by David Rechter.
Other titles: Mentshn fun Godlbozhits. English
Description: First edition. | Syracuse, New York : Syracuse University Press, 2017. |
Series: Judaic traditions in literature, music, and art | Includes bibliographical references. |
Description based on print version record and CIP data provided by publisher; resource not viewed.
Identifiers: LCCN 2017026007 (print) | LCCN 2017027955 (ebook) | ISBN 9780815654186 (e-book)
| ISBN 9780815635529 (hardcover : alk. paper) | ISBN 9780815610922 (pbk. : alk. paper)
Subjects: LCSH: Jews—Poland—Fiction. | Shtetls—Poland—Fiction. | Poland—
History—1918–1945—Fiction. | Jewish fiction. | GSAFD: Historical fiction.
Classification: LCC PJ5129.R315 (ebook) | LCC PJ5129.R315 M4513 2017 (print) |
DDC 839/.133—dc23
LC record available at https://lccn.loc.gov/2017026007

To the memory of

MAURICE FRIEDBERG

Contents

The People of Godlbozhits
1

Translator's Foreword

Leyb Rashkin's *The People of Godlbozhits* is a big novel, with big ideas, and a big cast of characters—characters who, at times, can be vulgar, venal, venial, and even villainous. And when all is said and done, that is the great appeal of the book, a vivid cross-section not so much of the fortes and foibles of the denizens of that shtetl, but of their dense and complicated web of humanity. At six hundred pages in the original Yiddish it offers a daunting prospect, but its brisk and oftentimes lively prose—what one commentator detracts as "blatant journalistic devices" and another lauds as "charming" pamphleteering—debunks that apprehension.[1]

Leyb Rashkin (pen name of Shol Fridman; 1903/4–39) was born in the shtetl Kuzmir (in Polish, Kazimierz Dolny nad Wisłą), the prototype for the shtetl Godlbozhits.[2] While writing short stories on the side, he had several jobs, including as administrator for a Jewish cooperative bank, an institution that figures prominently and critically in the novel. *The People of Godlbozhits*, Rashkin's only novel, was published in 1936 and won the Peretz Prize of the Polish Jewish PEN club in 1938.[3] Rashkin would ultimately perish while fleeing the Nazis to the

---

1. Chone Shmeruk, "Jews and Poles in Yiddish Literature in Poland between the Two World Wars," *Polin: a Journal of Polish-Jewish Studies* 1 (1986): 184; Y. Y. Trunk, *Di yidishe proze in poyln in der tekufe tsvishn beyde velt-milkhomes* (Buenos Aires: Tsentral-farband fun poylishe yidn in argentine, 1949), 101.

2. Shmeruk, "Jews and Poles," 184.

3. Leonard Prager, "Rashkin, Leyb," Jewish Virtual Library, http://www.jewish virtuallibrary.org/jsource/judaica/ejud_0002_0017_0_16454.html; some biographical

Soviet Union. What he left behind was a remarkable microcosmic depiction of a shtetl—indeed, in the words of one critic, a "civilization"—one that would soon cease to exist.

Why this book languishes unfairly in obscurity is a good but not a difficult question. Historically speaking, the Second World War and the author's death at its outset were not, shall we say, auspicious. A six-hundred-page book, moreover, will always be something of a challenge. But of course, translation is key. Without a readership, all works will wither. As Mikhail Krutikov notes

> Of two debuts that were awarded literary prizes—the seventeenth-century historical fantasy *Der sotn in Goray* (Satan in Goray; serialized in 1933; published in book form 1935) by Isaac Bashevis Singer and the realistic shtetl novel *Di mentshn fun Godl-bozhits* (The People of Godl-bozhits; 1936) by Leyb Rashkin—one became famous as the first step in the most successful Yiddish literary career of the twentieth century, whereas the other fell into oblivion because its author perished in the Holocaust.[4]

A carefully crafted public persona with a healthy dose of self-promotion and an active program of translation into English go a long way on the road to a Nobel Prize. But they are not part of Rashkin's story.

The People of Godlbozhits presents the fictional Polish shtetl of Godl-bozhits in the early interwar period, sometime in the 1920s—a toy that had been batted around by great powers in a great war. The running subtext of most of the characters' lives reads like some version of the "just trying to get by" theme. Everyone's a wheeler-dealer of some sort or another, from conniving procurer to fine-upstanding burgher, from rabbi to rabble-rouser. No one's immune from need (of some kind),

---

details differ here from those found in the *YIVO Encyclopedia of Jews in Eastern Europe* (Krutikov, "Yiddish Literature," 2080), and Volf Gliksman, "Rashkin, Leyb," in *Leksikon fun der nayer yidisher literature*, vol. 8 (New York: Alveltlekhn yidishn kulturkongres, 1981), 407–8.

4. Krutikov, "Yiddish Literature," 2070.

and no Jew is immune from the insidious anti-Semitism of the system itself. Though more often than not, the residents of Godlbozhits treat anti-Semitism less as a social ill than as a practical matter, a fact of life. When, for example, the pharmacist, Isidore (Itsik) Sonnenschein's conversion is derided as self-serving and insincere, he may take umbrage and may even express it, but he knows it changes nothing. Indeed, as the plot rolls toward its more roiling and boiling moments at the end of the novel, we see all the more clearly how *plus ça change* . . .

But for all of the virulence and violence of survival—driven out by war, driven to extremes by want, driven to wantonness by demoralization—the Jews in *The People of Godlbozhits* keep coming back, "building and building anew like indefatigable ants."[5] This sense of perseverance becomes something of a maudlin undertone throughout the novel. Kuzmir is a famously picturesque shtetl, and for that reason it was a favorite among artists. At one point in the novel, the editorialist Eyges and the painter Tykociński debate the nature of art and its relation to life. Tykociński is the conservative romantic for whom change is anathema:

> But of course the repairs to the old roofs brought the painter Tykociński to despair. Just when a shingle roof, spotted with green moss like the nostrils of an old snuff-sniffer, begins to bow wearily under the weight of its years and the roof produces a little hump, a little gold hump, just then a Jew starts rolling out a spool of tar and cardboard and spoils the whole effect.
>
> "Barbarians!" Tykociński cries. "Do you even know what you're destroying?"
>
> "And when it's dripping into my bed, is it your concern?" the Jew answers, also with a question.
>
> "Can't you fix it with shingles, like it was?" Tykociński screams.
>
> "Today there aren't fools like there used to be," that petty bourgeois soul yells back down. "Shingles are not so durable, and are three times as expensive . . . It's money! . . ."

5. Trunk, *Di yidishe proze in poyln*, 99.

"Money! Money! . . ." These people would sell everything for money, even their grandfather's spice box, even their grandmother's head kerchief . . .

Eyges goes on to agree, except for Tykociński's too easy dismissal of progress. Tykociński, for his part, rejoinders that

> when I see an old, bowed roof, covered with mildew I am reinvigorated like a tree in springtime. I still remember the flavor of the old Godlbozhits with its polluted stream flowing through the marketplace. And under the water it teemed with mysterious life, and above it a greenish gold mold winding like a magnificent snake, like a kilometer-long colorful serpent through the shtetl. Even when the old-fashioned trash cans were cleared out and removed from the middle of the marketplace—even that I call cultural barbarism. Oldness must not be merely superficial; oldness must have a smell. When painting one must not merely see, but also feel what one's painting. Smell has a tone, a color . . .[6]

Tykociński's romanticization of the smell of garbage cans and its artistic value is meant to be humorous. His intuition that something of value has been irretrievably lost in the processes of modernity is far more serious. That the value of the past is left to a writer and a painter—to artists—to debate and to depict presents us with Rashkin's own novelistic rationale.

In his book on Yiddish literature in interwar Poland, literary critic Y. Y. Trunk devoted a brief chapter to Rashkin. In it he compares Rashkin's novel with the other great Yiddish novel of wartime corruption, Oyzer Varshavski's *Smugglers* (*Shmuglars*; 1920). To Trunk, where Varshavski is a painter, Rashkin is a sketch artist.[7] What they share is a finely tuned sensitivity to the cracks and fissures that the

---

6. Leyb Rashkin, *Di mentshn fun godlbozhits: roman*, 1935 (Warsaw: Yidishe universal-bibliotek, 1936), 210–12.
7. Ibid., 98.

catastrophes of history cause in a community. To Trunk's mind, the First World War—which Trunk sees as the central historical event of both novels (foregrounded in Varshavksi and backgrounded in Rashkin)—irreparably disrupted Jewish communal cohesion in the shtetl, which he describes as "degeneration."[8] Under this rubric as applied to Rashkin's novel, Trunk would no doubt include any number of other forces of modernity. The overarching question the novel asks is whether *change* is the same thing as *degeneration*. In a more jaded moment Rashkin notes how "Godlbozhits was a city of rogues and scoundrels who no matter how much you give them never have enough, and whatever favor you do them will be repaid by being pelted with stones."[9] Tykociński would surely agree. But for the rest of the residents of Godlbozhits, the question of change is far less clear-cut.

There are two axes along which the episodic plot of the novel aligns. The first is the ideological axis, a contest of capital and labor, between reactionary and revolutionary. Several subplots revolve around the machinations of the local leather manufacturers, the brothers Meierbach, and the agitations of their workers. And there is no end to the activities of the local cultural, political, and professional "unions." Bundists, Zionists, Mizrahists, and Communists vie with one another as well as the conservative "elites" and the bourgeois elements for relevance and influence. The novel refers to a number of institutions as a *fareyn*—literally, a union—which includes anything from cultural clubs to political organizations and parties to trade unions. The word occurs frequently in the novel, and in a number of fraught contexts, to the extent that the word itself becomes an ironic symbol for the growing disunity and fractiousness of Jewish life in interwar Poland.

The second axis is familial. The novel's very first chapter—"Pedigree" (*yikhes*)—makes explicit how family is a social tether, no matter how strained or complicated, and that political allegiance is often a function of familial affection or, more often than not,

8. Trunk, *Di yidishe proze in poyln*, 99.
9. Rashkin, *Di mentshn*, 108.

alienation. The great chain of genealogical lineage attests to the inter-generational distribution of antipathies. Many of these antipathies begin to line up along the first axis as well. And it all comes together as a heady cholent indeed.

The novel does not have a single primary plot but rather proceeds along a number of intersecting and tangential tracks. One charac-ter may have a chapter devoted to him only to disappear for three hundred pages before resurfacing nonchalantly. We feel in this the organic flow of life in the shtetl. To the extent that there is a pro-tagonist, it is Shimen Shifris, an orphan taken in by relatives. He is the smart but credulous youth, something of a goody-goody, but ready for intellectual pursuits. It is his journey from simple, religious upbringing, to secular education, work as a bookkeeper in the coop-erative bank, the successes and failures in love, and the eye-opening loss of political innocence that form the moral spine of the novel, scoliotic though it be.

In the great polar opposition that strains at the core of the book, Shimen Shifris's coming-of-age evidences not indifference but an inability to come to terms with the conflict. Class struggle is mirrored in a struggle to understand class. In one scene, Shimen is convers-ing intimately with his paramour, Zosia (Zenia) Lerner, a firebrand Marxist political activist. She acts as the raiser of Shimen's political consciousness but sees in Shimen's political naïveté a reflection of a kind of romantic innocence she desires as an antidote to all the human cruelties and crudities she has experienced. In envisioning their devel-oping relationship, Zosia demands:

> "You won't interfere with my work! Right? You know, Shimen, if you ever set a condition that I must choose between you and my work, I won't give it a minute's thought—I'd choose the latter . . ."
> "I know that," he said in a hushed voice. "I understand that . . ."
> "And that I love you, you know that too?"
> He was silent.
> "Why are you silent?" she searched his sad eyes.
> "But you know . . . I have already experienced . . ."

"Go on, child! You cruel boy!" she kissed his mouth, his eyes. "Go on, you handsome one of mine! I am not Feygele Rabinovitch; I can love, really love . . . sacrifice myself . . ."

And then, with her lush, enthusiastic voice she recounted some of her experiences, but only some, because she was actually a veritable bundle of experiences, and one evening, even a whole week, would not have been enough to tell everything about herself. For Shimen, the serious bookkeeper at Fayvele Shpilman's cooperative bank, every one of her topics was like a sensation. All of the people, feelings, and passions that Zenia talked about with her melodic, charming speech were beyond the limits of Shimen's provincial middle-class experience. Like an adventure tale for children about heroic hunters who do battle with a whole tribe of wild, man-eating Indians, that's how captivated Shimen was by that heroic struggle of the weary workers against the profit-hungry factory owner and his lawful defenders. He envied Zenia's intelligent comrades who sacrificed themselves completely for the workers' cause, who went off to prison and torture, persecutions and hunger for the pure and simple truth that speaks from the books of Karl Marx and his disciples.

In light of such hard, steel will, of such heroic deeds, Shimen cried out as one who had grown small, shattered, "It seems to me that we, petty bourgeois, will always be crushed between those two aggressive forces: the capitalists on the one side and the workers on the other. The former consider our work and our ideas inferior, and the latter don't trust us, they look at us like little parasites."

"You express yourself quite beautifully, Shimen," Zosia said. "Not clearly, but your own way. Did you read those books I gave you?"

But it was as though Shimen hadn't heard the question. Instead of relying on books that he had read he was trotting out his own, Shimen-Shifrisy ideas. He didn't want to be inferior.

"No!" he cried out. "We petty bourgeois are not between the hammer and the anvil. We are a great, great class! We are a great multitude, we are the axle on which the wheel spins. Here are the capitalists above, and here are the workers below, and we, middlemen, spin along by momentum and still always remain the axle . . ." Shimen was charmed by his own words, by his new thought. After

all, being a young petty bourgeois man hadn't been a gloomy existence for him. She, however, Zenia, was not, it seemed, swept along
by his improvisation. His original words made no impression on her.

"You know what, Shimen," she said indifferently, "you still need
to learn so, so much, and above all: to see, to observe reality. You
switch too often from one mood to another. That's the whole psychology of the petty bourgeois class. That is hysteria. You have no
consciousness of certainty. Every petty bourgeois has at one time
been inclined to fantasize about a brilliant capitalist career, and then
another time in turn about becoming a resigned proletarian. A capitalist becomes one of maybe ten thousand; but before our eyes tens
of thousands are proletarianized. So the question is: if indeed a proletarian, then why not a conscious one, a proud one?"

"But we, the petty bourgeois, are nevertheless the axle," Shimen
insisted. Zenia smiled.

"How," she asked, "can one speak about a disoriented, confused
petty bourgeois as an axle? One has to lean on an axle, an axle has to
carry a load, and the petty bourgeoisie are physically and mentally in
the process of decline and disintegration. That is, after all, its visible,
scientifically founded, almost biological, fate."[10]

In Shimen's not quite wholehearted plea for the bourgeoisie we see a
striving for meaning. Shimen's passion is not for his class per se, but
for the striving itself. In one sense he is trying to impress his intellectual girlfriend, and his "speech" sounds a little like a self-defense. But
the intellectualizing itself intoxicates him. Zosia, whom we later learn
has been in prison for her political agitation, finds his passion quaint
but endearing. Yet for all of his inarticulateness, Shimen has hit upon
a key thematic tension in the novel. He gives a voice of sorts to the
"silent majority" of the class struggle, the Jewish middle class, which
becomes a metaphorical expression for the feeling of being caught
between. And caught-betweenness can be the experience of the individual with reactionaries to the right and revolutionaries to the left;

10. Ibid., 310–12.

the experience of Jews in Poland among anti-Semites all the way from *starosta* (village mayor) to the *Sejm*; or the experience of Poland itself between Russia, Austria, and Germany.

Dafna Clifford notes how the novel understands the shtetl coming to grips with "the corrupting influence of secularism and political radicalism," and how Shimen "experiences the arbitrary brutality of both worlds."[11] This seems right insofar as the evaluation of corruption is in the eyes of a traditional community and traditional values. Shimen's own critique, conservative in its own way, is more modernist, more attuned to his own ambivalences than any ideological dialectic. That is what makes him an "interesting character" and not merely a caricature. As literary critic Chone Shmeruk put it, "It seems that in this book, the familiar, stereotypic, traditional elements which indicate mutual alienation, isolation and contempt are ascribed to the wealthy, and to backward people who are not aware of the import of their deeds and words. True human relationships are determined by class and shaped by ideology."[12] Shifris is the protagonist because he is the uncommitted bourgeois middle-grounder, prone, but not a slave, to these determinacies.

The People of Godlbozhits is not an easy novel to translate. As Trunk puts it, "Both in terms of diction and style, Rashkin's language is full of Polish-Yiddish idioms and localisms—that is the book's personality."[13] While ultimately Trunk may go a little too far in his understanding of the book's ethnographic veracity, there is no doubt of his accuracy in describing the "colorful kaleidoscope of Jewish types in the shtetl."[14]

11. Dafna Clifford, "Shtetl Kuzmir: The Reality of the Image," in *The Shtetl: Image and Reality*, ed. Gennady Estraikh and Mikhail Krutikov (London: Legenda, 2000), 122.

12. Shmeruk, "Jews and Poles," 185.

13. Trunk, *Di yidishe proze in poyln*, 98–99.

14. "From Rashkin's book one can get a fairly clear picture of Jewish life in a Polish shtetl in the period between the two world wars" (Trunk, *Di yidishe proze in poyln*, 101).

Rashkin's language meets the demands of that kaleidoscopic imagination and often puts daunting demands on the translator.

Take, for example, a passage in which the procurer Khaykl, the sexton's son, is salaciously describing the "goods":

> But if you just give me a signal, is getting a girl a problem for me? First-rate, *primo*, Warsaw girls with the real education, the real "twist." Real dolls for sure with great racks, little mouths, "hot-lips" . . . Not that bit of junk with the wide "yap" and a chest, you'll pardon the expression, sunken like a trough . . .[15]

(Incidentally, for the sake of comparison, here is how Dafna Clifford renders the same passage: "'But if you just say the word, is it a problem for me to get you a girl? First class, premier class, Warsaw ladies with real education and with the real 'knack,' in fact, your real dolls with a bosom you can rummage around in and what a mouth, talk about a tasty morsel—absolutely filthy.'")[16]

The word referring to a mouth and rendered alternately as "hot-lips" and "talk about a tasty morsel" is *zhamzhele*. As it was explained to me: "'*zhamzhen*' means 'to chew slowly,' the way old, toothless people chew when they work over a bit of food for a long time with their lips. When one refers to the mouth of a woman as a *zhamzhele* it suggests that it would be a delight to work such a mouth over slowly with one's lips."[17] This is the kind of succulent language that makes a translator cry with delight and frustration. This is one linguistic detail of many in but a few lines of a Yiddish procurer.

A larger stylistic feature poses challenges as well for both translation and interpretation. Rashkin is usually referred to as a realist or a

15. "Nor ven ir git mir a pips, iz bay mir a dayge a meydl? ershter sort, 'pervi sort', varshever pannes mit der emeser bildung, mit dem emesn 'drey', un take di emese lyalkes mit di gorndike buzems un mit a maylekhl, a 'zhamzhele' . . ." (Rashkin, *Di mentshn*, 356–57).

16. Clifford, "Shtetl Kuzmir," 126.

17. Yitskhok Niborski, personal communication.

naturalist writer. His prose, though, is often fairly clipped, notational (I mentioned Shmeruk's assessment earlier: "journalistic"). There is also often a fairly loose interchange between quoted speech and *style indirect libre*. This refers to a technique in which a third-person report of speech uses the diction and style as if it were quoted. In this way style indirect libre offers a means of muddling the distinctions between interior and exterior, between the "I" and the "it." For his part, Rashkin does not seem to be consistent about when he chooses to use this device or not. But sometimes in moving from quotation to report and back to quotation, he blends the associative and dissociative; in a speech by the factory owner Moritz Meierbach, say, we are meant to see his words simultaneously as those of a single character who is a leather manufacturer and those of all industrialists.

Names, too, can be somewhat fluid. Naming conventions were not hard and fast, and many of the characters used descriptive names instead of their surnames. For example, occupations are common: *komashnmakher* (bootmaker), *garber* (tanner); as are associated characteristics or evaluative monikers such as *meshumed* (scoundrel) and *Kozak* (Cossack). Khaykl is referred to as the sexton's son (*dem shamess zun*), which reappears in an amusing connection near the end of the novel. Khaykl is trying as usual to get out of a scrape and is giving information to a prosecutor, who makes a call to another official regarding Khaykl:

> "Hallo . . . Pan Wojciechowicz? . . . *Tak, tak* . . . We spoke yesterday . . . From Godlbozhits . . . Ah, *nie* . . . A trustworthy person . . . On my responsibility . . . A thoroughly honest person . . . Right away . . . I'll send him to you . . . His family? Pan, Pan . . . Khaykl . . ."
>
> "Szameszson," Khaykl helped.[18]

Khaykl supplies the prosecutor an ersatz Polish surname that sounds like a plausible patronymic. Khaykl is ever light on his feet and fleet of tongue, in this case a feat of *legerdelangue* meant to save him from exposing his embarrassing Jewishness.

---

18. Rashkin, *Di mentshn*, 519.

This creation of Polishness, puckishly satirized by Khaykl, is an important concern for the critics who write about the novel. Shmeruk and Clifford, the most recent voices on the subject, both give details of Rashkin's engagement with Polish language, culture, and literature (especially the classic Polish playwright Stanisław Wyspiański's 1901 play *The Wedding* [*Wesele*]). It is a complicated relationship, to be sure, and one which some see as the novel's ultimate criticism. As Trunk opines, "In Rashkin's book the shtetl disintegrates something like a legitimately dialectical antithesis to the great and ancient *synthesis* of Jewish life in Poland."[19] In this connection I have opted to retain the Polish forms of address when they are used in the original text. After all, part of the novel's energy has to do with the Polonized and Polonizing Jewish bourgeoisie, for whom the gradations of their facility with the Polish language really mattered.

In a shtetl of vibrant personalities, one of the more colorful features is the name itself: Godlbozhits. Dafna Clifford etymologizes:

> Indeed, the Yiddish sonorities of the name "Godlbozhits" hide a Polish substructure, *godlo*, or emblem, in the sense here of a national emblem, and *boznica*, the Polish for synagogue. Thus the novel is a study of the archetypal Polish Jewish small town, viewed from the historical perspective where the shtetl was [citing Eugenia Prokopówna] "that place where the Scriptures are studied, where in the synagogue and the *besmedresh* the simple and learned, poor and rich discuss and deepen their knowledge of God's truth." While showing us that the shtetl is no longer the embodiment of Jewish spirituality [I must ask, by way of aside, was it ever such an embodiment?] Rashkin also considers what identity, if any, is possible for the town once the connection to the synagogue is no longer central to the lives of its inhabitants.[20]

As attractive as such an assessment may be, Clifford falls into the pitfall of conflating actual shtetls and literary shtetls, and I assert that this

19. Trunk, *Di yidishe proze in poyln*, 98.
20. Clifford, "Shtetl Kuzmir," 116.

is an essential distinction.[21] In the *literary* shtetl that is Godlbozhits, even when we step back into the "pre-decay" stage in the first chapter, the synagogue never functioned that way.

As for the etymology, Clifford is right that with a name like Godl-bozhits, we feel the need to etymologize. Less strained and slightly more straightforward would be something along the lines of the ironizing or satirical naming tradition in Yiddish and Hebrew literature from the mid-nineteenth century: to give a few examples, *Glupsk* ("Dummy-town"), *Kabtsansk* or *Kabtsiel* ("Beggarsville"), *Kisalon* ("Foolsburgh"), and *Loyhoyopol'* ("Neverwasford"). In this case we see *godl*, from Hebrew for big or great; *boż-*, from Polish for God; and a kind of locative suffix. All together this makes the name an ironically inflected "Big God Country." Everyone had his big god to serve, whether Bolshevism, baronial capitalism, or a belly aching with hunger. Whatever God it was, who believed in Him is certainly open to interpretation.

Jordan Finkin

Bibliography

Clifford, Dafna. "Shtetl Kuzmir: The Reality of the Image." In *The Shtetl: Image and Reality*, edited by Gennady Estraikh and Mikhail Krutikov, 115–32. London: Legenda, 2000.

Gliksman, Volf. "Rashkin, Leyb." In *Leksikon fun der nayer yidisher literature*, vol. 8, 407–8. New York: Alveltlekhn yidishn kultur-kongres, 1981.

Krutikov, Mikhail. "Yiddish Literature: Yiddish Literature after 1800." In *The YIVO Encyclopedia of Jews in Eastern Europe*, vol. 2, edited by Gerson David Hundert, 2065–84. New Haven, CT: Yale Univ. Press, 2008.

Prager, Leonard. "Rashkin, Leyb." Jewish Virtual Library. http://www.jewish virtuallibrary.org/jsource/judaica/ejud_0002_0017_0_16454.html.

Rashkin, Leyb. *Di mentshn fun godlbozhits: roman*. 1935. Warsaw: Yidishe universal-bibliotek, 1936.

21. See Jeffrey Shandler, *Shtetl: A Vernacular Intellectual History* (New Brunswick, NJ: Rutgers Univ. Press, 2014), especially chapter 1, 7–49.

Shandler, Jeffrey. *Shtetl: A Vernacular Intellectual History.* New Brunswick, NJ: Rutgers Univ. Press, 2014.

Shmeruk, Chone. "Jews and Poles in Yiddish Literature in Poland between the Two World Wars," *Polin: A Journal of Polish-Jewish Studies* 1 (1986): 176–95.

Trunk, Y. Y. *Di yidishe proze in poyln in der tekufe tsvishn beyde velt-milkhomes,* chapter 16, 97–101. Buenos Aires: Tsentral-farband fun poylishe yidn in argentine, 1949.

Acknowledgments

Though the work of translating can at times occur in solitude, it is never a solitary endeavor. I have had the immense benefit of a number of keen intellects and generous individuals who have offered insights and suggestions at every stage of this project. I must heartily thank Seth Wolitz, whose knowledge of this novel's world and the implications of these literary works is simply capacious, and by whose support and encouragement of my work I am humbled; Gennady Estraikh and Yitskhok Niborski, whose help puzzling through opaque Yiddish idioms was inestimable; Allison Schachter, whose suggestions helped winnow coherent wheat from garbled chaff; and Margalit Tal, who helped me work through some Polish idiomaticness, which I never would have been able to tackle on my own.

David Rechter wrote the truly splendid introduction to this book. I am enriched to know him as a scholar and a friend.

Syracuse University Press has been a pleasure to work with at every stage. The Press sees value in promoting not only fine works of scholarship but also literary translations, and that is a boon from which we all benefit. My particular thanks are due to Deborah Manion for her professionalism and enthusiasm.

Translating a six-hundred-page Yiddish novel does not happen in a day. Or a year. For their forbearance, love, energy, humor, and the hundreds of kindnesses great and small I have greedily accepted over the course of this undertaking, my wife, Sarah, and our two boys, Dashiell and Emmett, deserve far more than these words of undying thanks and appreciation. My parents, Eleanor and Matthew, have supported me through this and all of my various projects. And while they always say thanks are not necessary, I offer them lovingly nonetheless.

Introduction

Fact and Fiction in Kazimierz Dolny

It is possible to read the entire sprawling narrative of *The People of Godlbozhits* without knowing a great deal about the real world in which these fictional folk are embedded, since reality in the novel serves merely as a backdrop to the emotional combat zone that constitutes the core of the book and that engages the reader throughout. But it is the historical reality of Jewish life that makes the characters who they are and that intrudes upon them throughout the book. We are plunged headlong into small-town Polish Jewish life in the 1920s and, while it is not strictly necessary to have a firm grasp of the details of the time and place of the novel's setting, understanding its fundamentals might nonetheless be helpful for an appreciation of the stories that unfold in Godlbozhits.

First and foremost, this is a world—Polish Jewry—that is no more. Dispatched into oblivion by Nazi Germany during the Second World War, Jews had lived in Poland since at least the twelfth century. By the beginning of the eighteenth century, Polish Jewry—living in what after 1569 was called the Polish-Lithuanian Commonwealth—had become the world's largest Jewish population. In the late eighteenth century, as Poland-Lithuania was divided up by its three powerful neighbors to the east and west, its approximately 750,000 Jews were dispersed among Tsarist Russia, Habsburg Austria, and Prussia, with the majority finding themselves under Russian rule. (A little more than two million Jews lived in Europe at that time, around 90 percent of the world's Jewish population.) In the new, or reborn, Polish Republic of 1918, most of these Jews were "reunited," although their divergent nineteenth-century experiences left an indelible mark on their culture, religion, and politics. Interwar Poland was home to just over three million Jews (3.1 million according to the 1931 census), some 10 percent of the general population and one-third of the urban population. In the eastern provinces, the proportion of Jews was even higher, exceeding 50 percent in many towns and villages.

It has long been a useful historiographical convention to conceive of Jewish history in modern Europe, from the middle of the eighteenth century, as a story of East and West, with the imaginary border between them dividing the premodern from the modern, the unemancipated from the emancipated, the unassimilated from the assimilated. This view reflects the common identification of Eastern Europe as a relatively backward and underdeveloped region, the mirror image of the "modern" West. By the late nineteenth century, Western European Jewry was a comparatively small religious-ethnic minority that had rapidly acculturated and modernized, whereas Eastern European Jewry was far more numerous, remained devoted to its own religion and culture, and mostly rejected assimilation or acculturation. While this is no more than a set of broad descriptive generalizations, it is nonetheless a convenient way of grasping some of this history's basic outlines. Interwar Poland was perhaps the classic example of an Eastern European Jewry.

The development of Polish Jewry in the 1920s and 1930s was of course dependent on political and economic conditions within Polish society. In brief outline, unstable center-right coalition governments maintained an embattled democracy until 1926, when the war hero Józef Piłsudski engineered a military coup and installed an authoritarian and paternalistic regime that survived until his death in 1935. From that point, Poland's military rulers—"the colonels"—became increasingly right-wing, nationalist, and quasi-fascist. The Catholic Church was very powerful in a society that was conservative, predominantly agrarian, strongly nationalistic, and relatively underdeveloped economically. Interwar Polish governments worked on the assumption that Poland was, or at least ought to be, a Polish nation-state; in other words, a state in which the Polish nation was the dominant force. In reality, however, one-third of the country's population was not Polish, but rather was composed of large minorities of Jews, Ukrainians, Belorussians, and Germans. In keeping with this approach, the state refused, for example, to subsidize Jewish education, as it was reluctant to encourage what it regarded as separatism. Its economic and social policies, too, worked against Jews, particularly in the 1930s. It was difficult for Jews to find employment in state enterprises such as schools, banks, and railroads; Sunday trade was prohibited, an obvious difficulty for Jews, since many did not work or trade on Saturday; and taxes were weighted against the urban (read: Jewish) population. Polish governments viewed these policies not so much as anti-Jewish, but rather as pro-Polish, which unfortunately often amounted to the same thing. The consequences of this cumulative social, economic, and political pressure were progressive Jewish impoverishment and a widespread sense of mounting crisis.

If barriers to Jewish acculturation remained strong in such an environment, the Polish Republic was nonetheless a functioning, if imperfect, democracy that was sufficiently pluralistic to allow for a remarkably dynamic Jewish society. The decades following the First World War saw a spectacular expansion of modern, secular forms of culture and politics. Hundreds of daily and weekly newspapers, mostly in Yiddish but also in Polish and Hebrew, appeared across the land. Jewish dailies in Warsaw enjoyed a circulation at their peak of almost 100,000. Yiddish theater flourished, attaining unprecedented popularity. Professional and amateur theater companies performed in hundreds of towns and cities, their audience mainly drawn (unlike general theater) from the poor and working classes. Poland was a major center of Yiddish literature, while Yiddish cinema also reached a wide audience—both local and international. Two of the most famous and successful of all Yiddish films—*The Dybbuk* and *Yidl mitn Fidl*—were in fact filmed in "Godlbozhits" (i.e., Kazimierz Dolny). Vilna was home to the most important institution in the development of modern Jewish scholarship, YIVO (the Jewish Scientific Institute), which in 1940 relocated to New York. Jewish education prospered as never before, with the competing Yiddishist, Orthodox, and Zionist/Hebraist school networks, along with the many state schools that catered exclusively to Jews, attracting hundreds of thousands of pupils.

Jewish politics was equally vibrant, spanning the ideological spectrum from left to right. Jewish political parties engaged in intense and fractious competition for support among Jews, while at the same time endeavoring to represent Jewish interests on the Polish political scene. These parties, and the movements from which they emerged, succeeded in mobilizing hundreds of thousands of supporters; youth movements were particularly popular, reflecting a deep sense of unease among younger generations regarding their future in Poland. Jewish politics was proverbially divisive and conflict-ridden, divided between assimilationists of various stripes, Hasidic and anti-Hasidic orthodoxy, and a bewildering variety of nationalist and Zionist parties: socialist, religious, extreme left-wing and right-wing Zionists, anti-Zionist diaspora nationalists, territorialists (socialist and otherwise), Bundists, and Folkists. Achieving even a semblance of unity among these bitterly antagonistic ideologies proved to be an impossible challenge.

The overtly internal focus of so much of Polish Jewish culture, politics and education were driven and sustained by the continuing ambivalence about Jews felt by broad segments of Polish society (reflected also in low rates of intermarriage and conversion). The Jewish economic profile, too, was distinct. While the majority of Poles were engaged in agriculture, most Jews—as one would expect from an urban population—were employed in commerce, industry, or the professions, and were far more likely than Poles to be self-employed. Jews occupied certain niches in the Polish economy: they made up almost half of all workers in the clothing industry and one-quarter of those in the food industry; few, however, worked in heavy industry. A small Jewish bourgeoisie was very important to the Polish urban economy, as was the narrow stratum of wealthy industrialists, merchants, and bankers, but Polish Jews were predominantly lower middle or working class, earning a living as small shopkeepers or in trades and handicrafts of all sorts, such as tailors, bakers, carpenters, shoemakers, and watchmakers. In this poorly balanced ethnic economy, poverty was a significant problem; prospects for improvement were dim and there was little expectation of assistance from Polish sources. As in cultural and political life, this too generated a kind of parallel society, in which hundreds of thousands of people received aid from local and national Jewish welfare and charity groups—orphanages, health care, credit unions, interest-free loan associations—sponsored by political parties, merchants' associations, private individuals, and Jewish communities.

Throughout the interwar period, then, Polish Jews constituted a large minority with a distinct economy, religion, language, culture, and politics; an urban people in a peasant country, they were, by and large, unassimilated. Acculturation and integration did of course exist, and must not be discounted. Nonetheless, it remains mostly true that Polish Jews were *in* Poland but not entirely *of* Poland.

The immediate historical background to the novel is the First World War (also known as the Great War), the most devastating and violent conflict the world had seen to that point, a catastrophe of unprecedented scope that killed and wounded tens of millions of people. Widely known as the "war to end all wars," it was unfortunately nothing of the sort. In Jewish historiography and collective memory, the Great War has long been overshadowed by the incomparably greater disaster of the Second World War and the Holocaust. But at the time, and for the following generation, the First World War was understood as a trauma of immense proportions for millions of Jews in Eastern Europe. A recurring Jewish refrain was that "while everyone is suffering, we are suffering more." Perhaps in this instance they had a point: a great deal of the fighting on the Eastern front took place in what were the most densely populated Jewish areas in Europe. The fabric of Eastern European Jewish society unraveled as nearly one million Jews were displaced by the spring of 1915, uprooted by the Russian military advance into the Polish lands and into Habsburg Galicia and Bukovina.

In areas occupied by the Russian army, its troops wreaked havoc: they carried out pogroms, indulged in mass rape, looted and destroyed homes, took thousands of Jews hostage, and press-ganged many others into forced labor. During these years of instability and insecurity, hundreds of Jewish towns and communities were decimated. Even the armistice in November 1918 did not bring an end to Jewish misery. Winston Churchill is said to have remarked to then–British Prime Minister David Lloyd George: "the war of the Giants has ended; the quarrels of the pygmies have begun."[1] For the Jews, tragically, these quarrels were deadly. In November 1918 in Lemberg, for example, nearly a hundred were killed and many more were wounded as Poles and Ukrainians battled for control of the former Habsburg city. Between 1918 and 1920, perhaps 60,000 Jews were killed in pogroms in the areas fought over by Polish, Ukrainian, and Soviet forces, and as late as 1921 over 200,000 Jews were still homeless. By that point, it was generally assumed that the worst was over and that the disasters were a thing of the past. International borders were nearly stable, the various wars had run their course, and Jewish rights to state protection of their religious, educational, and cultural activities were nominally guaranteed by international agreement.

Kazimierz Dolny (Kuzmir in Yiddish), Leyb Rashkin's hometown and the model for Godlbozhits, was spared some of the worst ravages of the war years. Following the ejection of the Russians, who had ruled since the late eighteenth century, it was occupied by the Austrians from mid-1915 until war's end in 1918—a period that provides the loose scaffolding for the novel's early chapters. Real events work their way into the story: as the Austrian army advances (sometimes generically called "Germans") the Russians expel the Jews from the town and the characters talk of Cossacks, hangings, and pogroms. Similarly reality-based is the account of the nearly two hundred Jews who drowned in the Vistula River in November 1916, returning home from work digging trenches for the Austrians near the town of Janowiec on the far side of the river. Kazimierz Dolny, however, escaped the fate of cities

---

1. Norman Davies, *White Eagle, Red Star: The Polish-Soviet War 1919–1920 and 'The Miracle on the Vistula'* (London: Macdonald, 1972), 21.

such as Vilnius or Czernowitz, which were occupied and reoccupied on multiple occasions and suffered the accompanying depredations of the crisscrossing armies, with dreadful consequences for Jews.

Jews had lived in Kazimierz Dolny since at least the fourteenth century, primarily engaged in trade, transporting timber and grain, importing goods and foodstuffs, founding factories (paper, porcelain, glass), and operating breweries and mills. Lying on the right bank of the Vistula River, nearly thirty miles west of Lublin and seventy-five miles southeast of Warsaw, the famously picturesque town became, with the advent of the railroad, a popular summer resort in the later decades of the nineteenth century. By the 1920s, some 1,400 Jews lived in Kazimierz Dolny, approximately 40 percent of the total population. In a word, it was a shtetl, one of the many hundreds of small market towns with a large Jewish population that dotted the Polish countryside. We can certainly spend time with the fictional Jews of Godlbozhits unburdened by any acquaintance with the reality without which they would not, and could not, have existed: the shtetl of Kazimierz Dolny/Kuzmir, the traumas of Eastern European Jewry during the First World War, and the vast and complex world of interwar Polish Jewry. Their stories can be enjoyed without knowing any of this. But a little background knowledge will surely help us to understand the novel, and its people, better.

David Rechter
University of Oxford

The People of Godlbozhits

❖ 1 ❖

Pedigree

The grandfather came from a long line of village Jews. For his whole life, summer and winter alike, he dressed in a wadded kapote, lined with a strong, unrippable material. Only the elbows were worn out of course. The grandmother, a tidy woman, couldn't stand seeing the dirty wadding creeping out of the holes. "Better an ugly patch than a pretty hole"—and she would cut out a patch from one of her old jackets, thread a needle with some old grey thread, and the grandfather's garment once again began life anew.

Nevertheless, the grandfather left behind a decent inheritance. Aside from the patched jackets and kapotes there were two mills, a fine piece of property, some furniture, cattle, horses, as well as a number of debts owed to him by some of the shtetl's respectable Jews, worth several thousands. And all of it given charitably, since the grandfather never lent with interest.

The grandfather used to tell of how he earned everything with his own two hands; from his father—that is, from the great-grandfather, he inherited nothing. On the contrary, the great-grandfather, who had been a tenant of the old lord, was such a poor man that he never had enough to pay his installment of the lease. When angered the lord ordered his Cossack to whip him, and when he, the lord, had a spare moment the grandfather would sing him *Mah-yofis.*[1] But as for evicting his little Jew from the inn—that the lord never did.

---

1. *Mah-yofis* (How Fair Art Thou): the opening words of a Sabbath hymn; to sing or dance *mah-yofis*, however, referred to a degrading performance of Jewishness

And even though the grandfather was a simple Jew, and deceit was alien to him, it was still believed that his ascent to prosperity began with the great-grandfather's servile *Mah-yofis*. The grandfather did once tell of how the land where the walled house by the mill stood, together with the old wooden cottage, had been given as a gift to the great-grandfather by the lord.

And here is how it happened:

The lord once returned with his guests from hunting. Everyone was quite cheerful, as they had shot a great number of birds, hares, and other animals. They ate and drank. And *when the heart of the lord was merry with wine,*[2] he says to the Cossack, his servant, "Bring me my little Jew, Yerukhem, right this moment!" (That was the great-grandfather's name.) When the great-grandfather enters, stooped and trembling, the lord says to him, "Yerukhemke, Yerukhem! If you dance *Mah-yofis* for me right here on the table, in your bare shirt, I will give you, once and for all, your inn together with the land on which it stands."

And he burst out laughing, the lord did—he was already apparently quite drunk—and the noblewomen joined in the laughter.

So, what do you suppose happened? The grandfather Yerukhem didn't take long to think it over and threw off his jacket. To get an inn of his own for such a trifle and not to have to suffer any more worries over rent! And when great-grandfather Yerukhem got down to his under-tallis with its black stripes and started shaking its long fringes one of the noblewomen present grew frightened, as if she were witnessing some kind of witchcraft. And from that fear she let out a shriek and fell down in a faint.

The guests, all great lords, suddenly sobered up, taking offense and growing angry at their host for the noblewoman's fright. Only with great effort did the lord convince them to forgive him for the

---

before Polish audiences and eventually came to mean sycophantic or toadying behavior. See Chone Shmeruk, "*Mayufes*: A Window in Polish–Jewish Relations," *Polin: Studies in Polish Jewry* 10 (1997): 273–86.

2. Esther 1:10.

dirty Jew. And all of his wrath was poured out onto the great-grandfather; he was ordered to receive twenty lashes.

But the lord kept his word: the promised gift, the inn, he gave to the great-grandfather. A trifle! Such an insignificant thing for noblemen in those days!

Some say, however, that the grandfather's wealth began with a treasure: a pot of gold coins that the grandfather had dug up from the field the lord had given to him; a treasure that had been buried by the lord's great-great-grandfather in war-ridden times. Somewhere there were supposed to be signs indicating where to find the treasure. But no one could ever learn for certain from the grandfather. The grandfather answered every trick to get him to tell the story of the treasure with a mysterious silence. He only explained that on his travels he often came across valuable finds. Once he found a great sack of grain that he could hardly lift onto his cart. Another time he found an axe by a tree in the middle of the forest. And still another time a coachman's pail in the middle of the road. And once it even came to pass that the grandfather's life was saved by a miracle.

The grandfather always tried to return home from the city when it was still daytime. Once, however, he had to stay in the city a little longer than usual, and when he entered the forest it was already pitch-dark. The grandfather was very frightened because thieves were known to prowl that forest. Suddenly—stop! His horse came to a halt. So the grandfather yelled, "Giddyup!" and gave it the whip. But the horse stood still. The grandfather got down off of the cart to take a look at what was the matter. It was dark so he groped about and found what felt like a log or a tree in the middle of the road. The grandfather was a strong man so he didn't need to give much thought to lifting the log and removing it from the road. But the log let out a cry: "*Meh!* . . . *Meh!* . . ." This rather frightened the grandfather, but he soon discovered that this was no log but . . . a calf, a giant calf. "A real bargain," the grandfather thought to himself, and tried to lift the calf into his cart. But, no go; the calf was much heavier than a log.

Only with great effort, labor, and various kinds of peasant's tricks did the grandfather get the heavy calf up into his cart. He braced the rump, supporting it with a pole, and in this way brought it up and around. From all of this he worked up a good sweat.

So he drove on, hurrying his horse, and when he came to the edge of the forest he suddenly noticed that his cart had grown lighter. He looked around—the calf was not there. So the grandfather got down off the cart and took a look behind the cart; for all that, what a loss, such a valuable find! Maybe it fell off not too far back . . . But then he, the grandfather, heard a *"Ha-ha-ha!"* and *"Ha-ha-ha!"* and *"Ha-ha-ha!"* Laughter, human laughter, that made the whole forest echo. The grandfather lifted his eyes and there, standing in the middle of the road, was a demon with his tongue sticking out down to his belt, giggling . . . It was more dead than alive that the grandfather made it home.

And when people asked the grandfather in his later years, "Grandfather, tell us what a demon looks like," the grandfather answered evasively, "These days demons are no longer common. Hasidic rabbis have driven them off into the desolate wildernesses. Fearful folk like you've got today couldn't handle it."

———◆———

One thing is certain: the grandfather did not need to depend on the lord's benevolence. The young prince, the old lord's son, was always off abroad, and there in those foreign theaters he likely heard far more beautiful songs than the great-grandfather's *Mah-yofis*. Bit by bit he had squandered all of his inherited estate. One portion he sold, one portion he subdivided, and one portion the peasants tore right apart. Nor did the grandfather stand idly by: he bought up his two mills for next to nothing, and fields and forests besides.

And so it happened that the grandfather himself became a great landowner, a great lord. But then the city with its enticing honors intruded and ruined the grandfather's efforts. The grandfather, who had always been somewhat boorish like a peasant, began in his later years to refine and improve himself. And when he heard the groom's sermon at his younger son's wedding he said to himself, "Abandon all your fields and forests for one word of the holy Torah."

It started with a good deed. The grandfather was a very hospitable person. One could justly say that whoever came to him hungry left full. On the grandfather's farm there was an especially large house for guests. Bread, butter, and sour milk were never absent from the table. No Jew passing through the village ever left without praying and eating his fill. For lunch there were great pots of borsht. In the grandfather's village no Jew could die of hunger.

A story is told how the great timber merchant Reb Itshe-Volf once bought a forest in the area.[3] As a result, people started gathering in the grandfather's guest house: merchants, brokers, and woodsmen. Every day fresh cheeses were set by the hearth, but they never stayed long enough to dry out since people kept snatching them down. This company of woodsmen was quite a company of trenchermen. No evil eye! The grandfather happily indulged them. But why was it that Reb Itshe-Volf himself was often absent? The company of woodsmen gave each other looks. "Hmmm . . . Hmmm . . ." You're thinking Reb Itshe-Volf was not a good Jew? While there was no question of his wealth, you ought to know that Reb Itshe-Volf was also a very learned man, the greatest scholar, the wisest man in the city, a contemplative Jew and a most God-fearing man. It was no mean thing to be an "Itshe-Volf." He observed his Jewishness to the smallest detail They, the woodsmen, were quite doubtful whether such a Jew as Reb Itshe-Volf would partake of anything, willy-nilly, in an unfamiliar house.

To this the grandfather responded that for him it was not "willy-nilly an unfamiliar house," and that even a Jew like Reb Itshe-Volf was not exempt from helping another Jew fulfill the commandment to welcome guests.

"Well then," the woodsmen answered dismissively.

The grandfather said no more about it. But one time he did get up very early, took his knotty stick in his hand, and set out on the road. The grandfather had to wait for quite a long time, having forgotten

3. In Yiddish, Reb is a form of address used before a man's first name, the rough equivalent of Mr. in English.

that wealthy Jews don't rise so early and that such a Jew as Reb Itshe-Volf would not leave before praying. At about eight o'clock the timber merchant came riding by in his own britzka. The grandfather approached him:

"Good morning, Reb Itshe-Volf."

None too happily the wealthy man ordered his Gentile driver to stop the britzska.

"Good morning, a good year. What do you want?"

"Is something wrong," asked the grandfather *prosto z mostu*,[4] "that would keep Reb Itshe-Volf from ever stopping at my house? Does Reb Itshe-Volf not know that a Jew lives in this village and that one ought to give him the pleasure of performing a good deed?"

"Are there so few good deeds in the world," asked the timber merchant, "that the welcoming of guests is necessary?"

"There you have it," said the grandfather, "there's no synagogue here, and I'm just not able to study the little letters."[5]

"My dear sir, I just don't eat when away from home," he said, wanting to extricate himself, "for fear of lax standards of kosher butchery."

"Meat we eat but once a week," replied the grandfather, "and our milk, cheese, and butter are the most kosher. My wife herself supervises the dairy."

"Be off in good health!" The merchant was growing impatient. "Why are you being so bothersome?" And to his driver, "Macieju, drive!"

But the grandfather held back the horses.

"You'll please get down, eat up, and then you may drive on," he said quite calmly.

"Such a strange impertinence from a village Jew!" cried the wealthy man.

"You had better come with me," said the grandfather, still calm but already starting to get a little agitated.

4. *prosto z mostu* (Polish): bluntly.
5. *kleyne oysyelekh* (Yiddish): literally, little letters, refers to Jewish sacred texts.

"Show respect, ignoramus!"

"You really should be coming along with me," the grandfather asserted, now angry.

And when Reb Itshe-Volf tried to argue the grandfather raised his knotty stick, "I've already told you! I won't break your bones! *Mne!* A Jew should want the whole Leviathan and the Wild Ox?!⁶ And what am I? Maybe not a Jew?"

So, do you suppose after that Reb Itshe-Volf *wasn't* the grandfather's guest? And what an odd guest! Listen and be amazed: He, Reb Itshe-Volf, then became the grandfather's in-law.

That pedigree, which the grandfather got stuck with, was perhaps his greatest misfortune; otherwise his children's children to this day would still be healthy, well-established farmers.

And maybe this was the problem: the city was too close; and it, the city, was too enticing, with its comfort, refinement, and easy profits.

In any event, from that day on Reb Itshe-Volf was a regular guest at the grandfather's house, often staying for the Sabbath. And those were real Sabbaths—true rabbinical events with Torah and all good things.

It's all much easier said than done.

The grandfather really was a completely honorable man, but he was still a villager in a caftan, and Reb Itshe-Volf was the ample burgher with the lambskin hat and the polecat-fur coat. Furthermore, in the matter of the "little letters," there was a minor difference: Reb Itshe-Volf knew three hundred pages of Talmud by heart, while the grandfather "also" knew how to recite aloud a chapter of Psalms from the prayer book. In short, from time immemorial there had never been such a pair of in-laws. And nevertheless the fact remains: the grandfather's younger son married Reb Itshe-Volf's daughter.

That said, everything must have its cause, and in this case the cause was the fact that one bright, beautiful day Reb Itshe-Volf learned that

6. In Jewish folklore the whole Leviathan and the Wild Ox are the two delicacies to be served to the righteous when the Messiah has come.

he was, God preserve us, out of business. As it neared Danzig a large raft of his lumber was scattered by the wind in every direction so that no two pieces of that wood could ever be gathered back together again. To that misfortune was added such a great fall in the price of lumber that it didn't even pay to chop it down, and he had to forfeit his deposit to the noblemen. Which is the long way of saying Reb Itshe-Volf had lost, God preserve us, his swagger, and only had a little money left. With no other alternative he began to borrow on credit, where possible. Reb Itshe-Volf had actually always been a debtor, with various monies in dowries and lawsuits. The difference being, however, that where once people brought those monies to him as a trustworthy man, now he had to borrow at a cambio, to pay interest, and, in order to get that money, to visit such holes and such creatures he would never before have had anything to do with. And one should know that in those days it was something unknown to go to banks for such loans.

In short, around Chanukah time Reb Itshe-Volf borrowed from the grandfather a thousand rubles due back at the beginning of the month of Adar. But by Purim no money had been repaid. Then it was the beginning of the month of Nisan, and Reb Itshe-Volf had made no appearance.[7]

On the eve of Passover the grandfather rode into the city to buy matzah. When he inquired of some people after Reb Itshe-Volf's finances, they answered, "As secure as in the bank." But when he asked someone else he was told how Reb Itshe-Volf was quite short on capital. So the grandfather thought it best to ask Reb Itshe-Volf himself.

The grandfather entered Reb Itshe-Volf's house through the kitchen door—the grandfather hated barging in through the main entrance. Coming into the kitchen he found Reb Itshe-Volf's wife. "Is Reb Itshe-Volf at home?" the grandfather asked. "Left not long ago," was the answer he got.

---

7. Adar is the Jewish month roughly between February and March; Purim is celebrated on the fourteenth of Adar. Nisan is the Jewish month roughly between March and April; Passover begins on the fourteenth of Nisan.

The grandfather was a simple Jew, but he was also a man one had to be careful with. While still outside he had noticed through the window Reb Itshe-Volf's wife saying something into the next room and how her face reddened as she spoke. So the grandfather thought, "I'm being had. He is at home. He's hiding."

"So, why is he hiding from me?" The grandfather grew rather angry as he left the kitchen. "So be it, if he doesn't have the money to pay back the debt then he doesn't have it. But what am I, a bear? Or a thief?"

So he spun his axle right around and headed back into the timber merchant's kitchen.

"You'll pardon me, Reb Itshe-Volf's wife, if I wait here for your husband," the grandfather said, and not waiting for an answer he stretched himself out on the kitchen bench.

A half an hour went by, then an hour. The grandfather saw how agitated Reb Itshe-Volf's wife was getting, pacing back and forth. As they say, what an aggravating nuisance a village Jew can be! But no one spoke; Reb Itshe-Volf was still a debtor who owed a thousand rubles. The grandfather sat as though it had nothing to do with him.

Suddenly the door to the next room opened and in came Reb Itshe-Volf. Ashamed, he hid his face in his beard.

"Forgive me," he said to the grandfather.

The grandfather went into the next room. Reb Itshe-Volf asked him to sit.

"You've come for your money," said Reb Itshe-Volf gloomily, his lips quivering.

"Money, no money," the grandfather said reprovingly, "But why are you hiding from me?"

"I'll tell you the truth," answered Reb Itshe-Volf, "I'm ashamed before you and . . . I'm afraid of you."

"Afraid?" said the grandfather astonished, "What am I, God forbid, a thief? A bear?"

It was either because of the grandfather's speech or his mild face, but Reb Itshe-Volf was reassured so he took hold of his beard and gave his explanation:

"I well remember, Reb . . . Reb . . . Forgive me, what's your name? I well remember the knotty stick you raised at me when I didn't want to get down off my britzska. Having merely offended you, you were ready to tear me apart; how much more so now that I owe you a thousand rubles."

The grandfather was a little embarrassed. He reproached himself, "A Jew causing pain." Then he asked, "Reb Itshe-Volf, can you not repay me the debt now?"

"I cannot now, it's forbidden," said the timber-merchant.

"And when the holiday is over," the grandfather said as if to himself.

"And when the holiday is over," repeated Reb Itshe-Volf.

"And when the holiday is passed," the grandfather continued, "Huh? Offended? Why so quiet? You want to borrow a few hundred more? You're afraid you won't be able to pay it back? Where is your trust, Reb Itshe-Volf?"

So anyway, to cut a long story short . . . The grandfather lent him another three hundred rubles. And a few weeks after Passover Reb Itshe-Volf succeeded in selling a full shipment of lumber, so he was able to pay back the whole debt with a big thank-you bonus since, as was said, the grandfather never took interest.

Reb Itshe-Volf should not have harbored hatred in his heart for a rustic Jew, nor should he have remembered the passage from the Talmud, "A rustic Jew one may tear apart like a fish."[8] Rather he should have conceded that you have to go and learn trust from a village Jew.

Yes. That was quite a story. But miracles don't happen every day, and just as poverty had attached itself to Reb Itshe-Volf, so it didn't want to leave him. He descended lower and lower—and with every passing day he became, God preserve us, a poorer man.

And so it happened that Reb Itshe-Volf married his daughter into the grandfather's family.

And maybe the grandfather wouldn't have wanted to rise to such a height. But on the one hand Reb Itshe-Volf's rebbe himself had

8. Tractate Pesachim 49b.

intervened, a thing from heaven *that* was; and on the other hand the grandfather was well experienced in matchmaking with his first son who, unfortunately, had fallen into crude hands and led a life full of torments. At any rate, it seems the matter was destined to be.

The story of his older son's match was sufficient to show that the grandfather, though a simple man, enjoyed a joke even if it left him with a heavy heart.

That first match the grandfather made with a city miller, a Jew very much like himself. But as it later turned out, he was a rude soul and a miser. After the date of the wedding had been agreed upon, the grandfather asked, for no particular reason, "What does my in-law think is the better way to come, by cart or by train?" (Trains had only recently come into use.)

The grandfather's in-law answered as though speaking to a wearisome dullard, "Go keep your trains! As far as I'm concerned you can slide on your ass."

Well, don't ask . . . The grandfather did slide! Oh, how he slid!

The bride had been seated, the girls danced, the jester sang his celebratory songs, the musicians played—but the in-laws on the groom's side were not there. It turned nine o'clock, ten, then midnight—still no groom. The girls fell off their feet, the candles went out, riders were dispatched, and people worried, maybe some misfortune had befallen them? But nothing: no one had heard or seen anything.

First thing in the morning, at about three o'clock, the in-laws and the groom arrived healthy and in one piece, as though it had nothing to do with them. Well, don't ask what happened then! Fighting nearly broke out. It seemed that the match was on the verge of dissolving when others interceded and made peace. But the bride's shame! First go make a new wedding, then prepare a new feast so the guests might guzzle and gorge themselves. At the thought of it all the miserly miller grew steely.

At the serving of the wedding soup, when he had calmed down a bit, the in-law on the bride's side grumbled irritably, "Couldn't have ridden . . ."

"Didn't ride at all," said the grandfather.

"What does that mean, in-law?"

"It means, we slid . . . according to my in-law's advice."

"My in-law is mocking me! What does that mean, 'slid'?"

"Slid . . . yes . . . *on our ass* . . ."

Oh, the grandfather knew how to play a nasty trick and also how to rub it in. But with this match the grandfather had fallen into the hands of a lout, so he continued to rib these genteel people, and wore himself out badly.

He was what he was, but for his children things went like they do for an evildoer in the next world.

The grandfather's younger son—Yerukhem was his name, after his great-grandfather—didn't lead a sunny life. As a boy he liked horses, which drew him to the mill, to the fields, to the fish pond; but instead he had to sleep in the city at his teacher's house on the bed by the kitchen stove, and to study the holy Torah. Little Yerukhem would always run away from home, and every time he was led back into the *kheyder* with great "pomp." As punishment they would whip the boy in the morning. And the teacher didn't merely whip him with the leather whip, no, all the students held rods in their hands and each one gave him a lash. The custom with such a beating was that if a boy bore the whippee a grudge he gave him a powerful blow, and if he was a "friend" he gave him a light lash, for appearance's sake. But since all of them bore a grudge against this village boy, as against a "Maciek," some Christian kid from the village, each one laid into him with full force. Little Yerukhem never cried—he was stubborn—but he hurt nonetheless, and he swallowed his tears.

Then, when he was married off to Reb Itshe-Volf's daughter, and they stuffed him into a silk coat lined with fur, it went even worse for him: His young, pious wife constantly tormented him with her modesty, with her sevenfold thirty-six immersions in the ritual bath. And it was a very long while before he got used to her.

And, incidentally, the grandfather didn't feel particularly good about all that silk either. Just imagine: for his whole life a man is used to kapotes of peasant material, and now, in old age, at little Yerukhem's wedding, he had to hoist onto himself the "silken garment." But he had better know, people whispered in his ear, that from then on he was Reb Itshe-Volf's in-law.

So, in any event . . . The grandfather told of how it felt so airy in his silk garment that he couldn't shake the feeling he was walking around in his underwear.

However, once Yerukhem had grown accustomed to his wife, and that pious woman had grown accustomed to her husband, it all went as through a bag full of holes. Henele—that was Yerukhem's wife's name—constantly had her belly up to her nose. She was bestrewn with children, like a goat with droppings; a child every year.

After twelve years of living together as man and wife they were missing only two to make a dozen. Their house was always festooned with damp swaddling. Three babies were carried over to the other world from various epidemics: smallpox, scarlet fever, diphtheria . . . A fourth, when already a bigger child, the gravedigger took into the bosom of his large black coat. And then finally, after the respite of some pleasant years, Henele gave birth to a small, actually quite a tiny, baby—two months premature. And with that "scratchling," Henele's womb closed.

That birth took place during the war, while grenades were flying over the shtetl, in a cellar among misery and pain. Its father was not present. Cossacks had dragged Yerukhem off as a "hostage" and hanged him together with a quorum of Jews outside of Prashnik. Of this outrage, of her husband's martyrdom, Henele only learned later when she left her confinement and the Austrians were in the shtetl.

She accepted this misfortune almost with indifference. She said nothing; she neither cried, nor lamented, nor tore the hair from her head. She began to pray a lot, reciting her women's prayers with a dry voice. She recited them day and night, and there was no end to her recitation.

She went mad from her miseries, Henele Reb Itshe-Volf's daughter did, and so finally, one day when no one was at home, she threw herself from the balcony and died with much suffering.

Such an end for two parents and eleven children. The infant was given to one of the peasant women in the village to raise; the rest of the children who were still alive were taken by family in various cities. The grandfather was a very hospitable person, so having his grand-children being warmed and fed at strangers' tables . . . Woe to their parents in their graves.

The oldest of the orphans was named Nosn, and he became a simple worker, a tanner. The next oldest was named Shimen—Shimen Shifris was his name. He was educated, ably wielded a pen, and made a career for himself.

⇥ 2 ⇤

Aunt Mitshe Has Orphans; Little Yosele Violates Yom Kippur "by Coercion"; The Pharmacist Dreams a Dream

When the two miserable little creatures were brought into Aunt Mitshe's house she let out a heavy sigh at the great misfortune that had befallen her sister's house. But even then she thought, "Two more mouths . . ." Because, doing the sums: "Mine, yours, ours, and others'—that now makes eleven, eleven mouths to feed."

"Alas, alas! This awful war . . . Woe to their poor mother in the grave! Her children with their little heads . . . Alas, alas! . . . And of course it's all bathed in milk and honey."

All groaned out, Aunt Mitshe took her warm wool holiday shawl out of the chest—a gift and a remembrance from those good years in Danzig—and even though it was hot outside she wrapped herself tightly in that shawl, took those two miserable creatures by the hand, and went out to see the Jewish pharmacist.

Aunt Mitshe had little babies of her own at home, and all she needed was for those children to catch that foul scabies.

In the pharmacy the pleasant little pharmacist's wife was engaged in a heated argument with the tall *Pan* Władysław, a thin student in a small, worn-out fraternity cap whose leather visor mingled with his blond locks.[1] His father, the Endekist nobleman

---

1. The novel uses many Polish forms of address throughout; the following list indicates the form of address and the appropriate addressee: Pan: a man; Pani: a married woman; Panna: an unmarried woman; Państwo: a married couple; Panie:

15

Galewski,[2] hated him, Pan Władysław, for two things: First, he had wandered about idly for years, neither finishing his studies to become a lawyer nor lifting a finger to help in the economy. Second, he was to be found day and night at the Jewish pharmacist's—the devil knows the idle bum whose business is with Jews!

But Pan Władysław did not like the Jewish pharmacist so much as his pleasant little wife with the dark smoldering eyes; and not so much herself as her hot temper. There he stood—forgetting even to take off his hat—looking with exultant eyes right into her plump red mouth grinding like a mill:

"It seems to me the mobilization went the same for the Christians as the Jews," she said excitedly, "and still the Christians accepted their fate with complete dignity; you never heard a peep. They understand that the earth, where one gets one's bread, for that earth one must bear one's breast and give up one's life. And the Jews—holy mother! What noise, what wailing, what screaming—just like at a Jewish funeral."

Her husband, the pharmacist with the Vandyke beard, who was standing behind the partition mixing a prescription, found it extremely distasteful.

"Stefe, leave Pan Władysław alone. What do you want from him with your stories?"

"Leave him alone? Why leave him alone? It's about time to reform this 'ciemnota,'[3] this 'chałaczarstwo';[4] all of our misfortunes arise from this separation. Why do they say that Jews are spies? Maybe because they jabber in Yiddish? The intelligentsia suffers over them."

---

vocative form, when addressing a man, often used before a title or profession; Panowie: a group of people.

2. Endekist: The National Democratic Party, a Polish nationalist party, founded in 1893 and familiarly referred to as Endecja (a member being an Endek or Endekist), was avowedly anti-Semitic.

3. *ciemnota* (Polish): ignorance

4. *chałaczarstwo* (Polish nonce word): gabardinism, gabardinery (from *chałat*, "gabardine"), referring to the coats traditionally worn by Jews.

"*Prawda . . . prawda,*" the student agreed.[5]

Seeing the Jewish woman with the shawl coming in with the two little Jewish children at her sides the pharmacist's wife called to her husband, "Isidore, come here, *your* customers are here."

And to Pan Władysław:

"Come into the house for a moment, Panie Władysław, I'm not needed here—those are *his* customers . . ."

Pan Władysław smiled happily.

"Ha-ha-ha . . . His customers . . . Well put."

"Oh dear, Mitshe . . ." The pharmacist wondered, "How many children does Mitshe have? Ten, *keynehore*,[6] that I know of, and these snips of things here I haven't seen before."

Well . . . Better that the Pan Pharmacist not ask. God's wrath had been poured out on these children, on these orphans. She, Aunt Mitshe, remembered very well the war with Japan. That's quite a story . . . Maybe ten years ago, maybe more. People said, having read it in the papers, that somewhere over there there was a war going on between the Russians and Japan. When Asher Belfer returned home from his military service he told of many wondrous things, of Kalmyks with their little eyes, and of how at home he, Asher, had been a teacher's assistant, but there among the Russians he became a baker and baked bread for the soldiers. But a war—with people going to the front? In this country? In this very province? That she couldn't remember in her lifetime. And you should know, Aunt Mitshe was no little girl, she didn't turn eighteen yesterday.

The Pan Pharmacist would do well to hear her out: People were saying that on the eve of Tishe b'Av: *mobilization . . .*[7] They obviously knew the telegraph poles had to be guarded. Why do they have to be

<hr />

5. *prawda* (Polish): true.

6. *keynehore* (Yiddish): literally, no evil eye. It was considered bad luck to enumerate precious things especially children. Doing so required using apotropaic expressions such as *keynehore*.

7. Tishe b'Av is the fast day falling on the ninth of the month of Av, a somber holiday commemorating a number of calamities that befell the Jewish people.

guarded? Because the Germans will fly over in their airplanes and sever the wires. In any event, they're guarding. Then it's no joke? They take Jews with beards, stick tin badges on their caps, and put axes in their hands. Because when the Germans come in their airplanes they will certainly ask about the Jewish thieves. It's no use: people say guard, and they guard, as though they're children playing a game. But they'll soon learn that it's not as easy as it sounds. Fathers are taken from their children, put in soldiers' clothes, and then sent to the front!

What can you do . . . Those living grass widows, poor things—it was so miserable for them—they wept and wailed themselves out and then kept quiet.

But here—no one knows wherefrom or why—a troop of soldiers entered the city: Cossacks, Kalmyks, and dragoons. And a rumor spread that the rabbi, our Yerukhem, as well as other fine burghers from Prashnik, had stuffed the veins of slaughtered geese with gold ten-ruble coins, packed them in crates, and shipped them to the Germans.

"A foolish, idiotic charge," said the pharmacist, upset.

"It's not at all foolish, Panie Pharmacist. What miserable anger! It's not at all foolish. Did you know our Yerukhem? Alas, alas . . . And the rabbi of Prashnik with the white beard you probably also knew. The ten finest Jews of the city they . . . in the forest . . . from the trees . . . Oy! . . ."

"Hanged?"

"Yes, yes, kind Panie. And my sister, did you know her? You probably knew—you're from there—she went mad from her miseries."

"Went mad . . ."

"Yes, yes, you kind man. Went mad and threw herself from a balcony."

"*Borukh dayen ho-emes*," said the pharmacist piously.[8] "I did, I did know her, a precious woman."

---

8. *Borukh dayen ho-emes*: Blessed is the True Judge; this formula is traditionally said on receiving news of someone's death, usually someone close.

"Woe to that mother in the grave!" Aunt Mitshe lamented. "She left behind miserable orphans to God's mercy. But just look at what that looks like after only a couple of months."

And Aunt Mitshe took the cap off of little Shimen's head in order to show the pharmacist the scabies.

At that moment Shimen let out a shriek, "Auntie, Nosn's pinching me!"

"Don't," his aunt gently reproved him.

The little zealot was standing with one hand on the hat on his head, and with the other he was pointing at the wall above the clock.

"You can go with your head uncovered? There's a *Matka Boska* hanging on the wall."[9]

The pharmacist pretended not to hear and promised to prepare some ointment, taking several silver coins from Aunt Mitshe.

Barely managing to drag her feet due to her hardships the aunt started to leave, but when she got to the door she turned around.

"Yes," she said, "and who do you think made up that false accusation against my brother-in-law? Who do you think if not the village clerk who always drained money and blood from Yerukhem?"

"The clerk of the community of Prashnik? Impossible. I know him well. Sure, an anti-Semite, but an intelligent man. How did you get that idea?"

"Oy! How I got that idea . . ." Aunt Mitshe shook her head. "One of the townsmen who incited the Cossacks had a falling out with the clerk and told him off to his face—he did, the murderer!"

"And he—what?"

"He was made, he said, a laughingstock."

"*Boże kochany!*"[10]

With skilled hands the pharmacist chose some oil from here, a powder from there, and doggedly mixed together an ointment for

---

9. *Matka Boska* (Polish): Blessed Mother; an icon or image of the Virgin Mary.
10. *Boże kochany*! (Polish): Dear Lord!

Aunt Mitshe's orphans. His thoughts were somewhere else; his mind worked quickly.

"Maybe convert? Said and done?" His deceased father, the barber-surgeon with the white beard, the angel from the underworld who in the next world smacks you in the face, stood in his way: "It's a risk, Itshele, a great risk . . . It may very well be that there is a 'next world.'"

But Stefe . . . She, Stefe, is still right all the same: the bailiff comes every day and warns, "Tomorrow could be too late." The priest writes notes. He oughtn't be suspected of being only interested in their souls, though the souls of lost little lambs are also dear to him. Rather, he exhorts them for their own sake. It is the voice of the Lord God, the voice of His divine Son and of the Holy Virgin that speaks through his mouth: they should reflect and save their soul and their body; they, intelligent people, without Jewish superstitions, must not, dare not, risk their lives and the lives of those who will come after them . . .

And there, in the other room, the dark-eyed Stefe was sitting on the sofa with the tall student, her hands pressed to her heart, a tear in her eye. She was beseeching him ardently, as one does to a god, with great feeling and devotion:

"Look, Panie Władysław, convince him . . . Let us go over to your faith . . . Let your father talk it over with Isidore . . . Now is the time . . . So that he might forget he once had anything to do with Jews . . . In all seriousness, completely over to your faith . . ."

The tall student cooled her warm hands in his cold ones, and from time to time gave them a kiss.

"Yes, good, I'll talk it over. But just calm down, Pani . . . Calm down, Stefe . . . Dear . . ."

The tall student stole out through the back door of the pharmacy and shuffled off in the shadow of the houses. Ah! That's the real Jewess Rachela.[11] And why would she convert? So that he, a fine upstand-

---

11. Rachela: Rachel; also a reference to a Jewish character in Stanisław Wyspiański's play *Wesele* (*The Wedding*). See chapter 34 for Rashkin's fuller use of

ing Christian, should suffer pangs of conscience over having an affair with a married woman? What did it matter to him if he goes to hell, that little Jew with the clipped beard! Such an easygoing and harmless man. It's only right to make him work in the pharmacy at night and then get into his bed. She really does wear the pants.

At home he mentioned it to his father, the nobleman Galewski, "Ought one not persuade the Jewish pharmacist to convert, otherwise the Russian soldiers will hang him."

"Persuade? Persuade, you say?" The old lord twirled up a mustache. "Why don't you ask if I would like to have that Jew as an in-law in our community? Don't you see . . . They're already getting at you, those yids, through all the chinks in the fence. What is this, a refuge for every scabrous rogue? I tell you: those priests and missionaries should be flogged—who asked them to afflict us with those locusts?"

"But, father, he will convert," his son argued.

"It's all the same . . . A converted Jew is still a Jew—all the same. It's blood, child, understand? Accursed blood. Those priests' policy is a sham, I tell you. Were it not for the baptized Jews of the Middle Ages, who ate away at our country, Poland today would still be Poland . . .

"And the 'Golden Liberty' of the nobility?" said his son ironically.[12]

"You're all so . . ." he waved his hand dismissively and left.

———•◦•———

Everything happened just about the way Aunt Mitshe had foreseen. Stefe and the priest were right.

At first people didn't think of him, the pharmacist. Neither him nor even those like him. The poor women of the back-alleys, the "spare" women, with kerchiefs on their heads, wailed and lamented. Thursday they said: *mobilization*; and on Saturday several Jewish

this famous Polish play.

12. The Golden Liberty are the special rights and privileges of the Polish nobility during the period of the Polish-Lithuanian Commonwealth.

craftsmen, fathers of children, broke into the synagogue like thieves. Oyzer Fisher, with his Gentile face, banged his coarse fists on the lectern.

"Make with a couple rubles to leave for my wife! Give 'em here, I tells you! Give 'em here, the Devil take you, fine Jews! If not, it'll be your ruin! Hey, people! Go to the rabbi! It's no Sabbath! For us it's Tishe b'Av and you're gonna celebrate Sabbath?! They'll make off with everything!"

Well, anyway, they made it through. With glazed eyes, profaning the Sabbath on a matter of life and death, little Yosele went from house to house collecting various sums and gave them to Oyzer. And then Oyzer bid his farewell to the city from the mountain, "The Devil take your mothers, fine Jews! The guts from your belly!"

Then for whole weeks on end soldiers poured through the city. A little bird flying overhead could drop a feather and every soldier, no matter how badly off he might be, would leave some kind of a ransom: a zloty or two, sometimes a ruble, and sometimes even a new three-ruble coin. Old, damp tobacco passed through hands very quickly, rusty spoons, old-fashioned trouser buttons—everything became saleable merchandise.

Then they put out little Yosele's lamp and plundered his goods.

Then God sent his help: on Yom Kippur, in the middle of prayers, there came the order: *open the stores.*

So little Yosele, in his great white robe, standing at the cantor's lectern, rocked back and forth singing, crying out in a lamenting voice: "*Ha! . . . Ha! . . . Ha! . . . Ha-m-e-l-e-kh!*[13] Master of the Universe! You know its meaning best: *dine de-malkhuse dine.*"[14]

And he went behind the cupboard in his store, stuffed the banknotes into his coat pocket and the coins into his pockets, and gave

13. *Ha-melekh* (Hebrew): the King; the beginning of the introductory prayers on Rosh Hashanah and Yom Kippur.

14. *dine de-malkhuse dine* (Aramaic): "the law of the land is the law," a Talmudic precept (see Tractates Bava Batra 54b; Gittin 10b; Nedarim 28a).

orders to his daughters in Hebrew, because on Sabbaths and holidays he only spoke Hebrew, "Keep an eye out for Russian soldiers! Make change for ten zlotys! Maybe we'll make it out it of this shameful pillaging, praise God, with a little something extra!"

And from time to time he fixed his eyes on heaven.

"Sweet Father! You well know: *dine de-malkhuse . . .*"

Then the Russian General Staff, having earlier secretly spread among the soldiers the poisonous libel that the Jews were everyone's affliction, that the Jews were spies, now openly ordered: Here, so close to the front, *all Jews are to be expelled, spies hanged!*

The front was nearing Godlbozhits. The Germans were right on the other side of the Vistula. With Schadenfreude the bailiff let it be announced: *All the Jews must leave the city!*

"Where to?" one Jew asked terrified.

"To your wife in her underwear," the bailiff wisecracked, and all the townsfolk laughed in amusement.

"To severe cholera!" the bailiff said more quietly in the circle of the wealthy Christian citizens.

The townsfolk survived. The townsfolk had suffered through maybe ten pogroms, and—in Godlbozhits—couldn't bring themselves to talk about it. Perhaps two days before the expulsion of the Jews from the city the police had driven back a whole band of peasant men and women carrying bags, sacks, and coarse sheets. They had been told the Jews were being plundered in the city, so why should they be left out? Why should the burghers get all the Jews' belongings?

They were delayed, but they came nonetheless. Two days later, as the Jews left the city, the locks of their cellars were broken off, and those fine citizens, those "*proszę Pana*s," carried out their plunder without a war.[15]

The pharmacist with the Vandyke and his pleasant dark-eyed wife lived to see it with their own eyes.

---

15. *proszę Pana* (Polish): a term of respectful address, something like honorable gentlemen.

Here's what happened: When the order was given—*Jews out!*—the pharmacy couple were left in a dilemma: Did that include them or not? They hadn't yet converted, but they were on the very eve of doing so. They just hadn't had time to take care of the formalities because the priest had been so frightened by the war that he had fled for deepest Russia.

Then the dark-eyed pharmacist's wife took the initiative: she went to the military commander of the city and presented the matter as it stood. She received permission to stay.

In the morning, a second commander came into the city, and he likely never gave any thought to whether there was a pharmacist in the city, let alone would it even have occurred to him that that pharmacist might be a Jew.

But to a group of people in the market the bailiff let slip a little "witticism": "Just look at the pharmacist with the little clipped beard. Doesn't he look like a spy?"

"A spy, *jak Boga kocham!*" the drunk shoemaker chimed in.[16]

He then diligently went into the pub and had one drink after another, and the shoemaker's apprentice repeated everything: "By all the Saints and Jesus' mother—a spy!"

The drunkard then dragged himself to the military staff. There he received a silver half-ruble and a kick in the ass.

But they did seize the pharmacist, ordering him readied for the gallows.

The pharmacist's wife nearly fainted, falling imploringly at the commander's feet.

The commander asked, "You have a permission to stay?"

"The last commander gave a verbal permission."

"That's worthless. Besides, the order came from higher up, and the city commander cannot rescind it."

"But Your Honor or what-do-you-call-it . . . We've already received the first sacrament, we are Christians in our hearts . . ."

16. *jak Boga kocham* (Polish): I swear to God.

"To hell with your hearts! There's a war! Do you understand?! Your husband is a German spy! An enemy! We have proof: he delivered secret messages by string, like this!"

He was saved, the pharmacist was, by a real rabbinical miracle. The trumpets had suddenly sounded the alarm: *Fall back*! The commander, together with all of his staff, hardly had time to jump onto their horses, leaving the pharmacist, half-dead, next to the gallows—unhanged.

That same night, as grenades flew over the city, the pharmacist's dead father, the barber-surgeon with the white beard, came to him in a dream and said that he had interceded with the holy rabbis in the other world on his behalf, that he never gave the holy patriarchs a moment's rest till he had gotten him, his son, cut down from the gallows. His dead father took that opportunity to get him to promise that he would remain a Jew for as long as he lived.

And only those people of Godlbozhits who knew nothing of the pharmacist's dream were astonished at the great change that came over the pharmacist, the convert. Not only did he become more pious, the pharmacist did, but at every anniversary of his father's death he had a candle lit in the synagogue, and every Yom Kippur eve he came to the synagogue for Kol Nidre.

✧ 3 ✧

How One Moves In and How One Moves Out; How Austria Won the War

Like a chased, tormented dog, Godlbozhits ran off frightened, and looking over its shoulder howled, "Oho! My tail's been shot off!" That whole section of houses on River Street and Bath Street had burnt down. No matter—as long as everyone survived.

The study house and the synagogue escaped the fire because of the holy Torah scrolls. Nearby, the town hall and little Yosele's house, too, enjoyed the benefit of that protection.

The frightened, oil-painted walls of little Yosele's rooms certainly didn't express a scornful "Huh? Beggars! What are you doing making yourselves comfortable here?"

And at first the beggars weren't so brash as to touch the illustrious oil paint, instead piling their bedding rags in the middle of the room with a "Pardon us, Reb Yosele's floor, just for a moment . . ."

Then they grew steadily bolder, those beggars did—they stretched out in Reb Yosele's canopy bed.

Here's the story: Expelled from the city, each person fled according to his own ability. Some quite wealthy Jews, the industrialists Wiszniewski and Meierbach, for example, ran as far as deepest Russia; Reb Yosele drove by automobile to Warsaw; Jews of middling means got stuck in a cart on the road in some small shtetl; and the truly poor could scarcely drag themselves to a little village.

Now they, the beggars, were the first to come back. Finding their own homes burned, they lay down where they could: first in little Yosele's rooms, and then even in the study house and the synagogue.

Like the dove that Noah sent out from the ark after the flood little Yosele, sitting in Warsaw, kept his ears pricked up.

"Huh? Are they still shooting?"

"What's the matter, Reb Yosele? The Russians are gone and the Austrians are in the city. More than half the people have already returned. A few beggars are scratching about in the cellars. You didn't leave anything there, did you, Reb Yosele?"

"No, thank God. Managed to bring it with me in three trucks."

"Wait a moment, Reb Yosele. Your house is by the river?"

"No. Why?"

"River Street and Bath Street were burned down."

"Oh my gosh! And the town hall? And the study house?"

"They survived."

"Thanks and praise to God! Because of the holy Torah scroll. Right between the study house and the town hall, that's where my house is."

"Just a minute, Reb Yosele. Pinye told us that there's a whole barracks quartered at your house; all the poor people from Bath Street moved in there."

"They'll move out, with God's help."

"As Pinye told it, your watchman is selling cigarettes from your stores."

"He'll go back to cleaning the gutters, God willing."

"But listen, Reb Yosele, just listen to this story. Tuvye Vaks, Wiszniewski's and Meierbach's broker, moved into their factory, got all the merchandise in order, and sold it."

"Really? Tuvye Vaks? That would make him, by my reckoning, a wealthy man."

"And what of the Wiszniewskis? And the Meierbachs? Really all gone?" asked this inquiring soul.

But he never got a response because even though the beggars had moved out of little Yosele's rooms, Godlbozhits was still all topsyturvy: great merchants had fallen from their places, and indigent Jews had become well-to-do. The study house was utterly unrecognizable: of the five packed benches of regulars and Talmud scholars there remained but a quarter of a table; at the Eastern wall there was a motley mix of once fine upstanding Jews, the parvenu rich, and coarse youth. It seemed that God himself had gone bankrupt.

Moyshe Soyfer could not stand it that those filthy bumpkin buffoons seated themselves at the tables for Talmud study, and just as the saying goes in such cases—that potatoes are expensive and bread is a rarity—so he thought to himself that a word of Torah had become a useless thing here. But one may be permitted to tell a story, so here's the story he told:

"Once the Prussian kaiser invited the Russian czar for a visit, the czar who was, as everyone knows, his cousin. They went out for a coach ride over the streets of Berlin. The Russian czar was astonished at how on all of these wide streets they never saw any long kapotes, or beards or earlocks. So he asked, 'Here in Germany are there really no Jews?' The German kaiser answered that there were indeed Jews, but one doesn't recognize them because they all wear short jackets and shave their beards and earlocks. The Russian czar again wondered aloud: 'But look,' he said, 'I make numerous decrees against beards and earlocks, forbidding long kapotes and harassing those who wear them, and still it makes no difference. But here they say there's freedom, equality, and you nevertheless can't recognize a Jew?' To that the Prussian kaiser answered, 'Miseries make Jews, freedom unmakes them.'"

—•—

The old folks of Godlbozhits went on living with their memories of the past. But little Yosele, even though he too was no longer a young man, had a young man's evil inclination. When a woman died, little Yosele said, it's just like eating an onion: the eyes cry and the heart is pleased. In keeping with that philosophy he, having lost his third wife in one of the war's typhus outbreaks, made no delay in marrying for a fourth time—this time to a tall, solid woman, a real beauty. More than anything, in those days when the Imperial-and-Royal district commander was in charge a woman like that was as good as a permit for a wagonload of oats and a wagonload of wheat. You can get the wheat and the oats from the peasants for a song. They don't want to give it up? Piffle! Just take along a gendarme with a gun. While on the road you might also come upon a real bargain: a porter dragging a child's sled. What in the world would a porter be doing in the middle of the week playing with a child's sled? "So . . . By jingo! You're smuggling, you damned Jew!! Well, pardon me, I'll just go and carry it on this big wagon . . ."

And Moyshe Soyfer could again sit in the study house and argue:

"Huh? Our Yosele! And Zaynvele the pitiful tailor? What was he? A common tailor, a patcher. And what is he today? An entrepreneur! An Imperial-and-Royal supplier! And Tuvye Vaks, the Meierbachs's boot-lick, did you hear? Get this, the factory is now his. Moyshe Kripnik sent two steamers down the Vistula, and Reb Shmuel Rabinovitsh—with all due respect to him, honorable Jew and honorable man that he is—I mean, what was he? A woodsman his whole life, who went with the rafts on the Vistula, and never on Sabbath; and today—quite a big shot, a 'ya tebye dam!' Well, now Shmuel the woodsman is the great timber-merchant, and Reb Ayzik Danziger can go to an old-age home. So it's well worth asking the question: Is it worthwhile to destroy a world so that Zaynvele the pitiful tailor should have someone to supply moldy cheese and rotten turnips to?"

⇥ 4 ⇤

Abele Babisker's Will

The war ruined Moyshe the teacher's teaching. So he hopped onto a peasant cart and went from village to village, and from city to city, drawn to Godlbozhits, which, as people said, was the city to be in after the war. As the saying goes: Where there's bread, there's Torah.

When they got to Babisk the peasant hurried the horse on because it was already getting dark and the roads weren't safe. They wanted to get across the river before dark.

But when they reached the top of the mountain, and the first lights began to show on the far bank of the river, a burly Jew in a fur cape suddenly appeared in the middle of the road and stopped the cart.

"What's with the hurry?" he said in a coarse voice. "At any rate you won't be getting the ferry anymore today, even if you protest all night. No worry, in the village at least you can spend the night with Jews."

The teacher was quickly persuaded. "We're Jews after all, and from a villager you'll get a bowl of borsht and a piece of bread." But the peasant cart-driver was stubborn: "No, no!" He'd rather be stricken with epilepsy, the peasant would, than spend the night here. Here in Babisk, his friends told him, there have always been horse thieves who, if you but looked away for a second, would leave you in an empty cart.

At this the villager made a suggestion: he, the peasant, could sleep on his cart in the stable and his horse could stay nearby. Finally he persuaded him, the stubborn peasant, and turned the cart off toward the village. The villager led the peasant and his cart into the barn and went himself with the teacher into the house. Now the villager reached out his big paw and offered it to the teacher.

"Greetings to you."

"Greetings."

"Where're you coming from?"

"From here and there."

"And what's your business?"

"This and that."

"Have you not heard of Abele Babisker?"

"No."

"Well . . . Let us say our evening prayers," said the villager, "then we can chat."

And what prayers they were! The teacher prayed, as was his wont, by himself, quietly. But the villager prayed loudly, word by word, those words like pearls strung on a string. The teacher had never heard such praying, even from a rebbe.

Then they washed their hands, made the blessing before the meal, and ate potatoes with borsht. Just before the blessing after the meal the villager asked again, "Never heard of Abele Babisker?"

"Eh? . . . Maybe . . . Abele . . . Abele the horse thief? I did hear of him, from the Godlbozhits Hasidim."

And then the teacher remembered a little more.

"Right, right . . . People told of the wonders of that Abele. He held court, so they said, like a rebbe."

"What a court! It once happened that a Hasid came to the rebbe on the Sabbath. As was the custom when a Hasid came to the rebbe, he'd bring along with him his prayer shawl and phylacteries, as well as some provision for the road, all packed in a kerchief. While on the train he stretched himself out to sleep, and someone stole his bag. What does a Hasid do when he wakes up and realizes his misfortune? He takes someone else's bag . . . Meanwhile, instead of going to the rebbe, he makes for Abele Babisker. Anyway, why am I talking your ear off? That Hasid became an expert in his specialty of Sabbath load-lightening."

"What are you saying?! He became . . . a thief?"

"Well, believe it—a thief. This Abele we're talking about was a Jew who knew what's what, and could also do you a favor."

"So I've heard, so I've heard. He was also a very charitable and hospitable person."

"What a host! You heard the story of the rebbe's horse?"

"I've heard some of it and some I haven't heard. It's a bit hazy, like a dream . . . Huh? Right . . . Something of a miraculous tale: The rebbe had a pair of small horses for his coach, and once overnight they grew larger, like aristocratic mares. Meh. Who knows their ways? It's not for us to know. And certainly there were also prayers involved. But you're not going to tell me that for the sake of a couple of horses the rebbe was really and truly going to perform a miracle before the world."

"And what a miracle!" the villager interrupted. "And not just one miracle, but miracles and wonders, as the verse reads: '*Rov nisim hifleyto ba-laylo.*'[1] And so what should happen but that same night the stable of Chief Strażemski burned down. And what a fire it was! The whole kit and caboodle. The goy ran out in his underwear, wringing his hands: 'My sweet little horses, my dear little chestnut horses!' And those were the real pair of horses. And so, the straw roof burnt up, and he saw with his own eyes how the little creatures were fried up . . . But why am I talking your ear off, Reb Jew? It was a miracle with a Mighty Hand at the middle of it. Abele's apprentices were eager to learn, and Abele had himself once been a 'choirmaster': the rebbe's little nags had been led beforehand into the goy's stable and the goy's steeds into the rebbe's stable. And then: '*Boyrey meoyrey ho-eysh.*'[2] And you're going to call that theft? When he saw with his own eyes his chestnut horses burn?"

The teacher's collar suddenly started getting tighter; he scratched his neck.

"*Mne* . . . What can you say . . ."

"Indeed, what can you say," said the villager as he continued his tale. "Abele Babisker was a font of kindness. The rebbe was entitled to the gift. He justly deserved it. You want to know why? Then listen

---

1. (Hebrew): "You performed many miracles at night"—from a liturgical poem for Passover.

2. (Hebrew): "He who createth the light of the fire"—part of the blessing over lighting the special candle at the conclusion of the Sabbath.

here: Abele's only son was sent off as an apprentice to a teacher in Godlbozhits, and for years never saw his home. Abele sent his son to the best teacher and paid better than the finest Godlbozhits burghers. And still, when it was time to get the lad married, all the brides disappeared and all the matchmakers evaporated. So everyone flattered him, trembling before him as though terrified, and this 'Reb Abeshi' and 'Reb Abele'—*he* had to go all the way past Warsaw looking for a bargain. And Abele wasn't a bad man: if it was a poor man coming to him he'd let him bring the goods into his house; if it was a rich man he'd pay him for his troubles. His crew weren't required to toil away at night when everyone was asleep or to risk their lives needlessly . . . And you should know that people came to Abele as they would to a rebbe because there was no bit of work in the whole district Abele didn't know about. In short, *this* was 'Reb Abele' and 'Reb Abeshi,' and still no one wanted to marry into his family. Then Abele went to the rebbe, wrote out a check right in front of the rebbe's assistant, leaving a hefty donation, and what do you think? The rebbe decreed—he had seen with divine inspiration—that Moyshe Soyfer's daughter should marry Abele Babisker's son, but Abele had to pay six hundred rubles, in addition to the trousseau and gifts. The bride was no beauty, as you might imagine, and no young maiden either, and, you'll forgive me, utterly destitute. But, for all that, Abele Babisker had an in-law— Moyshe Soyfer! And apart from pedigree Abele was not disappointed: his son to this day is a well-off synagogue trustee in Godlbozhits. Jews could do worse."

It seemed that the teacher hadn't really been listening, or that Abele's only son hardly interested him. He still couldn't digest the story of the rebbe's horses. He trembled and his shoulder itched, and he stuck one sleeve into the other.

"Well," he suddenly interrupted the villager. "These are not ordinary matters . . . But the real miracle is that the nobleman didn't recognize his horses at the rebbe's. Otherwise it would have been, God forbid . . . It shouldn't be mentioned . . . The rebbe, going off in chains."

"What a story! Who says that he didn't recognize them? When the goy saw the rebbe's coach he nearly collapsed in an epileptic seizure:

'*Tak kak moi*,' he kept repeating.[3] But what could he say, since he saw his horses burn with his own eyes . . ."

"Didn't recognize his own horses?! Wow . . . wow," said the teacher, scratching his shoulder. "It's called a delusion."

"Why should he have known them so well when it was only two days earlier that Abele had given them to him as a gift?"

"What do you mean?"

"Those same horses . . . Hush money. Chief Strażemski deserved it. Was it nothing? A pair of horses taken from some yard and led into his stable—you think it was a trifle for Abele's crew? The police after all were completely . . ."

The teacher, it seemed, didn't understand a single thing of the whole tangled mess. He just stared at the villager's mouth and blinked his eyes. The villager himself was already yawning.

"Anyway," he said, standing up. "The Russian's gone, the rebbe's gone, and Abele's gone. The Austrians flushed out Abele's Hasidim one by one. Do you play around with an Austrian? He'll hang you for any old thing, so just go take chances with your life . . . So there it is. We'd better go to bed:

El melekh neeman. Shma yisroel, shma-a yis-ro-el, shmaaaa . . ."

———◆———

The teacher couldn't close his eyes the whole night. He kept feeling as though he were sleeping on chicken's feathers and that the mezuzah on the door was improper and invalid. At dawn he was awoken by a din outside.

Apparently overnight someone had stolen the peasant's horse and he was left in an empty cart. The peasant was tearing the hair from his head: "*Matka Boska! Matka Boska!*" And the villager asked stupidly, "Everything's *yak to biło*?[4] You survived the night?"

---

3. *tak kak moi* (Russian): but they're mine.
4. *yak to biło* (Polish): as it was.

Just then a peasant from Babisk who happened to be passing by called together a gang of peasants: "Give back the horse, you thieving mug!"

"*Żyd złodziej*!"[5]

"Don't we know you, Abush? You horse thief! You gypsy!"[6]

"Do you think we're among Russian soldiers?!"

Someone noticed the teacher at a distance:

"So you've got there your thief's accomplice!"

"*Cygańska morda*!"[7]

A young peasant yanked a stave off of the cart and made straight for the teacher. The villager blocked his way.

"Just think it over," he warned the peasant with a finger, "because you'll pay for it."

So the peasant with all his murderous rage hit the villager over the head with the stave.

The villager fell, gushing blood. The other villagers scattered. The teacher ran into the house, crying for help. But then he noticed that there was no one left in the house and that he was screaming at the empty walls.

So he took a scoop of water, moistened a rag, and began washing the villager's cracked-open head. But by then the blood had begun to flow and gush out in streams. The villager moved his hand, wishing to say something:

"No more Ab-ele Ba-bis-ker . . ."

"Help! Save him!"

The gendarmes and a doctor came later. The teacher was interrogated and it was all written down. Moshke, Abele's only son, the synagogue trustee, also came from Godlbozhits. His father was lying unconscious, one eye swollen like a mountain.

---

5. *Żyd złodziej* (Polish): Jew thief.

6. Abush is a Polish diminutive of Abele's name.

7. *Cygańska morda* (Polish): Gypsy mug.

People whispered, "We always knew he would die a violent death."

Right before his agonizing death Abele Babisker regained consciousness:

"Moshke? Is that you?"

"Yes, father."

"So? How is it going with the committee?"

"I'm an equal partner with all the other trustees."

"No use . . . Must become a rebbe . . . Like your father was."

"What do you mean, father?"

"What do you lot call the 'head of the community'?"

"President."

"Yes. That's what I mean: you must become the president."

And returning from the funeral where he said Kaddish over his father's grave Moshke confided to his friends, "D'you think that's what I'm striving for? As far as I'm concerned someone else can be president . . . But what's done is done. I have my father's will. And for my father's will I'll go to great lengths!"

✤ 5 ✤

The Heir to the Old Rabbi's Throne

Those "friends" gave their help. There were several of them, those strong young men. The chief among them was Yoyne Roytman, a giant of a man and a Cohen. When he performed the priestly benediction in synagogue the very walls shook, and among the horse cabs to the railroad station only he was visible, and only his monstrous voice could be heard. To his credit it should be mentioned that he was the first to bring some semblance of order to the draymen's world by instituting a system of "tenure" and "lawsuits"; after all, up until that time there had been nothing but quarrels and fights among the coachmen. For not submitting to Yoyne's arbitration you were compensated first by having your ribs knocked in, then a fine, and then a new "lawsuit." No matter—one could rely on Yoyne as the "rabbi": he had received his ordination from the Babisker "rebbe," Reb Abele, and was one of his best students, a specialist in stealing elite saddle horses from the Russians. And since Austria came in he had made a living, like all Jews, from honest toil. That, at any rate, is how Yoyne accounted for himself.

The second was Khaykl, the sexton's son, the eater of unkosher foods, who once ate kishke in the Polish pubs, and then another time carried the bags of some rebbes who had come to visit the graves of their parents. That was his good deed.

The third was Oyzer Fisher who had only just returned from the war and a prisoner-of-war camp. This Oyzer brought home from the front all the more toughened fists. But the light had gone out of his eyes, and his face had become that of a simpleton. He had been poisoned with the gas the Germans released in the trenches. His mind had dried up as a result, his face swollen—no longer the same Oyzer.

Then there was his family on his father's side, and next his family on his mother's side—that is, the family of his in-law Moyshe Soyfer. Altogether Moshke, Abishe's son, reckoned that half a city was his own flesh and blood.[1]

And the old rabbi . . .

"They should just send Yoynele Roytman, Khaykl, and Oyzer over to him. They wouldn't need to say anything. He, the rebbe, should just look at them."

"Who's knocking?" the old rabbi's voice could be heard from inside.

No answer came. Only the hawking and grunting of a regiment of soldiers.

So the rabbi lifted himself from the bench, dragged himself over to the nearby door, and said testily, "Mayerl, come in here. Someone's knocking. Seems they're not Jews."

Mayerl, the Crown Rabbi, walked with little steps to the door at the front of the house.

"The rabbi is not well," he yelled through the closed door. "He can't receive guests."

"Open up, little rabbi," cried back Yoyne Roytman. "We need to see the real rabbi, a municipal matter."

Mayerl leaned a long finger against his cheek and thought for a moment. He then opened the door.

"Good evening, Rabbi!" Yoyne greeted him cheerfully, setting his feet firmly in place, shoving his hands into his trouser pockets, a good-natured smile spreading across his face.

Out from behind his shoulders, on either side, Oyzer Fisher and Khaykl the sexton's son stood watching.

---

1. Hereafter Moshke is usually referred to by the patronymic Abishes—that is, Abishe's son.

All at once the old, stooped rabbi seemed to grow more stooped, staring mutely and frightened at Yoyne's ugly mug on one side and at Oyzer's hands on the other. And suddenly he flopped down onto a chair.

With little steps Mayerl ran up, imploring the group, "Not now, Jews, the rabbi is ill."

It seemed the hoary rabbi was so frightened that he was stricken suddenly with diarrhea and the shivers. He had to be undressed and laid in bed.

The men gave up and went away. On the way out Roytman opened the door to Mayerl's room and called out "Good evening" to Mayerl's young wife.

"Mayerl!" Roytman slapped him on the shoulder in a companionable way, "You've got a wholesome woman!"

But just then Mayerl had bigger worries. He felt the responsibility of the moment. It was possible that tomorrow or the next day he would have to take on the heavy burden of being a rabbi among Jews, a fact that was still not even mentioned.

He consulted his wife, Frumtshe, of whom, ever since she had come to Godlbozhits, it was said that she was very well educated, that she read French novels, and that she conferred with the governor-general. She seemed the equal of any Jewess in Godlbozhits. True, she did have a sharp tongue, reviling the city and the synagogue trustees with vehement curses. The city, you see, had done good business without her. Since the old rabbi had brought over his grandson Mayerl and his missus two years ago, the city had suffered nothing but a financial drain. The young rabbi's wife complained incessantly that the community was cheating the old rabbi, giving him nothing to live on, all despite the fact that the old rabbi, who—may he live to a hundred and twenty—had been rabbi in Godlbozhits for more than forty years, had not asked her for such a kindness.

The old rabbi couldn't stand her, his grandson's wife, and the way she constantly made demands. All told what does such a rabbi need who for forty years lived on red borsht and dry bread? Who for forty years had been writing a casuistical commentary on Tractate

Zevachim? And who for forty years collected money, groschen by gro-schen, to publish it?

True, the last few years they did need a crown rabbi to keep the books. But what had they done until then? It had been two years since the young rabbi's wife had abandoned the material world, and after all, a man needs someone to cook him a bowl of borsht.

The old rabbi complained to the burghers:

"And what a hue and cry there would have been if the Godlbozhits rabbi might in his seventieth year have cooked his own borsht? Because that's more difficult than a treatise on Zevachim? And in any case three hundred in gold was collected and squandered on who knows what. These forty years of work on holy purification want to see the light of day. So, could you at least promise me, Mayerl, that after my death you will publish this book?"

Mayerl promised, as one promises a child the moon. He saw how his hoary grandfather had day and night, with running eyes, spread his tiny curlicue handwriting over the paper, writing and writing those minute little letters with his goose quill so he could fit that much more on each sheet of paper.

The old rabbi lay in bed with his eyes closed, suffering from acute stomach pains. Mayerl implored, "That's, God forbid, what will become of him, your grandson—to go begging, or become destitute. Since he's ill-suited for business."

"You think my sons will give up their inheritance to *you*? Ley-bele received his permission to teach from a greater rabbi than your grandfather."

The old rabbi chewed his toothless gums and then suddenly grew angry.

"Can't you become a water carrier? Can't you become a street sweeper? Do you want to be a dog-beater like your grandfather was?! You coddled puppy! You want to accept the responsibility for a city-full of souls? When you have to go into people's houses asking them to come to you with their problems. Half a city of impious clean-shaven men, half a city of women with their own hair. Dear child . . . Don't lay such a chain upon yourself."

The young rabbi's wife cried; Mayerl wiped his tears. He was stubborn, the old man: Absolutely not! No one should lay a hand upon him. But about a half an hour later he again called for Mayerl, "Go call the burghers together."

They came, the burghers did: Reb Ayzik Danziger, Reb Moyshe-Mendl, Motele Perl-Tsvetes, and Reb Elye Graf. The old rabbi was sleeping. They were in the other room. A lively conversation was underway:

"For a quarter of a potato one can demand five krone. The Jews are at fault because when a peasant comes into the city he's pounced on like a jewel; why shouldn't a peasant be sitting pretty?"

"Always the Austrians . . . You didn't get this with the Russians," said Reb Elye Graf wistfully.

"Piss off!" Reb Moyshe-Mendl came down as though from the roof. "They want to turn Godlbozhits into a city with 'lectric plants. Otherwise wouldn't I be able, y'know, to endure it? Otherwise, wouldn't the young people here, y'know, be able to dance with the girls? Otherwise, wouldn't those lewd women, y'know, be able to go about without wigs, in their own hair?"

Reb Elye Graf was not at all impressed.

"It's German fashion," he said. "In Carlsbad, for example, women have been going about in their own hair for years. The rebbe, Reb Motele himself, of blessed memory, told me that."

"You should have the rebbe, Reb Motele, ask me!" Reb Ayzik interrupted. "In Prussia I saw the very same some twenty years ago."

"But we all knew," groaned Reb Moyshe-Mendl, "that the Germans would bring all manner of evil things, God save us. And the 'Party,' curse the name?! Before the war who heard of parties? So listen . . . To me there's still no difference, but I'm telling you, Ayzik, that this won't happen in my house. Come what may, but in my house there'll be no lamps lit on the Sabbath!"

Reb Ayzik Danziger, in whose house the Party had its accommodations, felt the slight. Nevertheless he restrained himself and asked with sullen resentment, "And who's stopping you? Seems they'll let you in? And if they let you in they can still beat you."

"And so what if you're beaten," Reb Moyshe-Mendl interrupted. "They still don't kill right away. I'm telling you that we have to go into the study house and cry out: *He who is for God is with me!*[2] On Friday night the whole study house should go to see the Party. I would just like to see who's stronger, me or them?"

"So, go, go . . ."

"But that's how it is whenever you spruce up your kapote. Apparently we're not violating '*Loy taymoyd al dam reyekho*'?"[3]

Motele Perl-Tsvete's stood off in a corner, looking out at the balcony and tugging on his beard. As always he was absorbed in the upper realms and wanted to figure something out through philosophical investigation.

Reb Elye Graf turned his stool and said quietly, "You've surely heard of the new Party that they're going to set up? Whose head do you think is mixed up in that? Not Mayerl's?"

"What's this again about a Party?"

"Mizrahi . . . Zionists, too. So-called Jewish Zionists."[4]

"D'you hear . . . That Mayerl's truly an arch-sinner."

"You'll see, he'll be the Godlbozhits rabbi for a hundred and twenty years."

"How you're blathering on."

"How you're listening . . . In time he'll be managing all the sides. And the Mizrahi, what do you think? And why have we been summoned here? Eh? No matter who's pretty, I'm clever."

Reb Elye Graf was triumphant. All that was left was for Motele Perl-Tsvetes to agree with him. The latter tore himself from his thoughts for a moment, scratched the middle of his back, and said only, "So be it, I believe everything."

The door opened. Moshke, Abishe's son, came in and, standing in the middle of the room, asked, "The rabbi called for me?"

---

2. A slogan derived from the words of Mattathias in the Book of Maccabees.

3. *Loy taymoyd al dam reyekho* (Hebrew): "Thou shalt not stand idly by the blood of thy neighbor" (Leviticus 19:16).

4. Mizrahi refers to a religious Zionist political organization in Poland in the first third of the twentieth century.

The respected burghers looked at one another: what wondrous times . . . new burghers . . . Moshke Abishe's son . . .

Mayerl's head popped in as well. One has to hear from every class, from every stratum. One just couldn't know. Moshke after all was a synagogue trustee, and it was rumored in the city that he would become president as well.

The hoary rabbi opened his eyes.

"Eh, Moshke? Is that you? Sit . . . Anyway, so I hear you're a real mover and shaker in the shtetl."

"A trustee, Rabbi, like all trustees."

With difficulty the old rabbi lifted himself on his pillows.

"Anyway, Mayerl has surely already spoken with you? You won't oppose it."

"Yes, Rabbi. Just the opposite, I'll help as far as I can. But I would like to ask the rabbi to persuade his grandson not to oppose me either."

"What do you mean?"

"What do I mean? Livel'hood . . ."

"Livelihood—war," groaned the rabbi.

"I will do it especially for you, blessed Rabbi."

"For me? For me?" The old rabbi had a coughing fit. "I . . . I need nothing . . . Summon Motele Perl-Tsvetes."

Motele folded his handkerchief in his hand, winding it around his finger in a pyramid, and unwrapping it again. He made no response to what the old rabbi said.

How could he respond? That Mayerl was as suited to becoming the Godlbozhits rabbi as I don't know who. And here Mayerl's grandfather argued, "Believe me, Motl, he's qualified. For this modern world he's a perfect fit."

It seems that he, Motele Perl-Tsvetes, was not at all "this world"; but Moyshe-Borukh the water-carrier and Moshke Abishes were "this world" . . .

Nevertheless, he promised to be helpful. Did he have a choice, when the old man took him by the hand and pleaded?

For what purpose? Could one really jump in and refuse something to this saint of his generation, this innocent man, in his final minutes?

It was because of this that, when the old rabbi did pass away and the dispute over who would become the Godlbozhits rabbi heated up, Moyshe-Mendl and Elye Graf could tease him, "You see, Motele, earlier you railed against Mayerl and now you're still helping; you're always on the side of truth . . . eh?"

He was exasperated by the arguments, but for all that he just didn't have it in him to respond. So he simply swore, "Because you're idiots it's my fault?!"

"But you love the truth . . ."

"So? What's the problem?"

"Then you'll have the true rabbi: Mayerl . . ."

"So, if I can bear it, why can't you?"

The study house was filled with his shouting; and the more aggravations that were added to the whole matter, the louder he yelled.

And to the people of Bronitz, the Hasidim of one rebbe, he cheerfully opened his heart, "Y'see: for all that I love the truth . . ."

"You mean the new rabbi?"

"Yes. He's the true bailiff, the true impudent man, and the true arch-sinner."

⇥ 6 ⇤

Civilization Flourishes
and Judaism Is Laid Waste

With all the power of his weak heart, Motele Perl-Tsvetes plowed his way into the thorny problems of Tractate Yevamot. He taught a boy with a solid mind, an eager lad. Shimen was the boy's name.

The boy sincerely tried to follow with his child's mind the teacher's difficult commentary, his casuistical interpretation. He then began to feel the proper meaning of studying Torah for its own sake. His little eyes sparkled like struck matches, his ears blushed rosy and translucent, his little voice echoed clearly. The world and all its vanities, with all its base desires, with all its foolishness and frivolity, sank away somewhere into the void, disappeared before his eyes. He drifted over the fields of eternal life, ate of the tree of life, as it is written of the holy Torah: "It is a tree of life for those who hold fast to it."[1]

However, sometimes a weariness overcame him, and then he would remove the harness and let the teacher go on ahead. At those times he merely repeated the teacher's words, while his thoughts flew far out over the market where the fair beckoned with its bright colors and a man in a red cap tossed hairpins, gesticulating and yelling: "For frrreee! For frrreee! . . ."

Sometimes in the middle of studying, some good friend of the teacher's would stop by to chat a little with him. Sometimes his wife called him back to his business. Then Shimen could breathe free for

1. Proverbs 3:18.

45

a moment and look out through the window at the market; how his heart longed for it. But such a miracle did not happen often, and little Shimen slaved away. The lessons dragged on into eternity and all he was left with was the hope that some catastrophe might knock down the teacher's house and set him free.

Sometimes it happened that the teacher noticed his student's unusually loud repetition of his difficult commentaries. In those cases, too, the teacher would close the Talmud and look into the little one's face, shrewdly and with a smile, as if to say, "Buddy, I've got your number . . ." But in those cases Shimen felt ashamed, very ashamed.

Little Shimen was well aware that this was a seductive play on the part of the Evil Inclination, that it was Satan with his peasant women from the fair barging into the middle of his studying in order to disrupt his learning, and he endeavored to hold strong against the Other Side. If That One danced into the middle of his studying he'd catch hold of him by his desires, by his tricks. It became clear to Shimen that the true Evil Inclination lay in the stick game *pyekure*. So first off he made a vow no longer to play with sticks. Then little by little he also refrained from all the other the games, like hide-and-seek, *kame-kame-tir*, *griske*, and hopscotch. He, little Shimen, set out slowly to lure Satan till he could catch him, tie him up with rope, and throw him into a deep pit.

And on the other end he applied himself all the more diligently to Judaism, to piety. He imitated his teacher, Motele Perl-Tsvetes's every step, his ways, his behavior; he prayed and recited Psalms with great devotion. He also decided that as soon as he was bar mitzvahed he would go to the Bronitzer rebbe for Rosh Hashanah.

And nevertheless it did once happen that the Evil Inclination overcame him. Little Shimen played some silly trick that incurred severe consequences, as it says in the verse: *"Aveyre goyreres aveyre."*[2]

2. *"Aveyre goyreres aveyre"* (Hebrew): "One sin leads to another" (Tractate Pirkei Avot 4:2).

Once—it was a Sabbath afternoon—Nosn said to his younger brother, "Shimen, are you coming along to war?"

Shimen answered, "It's forbidden. It's forbidden on the Sabbath."

"Idiot," he explained, "is it a real war with guns? It's obviously one with pebbles."

"It's not permitted with pebbles either," Shimen protested. "It's 'forbidden to carry.'"

"Carry-shmarry," Nosn teased. "You're such a goody-goody. All the other kids are allowed, but he's 'forbidden to carry.' You don't want to? Then I'll go by myself. But I've got a bone to pick with you."

"I'll tell on you to auntie," Shimen threatened.

"So come then. You'll only watch."

"But I won't throw any stones."

"You won't."

"Promise?"

"Guns!" Nosn was already growing impatient.

Shimen was beginning to yield.

"Will you let me stay in the 'fort'?"

"Yes," Nosn agreed.

In any case he only needed Shimen to come along so that Aunt Mitshe couldn't throw that goody-goody in his face, telling him to learn a thing or two from Shimen's quiet manner, his piety. But that aside, Shimen was useless for "war," a real dud; he threw pebbles clumsily with his left hand, like a girl.

They went down to the river. The "Russians" had already barricaded themselves in the burned-out ruin of a brick house with little turrets. The "Germans" and the "Austrians" were scattered all around, hiding behind the damaged walls and the tall, narrow chimneys of burned-down wooden houses. And the bolder ones were out in the open field.

A simple assault was under way. Regularly, minute by minute, large pieces of brick rained down from the fort. The Germans attacked with pointed whizzing stones that the littlest kids gathered and prepared for the soldiers. From time to time a face would appear in one of the fort's window-holes, and shortly thereafter a stone would whistle by.

Shimen was protected behind a high wall and could laugh at the bricks that kept flying over his head.

But standing by idly like that and the fear of sticking his head out began to bore him. He suddenly started to regret the whole thing. He didn't need to go on a Sabbath walk. He needed to study a chapter of Talmud. What would his teacher say if he heard about this? "What? Such a thing? Little Shimen, the good boy, with a good head on his shoulders, such a thing?"

Nosn fell in behind the wall. Shimen caught hold of him: "Nosn, come home, auntie . . ." But Nosn didn't even turn to look at him. He jumped up to a window-hole, stretched his hand out like a string, and let fly a stone that made a whine in his ears. Another stretch of the hand, and another throw. *Zh-u-u-u* . . . it whistled as it whipped through the air.

More boys fell in. Shimen heard: "They're attacking!" His courage failed him. He was frightened, and braced himself out of fear, listening.

The enemy was near, and their cries could already be heard and singled out. Alarmingly big stones were falling now, hitting the opposite wall and spraying debris everywhere. And they began to hail in from the open walls on the left and the right, so that even behind the wall you were no longer protected.

Aside from Shimen and his brother, everyone was now wild with excitement. Shimen trembled, and Nosn was pale, gritting his teeth. He leaned against the wall and listened. Someone from the other side had already even stuck his head in and with a wild cry threw a brick. Then Nosn gave a brief command to his comrades, "To arms!"

Alone he leapt up onto the parapet and with wild abandon he jumped off.

"Hurrrah! Hurrrah!"

With a cry of "hurrah," his comrades followed him out. Things whistled and howled all around, and suddenly—the stones stopped falling, the screaming faded. All was silence.

Then Shimen took a risk and looked out through the window-hole. Nosn and his comrades were already far away, at the other end of the street. On all sides they had surrounded the "Russian fort," its wall and its turrets, and from very close, from the middle of the street, they attacked.

All of a sudden little Shimen was no longer afraid. He drew inspiration from his brother, and a spirit of war had entered him. Swift as an arrow he made it across the small stretch of road separating him from Nosn, gathering the biggest stones and clumsily lobbing them at no particular target.

"Hurrrah!" he yelled louder than anyone, deafening himself; and his fear, well, dead is dead!

And when the "fort" was "taken," little Shimen was in the first line, throwing a giant pebble through the window-hole, like that Roman who threw a burning torch through the window of the Holy Temple.

Dead is dead!

But once the enemy had been driven out and the conquerors had pursued them and pressed them on to the river, there Shimen stood— the only conqueror in the fort—wiping blood from his cheek. Red blood—he saw it and at once thought to himself, "A hole in my head."

Maybe his wound hurt, but that's not what he was thinking about just then. "Sabbath . . ." He had violated the Sabbath. What was auntie going to say? What was his teacher going to say? "Eh, Shimen, this is how you lets the Evil Inclination lead you around by the nose? You throw away the Mishnah and the Talmud in order to go toss stones with ne'er-do-wells? Such a thing? A good thing?

"And do you know, Shimen, why God's only punished you? Do you know why, among all the boys who were throwing stones, it's only you who's gotten a hole in your head? Because you shouldn't be a ne'er-do-well like all the other ne'er-do-wells; because your teacher is Motele Perl-Tsvetes. Because you have a good mind and the Other Side latches on to such things. *Today it will tell you 'Do this!' And tomorrow it will tell you 'Do that!'"*[3]

___

3. *"Today it will tell you 'Do this!' And tomorrow it will tell you 'Do that!'"* is a paraphrase of the Talmud's description of how the Evil Inclination works: "Today it says

He was very sad and filled with regret. It was not so much the pain that concerned him but the fact that he had a hole in his head and a gashed cheek. How could he show his face at home, to his uncle, to his aunt, and even more so to his teacher?

He stood in the middle of the path to the deserted River Street holding his cheek, still dripping blood, as tears welled up in his eyes. He hadn't noticed the noblewoman who had approached him, trying to take his hand from his cheek. He didn't let her.

She asked him something in Polish. He understood her but couldn't answer. He hid his face further and burst out in sobs.

"Who made you bleed?" the woman asked. The little boy didn't answer.

So she took him by his little hand and gently led him along. He no longer put up any resistance and followed her.

She took him into the pharmacy and asked for iodine. With a practiced hand, like a nurse's, she applied the iodine to his cheek and his head. Then she asked, "Will you come with me?" She spoke Yiddish with a Lithuanian accent. With her kindly smile she tried to coax him to trust her.

Little Shimen sighed deeply and at the same time raised his eyes for the first time, taking a look at this "Jewish noblewoman." He soon lowered them again and silently nodded his head yes.

The pharmacist's wife was waiting for them to leave. She walked over to the glass door and watched them as far as she could. She then turned to her husband, "Isidore, do you know who that was?"

"What does it matter to me," the pharmacist rudely answered his wife. He, the pharmacist, had been very nervous of late. He had made a delivery on the sly of large quantities of saccharine, earning quite a lot on the shady deal. But this constant living in fear had made him mean and anxious.

---

to him 'Do this,' and tomorrow it says to him 'Do that,' until it says to him 'Worship idols' and he goes off and worships idols" (Tractate Shabbat 105b).

And thinking it over, he didn't care a fig about "them." He was still a pharmacist, not some wandering Jew. He needed that "sweet" for medicines. All useless pipe dreams. Huh? What d'you say? Not a fig!

He was talking to himself as if to someone he could trust, laughing to pluck up his courage, even though his stomach was cramping up; but between you and me, he was a coward. And he could never talk about business with his wife, though she always had plans for business deals abroad.

"Why aren'y you saying anything about that little overcoat, Isidore? Oughtn't a lady from a wealthy home be embarrassed to wear a dark cloth overcoat on a summer's day?"

"Who are you talking about?!" asked the pharmacist irritably.

"Don't you know who that was? That's Broderson's daughter, the one who was in here just now. The Brodersons from the villa . . ."

"Re-e-ally? Broderson? That's Broderson's daughter? Must really have come down in the world, that Broderson." Out of habit the pharmacist tried to shear through his Vandyke with two fingers, quite forgetting that, though he always used to do that when thinking of two things at the same time, he had already shaved off his beard some time ago.

A female customer whispered something with a flattering smile to the pharmacist's wife.

"Isidore, listen to what I've just learned!" the pharmacist's wife called out with the glee of poorly concealed schadenfreude. "The Panna takes her lunch in the soup kitchen. You know, Isidore, all else aside it really is a shame, a young lady from a good family. We'll have to give some thought to doing something for her. Well, some kind of job maybe. One can't really let a young lady from such a wealthy situation hit rock bottom."

And the women who peeled potatoes in the soup kitchen chatted among themselves, "Woe is me! I've got nothing to live on!"

Tsiml Cossack was pinching her cheeks, tearing out pieces of flesh.

"Y'know who we're making lunch for? That Broderson shikse . . . You remember that coach with the pair of horses? The cobblestones in the market shook."

"His smallest donation was a ruble, and on Passover he gave away three hundred. He bought the villa for his daughter as a birthday present."

"Today's wealthy men aren't worth his littlest nail! A Jew wouldn't starve with a penny of his. And his politeness, his refinement? You'd think they'd dress rich maybe, or his daughter? A wool skirt—so very modest."

"How the world's all gone to pieces. They stayed in Russia and the young lady in Warsaw. In any event, here at least she had a roof over her head."

Tall Chana said, "Whatever, so today there are other wealthy people. Just look at how they don't give it all away at once. Here Mekhele Podreytshik's got money so God gives him a daughter with a crooked shoulder."[4]

"So you're adding another worry!" one of her neighbors interrupted. "She'll get a husband quicker than your daughter."

"'Get' you say? She's already got one. And with whose money is Berl Treger's son studying?"

"Well . . . He'll become a doctor, you'll see. He'll give them a great big fig, both the father-in-law and the hunchback."

"Eh, Mekhele Scoundrel doesn't just give money away for no reason."

"Well, well! A new worry," Tsiml Cossack cut in, blowing her nose in her apron. "I'm more worried he's buying up all the potatoes, since you can't get a quarter of what the potatoes are worth from a peasant."

"That's why you've got bread," crowed one woman, as thin as a woodchip. "Moshke Abishes's rationed committee bread. I shouldn't sin by complaining, but it's clay, not bread."

"No worries, Moshke Abishes and the trustees bake challahs like the sun."

"Y'hear? I give him my ration tickets, and he takes one away. I have, he says, only six children, not seven. So, what does it matter to

---

4. *Podreytshik* (Yiddish): literally, entrepreneur.

you if I take something for my husband's sister? It costs you more? You're giving your own?"

The woman like a woodchip crowed, "So, go argue with him and he'll just keep cursing you like a dog. But the rabbi? Beats me! The rabbi has maybe fifty tickets."

"Anyway, he keeps the books, writes himself in for life."

"What does the rabbi need with so much bread?"

"What an impressively wise woman you are! You can't think of a reason? So one takes some flour, a ruble a pound. And sugar's not worth anything? And kerosene? And candles? And salt? And who knows what else?"

"Never mind the salt. So whatever comes in he sells? He weighs with a three-pound weight what sat for maybe a year in salt. Five ounces were definitely missing."

"Anyway, Moyshe Soyfer's daughter lived through it. Time was one would have let him have it (knowing, alas, who his father was), but now—a well-to-do president."

"Woe is her, upon my word! Or else what, she gets a what-for from him? He just slinks off to Malke, Leyzer Beker's wife."

"And what about Leyzer?"

"Take a shit on his head and he'll call it a shako! Or what, does she go asking his permission? And not with the gendarmes?"

And Tsiml Cossack came to the conclusion, "These rich folk today bring nothing but miseries!"

Still, it seemed that such heartbreaking pity for Broderson's daughter was nothing but gossip, because when little Shimen came home he right away told his aunt a tale about how he fell down on the mountain where he was taking a walk, and about how Miss Broderson put iodine on his wound, and as proof he showed her the piece of chocolate wrapped in the cambric handkerchief that the Pani had given him. She had also wanted to treat him to a white cake, but, as little Shimen boasted, even though the Brodersons were Jews he knew that they fried food in pork fat and that they baked foods with milk in pans used for meat, so he didn't take even a bit of the unkosher cake.

And Shimen went on: The Pani wanted to teach him how to write, for free. The Pani showed him a book with little pictures of people in it and told him to read. So he said he didn't know how to read, he only knew the letters. So she, the Pani herself, read aloud and told him to explain. So he said in Yiddish that he understood but he couldn't explain it in Polish.

"She's going to come to the house for a lesson?" Aunt Mitshe asked.

"No, I'm going to go to her."

"That's not seemly. She'll turn you into a goy, like those youths in the Party."

"The Pani said that everyone will learn to read," said Shimen.

"You, child, are something different. You are Motele Perl-Tsvetes's student."

Shimen considered this for a while and answered deliberately, like a grown-up, "These days, if one can't write, one is not a person."

"That too is true," his aunt groaned and thought to herself: "A rabbi? Who knows. He should at least be an honorable Jew: a merchant who knows how to study."

Later, little Shimen went off to the chairman of the Party and delivered a note from Miss Broderson. The chairman of the Zionist Party was an old bachelor with a tiny trimmed beard, two pencils—one red, one black—in the front pocket of his jacket, and a lame-footed, dancing little gait, like a baker rolling a bagel. The chairman read the note, cleared his throat importantly, and sent little Shimen with the note to the secretary.

Eventually it was discovered from the note that Miss Broderson wanted to set up a school in Godlbozhits—its first school for Jews.

The first thing that needed to be done, Miss Broderson maintained, was to go to the rabbi. To him, the leader of the city, and on from there . . .

The chairman covered his mouth, gave a meaningful little cough, and smiled a knowing smile at the strange idea of a female assimilationist (what did she think, a rabbi was a priest?). But nevertheless he agreed, "Let's go to the rabbi."

The young rabbi received them in the front room, averting his eyes from the woman and stretching his neck toward the ceiling like a gander. Then he grew very angry: What were they complaining about! People were dying from hunger, the mikveh was still in ruins from fire, and now—go take your 'schools'! 'Schools,' they say! Otherwise, what, they won't be able to light the lamp Friday night?

Miss Broderson tried to convince the rabbi: On the contrary, she was actually asking the rabbi if three times a week he would give a lecture on religion, that he might assume the protection of the school. To take an example: the priest among the Christians . . .

But she was left with no one to speak to. The young rabbi had left her standing there without so much as a "good-bye" and went back into the house.

Waiting for him inside were Moshke Abishes and the finance committee.

"What a nuisance!" spat the rabbi. "What a bother!"

And losing no time he got right down to business:

"As a matter of fact all of the surplus receipts are mine. After all, who keeps the books? The rabbi. However, I don't want to go busying myself with divvying it all up. Well, all right, I understand—here, take a percent too. But the whole 'thou shalt not steal'? Out of six sacks of sugar you send me three pood? *Feh!*"[5]

———•———

Meanwhile they, the culture-bearers of Godlbozhits, the chairman and the teacher, went to the children's fathers.

"Well, we'll see," one of them responded.

And another: "I need the girl in the store, and the boy goes to *kheyder*. I can't tear him away from his studies."

And a third: "But let me see a 'prospectus'."

And a fourth: "My wife handles these things."

---

5. A pood is Russian unit of weight equaling roughly thirty-six pounds.

And his wife: "How much does the Pani want a week? I can't afford a lot!"

And her intellectual neighbor: "Oh, how I've dreamed of a school! The children grow up like wild beasts without education. It's a shame I have only boys. The Pani understands they're *kheyder* boys; my husband handles that."

Her husband: "Even though I didn't study in a school, I can still compete with you in 'fractions.'"

Miss Broderson: "But this is not about you, Mr. S—, it's about your children."

"My children? Why is the Pani making such a fuss about my children? They have a father, may he live to a hundred and twenty."

So Miss Broderson gave it a lot of thought. She stopped going to people's houses. Instead, she dragged the big cross-leg table from the veranda into her house, set up an inkwell on it, and started with one student, for free.

Shimen Shifris was that first student.

The next morning two more came, and after about a week the whole table was already full. No sooner did the girls' lesson end than the boys poured in. In the evenings young men came in for lessons, the ones who were embarrassed to carry around books and exercise books during the day; and in the evening they carried their writing gear under their kapotes. They came, these marriageable young men who had for so long wandered among the desks of the study house, always brimming with questions they now needed to have answered from the mouth of the all-knowing Miss Broderson. Oh! She was such a creature, that Broderson, that precious woman. A lesson at seven in the morning, a lesson before noon, the boys in the afternoon, in the evening another lesson. She taught not only reading and writing, but also about taking off one's hat when greeting someone, and about how the girls should curtsy.

Once, that intellectual woman, Etele Shteynbok, met Miss Broderson at the magistrate's house, made a deep curtsy as she had seen among the schoolgirls, and demanded, "*Proszę Pani*, why does the Pani not want to take my children for school? Maybe I can't pay as well as the others? Believe you me, all you rich folk still don't own my garbage . . ."

Whether it was the curtsy that this grown woman had made, or her language, but Miss Broderson turned as red as a beet. In any case she couldn't call to mind what children these were because lately she'd been so overloaded with work that she couldn't refuse a single child.

But Etele Shteynbok left satisfied: she, that teacher, ought to know that even Etele Shteynbok could be allowed to take a lesson or two in her house as well. Because her husband, Leybele, who squared his shoulder and smoked a pipe, he traded in lumber he did. He was a partner in the factory that made pressed cabbage and dried potatoes he was.

Like the Sambatyon, Miss Broderson did not rest.[6] Just then, for example, she had to endure a battle with the boys who would under no circumstances sit in class with their heads uncovered. Little Shimen was particularly worked up; he studied for free but he stirred up a rebellion among the boys. He was a devotee of the study house, knew all the laws of the Torah, and got all the boys to say, "The rabbi says no."

If the rabbi said no then all really was lost.

She, the teacher, couldn't and wouldn't struggle against religion. But she was desperate: what would the inspector say about this?

And the boys kept getting more and more brazen. In the middle of lessons they pestered her with questions about milk and meat, about the Garden of Eden and Hell—all the things she had never heard about in her father's house.

One time, little Shimen, the best student, asked with feigned humility, "*Proszę Pani* . . . Is it true that those who fry chickens in this world will themselves be fried in Hell in the world to come?"

That was some nerve! She turned red, the teacher did—turned red and burst out laughing.

6. In the Rabbinic tradition, the Sambatyon refers to the mythological raging river of fire flowing constantly for six days of the week and stopping on the Sabbath, making it forever impassable for Jews.

He, that insolent boy, had wanted to needle her—her, the Jewish Gentile.

And when she stopped laughing she thought for a moment, put a stern expression on her face, and ordered, "Everyone, hats off! Those who don't obey are to leave class at once."

So everyone, except for little Shimen, removed their hats and remained seated, neat and quiet, like cowards. Stubborn little Shimen did not go to school for two days after that. On the third day he came with tears in his eyes, apologizing: He . . . He wanted to study.

But by that sacrifice pious Godlbozhits had still not atoned. So it was her desire, the teacher's, for the children to put on a performance, a play; she had gotten the young people of the cultural union also to put on a theatrical production. She aimed, that evil woman, to destroy Judaism in Godlbozhits.

But Godlbozhits wasn't sleeping either. A group of Jews with Reb Elye Graf and Reb Moyshe-Mendl in the lead raised such a ruckus at the rabbi's that half a street came out to see what was the matter:

"The rabbi keeps quiet and does nothing! Such a blasphemy! Young men and women together! Theater! No! Your grandfather, of blessed memory, your grandfather, Mayerl, would never have allowed it! Going about bare-headed! No matter the consequences—never would have allowed it!"

"What can be done? What must we do about it?" the rabbi asked.

"First of all, every father should take down his son's trousers at home and knock him a 'how do you like that' and a 'say you're sorry,' till he gets swollen; and they should grab their girls by the hair: 'You're staying at home, hussy!' But you shouldn't be satisfied just with that; the rabbi should go with them to the city commander. Even to the district commander . . . Franz Josef himself, his glory be exalted, also supports religion!"

Then the rabbi whispered a secret to them: The commander is a Jew. Well, yes, don't they know? The new commander, he means. What's his name? Stänglmeier. And if he's a Jew, they ought to know, he's probably a bigger heretic than a Gentile. Moreover, he, the rabbi, had heard a rumor that the new commander and Broderson's daughter knew each other, and if so, then all their work would be for nothing. What will come of screaming? You can't argue with these people now. He, the rabbi, was about to bring in flour for the holiday. It's possible one might yet need Broderson's daughter for a favor. What did they want, that the city would, God forbid, be without Passover flour? Matzah for Passover is a commandment from the Torah, but theater was banned only by later sages . . . What, didn't they know how to study?

But Moyshe-Mendl was not placated. "The rabbi is in a flippant mood," he said right to his face. "Your grandfather knew much better how to study, and he did not so lightly brush aside a ban."

Reb Moyshe-Mendl handpicked several important citizens and went off with them to see the district commander. Not to worry, a Yid like that would hash things out with him. Then they'd see who's right.

"On the other hand," Reb Moyshe-Mendl gave his interpretation, "if he sticks me in jail, there I'll sit. When a fire's burning, don't look!"

The district commander received the delegation, but he could not communicate with them. Moyshe-Mendl explained to the rest of the Jews, "The nobleman speaks pure German."

Meanwhile the district commander rang a bell and ordered someone be called in. Lieutenant Stänglmeier entered.

The Jews of the delegation quickly saw that the game was lost. If "the hand of a Jew was in the middle of it" . . . After all, he was called the Jewish gendarme. Moyshe-Mendl still decided to see it through to the end.

"Tell him, that nobleman of yours, the chief, that theater is for' den among Jews, Heaven protect us from all evil spirits."

And the lieutenant of the gendarmes:

"The Herr district commander says that he does not und‹ why young people should be forbidden from enjoying themsel›

Moyshe-Mendl:

"Tell him, the nobleman, the chief, that the Emperor Fr‹ himself, his glory be exalted, is also no opponent of religion."

The lieutenant:

"The Herr district commander says that his royal maj› opponent of theater—is in fact pro-theater."

Reb Moyshe-Mendl hesitated for a moment, then whispered, "Tell him, the nobleman, the master, that the emperor, his glory be exalted, is not a Jew, and such is permitted to idolaters."

The lieutenant of the gendarmes was at a loss. He labored hard to explain, but to no avail. Perhaps he hadn't completely understood the Talmudic locutions. The district commander shook his head back and forth, unable to comprehend.

And so theatrical performances went on all the same, and more than once. At first the rabbi persuaded them to have the female roles played by men in disguise; but later men and women, very freely, acted together. In fact, people came to the performances and enjoyed them immensely. Even in the study house, during prayer, people discussed the theater.

And in that same study house Moyshe Soyfer sat by the stove—the wider world concerning him like last year's snow—he sat in his wonted place for chatting, slapping his belly.

"Huh? What did I tell you? Miseries make Jews, freedom unmakes them! You wanted the Austrians?"

That's how he teased Moyshe-Mendl who from the beginning of the war had sided with the "Germans." Moyshe-Mendl fled from the stove. He couldn't listen to that loafer speak. For him everything was alright, as long as it showed that with the Russians it was all sweetness and light. Moyshe Soyfer still couldn't forget the white rolls of the evil kingdom. Aside from that, that is, did he understand one jot of political science?

And meantime the young rabbi had received a permit to import a cartload of Passover flour. He mulled it over and brought in two cartloads instead. But the Jewish commander had—you'll pardon the expression—eyes in his hindparts and confiscated all the flour.

With no other option Mayerl the rabbi put on his pitiful little *spodek* and, with large strides, clambered his way up the mountain to the school of Broderson's daughter.[7] He jumped like a stag over boul-

---

7. *Spodek* (Yiddish): a fur hat.

ders in order to fulfill a commandment: after all, the seized flour was
not just any flour, but flour for Passover, flour for making matzah,
and if it stayed in the gendarmerie there might be the suspicion of
contamination. The one consolation was the fact that the commander
was a Jew—a Jew with a defect, true, but still a Jew. A Jewish kishke is
beyond value. You never know . . . People say he prays every day.

Seeing the rabbi just outside the classroom the boys hastily put
on their caps; Miss Broderson turned red with anger and advanced
toward him, ready to defend her civilizing conquests. But how astonished was she when she heard the rabbi's request.

"How did the rabbi get that ridiculous idea in his head?" she blushed.
"I don't know the commander any better than the rabbi does. He comes
to me for a lesson in Polish, and that's the whole of our acquaintance."

"The Pani speaks German well, so the Pani will be able to present
our case to him," the rabbi entreated.

"But the Herr Rabbi must understand: I cannot, it's impossible for
me to go there. Moreover, I certainly wouldn't succeed in persuading
him."

The young rabbi didn't give up.

"The Pani *will* convince him. It's a matter of fulfilling a commandment. Otherwise, it's possible the city might, God forbid, go without
Passover flour."

And once again the rabbi supported his position with an example
from history, from Jewish history. She, the Pani, had likely read how
one Queen Esther once saved the entire Jewish people from destruc-
tion, Heaven protect us. Yes? That's also what's described in Polish
history.

"Probably . . . Read something . . . ," she didn't remember. "Maybe
read something . . ." She felt it would be very, very unpleasant to go
and discuss a matter of smuggling, but it was no use: she would do it
nonetheless.

She put on her little prewar black velvet hat and her worn out black
coat, and went off to see the commander.

Lieutenant Stänglmeier was pleasantly surprised: What a guest!
Welcome! But . . . he would not refuse her, the *gnädige* Fräulein. If the

gnädige Fräulein took the effort to come all the way from the mountain to see him . . .

He would not refuse her. How could he refuse when Fräulein Broderson possessed such large, grey, clever eyes, such an exceptionally intelligent face? "Of true nobility," thought Lieutenant Stänglmeier.

The whole matter was so unpleasant for her. For one person she would not intercede, but here it was a matter of an entire community. Poor Jews must have their ritual Passover bread.

"Well, good," he would not refuse her. But the gnädige Fräulein must forgive him, *bitte sehr um Verzeihung*: In these matters the gnädige Fräulein is quite naïve. He, Lieutenant Stänglmeier, is certain that half of the flour would be smuggled.

"Ah! Impossible!" Miss Broderson defended herself heatedly. "The rabbi himself came to me about this matter."

"Ho, ho!" He, Lieutenant Stänglmeier, it seemed, knew the shtetl better. "The young rabbi . . . *nicht wahr?*—he had a mystical appearance. *Ein guter Vogel*, this rabbi. It is unfortunately so, gnädige Fräulein."[8]

The following afternoon Lieutenant Stänglmeier came to Miss Broderson for his Polish lesson.

"Well, I have already ordered the flour released, gnädige Fräulein," he announced.

"Thank you very much, Herr Lieutenant."

"Think nothing of it, gnädige Fräulein. Well, was I right or were you, gnädige Fräulein?"

"What do you mean, Herr Lieutenant?"

"A full shipload of the flour was smuggled over to the other side of the Vistula."

"Impossible, Herr Lieutenant!"

"It's true, gnädige Fräulein. It was the rabbi, in partnership with the president of the Jewish community, that Moshke Abishes. I've already been informed. The Jews of Godlbozhits are now milling

8. *Ein guter Vogel* (German): a good bird.

buckwheat flour in the grain mills. *Ja, ja*. It's true, gnädige Fräulein. *Ein besserer Vogel*, your rabbi . . ."[9]

Miss Broderson could hardly believe it. She sat mute, as if paralyzed.

Then Lieutenant Stänglmeier bowed his head and, taking her hand with tender modesty, gave it a kiss.

"Don't be angry, gnädige Fräulein. You do not understand the world . . ."

"But a rabbi?!" said the young lady, her face burning with shame.

"It's no matter, gnädige Fräulein. The war has turned everyone into smugglers and thieves . . . Beasts . . ."

"And what about you, Herr Lieutenant?"

Lieutenant Stänglmeier once again elegantly kissed her hand.

"And what about you, gnädige Fräulein?"

He lifted his head, looking into her eyes affectionately.

She lowered her eyes. In the silence of the evening, in the twilight darkness in the room, something began to take shape. Something finer and more ethereal than spiderwebs.

9. *Ein besserer Vogel* (German): a better bird.

→ 7 ←

Uncle Melekh and His Household

On the ruins of Uncle Melekh's burnt-down house wild little trees had begun to grow. Both walls, the front wall and the one that went down to the river, still continued to conceal the poverty of the backstreets. Now, too, since Uncle Melekh's house had burned down together with all the wooden houses that once lined Bath Street and River Street, those two walls stood with their window-eyes put out, with their balconies propped up like broken old men leaning on their canes, and concealing from the marketplace the shame of naked chimneys, scattered bricks, and crumbling limestone.

There, in the back streets, poor people rooted around with sticks and scraps of iron, picking out a hinge, an oven door, some bent, scorched nails, half of a burnt floorboard, a whole brick; everything arranged in an order—*jakby nie byl szabas*, "as though it wasn't the Sabbath"—to be used for rebuilding a house.

But that Uncle Melekh, or as people called him, Melekh Mitshes (because he relied so heavily on his most capable wife), he left everything to rot in the ground. He was utterly neglectful and never lifted his hands to do a thing. For one thing, he was consumed with jealousy that all the fine houses of all the fine Jews in the city managed to remain standing, while only his house, which had nothing to be ashamed of compared to Ayzik Danziger's and little Yosele's houses— his house was the one that had to burn down.

Second of all, he, to his great misery, had started listening to his children. Nothing: he understood nothing, he saw nothing, he was not an up-to-date person. His Arn—the older lad with the tiny trimmed beard—his Arn nodded his head up and down and said, "Are you going

64

to put everything you've got back into the house? A year won't even have gone by and there'll be war again."

Meanwhile, wood from the state-owned forest was beginning to be distributed to those who were burned out. Whoever was able to grabbed enough for some kind of a dwelling. But that Melekh Mitshes—who could have gotten ten times as many boards as some poor man—that same Melekh Mitshes didn't make use of a third of his consignment of wood. And what he did take lay in the courtyard with its bark still on, soaked by the rain; it attracted worms that began gnawing away at the logs. The wood turned black, like cinders—and still nothing.

"Well, Arn, where's the war?"

"So now I'm supposed to build?" Arele brushed off his kapote. "Go, put all your effort into that 'housey' of yours. You invested whole life in that house. Couldn't you have made your children respectable people?"

Now it was easy for him to say to Arele, "So I'm supposed to," when Uncle Melekh was such a fool, having let go the reins and made his son a wealthy merchant.

So he gave it some thought, the uncle did, and hired a peasant and began to remove the bark from the worm-riddled trees. The worms burrowed deeper into the wood, and he, the uncle himself, with the help of only that one peasant, began to plane down whole unhewn boards for the walls. He lay the boards one right next to the other over the burned-down house, which was connected to the store, and over those he spread clay and dirt so thickly that it seemed no rain would ever soak through. There was no money for a roof, and Arele the "Scoundrel," who did have money, didn't want to contribute any.

Now the uncle took some rags that had been floating around the front vaulted store and brought them into the house. The bedding was soaking wet with damp. The vault, which still had no roof, had a peculiar quirk: if the sun was shining brightly outside, it started to rain inside. The uncle did what he could. He put out soaking pans, pots, plates, all to catch the water; over the vault he laid scorched, banged-up sheet metal. It all helped like cupping a corpse. One rotted alive inside. At around two in the morning Arele came. He took some cold dinner, looked around to see if everyone was asleep, and pulled out his wallet, arranging the bundle of crowns with the Russian hundred-ruble notes. Then he tucked the bundle under the head of the bed, and got into bed with his boots on.

He always dawdled stubbornly before going to bed, and if he wasn't tired he would spend an hour picking the lice out of his shirt.

But his old father was amazed that such a young man like that, not at all coarse, and on the surface very clean cut, that a young man like that could wear the same shirt for four weeks, crawl around in a puddle without a floor, and not pull out a hundred and say to his father: "Here, father, build a roof over your head."

It was incomprehensible how a young man like that, a wealthy chairman there among the women and the Party with all that "would you be so kind" and "please have a seat," a person always going to see pharmacists, a person, it seemed, who dealt with people all the time, how a person like that could go around scratching his shoulder all the time. Uncle Melekh was curious what he, Arele, would do if he were seized by an itch in the middle of talking with the pharmacist's wife.

Put frankly, there would have been no harm in knowing what Arele did day and night there in the pharmacy. Uncle Melekh would have given however much to know that the pharmacist's idea to get him to sell him that ruin of a house came from the mind of none other than Arele Scoundrel.

Recently, the pharmacist had sent word to him: If he, Uncle Melekh, would forget that on that site once stood a brick house, and if he didn't put up a fuss, he, the pharmacist, would buy it. But he, Uncle Melekh, had to remember that it was nothing but a bare patch of ground, and that it would still cost a good deal of money for the ruined walls to be cleared away and for the lot to be brought up to the condition of a good piece of property.

So what did Arele say? "Let him pay ten thousand, I'll shut my eyes and grab it up."

If so, if Arele was talking a blue streak, then he could sell him, the pharmacist, an illness! A malady! An affliction!

So much work that fine sonny boy did on the house! Suffer he did . . . Laid stone on top of stone . . . Lickety-split—done and dusted. He would finally sell it and grab up the dough.

So, let them both wait a bit more.

He, the uncle, went ahead and half rebuilt the store. For a family made up of mine, yours, ours, and everyone else who found a warm place there—all told eleven souls—one house was maybe a bit too small. They had to use half of the store for a bedroom. The other, front half was stocked with some merchandise: a little box of sweets, some millet, half an ounce of pepper, a bit of tea—as long as we're left with a window to the sky.

But the uncle himself was not meant for that kind of detailed business. Before the war he, Uncle Melekh, had been accustomed to wagonloads of herring, kerosene, salt; and now here was all he had: half an ounce of pepper. He'd never had any patience for it. What's more, the way prices behaved! Before the war a price was a price, but now—today something cost a crown and tomorrow it would be double.

New movers and shakers had sprung up: Mekhele Podreytshik, Leybele Shoulder, Moshke Abishes and, above all—women. Among them, the Austrians, without a woman you couldn't do business. Otherwise all you could do was smuggle.

Of course, if you asked him, Uncle Melekh, for his opinion, it would be something different. But whether or not you asked him, she, his daughter, the fat Yente, did what she wanted. She could even go get herself hanged for all he cared.

But Yente was not what would be called a real woman among the Austrians. True, she was a healthy lass with fat, ruddy cheeks; but the Austrians weren't Russians. An Austrian preferred a thin girl with rosy little cheeks, or even a grey, joyless face. Girls or women, it didn't matters, as long as they were tall and thin.

Such a Yente could at most attract the dark gendarme who was actually not a gendarme at all but just a cook for the gendarmes. Even so he could still do you a favor. But with him there was always some aggravation: at best, with a store full of customers, he'd lift up Yente's skirt just for laughs.

Of course, among the Austrian gendarmes there were only noble men who knew how to treat ladies. The dark gendarme, on the other hand, was a dyed-in-the-wool peasant, and you can't make a silk purse out of a sow's ear. One way or the other, it was a living—so say one's enemies.

The only people who did well were the ones on the committee and the others who supplied the military with beets, carrots, and little dried apples. Half a city revolved around those little dried apples. Fine whole apples, you see, the orchard owners sold raw. It was simply not profitable to dry healthy apples, because after drying they were only worth a tenth their value. But apples that were partially or completely rotten could be cut into slices and spread out on the "cord" to dry. Arele was one of Mekhele Podreytshik's suppliers. He bought up the little apples from the orchard owners, collected them, and sold them again to Mekhele.

One time Arn bought from a peasant the previous year's moldy apples that the peasant was going to dump into the river. He, Arele, bought them all for a song. He gathered barrels and tubs, poured water into them, and started to wash the apples. Apart from the uncle, he set the whole family to work. The aunt boiled pots of water; Nosn got into a barrel with his boots on and stamped and stirred; someone scrubbed another barrel with a floor brush the way one scours a muddy floor; Shmuel put the washed apples in a basket and took them up to the attic to let the excess water run off; and Arn himself did nothing, just running around here and there and giving orders at full blast.

Aside from the father, the group was only missing Yitskhok, Uncle Melekh's son, who worked for Tsadok at the tannery, as well as Yente, who was in the store with the dark gendarme. That revolting goy still didn't want to leave, even though the doors of the store were already closed and Yente was about to put out the lamp.

The house was inundated by dense steam and the stench of a tannery. That was the smell of the fermenting mold. He must have been a great risk taker, that Arele, if he could buy such merchandise, such worthless goods. But he was lucky, Arele was: that merchandise might well have been worth nothing, being completely moldy, white as snow with mold, but when Arele got hold of it it turned to gold.

When the water from the little apples had run off a little, Arn ordered them to be packed in sacks so that they wouldn't get lost on the road, and he left them in the sacks for several days in the attic to let the wind blow through them and dry them off a bit. Then he set the family to work again: each one took a sack on his shoulder and in the middle of the night they brought the whole supply into Mekhele's storehouse.

In the morning when they came to take a look steam was coming off the sacks like out of an oven, that's how rotten they were. Anyone else and Mekhele would have ordered him to throw it all into the river. But Arn was a good chap, a dependable supplier, and knew all of Mekhele's secrets. A little more, a little less—they'd come to an understanding on the price.

There, in Mekhele's storehouse, those few sacks of spoiled merchandise seemed like a drop in the ocean. They were emptied onto the heap—as high as two men—mixing in here, mixing in there, and it was done.

From that deal on moldy apples Arele earned a nice handful of money. Price aside, he had increased the weight by 50 percent with the water. That was nothing as far as he, Mekhele, was concerned! Did that Arele need to pour water in? Why, Mekhele immersed them himself.

But in any event, Mekhele did pour in the necessary amount of water. People were still bringing baskets of rotten raw apples, ones that had already turned black as coal and looked dried up. Those rotten things were cut into slices and mixed into the heap—another drop in the ocean.

Mekhele loaded wagons full of that rotten stuff. It went into "fruit soup" for the Austrian troops as well as the civilian population who worked forced labor in the trenches on the other side of the Vistula.

On their way back into the shtetl those people brought spotted typhus which then spread among the houses of the poor. Moshke Abishes, for his part, helped the dysentery along by adding portions of straw and clay to his bread.

Sometimes a poor woman would beg him, weeping, "Reb Moshkeshi, give me a 'mix' loaf. I can't, God forbid, eat that other stuff. It's all clay, though I shouldn't sin by complaining."

"Eat dirt, vile woman!"

He cursed like this or worse, the community's provider, while himself eating white challah. Mekhele, meantime, supplied the commander with little steamed apples, which were peeled and the seeds removed, as white as the sun and as light as down.

Arele, too, benefitted. From time to time he brought home some provisions from the committee. Moshke knew but didn't want to get into a fight with him. In general he, Moshke Bastard, knew the who, the where, and the how of things. This one gets a whiff, that one gets a taste—and here, here's a slap in your face.

But the essential thing for Arele was organizing the crowns: ones with ones, tens with tens, twenties with twenties, and hundreds with hundreds. He pressed them together in his wallet and warmed them at night under his pillow at the head of the bed. Eventually people said, "That young man has put together a pretty penny for himself."

Once, seeing Uncle Melekh in the street, a crazy idea came to the pharmacist's wife. She called to the Uncle:

"Panie Melekh," she uttered pretentiously. "Why don't you marry off your son? Why are you holding on to such merchandise?"

"Ha-ha . . . Holding on . . . That's well said. Doesn't he, that is, my son, do as he pleases? Is he a babe in the woods? On the contrary, maybe the Pani could prevail upon him? Maybe the Pani knows something?"

"I could find him a fitting partner," said the pharmacist's wife. "An educated Panna—but one who has no money."

Uncle Melekh shrugged his shoulder, "Two poor people going to a dance."

"Eh, Panie Melekh," the pharmacist's wife scolded him. "These days people don't consider money. An educated Panna is her own reward."

"Who does the Pani have in mind? Someone from around here?"

"Yes, from here."

"Who, for example?"

"For example, Panna Broderson."

"That's no small thing! Broderson and Melekh Zaydman. Well then—I'm open to the match, but what will Broderson say?"

"Don't worry about that! Pedigree is not an issue these days. Your Arn is a fitting suitor who can earn his money."

"Well then," Uncle Melekh spun back around on his axle. "I don't need to boast about my son. No, you don't think very highly of it. But if he wants it, he has a permission to teach."

"Eh, there it is. Today one needs to know how to read and write, not to sway around over the Talmud."

"Write? In the Russian times my Arn had finished four classes in the gymnasium. Does the Pani mean, God forbid, going to the 'school'? Writing letters, and grammar, and arithmetic, and whatnot? Yes, I'm familiar with such things. Me, as the Pani can see, I am a Jew with a long kapote, with a hat."

"So, Panie Melekh," the pharmacist's wife resumed her part of the conversation. "You marry off your children, you sell the burned-down ruin, you build yourself a house, and '*dziad z babą*,' you coast into your old age and you're done."[1]

Uncle Melekh grew clearheaded. He thought, "A pox on you! You call me over and pester me? All about my house?" And aloud he said, "'Sell' the Pani says? All my enemies should sell and all my good friends should buy. We still haven't, God forbid, gotten to that point. I still don't, God forbid, lack any food. I will yet build myself, God

---

1. *Dziad z babą* (Polish): grandfather and grandmother—in this case, an idiom glossed by the phrase following "you coast into your old age and you're done."

willing, a nice house on the corner. 'As there was water, so will there be water' . . .² So, Pani Pharmacist, *do widzenia!*"³

It all made him, Uncle Melekh, quite ill. Arele Scoundrel—he thought—leaves no stone unturned; just look how she leaves, that Sarah Scab, with her 'selling'! She should sell the shirt off her back!

2. "As there was water, so will there be water" is taken from a Polish proverb: *Gdzie woda była, tam woda będzie.* See Chone Shmeruk, "Jews and Poles in Yiddish Literature in Poland between the Two World Wars," *Polin: a Journal of Polish-Jewish Studies* 1 (1986): 176–95; here: 194n33.

3. *do widzenia* (Polish): good-bye, good day.

→ 8 ←

And These Are the Rest of Melekh's Children

Uncle Melekh didn't berate Arele in front of everyone. Uncle Melekh loved each of his nine children in his own way. And not only his own children—the orphans and stepchildren, too, he looked after as far as he was able. The odd ruble he slipped to lame Moyshele so that even his mother herself might not know about it. The uncle pitied the cripple who was no ignoramus, who knew a page of Talmud, and made a living fit for one's enemies: he was a coachman, and an unlucky coachman at that—every month another horse died.

And that lame man barely scraped together enough for a new horse, usually one without equal: an old mare, blind in one eye, with a sagging head. He would wave his whip forbiddingly and threaten:

"People! Go away! I mean to drive!"

While he started out to the railway at seven o'clock in the morning, it was around ten o'clock that he had finally budged from his place, and by two in the afternoon he had made it to the train. He tarried too long over those few kilometers from the city to the train station—by that time, one could have made it to Cracow. But really it was only the bag-carrying Jewish women who travelled with him, piling the cart high with bags of feathers, boxes of eggs, kerosene cans, and empty herring barrels. The wagon nearly broke under the load; there wasn't even room for oats for the horse, and someone was already talking about dinner for his wife.

Nevertheless Tsadok, Uncle Melekh's son by his first wife, was a wealthy man. Although it was rumored that he had stopped giving all of a sudden. Tsadok did not possess a nobility of spirit, and in all his body and soul there was not what lame Moyshele had in the nail of his little finger. Let's be frank: Tsadok was his father's son, only with haughty little up-twisted mustaches, instead of Uncle Melekh's simple "Good Sabbath." And what do you think Uncle Melekh was before he became a stone-built-householder? Old Jews still remembered his father whom Tsadok was named after. Uncle Melekh's father was an ordinary man, a quite simple Jew. A chapter of Psalms, maybe a section of the Torah undertaken with great effort. But he did not intend to be Reb Simkhele Eybeshits's in-law—far from it.

But as you probably know: God sits above and commands below. Tsadok was a fuller, a good trade in Russian times—you made twenty, twenty-five rubles a week, while Reb Simkhele Eybeshits with all his pedigree and his dry-goods store in the middle of the market was a very poor man, heaven preserve us; he went bankrupt, very badly bankrupt, and had to resort to making ends meet by teaching. What is such an unfortunate Jew to do when he's got a grown daughter hanging around at home? He should propose a match for her: one of Reb Leybish Peysakh's grandsons, a widower with two children but a scholar, God-fearing and prosperous, *keynehore*. Well, what do you know? She, his daughter Mirele, didn't even want to hear anything of it.

When an old maid wants to hear nothing of a match, and such a respectable match as Reb Leybish Peysakh's grandson at that, it is no ordinary matter; there's something going on there, something must be wrong with such a girl. But after all, no one will say that a grown, unmarried girl really wants to turn into a spinster with a grey braid. It seemed that the obstacle was a heroic, dashing young man, with dark upturned mustaches, with two coal-black, sparkling eyes, that swore to her, Mirele, "eternal" love—Tsadok the fuller was that obstacle.

But the most interesting thing was that when the story of Mirele's "love" got around the city and everybody was talking about it, her father, Reb Simkhele Eybeshits, could never even have dreamed of something like it, and kept pestering the widower, Reb Leybish Peysakh's son. Maybe Reb Simkhele did know something, but he saw fit to keep it to himself and act as if he didn't know. In just the same way, but from the opposite side, Uncle Melekh pretended not to know and one time he even grabbed the matchmaker by his lapels:

"Listen up, go tell him, my in-law Reb Simkhele, that if he doesn't like the match I can get him out of it. What? It's beneath him, such a fine Jew? What, he can strain his hemorrhoids better than me? You understand what I'm getting at? To be 'my in-law' out of the blue and all of a sudden. That's no small distance: Reb Simkhele Eybeshits and—Melekh Mitshes."

But apparently something bigger was involved. The matter had been ordained in heaven. He, Reb Simkhele Eybeshits, therefore had to surrender; he passed away. And grass hadn't even begun growing on his grave when the wedding between Tsadok and Mirele took place with full pomp, except there were no musicians, since it hadn't been a year since the funeral.

A year of war, and it seemed all of it would be "once upon a time" . . . That's the way the world had turned. Tsadok Beyger (he was no longer called *Beyger*, but rather *Zaydman*—how grand!) had become the finest burgher in the city. He bought up all of the *ato horeyso*'s,[1] he got all of the best *aliyes* in synagogue, every Sabbath he made a kiddush. And she, Mirele—she was utterly without equal! It makes you want to laugh: she has two little children and it's already settled, one will be an engineer, and the other a PhD. That is, she is all ready, pocked and measled.[2] And perhaps they would be great scholars like their grandfather, should they take the effort? Oh! Then we should be worried . . . They are already going about with their heads uncovered and people speak to them only in Polish.

1. *Ato horeyso*: The first words of a series of verses recited in the synagogue during the holiday of Simchat Torah. To be given the honor of reciting them was a privilege that was often was auctioned off.

2. *gepokt un gemozlt* (Yiddish): literally, "pocked and measled"—refers to measles and chickenpox, which are the necessary tribulations early on in childhood and figuratively any new experience; this idiom therefore has to do with being well seasoned and experienced.

But she, Mirele, had what it takes to put on airs. Tsadok had become a wealthy industrialist. He had gotten rid of that fulling business and had taken up tanning hides on his own account. Was it all smuggling when the Austrians were in? Well, you followed a bit of advice: for this gendarme a small coin, for that one a pair of gaiters. He had shoulders, Tsadok Zaydman did, and it was believed that eventually he would receive a consignment from the district command as well.

Tsadok, however, did have one flaw: he was a big dreamer; he loved to twirl his mustache and divert himself from his affairs. He couldn't stand it that Moshke Abishes stole from the poor people, giving them nothing of what the Committee owed them. What does it matter to you? As long as he gives you your share. On the other hand, would it be better for him to stick to his own affairs? A man is from head to toe pure smuggling! Why do you stick your nose out at him? No! He won't sit on his backside, pardon my language, waiting for Moshke to push him out; and if Moshke gets involved, how he will howl!

And in case he, Tsadok, should forget about the community's affairs, then there are others, good chaps, to keep him to it. That is, who will stand up for the community if not he, Tsadok?

The industrialist Moritz Meierbach and the older Broderson along with his wife had just returned from Russia. Well, Meierbach still wore a black bowler on his head and a narrow overcoat that kept his girth straining at the seams. That great wealthy man Broderson, however, was returning naked and destitute, in rags and tatters. When all is said and done, God still pitied this man who once owned five houses in Moscow, not counting a managerial pension from Brodsky of three and a half thousand rubles a month.[3]

Moritz Meierbach rode in Yoynele's coach right into the middle of the market, got down from his seat, took the bowler down off his head, stuck both hands into his vest pockets, looked around, and made a sour face, as if to say: what've you done with my market?! And

---

3. Lazar Brodsky (1848–1904) was a wealthy businessman and munificent Jewish philanthropist in the Russian Empire.

since the market was empty, and no one was running out to meet him, he turned to the right, onto the path by the riverbank, toward his factory.

When still at the train station he had heard that his broker, Tuvye Vaks, had started feeling his oats at the factory. It mortified him, Pan Moritz, greatly. Their conversation was a brief one:

"Ah! Welcome back, Reb Moyshele! Thank God you've made it back safe."

Meierbach: "*Po pierwam,*[4] to you I am not 'Moyshele'; and second, why have you made yourself at home as though in your father's vineyard? Bolshevism is not here yet . . ."

And with every word anger flared up in Pan Moritz, and he gnashed his mouth so much that it started to foam.

But Tuvye Vaks was a sly fox, and he thought to himself: Why should he go picking a fight? What needed to be done, he did. Before Moritz Meierbach crossed the border he had already heard a rumor and immediately removed all the merchandise from the soaking barrels, from the "drums": prepared, half-prepared, and even raw hides. Everything was packed in sacks and sent to Lublin, to Ostrowce; the factory was left with only bare walls and empty vats . . . not even the tail of a single pelt was left.

And like a thief when caught red-handed, Tuvye Vaks pointed to the empty walls and said in his ungrammatical Russian:

"*Nikakikh, Reb Moyshele, kak tvoya—byeri!*"[5]

That is: He, Tuvye the broker, was not, God forbid, demanding to be paid for his efforts to protect the factory that entire time from an "evil eye" . . . That is—were it not for him, Tuvye, no stone would have been left standing. When he got there a whole city of poor people had spread out inside, dug around in the barrels with pieces of iron, spared no effort in befouling everything, and had set

4. *Po pierwam* (Polish): first of all, firstly.

5. Ungrammatical Russian—"There's nothing, Reb Moyshele, but if something looks like your stuff—take it!"

about removing even the screws from the machines. He had sent that riffraff packing and this was the fine thanks he got . . . That is: the hides? So that there shouldn't be any ill will between him and Moritz Meierbach he also left not even the hint of a single hide to be found. The Austrians confiscated everything, not even leaving a single head of a pin . . .

And even though he knew that everything Tuvye was telling him was a bald-faced lie, Moritz Meierbach didn't want to worry himself needlessly. To himself he thought: you can get nothing out of a pig's snout; and aloud he bragged:

"I gave that servant the old heave-ho!"

He, Moritz Meierbach, took a real shine to Tsadok; he talked with him, spoke to him not as one does to a young fuller or to a former worker, but rather to one of his own:

"Tsadok," Meierbach said, "I've heard you're a well-off manufacturer. Well, very good . . . Very good . . ."

"Er, we do some soaking in a little workshop," Tsadok wrinkled his brow, and the corners of his mouth smiled boastfully.

"Well, well, don't put all your eggs in one basket," Moritz Meierbach gave him a brotherly slap on the shoulder. "What do you think? Would it be profitable to get into soaking? Will they, the Krauts, give a permit?"

Tsadok's dark eyes began to shine.

"Don't ask, Panie Meierbach, gold lies in the streets! If only I had a place. With the Austrians one can come to an agreement. You just give them a pain in their side."

It was good for Tsadok to say that for his little workshop, for his "chicken coop," he needed eighteen and thirteen. He, Moritz Meierbach, would not roll up his sleeves like Tsadok and stand around a soaking bucket. He needed to start a factory; for that one needed money, and here he was with a hole in his pocket.

He started questioning Tsadok about who were currently the fat Jews in the shtetl, the Jews with money.

"Why are you asking, *who*?" Tsadok blurted out what was weighing on him. "You ask, *who*? Moshke the Thief . . ."

"Am I hearing you right, Tsadok?" Moritz Meierbach fanned the flames, "Moshke Abishes, that scoundrel, is leading a whole city around by the nose?"

"You call it a 'city'? A herd of beasts is no city! Stick them in a stable and give them straw to chew . . ."

"Nevertheless one must see about doing something," Moritz Meierbach said.

"What, what are you asking? The burghers must get together: you, Pan Broderson, the pharmacist, Reb Ayzik Danziger—an old burgher—they must consider that such a thing can't be ignored."

To Meierbach's face Tsadok displayed modesty by not including himself among the fine burghers; but behind his back he mocked him, sticking out his tongue and telling a group of people in the middle of the market, "Well, I duped him! You shouldn't ask . . . Pan Meierbach, I said, Pan Broderson, burghers! What else, you'd call them urchins?! Boy did I dupe him!"

But they, the fine burghers, duped Tsadok no less by taking him into their group: little by little he gave himself over to the Committee's work so that he forgot what world he belonged to, neglecting his own affairs; and even his wife, Mirele, whom he loved dearly, she too had no influence over him.

Tsadok, however, did get his way: he managed to get a paper from the district commander, So-and-So: a meeting was to be convened in order to select a new committee.

Tsadok Fuller and Meierbach went off to see old Broderson. The old man was not inclined. It was not for him, he said; he didn't know the city and he didn't want to get involved. No, his wife wouldn't let him.

"Panie Broderson," Moritz Meierbach replied, "we don't accept your excuse. The city wishes it, the city is asking."

Then Pani Maria spoke up:

"If the city's asking, Stasiu," she said. "Don't refuse, go."

Broderson put on his expensive mink coat with the beaver collar (this one, La Broderson said, she had succeeded in rescuing from the claws of the Bolsheviks) and left the meeting.

But in the study house where the meeting was taking place there was another "city" considering Moshke Abishes. There was Oyzer Fisher, and Yoynele Roytman with his band, all burning bright with "180 proof" that could set a blaze at ten cubits away. Only Moshke walked around soberly. Had he given them brandy? "I don't want any mischief here, Panie Broderson, I swear by my wife and my children that I had no idea whatsoever."

The meeting never really came to an agreement, but blows flew from all sides, and the first ones landed on Tsadok Fuller, "that vile fuller's apprentice, that cobbler-ass!"

"Such a good-for-nothing!" charged Moshke. "It's fine, I've handled him . . . It's fine, he's got some business for me . . . Re-mem-ber! Just you keep it in mind! My name is Moshke!"

Understandably old Broderson, whom everyone assured that the "city" was with him, never expected such a thing. He bore Meierbach a strong grudge. What had he gotten him involved in? "My one and only God! These are people?"

He threw on his expensive mink coat with the beaver collar and left the meeting.

Moritz Meierbach stayed. He was not Tsadok. No one would dare lay a hand on him. He could therefore settle up with Moshke:

"You see," he cried out and pointed at the palm of his hand. "Let hair grow here if you take the committee! I'm not Tsadok Beyger! You'll get nowhere with me by such tricks! You see, you're walking along, just so, and, honest, I need to earn some money, it's something else. But so . . ."

Moritz Meierbach didn't finish his sentence, got stuck right in the middle, and Moshke immediately sensed that the snot-nosed big shot was going soft. If so, one could soft-soap him:

"Panie Meierbach," Moshke whispered to him, "I don't want any mischief here, how can I have the whole committee in my house on the Sabbath . . ."

He didn't make mistakes, Moshke the Sly. Meierbach was agitated. Meierbach loved giving a person his due. Meierbach was not Tsadok

Fuller. Meierbach's father was Reb Meshulem Meierbach—a whole city treated him with respect.

As for Tsadok, that evening he hadn't gotten off with just those blows. When he got home he met a teary-eyed Mirele. What was the matter?

She answered that she wasn't angry.

"What do you want of my life?" Mirele suddenly unleashed a flood of tears. "Why have you burdened my head with a Moshke Abishes?! Such a crude creature."

"He, Moshke, came here," Mirele explained, "at first threatening that he'd report you, you could pack up the factory, Tsadok could pre-pare a couple of hides." She hadn't said a word. Then he started to bad-ger her, that she was guilty of everything; if she wanted to she could have stopped it. People still thought that he was the old Tsadok to her, that she could convince him to do anything.

And once again Mirele let loose a flood of tears, sobbing pitiably, and soon began talking again:

"When he, Moshke, saw he wasn't getting anywhere with being mean, he tried the nice approach: he too had a wife and children, he started crying, he too needed to make a living . . . He might die sud-denly without enough for the Sabbath . . . And what did he, Tsadok, think, that he had God by the beard?"

Suddenly, he, Moshke, grabbed a knife from the table. At first she was terrified, but then he handed her the knife and stretched out his neck, like a calf to the slaughter:

"Here, go ahead," he cried out, "slaughter! What's the difference how you do it? Just slaughter!"

She still didn't answer him, even though her heart was full, and then he, Moshke, left, slamming the door behind him and cursing that all this should befall him!

"Re-mem-ber!" he yelled, "*I have surely visited you*! Re-mem-ber!"[6]

---

6. "*I have surely visited you*": In Hebrew, *pakod pakadti* (Exodus 3:16).

And after all that—what had he, Tsadok, accomplished with all of his fuss? They, the gentry, had come to an agreement with Moshke: Broderson would become honorary president and, as befits such a station, would be little involved; Reb Ayzik Danziger would become treasurer, and that honor he soon gave to his son-in-law, Fayvele Shpilman. This Fayvele Shpilman had a head on his shoulders, ho, ho! And a pretty penny, too, he made off the Austrians, a real pretty penny! When Fayvele undertook a piece of business one could be sure it would be well settled. He subscribed to the principle "live and let live." What's done is done—he said with regard to Moshke Abishes—when a person has already made a go at the bread, one can't just take it and throw it away. "Take my advice, leave it alone, Tsadok, the world is not yours . . . Don't worry yourself over it—leave it be!"

"Have I wasted so much effort on this?" argued Tsadok.

"He, however, will not give it up," Fayvele explained. "That is, you understand me, some sticky tar. When Moshke gets his teeth into something, one had better be careful."

And again, everything was left to the old man, and worse still than the old man. Moshke Abishes divvied things up as before: bread, kasha, flour, sugar, kerosene. What's more, the bread was nothing but chopped straw, the kasha was mixed with sand, and the kerosene was pure mud, but in larger volume than there had been previously.

Moshke cursed again, and cursing he defended himself, "Now I have to share the theft with Tsadok Beyger."

In that there was a bit of truth. Moshke had always been a cunning man: throughout the whole quarrel he had sent to Tsadok's house the finest challah flour and white sugar. And Tsadok, who had already had enough grief, and who was not a vindictive person, gave up, boasting, "He should have a fit of vomiting! Ho, ho! Before me he trembles fearfully! He's got epilepsy!"

But the real imbroglio, quietly, was Fayvele Shpilman's. With his pious little eyes through his bifocals he winked cunningly to Moshke Abishes:

"Do you, you bastard!, recite the whole *Thou shalt not steal*? I like it when someone's a decent human being."

Fayvele Prashniker (he came from Prashnik) made a living from a thousand different deals, but committee loaves were business too. In point of fact, very good business.

But he, Fayvele, was hesitant about what to do with Moritz Meierbach. After all, he had grown on increasingly intimate terms with him. What does that mean? He had explicitly passed a business deal on to him. The whole wedding with the committee had come from Moritz.

And he, Fayvele, came to the conclusion: Done is done, they'd have to lend him a little money. Of course, getting security in gold for the mortgage he, Moritz Meierbach, wouldn't be implicated! Leather is the same as gold; he'd have the means to pay a good "interest rate."

And once again Fayvele unburdened himself to Moshke Abishes: He, Fayvele, had received from the district command a permission to supply ten wagonloads of scrap iron, barbed wire, and so forth—one down. The Godlbozhits iron merchants buy up scrap iron, and whose concern is that? Let them buy! If that's too little for the iron merchants then they'll buy up from the peasants used barbed wire and iron bars from the trenches. So be it, Fayvele thought to himself—profits. There's no gendarme for him to go snitching to. But the question still remained, why were they selling the used wire and iron bars to a foreign buyer? Did he want the wire, God forbid, for free? Didn't he have as much right as some foreign devil? "But it so happens," Fayvele admits to himself, "that Fayvele Shpilman shits on everyone's head."

"Don't you worry, Fayvele," Moshke Abishes said to him using the familiar *you*. "They'll soon get what's coming to them! I've known for a long time that with Jews it's good to go to synagogue, that when you catch him by the chin, he'll lead you by the nose."

But Fayvele Prashniker didn't want anyone to inform on Jews, God forbid. He asked only him, Moshke—Moshke was no fool—why this was happening to him? Whom had he, Fayvele, wronged?

To this Moshke had a verse at the ready: *"Al de-ateft atifukh"* or, as Moshke pronounced it in his uncultured Yiddish: *"Taftikh, taftikh*

. . ."[7] He had already sniffed around and asked Khaykl the *shames'* son: what, for example, were the Gentiles on the other side of the Vistula doing with Motl Ayznkremer![8]

Khaykl the *shames'* son—the one who walks around behind the rebbes carrying their bags and who gobbles down derma in all the Polish taverns—*he* wasn't born yesterday. Just give him a wink and he'll know what you mean.

And when the gendarmerie had uncovered a whole load of barbed wire from the trenches in Motl Ayznkremer's cellar, Fayvele went this way and that—he was a Jew after all. At first he didn't want to listen. "What!" he scolded. "You trade in illegal wire and I should go to prison for your sake?" But when Ayznkremer's wife came to him and unleashed a flood of tears—"Reb Fayveshi and Reb Fayvele, you will earn the world to come; after all, you're allowed to, you have a permit"—he saw that he wouldn't be rid of that woman nor could he stand her crying, so he intervened and went where he had to. He took all the blame himself, Fayvele Shpilman did: the wire was all his and was originally purchased for him.

If, however, Motl Ayznkremer thought that the commander would let himself be deceived, he had made a big mistake. The commander had a Jewish head on his shoulders. Maybe they'd get away with three hundred, maybe . . . But he, Fayvele, didn't know how they'd get the bribe to him. Have you ever trifled with an Austrian? He can advance you the money where you need it and then turn around and say that you wanted to pay him off, to bribe him . . . He, Fayvele, didn't know what was wanted of him. He was scarcely keeping alive as it was, and these days dealing with them was mortally dangerous.

Was he still bargaining, that Ayznkremer? "Maybe a hundred and fifty," he said, "would be enough?" For his sake, for Fayvele's sake, let him, the commander, give him his bonus. Let him kiss his hand that

7. *"Al de-ateft atifukh"* (Aramaic): "Because you have drowned other people other people have drowned you" (Tractate Avot, 2:6).

8. A *shames* is personal assistant or aide to a Hasidic rebbe.

he might allow the illegal goods be taken back. But why was he pestering him, Fayvele? Let him go on his own, let him go on his own to talk to him.

Since Motl Ayznkremer still had to ask forgiveness of the upset Fayvele, with a groan he paid out the three hundred crowns and thanked him, thanked him very much for the effort and for the favor.

But a little while later Moshke learned of Fayvele's quiet imbroglio, and he couldn't forgive it.

"Ass!" he yelled at Ayznkremer. "You couldn't come to me? For fifty I would have put you in the best position. With your head turned away you come to Moshke, and to earn a zloty you go to the rich men—Ah, you should go to hell!"

At first Motl Ayznkremer was stunned, then he spat three times.

"So be it, supposing a child has become sick, supposing the pharmacy has refused to help, supposing misfortune lurks everywhere."

✧ 9 ✧

Lozer Kohn Provides the Drowned with Shrouds, and the Rabbi Ties the Bundle of Eternal Life to Them

At about that time Aunt Mitshe met with a misfortune which was both a bit of bad luck and good luck. It was a day of judgment in Godl-bozhits that no one should live through again. Two hundred people were being ferried across from the other side of the Vistula, back from their work in the trenches, and barely thirty escaped with their lives. The rest, alas, all perished, the Lord protect and save them! Nosn was among the survivors. Can you really believe that Aunt Mitshe sent Nosn off to earn some money in the trenches? The whole city could be her witness that the orphans were in no need, God forbid, of going off to work. On the contrary, you should just have seen the teachers Shimen studied with and what schools he went to. However, Nosn didn't want to dedicate his mind to studying, and Aunt Mitshe should know of no ill she didn't already, that Nosn went to work in the trenches. Had she known she certainly would have let him straightaway.

But Aunt Mitshe—with all due respect to her—did actually know. It wasn't the first day that Nosn went off to work in the trenches, when it was again time for school, and Shimen's school didn't even cost her three kopecks; Miss Broderson taught him completely for free. But an extraordinary piece of good luck it was for her all the same, Aunt Mitshe, that Nosn survived, because otherwise she would have had that orphan on her conscience.

No less lucky, however, was Lozer "Komashnmakher," the boot-maker. It is possible that were it not for the tragedy with the drowned people Lozer would to this day have stitched bootlegs just like before the war and even earlier, not even making enough to buy bread. So one should know that even though Lozer had always been clever and knew how to study traditional texts, in his work he was still a failure—a common bootmaker who died from hunger three times a day.

All his joy came from the fact that he was a member of the burial society. Early in the morning after the tragedy with the drowned people Lozer Kohn set off to Warsaw with several other burghers for help. Their first task was to procure linen to give a proper Jewish burial to the dead that people managed to get out of the water. The community leaders in Warsaw were not stingy in measuring out the pieces of linen for burying the drowned. The catastrophe in Godlbozhits had caused a great deal of commotion, and from the other surrounding cities and shtetls, too, people kept bringing more linen. But in Godlbozhits itself Lozer Komashnmakher moved heaven and earth to get the rabbi to allow the dead to be buried in ersatz linen made of paper. The rabbi recognized that it was an "emergency," and in order to ask forgiveness of the dead for the shame of wrapping them in paper mats he had the following registered in the record book of the burial society:

> A great calamity befell the Holy Community in Godlbozhits, where on such and such day, of such and such month, in the year reckoned "And the plague took place," there drowned in the Vistula many men, women, and children; out of the need for great haste, and in order not to shame our deceased by delaying overnight, they have been laid to rest in paper garments. May their souls be tied with the bundle of eternal life.

Then Lozer Komashnmakher composed a letter to the Godlbozhits landsmen across the sea in America. In the letter were vividly described all the miseries which the shtetl underwent during the war followed by the great tragedy of the drowned which left in its wake hundreds of orphans without roofs over their heads, or clothes on their backs, or a piece of bread to eat, and without manners—that is, basic elementary schools. All of the trustees signed the letter and the rabbi added his signature. The letter was sent by express delivery.

Then Lozer went off to see old Broderson.

"Panie Broderson, the city is asking that you be put at the head of a relief committee for the orphans of the drowning victims."

Broderson pushed up his glasses and exchanged glances with his wife.

"Well, what do you say, Maria?"

"If the city asks for it, Stasiu," Mrs. Broderson said. "Don't turn them down. Poor, poor orphans . . ."

And Pani Maria Broderson wiped away a tear from her eye with the corner of a cambric handkerchief.

Old Broderson put on the mink coat with the beaver collar and went together with Lozer Komashnmakher to Warsaw.

In Warsaw it turned out that the wealthy big shot there in the American relief committee—a certain engineer by the name of Binyomin Rafalkes—knew Broderson well from back in Moscow. He had soon provided them with a small quantity of old clothes, some American flour, and a small crate of canned infant milk. Moreover, engineer Rafalkes soon promised to transmit by cable the whole letter from the Godlbozhits community with their plea for immediate aid. The director of the central American relief committee was profoundly moved by the terrible tragedy: "Three hundred people disappeared in the waves of the beautiful Vistula"—he ordered the telegram sent.

Herr Broderson said that the number of the drowned only amounted to a hundred and seventy? That was in point of fact an unimportant detail. You have to round off numbers, and you have to be able to paint a picture of need—"Little children wander about naked in the street, swollen with hunger." A director of a relief committee cannot be a dry statistician; he must have the feeling and talent to portray his spiritual condition to the American charitable donors. And so it is—Panie Broderson.

From then on from the golden land of America there began to float to Godlbozhits aid upon aid. The little orphans were clothed in large, old pants and twisted shoes with long toes. To crazy Yekl they gave a top hat full of holes; the soup kitchen offered dairy lunches of potatoes and rice; three teachers gave lessons in the women's study house to lads in rags and tatters: "*Komets alef*—o! *Vayoymer*—'said'; *vaydaber*—'spoke.'" That's what it looked like in the shtetl.

But Godlbozhits was a city of rogues and scoundrels who no matter how much you give them never have enough, and whatever favor you do them will be repaid by being pelted with stones. So they went, those insolent people, those spoiled poor folk, and informed on Lozer to Broderson, who was chairman of the committee, that Lozer was selling the white American flour, schmaltz, and infant milk in the stores, that the best American clothes with the silk lining he was selling for himself.

Broderson pushed up his glasses and exchanged glances with his wife.

"Well, what do you think, Maria? Do you hear what people are saying about our Lozer?"

And Pani Maria shook her head.

"Impossible, Stasiu . . . An honest soul, our Lozerl."

Pani Maria understood people. Pani Maria had a particular talent for discerning a person's true nature right from the very first glimpse. With his silky black beard and fiery eyes—like the ancient Hebrews—she liked Lozer at first sight; and later she liked him even more for his gratis and self-sacrificing work for the relief committee.

But the insolent poor folk, with Oyzer Fisher as their leader, were not satisfied with informing on Lozer to Broderson. Nor did they lower their eyes with shame when Pani Maria rebuked them for besmirching their benefactor. They went off to see the municipal commander and showed him the stores and other places where the goods and clothing from the American relief committee were being sold. The commander confiscated the discovered goods and launched an investigation.

That same day Sonia Broderson came home from school utterly upset and irate, "Such a shame! Such a disgrace!"

What happened? The gendarmerie had detained a wagon full of female smugglers. Apparently the women were dressed in conspicuously thick clothing, even though there had been no frosts yet. That was a well-known way of smuggling leather: you wrap yourself in it as far up as possible. The gendarmerie was certain this time it was also a leather-smuggling operation. How surprised they were, though, when the women who searched the female smugglers began unwrapping from them whole lengths of linen, like peeling an onion. Moreover, the case grew more remarkable because, generally speaking, linen was not something that was smuggled . . . The women were interrogated, threatened, and finally they confessed that it came from the linen that had been obtained for the "ritual burial" of the drowning victims. The women were in fact professional corpse-washers, and the linen had been given to them for a good reward by Lozer Kohn.

Old Broderson stood there amazed, pushed his glasses up onto his forehead.

"And what does the rabbi say about this? After all, didn't he have control over all of this?"

Sonia waved her hand: "It's better that papa not speak about that rabbi. Perhaps papa remembers the letter he wrote to the central committee asking why the aid for the elementary schools had not been sent?" So now an answer has arrived, that the money has been sent regularly every month to the local rabbi, and the rabbi feigns ignorance. Such a thing is unheard of! She, Sonia, knew him well, that local rabbi, and his Passover flour, but to take money from orphans one would have to be something far worse!

Old Broderson described the rabbi's ugly deeds to one of the burghers who could keep a secret, and that secret-keeper diligently questioned the rabbi.

The rabbi tried to defend himself: It was given here, given there, given for kerosene, to make ritual undergarments for the children. And when the account of the monies received still didn't add up he grew testy and answered in the following words:

"By elementary school, then, you mean the alphabet? If so, they'll grow up into Jews without Judaism, violators of the Sabbath and the Law. Elementary school means . . . studying Torah! Who teaches Torah? A rabbi! The Honor of the Torah—yes!"

So responded the rabbi, a person who had the prestige of an ancestry of maybe twenty generations of saints and holy men, while Lozer Komashnmakher could invoke no grand lineage. He had finally had enough of his head in the clouds as it had cost him enough energy and money to straighten out the matter of the linen and the American schmalz. Commander Stänglmeier had a clever head on his shoulders. You couldn't buy him off for a mere pittance. He approached it like a merchant: half for me—half for you.

At any rate, Lozer Komashnmakher abandoned the Americans' good fortunes. He, Lozer, who before the war had been a penniless beggar now had enough money to become a chief buyer of leather in Meierbach's factory. Moritz Meierbach said of him: "A common youth, that Komashnmakher, but a lively head he's got on him. The American committee? When he could, he would . . ."

Meanwhile, salvation came to the Jews of Godlbozhits from a different direction. The noble Lord Balfour issued his declaration concerning a national home for the Jewish people in the Jewish Land of Israel, and the Jews of Godlbozhits came to the conclusion that if rebuilding the Land of Israel were once again left in the hands of the boys and girls of a party there, then it might still be possible, God forbid, that in the Holy Land too lamps would be lit on Friday nights.

That Sabbath, therefore, the Rabbi gave a sermon in the synagogue on the *mitsve* of settlement of the Land of Israel and on the righteous kingdom—that is, England, which is one of the Ten Tribes from the other side of the Sambatyon. Then the rabbi addressed the women:

"And to you, women, I say: it is written in the verse: *So shall you say to Jacob's household*, that means to the women, whom one is commanded to speak to before the men. In Egypt, it is written, the women had the privilege that from their mirrors, in which they used to look at themselves, in order to make the men desire them and 'join' with them, the women had the honor of that privilege, that from their mirrors was made the washbasin of the tabernacle, that is, the Temple. But later— for women have light minds—the women sinned by giving over their jewelry to the service of idolatry, to making the golden calf, the *Eygel*.

To this day they cannot redeem themselves from that sin, and each one has a difficult labor, and each one gives birth with difficulty, that is the punishment for the 'sin of the golden calf.' And here is the proof, of the pious it is written: 'And the midwives complained to Pharaoh, king of Egypt, that the Jewish women were giving birth on their own, *for they are lively*—they are their own midwives.'[1] Now, when there are so many signs that the redemption is near, when the footsteps of the Messiah are heard, you women must redress the sin of the golden calf, you must give away your jewelry in order to redeem the holy ground from the Gentiles' hands, and in that merit Jewish mothers will have, like their grandmothers in Egypt, easy deliveries, will give birth to male children, and the savior will come to Zion and we will—Amen."

The lament that erupted in the women's section when the rabbi mentioned the sin of the *Eygel*, the golden calf, suddenly turned into a cry of joy. Women who had for years quarreled with their neighbors in the women's section now embraced one another, noses running, and kissing each other's faces. Then Tsiml "Cossack" took out a dirty handkerchief and exclaimed, "Give it here, kosher women, give here your jewelry for the Lando'Israel!"

So those simple women took off what they had: a gold chain, a ring, a silver bracelet; they threw them into the kerchief and said: "Lord of the Universe, kind Father, may it fulfill a *mitsve*!" The poor women, too, who owned no jewelry, did not want to be prevented from doing their part. So they ran home and looked for what they could: this one had a copper pan, that one a little brass Sabbath candlestick hidden from the Austrian confiscations; all these things were taken right into the home of the chairman of the Mizrahi—to Lozer Kohn.

And above, in the women's section, Tsiml "Cossack" and several other women went from "city" to "city," no one was exempt, each one had to throw something into the kerchief till they reached the Eastern wall where the wealthy women sat.

1. "For they are lively": Exodus 1:19.

But the wealthy women kept their hands at their sides. Little Yosele's wife answered that if she was meant to give something for the Land of Israel, she simply could not make a mockery by giving a little ring or some other trifle; if she was meant to give, that wealthy woman said, then she must give something valuable: her pearl or her diamond necklace, and that she could not do without her husband's knowledge. This was a matter that demanded deliberation. One had to think it over, discuss it. And if she was indeed meant to give, then she was certainly not going to give anything to Lozer Kohn. Since when was this Lozer Komashnmakher such a trustworthy person? Since he stopped "pulling two pigs through one hole"; that is, since he stopped being a cobbler? She, that wealthy woman, knew far more trustworthy people, she could herself find the right way to Warsaw, and even to Jerusalem as well . . .

And since the rest of the wealthy women agreed with little Yosele's wife—particularly with regard to discussing it with their husbands and entrusting their jewelry only to reliable hands—Tsiml tied up the kerchief with the few things there were in it, made a solid loop and slung it down through the little window into the men's section, right up onto the lectern, and yelled down:

"Here, Jews! Take it, Reb Lozer! This is from the poor women . . ."

And to those poor women she said:

"The same to them! Those rich women'll have no share in the Land o'Israel. Women, you've read the *Tsenerene*?[2] In the *Tsenerene* it's written that when the Messiah comes all the poor women will become rich women and all the rich women with their hearts of stone will become poor folk; then Satan will further strengthen their resolve, so that they will give no alms, and that they will be refused to greet the Messiah . . .

---

2. The *Tsenerene* is an immensely popular Yiddish Bible translation and commentary, originally compiled for women. It was first published in the late sixteenth century and has appeared in hundreds of editions since then.

The Zionists decked out their meeting hall with blue and white paper banners and sang Zionist songs; and every Sabbath the Mizrahists made a "Kiddush" with a greasy kugel, and every Saturday evening an end-of-Sabbath meal. Only the Bronitser Hasidim stood against the Land-of-Israel work. The Mizrahists drove them out of their superior study house and painted on its Eastern wall a Star of David with two lions. Then they, the Bronitsers, with Motele Perl-Tsvetes at their head, moved into a private home, bolted the doors and windows, and their mouths and ears to the outside, drank brandy and sang:

What are they doing in Bronits?
Oy, what are they doing in Bronits?
Oy! Oy! Oy! What are they doing in Bronits?

"They're drinking brandy, they're eating spice cakes at their feast, ha!"

"Oy! They're eating brandy, they're drinking spice cakes at their feast, ha!"

✣ 10 ✣

The Evening in Uncle Melekh's House

At last, having dawdled here and lingered there, he had to go home from the study house, Uncle Melekh did. It turned ten o'clock, eleven—midnight; he'd been listening to so many stories, and now outside there was such a downpour, such a rain, that even his nose didn't wish to stick out. But truth be told, Uncle Melekh would much rather take the pouring rain outside than his house with its bowls and soaking pails set out to catch the rain, and with the splashing on the muddy floor. One shouldn't sin by complaining, but "A stable, a chicken coop, not a house. He'll never get out of hell, Arele, when he won't let some kind of roof get put over his head."

At any rate, Arele had a job. He sat all night long at the Party groping the young women behind the stove, and during the day he snoozed till two o'clock.

And just in case that wasn't enough misery and heartache for you, Aunt Mitshe had begun raising chickens and ducks in that filthy house. Clearly the old folks were losing more and more of their minds every year. Otherwise it would be unthinkable that a person could let chickens wander around in such close quarters inside the house. Otherwise wouldn't they gobble down more than they were worth?

"Here chick, chick, chickee!" Uncle Melekh, who was outside, heard Aunt Mitshe calling the chickens together inside.

In the middle of the house, right in the mud, kernels had been strewn. The chickens pecked and grabbed, and the prattling rooster strode about haughtily, inspecting whether there was any disorder in his state; and only from time to time did he bend down for a kernel.

In the chimney—a drowsy fire from damp chips of wood. No matter how much you showed Aunt Mitshe that a bundle of wood costs less and smokes less, she could not break the habit of using wood chips. Dinner still didn't have it in mind to finish cooking—it wasn't yet two o'clock in the morning. The cat dozed on the chafing dish—it's more than likely that no roasted meat could be prepared in that glowing stove. Serves them right! Chickens and cats . . . Dogs were all that was missing!

And here every once in a while a drop dripped from the ceiling into your collar. Brrrr . . . Uncle Melekh went into the other room and turned up the lamp.

"Mitshe, maybe you've got something to eat?"

"Dinner is cooking," the aunt answered. "I'm going to add a piece of wood. Meantime, go pray your evening prayers."

"*Who makes the day pass and who brings the night . . . And who separates day from night . . . And who separates . . . And who separates . . .* Well, oh? Yitskhok? Nosn?"

He had the habit, Uncle Melekh did, of getting sidetracked during prayer and repeating a word ten times, and Aunt Mitshe could hardly understand his Hebrew.

"They're still at work," the aunt could hardly grasp what he meant. "Tsadok had to prepare a load of uppers today, so they'll come home late."

"*God living and enduring . . . God living and enduring . . .* ," the uncle continued to pray. "Well, oh? Shmuel? Yente?"

"So now there's a Party to add insult to injury," groaned the aunt.

"*God is a faithful king . . . God is a faithful . . .* ," prattled the uncle angrily. "Well, oh! Shmuel . . . *I give to him! I-I-I give!*"

And the uncle continued to pray more quietly, more restrained, and looked through the glass door into the store. There Shimen was sitting, his head propped up, and by a candle he was reading, studying something inwardly out of a book, ruminating difficult, incomprehensible words. The uncle knew that out of the whole gang there was maybe but one Shimen to have the makings of a respectable person—he wants to and will become a respectable person.

Meanwhile Aunt Mitshe had already prepared a pot of soup. Uncle Melekh washed his hands and with a dishrag he slowly wiped and dried them. No matter how much that pot of food stood on the table, wafting its steam, Uncle Melekh would not hurry in like a glutton and a drunkard. He took his time, chewing his piece of bread from the *grace before meals* for a long time, and said:

"Listen, Mitshe, I heard in the study house a nice story about the women's preacher."

"Who d'you mean?" asked the Aunt.

"Who d'I mean? That Land-of-Israel Jew."

"Lozer Komashnmakher?"

"Whatever I meant, you won't guess!" Uncle Melekh joked. "Tell me, I ask you, why were you in such a hurry to give away your diamond earrings? They wouldn't take 'em later? So I ask myself: Little Yosele's wife was also in a hurry? Reb Ayzik Danziger's wife, too, got all carried away and gave away her pearls and diamonds? They've got nicer jewelry than you."

Aunt Mitshe didn't give in.

"Rich people never hurry," she said. "All Jews give for the Land of Israel, and I too want to have a hand in it."

"D'you hear what people are saying," Uncle Melekh wiped his mustache with the edge of the tablecloth. "People are saying that that sly bastard has slipped all those things into his own pocket. They're saying that Tsiml Cossack recognized her brass candlesticks in Lozer's possession."

"My earrings," the aunt still remained firm, "he did not take; for my earrings I have a receipt from Warsaw."

"And what do you think, in Warsaw they're lesser thieves? It is what it is, after all you're going to say that I'm a fool. But remember what Melekh's telling you, that by the time your earrings reach the Land of Israel there won't even be a tiny diamond left."

"And what about the candlesticks?" the aunt was curious.

"Who d'you mean? Tsiml Cossack? She got them back. She cursed him out . . . the way Tsiml Cossack can. She announced to him how it was going to be: 'You think,' she said, 'this is Tsipore, lame Moyshele's wife? You two-timing cheat!'"

—•—

"There he is! Welcome! We should have mentioned the Messiah. Good Lord, where have you been roving about?"

Lame Moyshele, who had just then come in, did not even respond to the greeting. He put down his whip and lantern in a corner, pushed up his plush cap, and wiped his forehead with a wet sleeve.

"Mama," he asked, "maybe you could give me a scrap to eat, I'm nearly fainting from hunger."

"And where is Tsipore?" the aunt asked.

"May she be stricken with epilepsy! She's going around with that bastard."

He shuffled back and forth over the muddy floor, dragging his lame foot and cursing: "Epilepsy! A calamity!"

"Such a trollop!" the aunt said angrily. "And have the children eaten?"

"Miseries and suffering. The poor things have fallen asleep like hungry birds."

Again he shuffled about, that lame man, back and forth, unable to resist:

"Mama, give me a spoonful of food," he asked. "I'm falling off my feet . . . A whole day in the rain . . ."

Aunt Mitshe set a bowl of food in front of him on the table. The lame man didn't even make a blessing, slurping like a Gentile. This bothered the uncle:

"You ought to at least make a blessing," he said resentfully. "After all, you did learn it once."

"Uncle," said the lame man, "*vsyo ravno*.[1] It's all the same—*hejta, wiśta, wio* . . .[2] I'm asking myself, Uncle, just wait a second: why should

---

1. *vsyo ravno* (Russian): it's all the same, it's no matter.
2. *hejta, wiśta, wio*: Polish coachman's words to spur on horses.

he, that bastard, like Tsipore? Just some foreign woman? Really, a man has a wife, a kosher Jewish woman, and I'm thinking of that bastard. And if that Jewish woman gets sick, God forbid, oughtn't one bury her right away? What a dirty trick! How is that Jewish? But is he after all rather a goody-two-shoes, a real scholar, the rabbi's toady? Just hold on, Uncle—You're no fool . . .'"

"I've known him for a long time to be a heretic, a pork eater," said the uncle. "How you've made him into a wealthy resident! Came from the devil knows where, some piddling cobbler, a common bootmaker. And in Godlbozhits you get to be a respectable person!"

"Uncle is making fun I've made him? Lame Moyshele did? What could someone like me know? A whole day: horses, horses . . . *hejta*, *wiśta* . . . Uncle! Among horses you yourself become a horse."

"And If you don't take the nasty carcass and sell it properly you'll be a still bigger horse," said Uncle Melekh.[3]

"Uncle!" lame Moyshele said standing up. "I swear! What you think of me . . . I'll flay him alive!"

Uncle Melekh smiled wryly, and belched.

"A joke, I don't know your strength?! 'Tsipore, may you be stricken with cholera, just come home . . . ' So she goes home. But if you won't let her over the doorstep, she'd speak differently. Otherwise what, you'll live with her? After all, you're no boor, are you?"

Someone knocked on the window. A head appeared through the pane. "Who is that? Yosl?"

"Come on, Moyshe," someone yelled from outside. "Tsipore's getting married to Lozer Komashnmakher!"

The lame man grabbed his whip with one hand, the lantern with the other, and skipped out. Uncle Melekh remained seated, astonished: "Such a shame, such a disgrace." He, the uncle, was himself ashamed to leave, so he sent Shimen instead.

Even though it was pitch dark in the market, and pouring rain to boot, it was full of people. Everyone had crammed themselves into the

3. In Yiddish, horse (*ferd*) can also mean blockhead, ignoramus.

narrow alley between little Yosele's house and the study house. People were pressed against a closed door where Yosl Treger stood, ordering that no one be allowed in. A gang of children was making a ruckus and whistling, and Yosl Treger was cursing with all his strength.

And when Yosl thrust open the door of the house, and the crowd was let in, there was no one there. People laughed to themselves:

"He made such a fuss, Yosl Bandit did! A city full of sensible people led up the garden path, and a bunch of idiots jumping at the spectacle. Serves him right! A young man's ruin—that'll wake people from their sleep. I thought there was a fire, God forbid!"

So some regretted their interrupted sleep, and little Shimen meantime stood by lame Moyshele. They thoroughly searched little Yosele's house. The lame man lit every corner with his lantern.

"Look!" Shimen called out suddenly and pulled open a half-shut door to Butcher Shop Street. "Look! They left over here. The door is open."

Later Shimen described what happened to Uncle Melekh. He had quietly approached the group of porters by the pump and listened: everything about Tsipore was true. It was all true. They had shut her in with Lozer there where they stood in the house, and then they sent in two of the porters: "Hand over some money, it'd be best for you not to be here with the whole city all in one place." Did he have any choice, Lozer Komashnmakher? The longer he dithered, the more he'd have to pay; and he promised a good swig of brandy too to keep completely mum. So just then they let him out the other side door together with Tsipore, and meanwhile Yosl Treger gave the crowd the runaround.

Uncle Melekh listed to it all and merely said, "Don't go repeating things, Shimen, it's not for decent people." Then he yawned widely—he seemed to be getting sleepy already, scratched his shoulder, and read his evening prayers:

"God is a faithful king . . . Shema yisrael . . . Shemaaa . . ."

All of a sudden his jewels of children came in: Arele, Yente, and Shmuel trailing at the rear. Little Shmuel snuck in quietly, and it almost went poorly for him when he saw that his father was not yet asleep.

And the uncle, as though oblivious, chewed the words of his evening prayers aloud, while at the same time fussing over the belt of his pants. Shmuel took the opportunity to hide his face with his hands. Suddenly the belt swooped down onto Shmuel's lowered head, onto his bare hands:

"Take that, Party! You, too, in the Party?! So you're already an obstreperous kid too?! You're too sick to do your homework?"

And already calming down:

"No matter, when the young woman wanders around till one o'clock, the young man . . . People! Berele the Shitter's Party! But you, you little snot?! You're already trying to get around me!"

Shmuel didn't make a sound; he rushed into the back storeroom and threw himself down fully clothed onto the pallet, crying into his pillow. His mother came in with a bowl of food: No! He won't eat! His father emptied his whole bitter heart to him. It was his fault it was raining in? If Arele didn't want to give a penny then he was somehow to blame?

"But why aren't you doing your homework?" his mother gently chided him. "See, just look at Shimen . . ."

"Homework?" He had done his homework. He had not gone to the Party. Father was beating him for nothing. He had done his homework at Bebele's, didn't mother know who that was? Bebele Rabinovitsh, Shmuel Rabinovitsh's daughter. She had a separate room for doing homework. But at home father didn't even let a candle burn.

Arn and Yente had also come into the back storeroom. They were still enjoying the whole affair; they started laughing, and said: "All the same!" They, at their age, sat at home, stuck in that house, while he, such a little brat, was off chasing girls . . . Till twelve, one o'clock in the morning. What was he doing for so long there with Bebele, she, Yente, wanted to know? And just to torment him she sang him a little ditty:

That girl I love,
That girl I love,
With the blue eyes and the bright hair,

That girl I love,
That girl I love,
With the eyes so blue.

She meant Bebele with the golden hair and shining eyes. She had hit him right in his suffering heart. He shot back, "Yentoyl! What's wrong with you? Go make out with your gendarme!"

But then Arele jumped in, "Are you sleeping, or not?! I'll call papa right in here and he'll whup you with his belt so you'll not soon forget! Be-bele! Be-betshke . . . dear Bebush . . ."

"Go to hell, Arele Scuzz! Don't you want Pani Sonia? She's waiting for you!"

"Be-betshke . . . sweet Bebush . . ."

"Sonitshke . . . Sonyush . . ."

For a long time they traded insults, barbs, tearing into each other right to the quick till Arele grew tired of it and, as the older and wiser one, was the first to give up. He took off his collar, cuffs, vest, and stood there in his filthy underwear, scratching his hairy chest with pleasure. Then he smoked a cigarette and blew out the candle. It went dark, and only from the side of the store with the glass door did the light of a lamp shine weakly in.

Shmuel was already asleep, Yente was snorting and snoring. Only Arn couldn't get to sleep. He was not such a brat as Shmuel who just got beat up, cried, and was now already sleeping. Arele was already, knock wood, a real man, an adult. At night various thoughts crept into his head. During the day he never deluded himself into thinking he could approach Sonia Broderson, but in his sleepless nights that possibility seemed more realistic. He remembered that the pharmacist's wife talked about a match and how people praised him. There was probably no doctor coming from Cracow to snatch her away. A doctor would need it to be worth his while and today the Brodersons were beggars. Right here, then, in Godlbozhits, he was the only serious contender.

He did have one significant rival: Stänglmeier. But that was when Austria was in and he was commander of the shtetl. Now he went around in a stiff fedora, like someone who's seen better days, and courted that old maid, that pockmarked dentist. No, Arele wasn't afraid of him.

But he did fear the students in their fraternity caps who came driving in from Warsaw one after the other. There in Warsaw people were dying of hunger, they were eating potato peels; so they came to Godlbozhits, stuffing their gobs enough for two. And as soon as they had gotten their fill they started saying terrible things about the shtetl: that Godlbozhits was a dark hole, that Godlbozhits was a desolate hick-burg, that the people of Godlbozhits were animals . . . Flapped their gums and—gone.

All those students stayed with the Brodersons. There they were pampered; Sonia offered them lessons, gave them jobs at her school, and as a result people looked at each one of those students in turn as though he was Sonia's intended. That usually lasted until that one left.

But one time there came from the devil knows where a Litvak, a Hebrew teacher with little black mustaches, and as soon as he arrived he became a regular visitor to the Party, making speeches and droning endlessly in Hebrew.[4] Like a longtime resident offering his opinions in the Party: This he didn't like, that he didn't like; here the Star of David didn't have the proper angles, and there the minutes were written in a florid Hebrew, with mistakes. Arele, as both chairman of the Party and a Hebrew grammarian, might have tried to oppose him, showing him the door: "*Panie* So-and-So, I'm the chairman here so please don't criticize me." But Livshits—that was the teacher's name— had brought Miss Broderson with him, and Arele held her in esteem. The Litvak had managed an even greater feat: he had brought Miss Broderson into the Party, she had become a member—she who was well-known as an assimilationist. Soon she herself had also started getting involved, offering opinions, as though she'd been a bigwig at the Party for a long time. There was no doubt that at the first, most

---

4. Litvak: A Lithuanian Jew; often a stereotype in Jewish culture, Litvaks were known for their dry intellectualism, especially when compared with Polish Jews.

important meeting they would elect Livshits chairman, and he, Arele, would have a choice to clear his throat with dignity and say:

"So be it, let someone else be chairman . . . I don't crave that chair . . ." So it would be his choice to say this and nothing more. After all he wasn't going to go on to be secretary, or some other lower functionary there in the election; at his age he certainly couldn't bear someone else bossing him around.

And given the fact that the teacher Livshits—even though he had already been in the shtetl for half a year and had stuffed his gob enough for two—had still not started bad-mouthing the shtetl; and given the fact that the girls didn't consider him a suitable match for the highly intelligent Miss Broderson—all of this convinced Arele that they, Livshits and Broderson, were engaged.

And even if Arele might not have been jealous of all of the earlier students for such a thing, he certainly couldn't fail to envy Livshits. He even felt insulted: No. She, Miss Sonia, still didn't have to trade him in for such a shabby teacher.

On his damp mattress, where he tossed about from one side to the other, he pitied Pani Broderson that she was going to get married to such a pauper. And he also felt a little sorry for himself that he felt old, tired, and broken.

————

At around three o'clock Arn had barely fallen asleep. But that day had still not come to an end in Uncle Melekh's house. First Yitskhok and Nosn came home from the factory, both of them wearing their tanners' boots with the high bootlegs. Aunt Mitshe sat by the stove and dozed. Without saying a word she handed them the lukewarm dinner and immediately went of to lay down in bed. Nosn hurriedly drained his bowl and lay down next to Shmuel. Shmuel felt a light push and at the same time got a whiff of a tangy tannery smell. He woke up.

"Who's that?"

"Me, Nosn."

"So late?"

"We were finishing up a load of uppers."

Shmuel didn't ask anything else and stopped listening. He fell back to sleep.

Nosn woke him up.

"Shmuel . . ."

"What?"

"Haven't you heard?"

"What?!"

"That—at Meierbach's factory . . . That—with the strike . . ."

"What?! They'll shoot?!"

"What shooting . . . a strike and that's it."

"Who's striking? What strikers?"

"What strikers . . . The workers are striking."

"Why are they striking?"

"They want higher pay. Everything's expensive. Otherwise they won't work."

Shmuel sat up.

"And if Meierbach won't go for it? Oh! It's best not to pick a fight with him, he's prickly! Yente once sent me to collect a bill from the store. Well, from then on he never bought anything from us!"

"That was something different," Nosn said. "Here it's a matter of his losing money. Every hour costs him money. His customers are waiting for their merchandise."

"So he'll hire other workers."

"Just let them come! Heads will roll!"

"Really?! Those strikers?!"

"Absolutely . . ."

Again Shmuel didn't hear these last words. His eyes kept sticking together. He stretched himself out over the full width of the pallet and spoke from his sleep, "Nosn, move over."

"Where can I go? I'll fall off . . ."

"Let me take the edge and you can be against the wall."

They changed places, but Shmuel was still restless.

"It stinks," he complained.

"It's from the grease we coat the uppers with," Nosn defended himself.

For a while it was quiet. Suddenly Nosn sat up.

"Shmuel."

"What?"

"You know? I'm not going to work for Tsadok in that stench anymore. I can do without the favor."

"You don't want to work?" said Shmuel frightened.

"I'll hire myself out to Meierbach at his factory. I'll work with Russia leather—like a nobleman—that's it."

"And what will Tsadok say?"

"Tsadok? What am I, his slave? It's not enough for 'us' to work in that stench all day long, but he walks around back and forth, with his hands folded behind his back and curses! Shouting! You think he doesn't swear at Yitskhok?"

"And Yitskhok?"

"Yitskhok is a different matter. He's got sangfroid. If you spit in his face he'll say: It's raining. As long as there're still a couple of hours of work in your free time, as long as there're still a couple of marks . . ."

It grew quiet again. Shmuel snored. From the door to the storeroom, where the light of a lamp shone through the glass, came Shimen's stubborn and desperate voice repeating:

"Ich möchte gesingen, du möchst gesingen, er möcht gesingen. Ich möchte gesprungen, du möchst gesprungen, er möcht gesprungen."

✤ 11 ✦

On the Two Pairs of Eyes of Iser Meierbach

This is what Shimen, who was an eyewitness, described in the morning:

I'm sitting and reciting from my geography textbook. First I hear something like a groan, one and then another. From the ceiling lime starts pouring down, and before I can look around: *Craaash!* The lamp goes out and the sky looks in from outside: 'a peep show!' The uncle woke up right away, followed by the aunt and all of the children; only Yente couldn't be woken up—she was sleeping like a log. The Uncle lit the lantern and we all went outside—the whole front wall lay on the ground like a cake in the market. Stones had rolled clear off to the other side. The uncle looked like he'd lost his mind. He suddenly put down the lantern and clapped his hands together:

"Children! It's raging against me!"

And Arele clenched his teeth. It didn't matter to him.

"Otherwise," he said, "we wouldn't have known? It's nothing, such a wall, such a giant held up with sticks. Is it any wonder?"

And the uncle:

"Who knows if someone's, God forbid, to blame."

And Arn:

"It's got itself to blame! Four o'clock in the morning is to blame."

Early in the morning people from the municipal authorities began pestering Uncle Melekh: he had to remove all the stones and he had to put up a fence around the site. Godlbozhits was not some village where everyone just empties their slop buckets in the middle of the street, piling up stones and snarling up traffic. Your wall—clear it out and thank God no one writes an official report on you. You had a dilapidated wall, so knock it down and don't risk human lives.

As if he didn't have enough troubles with the aggravation of the damage itself, but people from the municipal authorities kept scolding and berating him. And hardly had he—that wreck of a man—piled up the stones, with his own hands and those of his little children, and cleared away the debris (Arele didn't lend a hand), than Arele came home with fresh news that the municipal authorities were going to forcibly confiscate half of the land in order to widen the road to the river. So it was set out in the new design of the municipal code.

Uncle Melekh was no fool. He listened and understood exactly the new design of the municipal code; but what's more, the whole thing smacked of the pharmacist who wanted nothing more than to get his land for pennies.

And if so, then to hell with him! From lame Moyshele the uncle borrowed his patched tarp, stretched it out over his house in place of a roof, and determined to live there for as long as possible.

And he would certainly have succeeded, Uncle Melekh would. He was a stubborn Jew, and no spoiled child. He was just as able to tolerate honey cakes as bread and onions; if needed he could be a train-traveling merchant, and if there was no money, here's half a bushel of rye carried in from the village on his shoulders.

But a misfortune befell him having to do with his wife. She, the aunt, had gone, heaven preserve you, completely "funny." A whole day and a whole night she kept the stove burning, constantly adding woodchips, and at one o'clock in the morning their meager supper was still not ready. When the Uncle would come home from the village weary and exhausted, he would never find her at home. Here she was with a woman giving birth, and there she was caring for a sick person; with her wide apron wrapped around her hips, she brought everything from her house, not forgetting a piece of bread, and late at night she returned home from her new mother, her apron undone and completely empty.

What was he, the uncle, going to do, yell at her, scold her? He saw it wouldn't do any good anyway—the woman was possessed.

But worst of all was the fact that the aunt had completely stopped sleeping. A whole night she sat by the stove, constantly adding woodchips to the fire; she never got undressed, and the cats lay at her feet, on her lap, and by the chimney.

One time her apron even caught fire and she was nearly burned alive. By a stroke of luck someone noticed and poured out a whole bucket of water onto her.

The children were beginning to go their separate ways: some went off to work and others found their bread by other means. Arele stuck to the currency traders and spent whole days in the village, scarfing down millet with milk and sleeping in the barns with the peasant girls. Yente, for her part, had a crush on a Jewish soldier in the garrison and robbed Uncle Melekh blind. There was nothing left for it—Uncle Melekh in his old age had to become a porch-sitter. Otherwise they'd steal the pillow from under his head: his crazy wife from one side and Yente from the other.

And just as the rope tightened around his throat Uncle Melekh let slip to the broker that if the pharmacist would pay four thousand rubles in gold he'd sell him his share. But he would take no other form of money.

To this the pharmacist responded that he, the uncle, was too hot under the collar—he would also take two thousand. As for the gold, that was no big deal. He, the pharmacist, owned valuables worth more than gold that he could easily convert to cash.

It took a fair bit of time before the municipal authorities set up their posts two cubits into Uncle Melekh's property. The municipal authorities were going to build sidewalks and sewers; and it wasn't enough that they had robbed Uncle Melekh of two cubits' worth of land, but they sent him a bill that he had to pay, in advance. They should have the pleasure for Uncle Melekh to live so long!

So the uncle asked the paver: Why were they starting to construct sidewalks right by his house? Little Yosele had a nicer brick house, as did Ayzik Danziger; they hadn't been burned down. So why did Melekh Zaydman have to be the first scapegoat?

The paver muttered: he didn't know; they ordered him to build, so he built. He, the uncle, should go to see the municipal authorities. Incidentally, he, the Jew, should move aside or he'd be sorry.

He doubtless didn't move aside, the Jew, but rather swore mightily: "Are you kidding? Why are you lording it over my property?" So a policeman came over and stuck him in the clink.

Then Arele with the two pencils in his front pocket ran over and went off to the pharmacist to intercede for his father. So the pharmacist went and posted bail for Uncle Melekh.

They let the uncle go. But the pharmacist—what was the good of his posting bail for all the Jews? You speak up at least for a person you know. But if it's not a person . . . It's a shame he didn't ask for at least ten thousand for the ramshackle house.

Ultimately the sale was concluded for two and a half thousand. The gold rubles were converted to Polish marks, and those marks to Leybele Shteynbok's and Shmuel Rabinovitsh's promissory notes.

Once again, Arele was deeply involved in the whole business. "What good," he said, "is gold to you, papa? So you'll keep it and live off your reserves? For the pharmacist, you see, it's all the same, he has the promissory notes, it's a converted gold coin, it's gold and diamonds, and in addition to that 10 percent a month. You know how much that makes? No less than double, more than double every year. You can sit and eat and still put aside a ruble. You need to have money? At any time you can exchange the promissory notes with Fayvele Shpilman or with little Yosele or with whomever you want."

And he prevailed, Arele did. Because at the moment when Uncle Melekh went to sell his house, Melekh Mitshes was finished . . . gone senile. That's how one deprives someone, heaven protect us, of his ability to communicate.

The house was in disarray: Yente got married to the soldier and went off with him to where he came from, and Shimen took his meals at Tsadok's. This was a beneficial arrangement. Tsadok had taken on a partner at the tannery, and Shimen kept the partnership accounts.

Moreover, Shimen taught Tsadok's children, forcing knowledge into their clumsy minds—an utterly futile task.

Yitskhok had been almost completely won over by his mother-in-law. People said that Milke, the village produce seller, had won him, Yitskhok, as a son-in-law with the soups that she cooked for him, and with the warm featherbed that she gave to cover him. Otherwise it would have been incomprehensible why he, Yitskhok, an educated young man who made a pretty penny, would take such a fat, idle girl as Milke's daughter. And if she had red, puffy cheeks, is that everything?

It was more than certain, though, that Yitskhok was well aware that his mother-in-law, Milke the produce seller, a widow, from time to time received dollars from her son in America. During the week, she went around the village, and on the Sabbath brought back a fat hen, a fish, some kasha, and a little flour. None of this cost any money, and one might say it was enough to live on. A penny saved is a penny earned.

There was one child Uncle Melekh did protect by disposing of his land. That was Shmuel. In the sale it was explicitly agreed upon that Shmuel would work for the pharmacist, and he was obligated to train him as an apprentice pharmacist. This is one thing Uncle Melekh did accomplish.

What's more, Nosn quarreled with Tsadok, with the uncle, and with everyone. He got his way. He went to Meierbach's factory. But he had a rough time of it there. He thought he'd quickly be given the Russia leather. No-ot so-o fast! First you have to work evenings at the damp hides: pushing, beating, and only then . . .

He assisted Jan working the raw leather right as it was taken out of the lime. This was not such a great feat. First, with the blunt edge of a scraping knife you rake off the hair, then you snip off the "membrane"; you cut off the ears and the remaining tufts of hair (the hair and the membrane especially for lamb's leather). This was not difficult work, but after eight hours bent over a board scraping away and all your limbs will ache. So Nosn didn't understand how Jan could constantly work overtime—that thin, emaciated Jan with the lusterless eyes, like evaporated lime, and with the drooping mustaches, like on a sad Cossack.

"Janye, how long've you worked here?"

"Ho, ho! Certainly gotta be thirty years already . . . Since I was fourteen."

"And always doing the same thing?"

"First at the lime vats, and then right here."

"And it still doesn't get tiresome for you?"

"It's all the same to me, as long as I'm earning."

"And how much do you make?"

"That depends. If there's free time you make more, and if there's no free time, you make less. It depends . . ."

"Where do you live, Janye?"

"Ho, ho! You gotta know everything? Anyway, you won't work here, you're too weak. I'm different, I'm already used to it. Lime's no plaything for you; it'll eat a hole in your hands. Oh! Just look at a pair of hands . . ."

Nosn looked at Jan's hands, eaten through with holes, and then at his lusterless face. Pain choked him for this peasant who seemed to have no bitterness in him. He talks to you and tells you everything without any anger; he doesn't get mad or curse. It seemed that the lime had leeched out of him all of the sap and nerve of a living man, and here standing before you was an automaton who kept scraping the hides from early in the morning till late into the evening, scraping and describing his joys and miseries with a dull indifference. Nosn kept at him.

"Where do you live, Janye?"

"In Rogów."

"In Rogów? But that's eight kilometers from here. You go home every day?"

"Of course. That's far to you? What about when I used to live on the other side of the Vistula and had to take the ferry every day, which made it ten kilometers?"

"Every day there and back?" asked Nosn with astonishment.

"Well, sometimes when you work till midnight and you have to speed up the job, then you sleep in the factory."

"Do you have some land, Janye?"

"There's five acres there."

"So you're not poor after all, Janye?"

"For you it's all the same: one piece of land or another. When you've got barren sand and it won't even yield to the labor you invest in it. When that's your crop, thin and paltry . . ."

"Did you give something for the strike?" Nosn jumped from one question to another.

"Oh, something . . . Wasn't worth it to strike."

"It was indeed worth it to strike."

"You say so?"

"Yes. They ought to know!"

"Quiet. He's coming."

Meierbach had arrived and with him was a tall man in a jacket and a bicycle cap. Everyone already knew: that was Meierbach's brother from Russia. He had fled the Bolsheviks.

The two were speaking to one another. The factory owner was explaining something to his brother, clarifying something or other. Soon he had thrown off his outer clothes and put on a pair of tanners' boots and belted on a leather apron.

No one understood: was Meierbach's brother to be a simple worker? Hypotheses flew from every direction; first, that the foreigner—or the Russki as the workers called him—was not his brother but a distant relative, because Meierbach wouldn't let a brother work together with all the other common workers.

The Russki himself shortly cleared up everyone's doubts. Yes, he really was a brother, but he didn't want to eat for free—he wanted to work. In Russia they didn't know: you work—you eat, you don't work—so go to hell.

On the Russki's face full of little pouches emptied of fat, there sparkled two cunning little eyes that seemed as though they were actually two pairs of eyes, since they beamed into you their work-weary spirit: "I love worn out hands; I hate noblemen. Eh? Moritz-poritz . . ."[1] And then they were burning you with their glowing wires: "A fire is looking

1. *poritz* (Yiddish): lord, nobleman.

for you, Ivan! Just yesterday you shined my shoes, just yesterday you kissed my hand, you boor! So here you go: Yosl the carpenter is my judge . . . shoot! Ural! They won't hold out another year, so let our hair grow! They must pay the price!"

What's true is true: he was no arrogant person, the Russki. A cunning lad, though, clever and wily. If he intended to do something, heaven and earth would be brought together and he got his way.

In the factory there was a doddering foreman who was always hanging about; the workers were tired of his bell and his rotten nose that he stuck everywhere. He, the foreman, was an Endek from the illustrious family Wiszniewski. Lineage he had coming and going: on one side his father received a gold medal and a confiscated farm from the Czar for delivering Polish rebels to the gallows; and on the other side his son, his jewel, had as a volunteer in the army joined a band of thieves on the Kresy and was convicted by the Polish tribunal of participating in acts of banditry.[2]

The foreman Wiszniewski was good for nothing more than pestering and annoying the workers with his rotten nose and his mercilessly long and deafening bell-ringing; and yet Moritz Meierbach kept him on. For a Gentile, and an Endek at that, Moritz Meierbach felt injured. "One must show them," he claimed, "that we are not the anti-Semites they are." And for another thing, he liked the Gentiles, the nobility—that is, not the riffraff. You could be the biggest anti-Semite, calling for boycotts, pogroms, you name it—no big deal; but strikers he couldn't abide. He had a sense of honor.

If so, the Russki promised, he'd give them both a dressing down. Wiszniewski must be the scapegoat. They had no need for rotten stinkers, and he, Moritz, would have to give the workers a 10 percent raise, however he could . . .

(Moritz Ox! Everything is double. If you won't give 10 percent by fair means they'll take 50 by foul.)

---

2. Kresy: the Polish eastern marches, which were hotly contested in the interwar period.

A delegation was sent with the Russki at its head. His cunning little eyes pierced: Forward! Have no fear, comrades, my name is Meierbach. Nothing is cheap. He must give in. He may get angry . . .

Mortiz Meierbach met them with his hands in his pockets, quiet and impassive, but suddenly he let loose his hands and started foaming at the mouth.

"Quiet! Enough! Stop snorting so out your mouth, Panie Moritz," the Russki trained his cunning eyes on him, "it won't help you. Everything's expensive; the mark's falling, eh? It's possible wages may need to go up again."

Moritz Meierbach calmed down a bit, saying, "Am I too not a person? Do I not understand that people need a raise? But one doesn't do this, one doesn't do things by force, it's not fair to the foreman, I'd die of shame."

"Wiszniewski?" the Russki continued. "To hell with him! He was useful if you soaked a hide for sixteen months. That stinker? Let him go ring his bell somewhere else. He won't work here, that much I know."

"You're giving me orders?!"

"Comrades," the Russki turned to the delegation. "Give me a moment alone with Pan Meierbach."

They left, and from behind the door they heard how the Russki let him have it:

"Moritzl, don't start in! Just don't start in. What you say goes. Do you want the hides to stay in the lime? Unless you want . . . Moritzl, give in!"

And the Russki left the office.

"Well?" he smiled cunningly at the workers. "Well?" And they understood, the workers did, they could count on him.

That's how he was, that Russki. You couldn't get a straight answer from him. He stood right by you beating the hides, in the stench, working like a good peasant, when in truth he was managing the whole factory. Running here and there, keeping an eye on things, he knew how to toss in a comment: A little more oak, another two or three minutes in the "drum," not enough lead acetate, too thin of a shaving. It's striking how he had it right on the dot every time. Just a few months ago when he first came to the factory he seemed to be no expert, feeling his way in the dark, but now he seemed more and more like an experienced manager.

Since the foreman Wiszniewski had been insulted, and he twirled his mustache and cleared out, the Russki gained in importance at the factory. He transferred all the old foremen—even the German, Fischer—all the people who had gone with the flag in '05 and since then were redeemed shop stewards.

The Polish mark kept falling, so every Monday and Thursday people had to demand wage increases. All of these quarrels the Russki now took up with the factory-owner personally, adding a couple of marks, a sop; but their work couldn't keep up with the continually rising price of bread, not by a longshot.

Until one day the Russki, while at his work, casually took out of his vest pocket a shiny stone, something like a little diamond, about the size of a nut. When he held it in the palm of his hand it cast glimmers all around.

"Well?" his two cunning little eyes sparkled. "What do you think, Nosn, is it worth a hundred marks? Maybe a hundred and ten?"

And he put it back in his vest pocket, like he was tucking away a piece chalk, or some trifle, as though he was not afraid of losing such a fortune.

It was clear to everyone: Iser Meierbach, Moritz Meierbach's brother, the Russki with the big tanners' boots, had brought back with him from Russia real dough, thick English pounds, gold and diamonds. Anyone who was a person and was capable could have made a pretty penny during the war, and Iser Meierbach, it seems, was a person who was capable.

And then people found out: Iser Meierbach had been a partner in the factory from the very first day he arrived, and even at the time he led that first action in the name of the workers . . .

And people kept talking: with the money that Mortiz Meierbach had saved up from his factory in Godlbozhits, and with the money that

Iser had brought with him from Russia, they were going to construct a factory properly, a real factory.

The structure that had till then housed the entire factory was nearly invisible, so many other buildings had been added. Masons and carpenters worked from very early in the morning till late at night. People kept delivering bricks, cement, and iron beams.

"So, Janye," Nosn recently said to Jan, "they're going to install machines that do all the work themselves, shave and roll the leather; they're not going to need us anymore."

"And I tell you," Jan answered, "that a machine without human hands is worthless. An expert like me they'll always need. A person works for thirty years . . . You don't learn that in a day."

"Forget it, Janye . . . A simple peasant can also learn from a machine."

Jan shook his head incredulously; Nosn cited his evidence.

"Everything I'm telling you I didn't make up; it's all known from the real world, it's described in books, exactly what's going on with the worker and the machines, it's all described precisely."

"Nah, you fool."

Still, he thought it over to himself, the thin Jan did, lowering his head, stubbornly scraping the hides, and his mustaches drooped, like on a sad Cossack.

⊹ 12 ⊰

When Shimen Shifris Got Up from Sleep

Shimen Shifris prepared for the exam. He worked a full day for his bread: gave lessons, kept the books at Tsadok Fuller's tannery, and first thing in the evening he undertook his self-education.

So that nothing could get in the way of his studies Shimen broke with the friends of his youth. He didn't play or dance with anyone, didn't go to parties, didn't befriend girls, didn't stand around chatting in the street. In the prime of his youth, barely a few grades into Gymnasium, and he gave the impression of a musty old student.

He was very much the diligent student. When in the evening he sat down to his Latin book he could pound away at that recondite language till daylight. Just as a sunbeam would begin stinging his eye in the morning he would say to himself: I'll just take a look how it is outside and then I'll come back. Useless to waste time going for a walk—that the diligent student would not permit himself.

However, as soon as he went outside a youthful vigor took hold of him, an early morning freshness that forced its way into his nostrils, his eyes, his breath, a freshness he could scarcely overcome to return to the suffocating air of that sleepy room, to the musty Latin book.

On the announcement board at city hall there had been pasted a new placard depicting: A Jew as a devil, a Bolshevik, with horse's hooves, offering a ruble bribe to an honest Pole with a four-cornered hat and Cracovian *sukmana*.[1] Underneath was a caption: "Down with the Jew-Bolsheviks! Vote for number eight of the National Democracy!"

---

1. A *sukmana* is a traditional Polish peasant's russet coat.

118

In two days there were to be the elections for the Sejm. Yesterday a Folkist heatedly read a speech to a gathering in the market that Noyekh Pryłucki had given in the Sejm. "Alas!" they complained, "those goyim who between them don't have a head like Noyekh Pryłucki!" Shimen was not proud of the fact that that worthless anti-Semitic placard had offended him.

The fresh air of the early morning inspired in him a longing for people. Better to engage in some trivial conversation than to stand around all alone in the middle of the market. From the house opposite, from his own house, Reb Ayzig Danziger was leaving with a walking stick in his hand. He circled the brick structure and inspected his estate from every angle. That eminent burgher was certainly not Shimen's friend. Maybe he didn't even recognize Shimen, but that young man, the diligent student, was now so drawn to the man that he summoned his courage and seized the opportunity.

"Good morning, Reb Ayzik. Up so early, Reb Ayzik? So Reb Ayzik is inspecting his house?"

The old eminent burgher looked at the young man, visibly recognized him, but could not remember his name.

"Listen here, young man," he said self-importantly, "I'm no longer a little boy"—he pulled on his grey beard, stroking it—"sleep is a thing of the past. Sometimes I lie awake for half the night and can't manage to fall asleep. So one lies there and one thinks: It seems—Ayzik Danziger, the proprietor of a house? Not so? . . . So one gets dressed, one goes to take a look—When? Where? A dream . . ."

"Is Reb Ayzik joking?" Shimen asked respectfully. "A burgher, praise God, till a hundred and twenty."

Reb Ayzik smiled bitterly.

"Me? A burgher?"

"Who else would be a burgher, Reb Ayzik?"

"Oh, young man . . . You're clearly not up-to-date," Reb Ayzik stroked his grey beard, combing it with his fingers, and mocking bitterly, "Ha-ha-ha! I am a burgher? Ayzik Danziger is a burgher! If he wants, he pays his rent, if he doesn't want to, then he doesn't pay. Is it possible you can do something for him? Yes, you see, when it comes to taxes, Ayzikl Danziger is a burgher; for taxes you don't go to the tenants. When they need to build sidewalks they come to Ayzik Danziger for money, not to the tenants. But do I have a say? Take my word: it's worse than Bolshevism. It's enough to make your blood spoil."

And Reb Ayzik kept fueling his pique: "Time was, before the war, when one wanted to undertake some municipal business, one consulted the burghers. So it should be: 'If one doesn't pay the communal tax one doesn't get a say.' Today, however, it's just the opposite: tenants sit in city hall and make . . . make sidewalks, power stations, garbage cans . . . It should stick in their throat! Till now they could walk on gravel, but now they need sidewalks, those refined people. And who is called upon to pay for it all? Naturally, the burgher."

Shimen tried to calm the eminent burgher, but he wouldn't even let him get a word out. He kept getting angrier and tapping his walking stick on the cobblestones, striking them so hard it started to make Shimen feel uneasy.

Suddenly the stones of the marketplace began to resound. From a narrow sandy side street came horses and carts dragging long logs, pine trees, from which dripped fresh sap. Peasants with whips in their hands used their tricks to steer and coax the long trees from that narrow, crooked street.

And in the market Leybele Shteynbok appeared with his pipe in his mouth. He shrugged a little shoulder and smoked: *puff . . . puff . . .* Leybele Shteynbok was a person whom nothing bothered. The Christian burghers had divided up the city's forest amongst themselves— they did!

"What's it matter to you," Leybele Shteynbok argued, "if they divide up the forest? Why doesn't it bother me? As far as I'm concerned they can divide up the stones of the marketplace as well. What d'you think this is, *your* Poland? Idiots! *Your* Poland?!"

Now, when that same Leybele Shteynbok together with Shmuel Rabinovitsh, those prewar paupers, Reb Ayzik Danziger's woodsmen—when those arriviste moneybags bought from the townsmen the wood from the city's forest, and then led the wood clatteringly through the Godlbozhits market to the Vistula in order to float the lumber by raft far away . . . to Danzig. Well, at that the old burgher, the former timber merchant Reb Ayzik Danziger, was sorely pained. His face turned blue with that grief, and for fear of having an apopleptic fit right on the spot he up and fled the market.

Now Shimen suddenly remembered that Meierbach had sent for him. This was a great honor for Shimen, and gave him much hope: who knows—maybe Meierbach wanted to hire him as an apprentice bookkeeper. But no, Meierbach wanted to give him, Shimen, the opportunity to "take down" an idea in writing . . . a memo, a communal matter. All the greatest lawyers got their work experience for free in the public institutions, all the greatest doctors paid, as long as they were admitted by a hospital. Did Shimen understand? The most important thing was practical experience. Even if he had gone to ten universities, without practical experience he wouldn't even be able to write down a simple request in the tax office.

So he, Shimen, should just listen well and pay close attention: the Christian community were going to sell the forest, divide it only amongst the Christian burghers, and the Jewish burghers would not even get a stick of wood. The memo was going be sent to the government ministry, so it had to be written with some flair . . . some Polish . . . something that would excite attention.

Beads of sweat appeared on Shimen's brow. With all his heart he wanted to write this well. This was his first step, it was a matter of pride. He wrote, and erased, and wrote again; and Mortiz Meierbach constantly shook his head: it lacked a bit of salt . . . a little pepper . . .

Until old Broderson came down from the mountain. The burghers had nearly dragged him down since he had such an aversion to communal affairs. Pani Broderson, as was her wont, gave him some encouragement: "If, Stasiu, it is a communal matter, then don't refuse," she said, and the old man put on his mink coat with the beaver collar and went off with the burghers.

He had merely dipped the pen into the inkwell everything flowed very smoothly:

For four hundred years Jews have dwelt in Godlbozhits, and by the grace of King Zygmunt various privileges were bestowed upon them, among them—the privilege of deriving benefit equal to the Christian burghers of the lumber of the forest to build stables and to erect granaries. This privilege was subsequently reaffirmed by other Polish kings and noblemen, lords of the city. Now there are those seeking to deprive the Jews of the right to derive benefit from the forest, a right of many generations' standing. And what will become of that wood? It would be exported to Danzig for the benefit of the Germans . . .

Right here he'd gotten hold of it, the old man! That's good: *for the benefit of the Germans* . . . Meierbach rubbed his hands with pleasure. It wasn't for nothing that he had said that only Broderson, and no one else, would be able to write it, for in addition to writing one must have an idea.

But all the scribblings and memos came a cropper. The Christian burghers divided up the forest among themselves as they pleased. Nor did they waste any time . . . they chopped down the trees and sold them to Leybele Shteynbok and Shmuel Rabinovitsh, the two newly rich war-profiteering timber merchants.

It would not have annoyed him, Moritz Meierbach, so much if nothing could really have been achieved. Ultimately he found his own solution: he transferred ownership of his house to his Christian watchman. A little scheme here, a little scheme there, the Christian burghers didn't want to get into a big fight with him—so he got his share of the forest. So it would not have annoyed him, Moritz, if the whole affair hadn't been scuppered thanks to a couple of measly million marks needed to grease some palms in a particular place. On its own one could be persuaded that it wasn't so bad for him, he could hold his own. For him the issue was the general run of Jewish burghers, the Jews—you see, whenever he remembered it, he ground his teeth. The same to them, those rotten Jews! Their job was to yell and scream, and if a penny had to be paid, every one of them hid, the same to them! Just try to take their rags!

And Leybele Shteynbok shrugged his little shoulder.

"I don't know why they care so much that the goyim divide up the forest. As far as I'm concerned they can divide up the stones of the marketplace as well. Idiots! *Your* Poland?!"

He'd have to live to at least a hundred and twenty, that Leybele Pipe. He was a cold fish. Nothing ever bothered him; he never got worked up.

Shimen remembered all of this as he watched Leybele Pipe's men, his clerks and servants, working over those great corpses of pines.

And all at once the clock on the church started chiming: eight o'clock. Shmuel, Uncle Melekh's son, had asked Shimen to wake him up. Shmuel slept in the back room of the pharmacy; he was a slugabed, people always had to wake him up.

Shimen knocked on the shutter.

"Shmuel! Shmuel! It's late, get up!"

"Hun? What?" Shmuel's voice could be heard through the thin shutter. "How is the dollar doing?"

"What dollar? I'm telling you, it's late."

"Alright, alright . . . I'm coming."

The shutter on the window opened. Shmuel stuck out his disheveled head, took a look around, and went to let Shimen in.

Shimen entered and fastened the door chain behind him.

"How can you sleep here? Won't you suffocate?"

Shmuel scratched his unkempt locks.

"You know," he said, "Arn was here yesterday, the dollar's worth a million."

"A million?!"

"Yes, Arele's buying up gold for the pharmacist."

"And he scammed Leybele Pipe's promissory notes to his own father," said Shimen pityingly.

"He ruined his father: because of those promissory notes there'll be a strike. What a ruin to make of an estate!"

"But Nosn always said . . ."

"Nosn?" Shmuel turned his head. "What's the point in asking him if the house matters to him. He can only keep his mind on turning that union on its head."

"You mean the Zionists?"

"I mean in the cultural union, they brought in a speaker. Nosn sides with them."

"And the rest of his friends?"

"What friends? The cobblers and the tailors and a couple of young women side with them, the workers. They are going to form a trade union."

"And Nosn's in the middle," said Shimen with pity.

"Nosn . . . He's in it all the way! There he'll be a big shot. When he gets a little older they'll make him chairman."

"In Berele the Shitter's union . . ." Shimen said mockingly.

"Ha-ha! That's father's word," Shmuel swelled with pride.

"Well, anyway, I'm going," said Shimen. "And you, get back to the pharmacy. He'll be getting in soon."

"You mean the pharmacist?" Shmuel waved his hand. "He won't be coming in early today. Yesterday they played cards till two o'clock; him, the doctor, and the clerk."

"The doctor too?" Shimen was surprised.

"Phooey! You should see a cardplayer. When they get worked up it's like being among real gamblers. And a little glass, too, they didn't pooh-pooh. Half past one in the morning I had to go get more liquor. And 'that' was also to be provided. That's when the clerk asked me . . ."

"And how did you answer?" Shimen interrupted him out of curiosity.

"Nothing. I don't know. Let him go to Yankl the broker, to Khaykl the sexton's son."

"And what did he say?"

"Didn't say anything. Otherwise—they'd be missing the 'goods' . . . One lends to the other."

"Jewish girls?" Shimen needed to know.

"All's I know . . . Elke the cook, peasant girls—all the same. Curse him! It seems he got her pregnant."

"Who?"

"The pharmacist, he should be taken!"

"Whom?" Shimen was burning with curiosity. "The pharmacy clerk?"

Shmuel mischievously squinted an eye.

"Wow! An impressive object! The shikse isn't better?"

"Kasia? A beautiful girl . . ."

"Don't you know what a swine the pharmacist is?! He torments her miserably, and he's never ashamed of it in front of us."

"And her? What a shame such a young girl," Shimen felt sorry for her.

"She's got a choice?" Shmuel said. "At home, with her father the drunk, was it any better? Dying for a piece of bread . . . Here at least she's got something to eat."

"And the pharmacy clerk knows about it?"

"Beast," Shmuel said. "Right in front of her, in front of the both of us, he kisses the girl, paws at her. The pharmacy clerk would from time to time exchange glances with me and grit her teeth."

"She would herself have wanted . . ." Shimen's mouth filled with saliva.

"Well," Shmuel said, "you'd have to have an insatiable desire."

And right then there awoke in him compassion for his coworker.

"Don't think," he said, "that I'm also cursing her. The pharmacist is really exploiting her. She works for pennies. She just recently told me that if it weren't for the fact that she had to take care of her poor mother, whom she sends the couple of pennies she makes, she'd have left long ago."

"But at least the pharmacist's wife treats her well?" Shimen asked.

"She torments her in her own way. She relentlessly proposes matches to her. You know to whom? To Hezl Poyer—a vulgar boy. She recently complained, the pharmacy clerk did; it was pitiful to look at her."

"And what was going on with the girl, does the pharmacist's wife know?"

"And if she knew, what then? He, the pharmacist, yells at her, such nonsense. Ho, ho! No way . . . Now she trembles in fear of him."

"It's late," Shimen suddenly realized. "I've got to go."

He ran home, took several books and some notebooks and went to his Polish lessons with Sonia Broderson. With those study tools in hand he strode confidently through the market as though the market belonged to him. He even greeted "Good morning" to a woman vendor, as if to say: "Even though I'm studying trigonometry, I'm not putting on airs; no truly learned person acts haughtily." Then he climbed the mountain to the Brodersons. Birds chirped and the dew glistened on the rejuvenated leaves. It had rained all night and starting in the early morning fragrant dews rose from the green earth.

On a bench by the door of the villa sat the Hebrew teacher Livshits with a wool kerchief around his neck; he always had a bit of a cold. He had made himself a fixture at the Brodersons, considered himself a fiancé. He strode around the villa half the day in his blue and white pajamas, in the manner of a burgher. Old Broderson gently mocked him: "My son-in-law . . ." And Mrs. Broderson said sulkily: "Who will you be? Brodski's son was in love with my daughter, wept for her footstep, and who else? Lawyers, doctors . . ."

And even though Madame Broderson far from consented to the match that her only daughter had herself brought into their home, she gradually grew accustomed to the idea that this little Hebrew teacher was going to be her son-in-law. Pani Broderson had grown accustomed to many things that were repugnant to her prewar, affluent customs. Just as long as it was not all of a sudden. A boardinghouse was due to open right here on the mountain, in their former summer residence. She—that is, Pani Broderson, the proprietress of five houses in Moscow (nationalized by the Bolsheviks)—was going to serve these newly rich war profiteers, these "Saltshes" and "Moritzes"; this was no just world, eh?

Even though some nice years had gone by, Madame Broderson was unable to get used to only one thing—to the Bolsheviks and the confiscation of her five houses in Moscow. She, an aristocratic lady with genteel manners and refined speech, cursed them, the Bolsheviks, every day with vituperative oaths, wished them all manner of plagues and violent deaths. Together with Iser Meierbach she regularly asserted that such a barbaric regime as the Bolshevik one could absolutely not last long. If it did last, it was only because of the backwardness and benightedness of the Russian masses. As a Polish citizen she was proud of the fact that the long enslaved and now awakening fatherland had, with God's help and His miracle at the Vistula, driven the Bolsheviks to the other side of the Dnieper.

Her husband, by contrast, was not so optimistically disposed. Old Broderson thought that Bolshevism would spread over the whole world and would ultimately make its way here. He offered his wife a word of consolation, "Maria dear, man is not a recalcitrant animal . . . A man can get used to anything. How many poor unfortunate of ours must get used to 'them'?"

By "them" he meant the Bolsheviks. And again he raised his drooping grey mustaches, twirled them, stretched them out like wire, one to the north and the other to the south, and intoned the slogan: "Long live Poland from sea to sea!"

Greater Poland needed to stretch from the Baltic all the way to the Black Sea. Such a gift did Broderson, the only Pole of Mosaic faith in Godlbozhits, have for his fatherland for the May 3rd holiday. He had prepared a long speech, a speech that had to overshadow the Nalewkis, the Wiszniewskis, all the greatest patriots of Godlbozhits.

The old man caught sight of Shimen outside the room.

"Well, Panie Shifris," he asked, "what's the news in the shtetl? What's going on with the forest?"

"They're taking it to the Vistula," Shimen answered.

"Really . . ." the old man let his proud mustaches droop. "I heard that Leyebele Shteynbok and that Rabinovitsh stuck their noses in, even gave bribes. Is that true? Jews no less?"

"So they say. Meierbach recently accosted Rabinovitsh and cursed him: 'You,' he said, 'are nothing but a thieving Hasid, you'd sell your own tallith and tefillin . . .'"

"And Rabinovitsh?"

"Nothing. 'Don't get in such a tizzy, Panie Meierbach,' he answered him. 'Don't insult me. Maybe you want a piece of the action?'"

"Ho, ho! Lovely things!" Broderson raised his shoulders. "And what do you hear about the elections?"

"Well, Jews will certainly get in: you, Meierbach . . ."

"Because I want it?" the old man grimaced.

"But who's forcing you to?"

This was asked by Livshits, who had been listening to the conversation the whole time and had not said a word. He couldn't hold his tongue any longer, he couldn't stand the old man's cultural work anymore. Each one used it for whatever purpose he needed. Sometimes it was Lozer Kohn, sometimes Meierbach, and sometimes even Moshke Abishes.

"And if they drop me," the old man defended himself, "is there anyone else?"

To the old man's prattle, Livshits had no desire to respond. He merely smiled to himself, cleverly, into his little black mustaches: is there anyone else? Zionist exilic politics would have an answer for that. He, Livshits, once he was a little more acclimated to Godlbozhits, must deal a political deathblow to all these Godlbozhits old-fashioned don't-rock-the-boat deal-makers: the Brodersons, the Meierbachs, the Lozer Kohns . . .

Nosn and someone else had arrived. Shimen recognized him, that shaggy cobbler with the mane of a philosopher, pale face and long beak of a nose. This was comrade Moyshe.

"Wait, Shifris," Livshits said to Shimen. "Here come the rrrrevolutionaries. You'll see something nice . . ."

The two approached.

"Can we see Pani Sonia?" comrade Moyshe asked.

"Hmmm . . ." Livshits did not know how best to nettle them. "Soon, she'll come soon. Might I know what it's about?"

"About the union, a union matter," Moyshe said.

"Union?" Livshits smiled slyly into his little black mustaches. "You already have a separate union, why do you want another?"

"We want to speak with Pani Sonia," Nosn interrupted impolitely.

"Hmmm . . ." Livshits turned to Shimen. "A relative of yours, it seems, that young man? It seems, a brother even?"

Shimen felt ashamed because of his brother, but he didn't get involved in the discussion. He just blushed.

Miss Sonia appeared in the doorway. With her grey, intelligent eyes she took in the situation. She saw that Livshits was agitated.

"Good morning, boys," she turned to the ones who had arrived. "What? For me?"

"Yes." The boys bowed politely. "May we have a few words?"

She went off with them to the orchard and heard them out with all earnestness. The boys made their presentation: since there were now two separate unions in the city, might their comrades attend the lessons that the pani gave in the culture union? They had come as a delegation from the trade union to ask whether the pani might consent to give them at least an hour, at least just history and natural science. They were not asking she do this for free. The union couldn't pay much, since they were poor workers' children, but they would pay something.

They did not go away empty-handed, those boys. The pani listened to them attentively the entire time, praised their plan for organizing educational courses, and promised her help, if time would permit; in any case, she would not ask for any money.

On the way back home Moyshe said triumphantly, "Well, what did I tell you? One must make use of all sympathetic elements. Even though Livshits is a Zionist, *she* sympathizes with us, with the workers."

"Don't get ahead of yourself," Nosn said. "She is still going to discuss it with Livshits; she still agrees with him more than with us. Nothing's going to come of it. I only went to humor you."

"So why is she giving me a private lesson for free?" comrade Moyshe defended his position.

"Private is different; to a union of cobblers and tailors she won't come."

"You, Nosn, are ever the pessimist."

"This has nothing to do with pessimism," Nosn couldn't find the right word. "You," he said, "so go on then, just pal around and buddy up to the aristocracy. You'll get a kick in the ass, and then you'll wake up and remember who you are and what people think of you."

"And I'm telling you that among them too there is a difference between people."

"Of course there's a difference," Nosn smiled disdainfully. "There's certainly a difference: one gives the dog a kick and the other pets him out of pity. Among us there's also a difference: one won't let himself be spit in the face and the other says, 'It's raining.'"

"The mind is working."

"Whose mind, and whose imagination . . ."

So the boys argued in a friendly way about Pani Sonia, while she had likely not thought at all about them. She probably thanked God that those boys had left and she could return to her Yakob.

"*Dzień dobry, moreh*," she greeted him furtively, and with two fingers combed a curl off his forehead.[2]

Shimen got embarrassed, blushed.

"What did they want, Sonyetshke, those rrrevolutionaries?" Livshits asked.

"That I might offer them lessons."

"Soon, right away . . . And Nosn Shifris needs instruction? But he's a real expert, a true intellectual, knows all of Marx's *Kapital* by heart."

"But what does that have to do with history?" Sonia didn't understand.

"Did you not hear how he recently held forth: 'We must go armed with Marx's works, we must conceive of history materialistically . . .' What a brat, what a nobody, and all of that so stupefies boys and girls that he'll become a leader!"

And again Livshits got worked up, all of him was trembling, he spoke with contempt, with irony:

"Socialists . . . You call them socialists?! I should know. I myself, as a Russian student . . . threw bombs . . . went to prison, hard labor, to Siberia . . . Today, whoever's got a mouth is a socialist, a revolutionary . . ."

He was getting very upset, Yakob Livshits was, a cold sweat appeared on his pale forehead, he was ready to catch another cold and again go hoarse.

---

2. *Dzień dobry, moreh*: the first phrase is Polish—good day; the second is Hebrew—teacher.

So Sonia was mostly afraid. She put her hand to his brow, calming him.

"Come now, don't get so agitated, Yakob, put the kerchief around your neck, there's a bit of a draft. It's really not worth it to get worked up over any little trifle. If it's that important to you, I won't go to them. It's not worth your health, Yakob."

But Yakob couldn't control himself, couldn't forgive anything. He kept remembering more:

"The whole world can insist that the Jews get back the Land of Israel and only Zalmen the bootmaker and Nosn the tanner—no. It's a lie . . . No one gave the Jews anything, except England . . . And go argue with them. And such merciful people! They're going to enslave the Arabs. Dr. Weizmann is going to enslave the Arabs, and Nosn Shifris is going to liberate them . . ."

Sonia laughed. It pleased her, but one couldn't tell for sure if it was the comparison of Dr. Weizmann with Nosn the tanner that pleased her or Yakob's white teeth behind his little black mustaches . . .

At any rate, he, Livshits, appeared completely sympathetic and sufficiently determined in such an agitated state. Sonia, however, always had to watch out for his health, remembering his tendency toward high temperatures, and the best medicine for that was laughing when he made a joke.

And Shimen Shifris also laughed. He laughed because he hated arguments; he laughed because now Pani Sonia could finally get to his lesson. He absolutely loved his lessons with Sonia Broderson. In general he loved learning and everything connected with it: studying, ascending, becoming a man . . .

———◆———

The next morning Shimen Shifris travelled to Warsaw to take the long-awaited exam. This was the first time in his life he had ridden a train.

At the door to the second-class compartment there stood what was apparently a gentleman, reading from an outspread newspaper. "French," Shimen thought, not a little surprised.

"Might I ask for the middle section," asked Shimen politely.

"*Bitte*," the unknown gentleman handed Shimen the whole paper without the least surprise, as though it was completely believable that Shimen read French, as though it was no big deal to him, Shimen.

"Do you often read French newspapers?" Shimen asked.

"I subscribe," the gentleman answered simply.

"You speak it as well?"

"Almost like Polish," the gentleman smiled.

Shimen timidly lowered himself onto the bench, as if someone had seated him there. After all, Shimen had started longing for home, longing for his uncle, his aunt, his cousins, for the whole shtetl for whom he, Shimen, was something of a genius, an intellectual.

Into his train car had come a girl with laughing eyes and hair pulled back like in a grandmother's head scarf. She was carrying a bouquet of flowers in her hand, and behind her—a troupe of young men with suitcases in their hands.

He recognized her, the girl, from a distance. And she him, of course, as well. Indeed, he helped her stow her bags.

The train gave a shudder. The young men kissed her slender hand, gave a shout, and dashed out of the train car. She laughed at them through the window, waving her hand good-bye: the same to them all and to each one individually.

The train moved. She sat down.

"You look familiar to me," Shimen ventured.

"So do you to me a little," she laughed.

"Your name is Rabinovitsh, Fele Rabinovitsh."

"I prefer Feyge."

"Feygele."

"That I like too. Are you going to Warsaw?"

"Yes, for the exam."

"What grade?"

"Eight."

"I heard that you are the most talented and hardworking student in Godlbozhits."

Shimen was embarrassed by the compliment. He was actually quite modest.

For a while the conversation did not take, and then Shimen said, "You know, miss, say what you will, but as I'm now traveling comfortably in such a swift train it seems to me that I haven't deserved it. I feel rather small compared to this great invention, compared to Stephenson . . ."[3]

"You are sentimental, you would be very good at music."

"Surely you jest," Shimen countered. "I have no ear for music at all. Recently I was out walking by myself on Lubliner Street and I heard the sounds of a piano playing from your window. It moved something in me, such a longing gnawed at me. But I don't understand music; and sentimental—oh, you're surely joking."

"Yes, yes," Feygele Rabinovitsh laughed. "Still, you are a bit."

"Not even a little bit," Shimen countered. "I have the reputation of being dry, of not carrying on romances with girls, of pounding away at the books day and night."

"That makes no difference," Feygele said. "But sentimental you are. I see it in your eyes."

"And you?" asked Shimen.

"I am a little bit too, when I play; but a minute later—gone! I love it when I'm surrounded by cheerfulness, camaraderie, dancing . . ."

"So you dance," Shimen laughed.

"But I neglect my playing, and that is a shame. My professor keeps complaining: You must play a great deal, and I am not long on patience."

"You study music?" Shimen asked.

"Yes, but I fear nothing will come of it. I cannot stick to one thing for very long."

"So you think," said Shimen with a smile.

"I have no patience," Feygele said coquettishly. "So I want to flirt with boys."

3. George Stephenson (1781–1848), was an English railway engineer.

And suddenly she broke into a wide yawn.

"I haven't slept a-a-a-all ni-i-i-ight, a-a-a-a-a-h . . ."

Then she burst out laughing at her own impolite yawn; she laughed a little provocatively until people started glancing over.

This oughtn't have mattered to Shimen, but it did bother him a little.

"Let me lean my head on your shoulder, Panie Shifris."

"With pleasure."

"But . . . it will be heavy for you."

"No . . ."

So she, Feygele, fell asleep on his shoulder. He, Shimen, observed that in her sleep she looked like a little child, like an angel.

→ 13 ←

On Love, Which Lives Forever, and on Coach-Driving, Which Is on the Wane

Shimen Shifris returned from Warsaw with a diploma in his pocket and despair in his heart: Feygele had given herself to him; but had he received love—no.

This seemed bizarre to him: could a girl, a woman, give herself to someone whom she did not love? Could a young girl have such a reckless attitude toward her most sacred possession, to her modesty?

Now Shimen had a choice whether to gather together all of her known boys and young men—desperate lovers and hopeless admirers—candidates for suicide, severe melancholy, and the insane asylum: he had a choice to assemble them and bait them.

"Bah . . . But to whom did Feygele surrender her innocence, her maidenhood? To me! Me, Shimen Shifris."

He was not going to do that, because, first of all, he was not one of those young men who brags that a girl has kissed them; and second, she, Feygele, would dismiss it all vulgarly:

"As long as you got rid of the slut," she would say, cracking up with laughter.

Who taught her to be so cynical? Who taught her such obscene language?

Among all of her many familiars, in fact, there was no shortage of "teachers." And if there had only been one—the writer Eyges with the black shovel-like beard—that too would have been enough to make her a "respectable person." At first this puzzled Shimen. When introducing Eyges to him Feygele had said: "I hate men who wear beards, and poets who speak obscenely." So who was forcing her to go around with Eyges? But later he calmed down. And when she assured him fifteen times over that it was only him, Shimen, that she loved? So when another one showed up, she also loved that one a little. She loved a lot of people. And what if Shimen tortured himself again: how can you love so many people the way you love your chosen one? Surely that wasn't natural? So she, Feygele, really didn't love anyone—him, Shimen, included. She couldn't love, she didn't know how to love, and—she jumped into his lap.

He obviously needed to stop being so naïve, Shimen Shifris did. Schoolgirls from the lower grades had made him aware: If you want to please a pretty girl you must have two things: a car, and . . . money.

Instead of a car it could also be a motorcycle. The main thing was—money . . . money . . . But the small-town Shimen just took that for idle chitchat. Here there had fallen in love with him, a poor student, that golden girl with sparkling, laughing eyes and hair pulled back like in a grandmother's head scarf.

That is, until that matter with the lawyer. Here is what happened: Feygele had given a piano lesson to a fourteen-year-old boy from a wealthy family. He was quickly moved to recount tales of his exploits with girls, as though they were games. She scolded him, and he broke down in tears, grabbed her hand, and started kissing it, confessing that he was in love with her, that he couldn't sleep at night, that she was everything to him, that without her he would die.

Then his mother came in:

"A fine thing you're teaching my son. There's nothing to talk about. So I really am paying you to corrupt my child . . ."

Feygele responded that her son had someone else to thank for his corruption.

What?! That some tramp should come and throw filth at her house?! Get out! Get out this minute!

Shimen himself found a lawyer, a Christian—Czeszniewski was his name—a tall, thin, blond man with freckles on his face. His waiting room was full of old inherited furniture, pictures, deer antlers, and crucifixes.

"Does this woman still owe you any tuition?" the lawyer asked.

"A month's worth," Feygele answered.

Did she, that is, in this way, by means of a scandal, by a false accusation, mean to get out of paying her debt?

"This," Feygele explained to him, "has nothing to do with money. That woman insulted me seriously."

"Of course," the lawyer smiled. "But the reason? The reason?"

"I've told you the whole truth. That truth no one can stand."

"Very well," the lawyer smiled and drew a bony hand across his brow, through his fair mane. "Very well, miss, but my motive is stronger, categorically stronger."

Now Feygele, too, broke into a smile.

Leaving the lawyer's she was completely drained and clung to Shimen's shoulder. Shimen was an extraordinary, dear young man. He had made a good choice: the young lawyer pleased her, and how lovely the way he drew his hand across his brow.

"Did you notice that stylish furniture? It was so cozy in there."

Shimen was silent.

Abruptly she noted his silence.

"Why are you so sullen?" she asked.

"Should I be dancing in the street?" he answered discourteously.

Feygele let go of his arm; she was angry. Shimen bit his lip.

The next day he came to her house. She had made supper and offered him weak, "goose" tea.

"Now that's tea! Some tea!"

"You may serve yourself," she said flirtily.

So he poured a nice glass of tea and set it on the table. She took a sip and smacked her lips.

"Ah, what excellent tea! What a wonderful thing to have such a boy! I never knew what a good housewife you are."

He gave her a kiss on the forehead, and said with dreamy eyes, "Truly, Feygele, when we get married you'll serve tea."

"Is that so?" she took affront. "That'll always be your job."

"Fine, that'll be my job," he agreed.

Then she jumped into his lap and covered him with kisses.

"You are my best boy, Shimen. I will no doubt be happy. My father says that I will make the best wife, if only I will love . . ."

"You do love."

"Who?"

"Who?" Shimen lifted a pair of foolish doe-eyes.

She noticed that and smoothed it over with a kiss, then threw on her coat.

"Forget it . . . oh dear! Forget it . . . silly! I really must be at the lawyer's."

They went down to the street. As always, when she was in a good mood she clung to his arm, to keep herself from slipping down the stairs. He was terribly happy, but he regretted that he had to go off to his lesson and couldn't go with her to the lawyer's. He accompanied her as far as the streetcar. They agreed that on his way back from his lesson he would go straightaway to see her because she would certainly be home by then.

But when he came to her house no one was there. She will surely arrive soon, he thought, and meantime he made himself comfortable, took off his coat, stretched out on the sofa, and daydreamed:

In their future life together, when he and Feygele were husband and wife, he would even be ready to take on the role of housewife. He, the ever shabby and needful-of-nothing Shimen Shifris, suddenly started to get fastidious about little things in his and, even more so, in Feygele's toilette. It displeased him that Feygele used pins where there needed to be a button, that she left unmended a little hole in her blouse that was getting larger. Just a year ago he was too lazy to brew tea and would drink water with sugar, and now it bothered him if the tea was not sufficiently bright, sufficiently amber-colored. He regularly hung around Feygele's house like an anxious proprietor, dusting the cobwebs out of the corners and smoothing out the curtains by the window.

Surrendering himself to these thoughts and waiting for Feygele Shimen tried to take a nap, but had little success. So he got up, went down to the street, bought some bread, butter, cheese. Then he went back up to the house and made tea. But Feygele still was not there.

He yawned and thought it didn't bother him that she was late, that there was really nothing to worry about.

But an hour later she still had not come, and then two hours—still nothing. So he went to the lawyer's.

The servant girl opened the front door halfway and stood fast like a dog on a chain.

"There wasn't . . . there wasn't any young lady. I should remember everyone? I don't take photographs."

The spring bolt snapped shut.

Shimen deluded himself that she, Feygele, was certainly already home. Of course they'd just missed each other in the street. So he set off on the way back, unlocked the front door silent as a thief, tiptoed through the dark hallway, quietly knocked, opened the door—dark, there was no one there.

He turned on the electric lights. The light bothered him, so he made it dark again, laid down on the sofa in his coat. Daydreaming images crept into his head, swarming like loathsome worms, like flies to sticky food on a summer's day. He turned from one side to the other, his collar became constricting, and his clothes heavy. A kind of a sharp pain stuck in his gut and couldn't get out. Were it not that he was thinking clearly he would have howled at the walls.

It was maybe half past midnight when she came home.

"Good evening," she laughed in his face.

He did not respond.

She walked over to the wardrobe, screened herself behind one of the doors, and threw on a nightgown.

"A-a-a-h . . ." she broke into a yawn and laughed. "A-a-a-h'm sle-e-e-e-py . . ."

Shimen got up, and pulled up the collar of his coat.

"Time to go," he said to himself.

"Wha-a-a-t's the hu-u-u-u-rry . . ."

"Good night."

"Go-o-o-d n-i-i-i . . ."

He left, and this time did not kiss her hand. He certainly handled himself admirably. To leave that way was for him a heroic act.

But that did not last long. The next evening he was again at her door. There was some noise inside: people's voices, glasses, and Feygele's sonorous laughter over all of it.

"A spree!"

He knew of these sprees from Feygele's friends who swarmed around her like bees around honey. He fit them like a fifth wheel on a cart. My hand—your hand, my foot—your foot . . . It disgusted him.

He quitted the door and could not sleep all night, tossing and turning on his bed, as dark thoughts like leeches gnawed at his heart, pecking like black crows.

The next afternoon he found a note on his table: "*If you want, come over, I'm not feeling well.* —Feygele."

He ran over every hill and dale.

"What's wrong, Feygele?"

She lay in bed, half-dressed, her face aflame, her eyes to match.

"I don't feel well," she said weakly.

He lay his hand on her forehead.

"It feels like you have a fever," he said. "I'll go get a thermometer."

The landlady had no thermometer. So he ran down to the pharmacy and bought one.

There was no fever. So he ran out again, bought sugar, tea, a lemon, hastily made tea, and offered her some.

"You have a glass too," she said.

"I'm not thirsty, Feygele."

"You troubled yourself only for me?"

"You're not well."

"Come here, Shimen. Why are you standing so far away?"

He walked over, sat down on the bed next to her, and held her head gently.

"Why haven't you given me a kiss?" she demanded. "For two days already you haven't kissed me."

He bent over her, lightly brushed his lips to her forehead, to her mouth.

"Do you love me?" she asked.

"Yes."

"Very much . . . love me?"

"Very much."

"So much?"

"So much."

"So why don't you say anything to me?"

"What should I say to you?"

"Say that I am a bad, thoughtless girl."

"You are good."

"You are good." She pulled him to her, pushed her cheek to his, then embraced him, kissing him long and passionately.

"You know, Shimen," she said seriously. "I am convinced that you are better, the best of all of those circling around me. They love me when I make them merry; you are always devoted and loyal."

He was silent, kissed her hands.

"They were here yesterday, and brought wine and chocolate . . ."

"Who?" Shimen asked hoarsely.

"You well know: them . . . Eyges and the gang, the show-off . . . Got drunk like swine."

"You drink, Feygele?" Shimen said accusatorily. "What good does it do you?"

She nearly threw him off of her.

"Go on! You're cruel. Remind me."

"Well, I won't remind you."

She cuddled up to him again.

"Shimen, do you want us to get married? Put up a chuppah?"

"If you want to."

"Of course I want to. Just soon—right away!"

"Soon, right away!"

"Go on! You're making fun." She pushed him away, and then pulled him back toward her.

"You know what I told Eyges last night? 'Pretty speeches,' I said, 'you make in the literature union: ethics, aesthetics. And then you come here and dirty things up."

"So, did he get offended?"

"Such a pig will get offended."

"But what did he say?"

"He got drunk, talked a lot of rubbish."

"But what did you do till so late?" Shimen inquired.

"Don't ask . . . I'm embarrassed . . . I'll tell you . . . You know that I tell you everything, but I hate being interrogated."

After a little while, "You want to know where I was last night?"

"If you wish," he said cautiously.

She recounted: The lawyer Czeszniewski kept her for a long time, asking her questions, and it was obvious that she had interested him; he was also pleasing to her, especially his long, bony fingers and his aristocratic manners. But more than anything she didn't want to leave that lovely office with the beautiful old-fashioned furniture. She began to feel somewhat at one with all of it. Then he began to show her a collection of various curiosities: pictures, wild ducks, stuffed sea creatures, shellfish, old weapons. All of the rooms were full of these things, and everything was displayed so tastefully.

Then he invited her to the movies. She knew that it wasn't appropriate, but she couldn't refuse—so she went. On the way back his very own car was waiting for them. You should see a car! A vision. They drove for a long time. She leaned her head on the white seatback. He embraced her head, a fine and aristocratic embrace; but she could not allow it. All of a sudden, as though thinking it over, he said, "Strange . . . you know? But I'm actually not in love with you."

She then asked him to drive her home right away. She said good-bye and got out. No, he didn't need to escort her to the gate. She could no longer look him in the eye, and even today she wouldn't be able to do it.

"But if Czeszniewski hadn't then told you the truth, you wouldn't be sitting here with me now. Right, Feygele?"

"Don't say that, because I hate him."

"Well then, I won't speak."

But it nagged at Feygele.

"What do you think, Shimen, I could convert for the sake of a Christian?"

"Like I know? What do you think?"

"I think . . . that for me that would be no obstacle, if I were in love."

"I don't believe it. And your father? Your mother?"

"I've already gone with a Christian once. I told you: with the son of the Godlbozhits *starosta*."

"Well, and then what?"

"Nothing. He once suggested I convert. But I burst out laughing and thought I was having a seizure! 'If,' I said, 'you love me, then you become a Jew.'"

"And he?"

"He . . . He looked at me like I had three heads, thought I was making fun of him. 'I,' he said, 'a Jew'?"

"And how did it turn out?"

Feygele waved her hand.

"Nothing happened. At first he threatened to shoot both me and himself. But the next day I didn't even remember."

"So why do you say that you would be able to convert?"

"Well . . . If it's not demanded of me. Of its own—maybe."

"You're talking nonsense," Shimen said. "Why would you need to do it if it weren't being demanded of you?"

"Certainly not," she agreed. "But you know, that Czeszniewski—it was very good of him to speak to me so openly and candidly."

Shimen thought for a while and responded, "It was calculated in quite a lawyerly way. He looked you over and thought: a poor teacher, she's not going to make the demands a girl tricked or deceived would make. From one side he played on your reckless dissipation, and on the other side on your honesty."

Feygele considered this and said, "Maybe you're right, Shimen. I really do look, in my hat, in my coat, like some wretched teacher. To play a game—yes, but without responsibility."

"And you, Shimen," she continued, "why aren't you so easygoing? Why don't you play the game? Why are you always so serious and anxious?"

Shimen answered darkly, "How would I know how to play? By six years old the teacher had brandished both whip and hellfire; by eight, Cossacks had hanged my father; by nine, my mother went mad from her miseries."

She put her hand to his mouth:

"Don't," she fell into his arms trembling all over. "Don't tell any more . . . I know . . . I'm shivering . . . It's cold . . . co-o-ld . . . Hold me . . . That's better . . . Just like that . . . tha-a-at!"

———•———

That evening, that promise, that love lasted—a day and the night. Now Shimen Shifris put that whole beautiful dream behind him. On the way back home he trembled in a rickety hansom over the beautiful Godlbozhits chaussée and listened to scraps of news:

"Well now . . . seems Shmuel Rabinovitsh has finally also gone bankrupt."

"That's not whatcha call bankrupt these days. They took a deposit from a German from Danzig for a two-thousand-pound load of wood and with it bought the Rogów estate."

"And the German's keeping quiet?"

"When you soil your prick, it's soiled."

"Well, and did they repay Uncle Melekh for the promissory notes?"

"They'll never deny him. Well, he has a choice to make about Ley-bele Shoulder, the Pipe, and about Shmuel Rabinovitsh—a couple of girls, one after the other—pure gold, 'pon my word! I've heard that in Buenos Aires there's 'livelyhud' aplenty . . . You yourself, Panie Shifris, wouldn't choke."

Shimen pulled up the collar of his coat. It was cool. He felt as though they were going to spit in his face. The coach bounced. Yoynele Roytman cracked his whip, pushed back his cap, and off they went!

And Yoyne went on with his tale:

"So Feygele Rabinovitsh comes driving by, and I tell you, Panie Shifris, as I live and breathe—a real officers' broad! So she comes driving along with that writer Eyges and someone else . . ."

"You know Eyges?" Shimen asked.

"Do I know that black-haired writer? Panie Shifris, you don't have as many hairs on your head as the number of times he's described me in the papers. If that was someone else, and not Eyges, then I'm no Jew, if I can't tell his face. But Eyges is a regular Joe, a good guy. Comes driving along—orders up a shot, and drives off—'Yoynele, come have a little drink,' and now you should see how he brought me a necktie! . . . A real silk necktie! . . . He tied it on me, 'pon my word, right in the middle of the market. You'll definitely see me on Sabbath, when I put on my new 'suit'."

"And how is work, Yoynele?" Shimen steered the conversation in a different direction.

"Not good. The motorcars are going to kill coach-driving. They've already killed it."

"People pool their money and buy a motorcar."

"You don't have to tell me, Panie Shifris. It's killing us! All the coachmen together don't have what one machine must cost. So you think a 'livelyhud' will support ten families with wives and children?"

"So what are you considering doing about it?" Shimen asked.

Yoyne explained:

"All the coachmen got together and had the rabbi issue a prohibition and a ban that no one may lay a hand on a motorcar. What do you think that ginger does, a fire take his brain?! He goes and sets up an automobile association with the mayor. You think maybe the *goy* invests a little money in the business? Not a penny. Does that ginger bastard need money? That ginger bastard has a sister-in-law in Argentina, a 'madam' in a 'little house,' and he sends her hundreds of dollars, the devil take him! . . . So I go up to that ginger: 'Hey, ginger bastard,' I say, 'Damn your madam, the whore! Why are you poking me in the eyes with the mayor—may you go blind in both eyes! You think I'm afraid? No doubt you and the goy'll get caught, or that motorcar will find itself in the river! No doubt you'll die a horrible death, or those rubber wheels will be turned to cabbage.

"The first day—the red-haired one hid. His driver spent the whole day driving with a police escort. Me—nothing, like they weren't thinking about me. Just let me see what was gonna happen. The next day—the ginger was there . . . mo-ther! You'll get it yet—I thought to myself. So I threw down my jacket, spat in my hands, and counted! One! Between the eyes. Two! Under the chin. Three! Between the shoulders . . . I didn't need any more—he was already down, leaking red soup . . .

"No doubt you think the ginger is a weakling? No doubt you think he didn't get up and pull a knife on me, the whoreson? Well—I like strong people! I hate beating up an empty barrel."

"And when he jabbed at you with the knife?" Shimen asked.

"Hopeless as well," Yoyne said. "Here I am: when I set about a piece of work, then let me imagine I'm already ninety years old. You don't die twice, my good man."

"And the motorcar really didn't drive?" Shimen asked further.

"Don't ask, Panie Shifris: as far as I'm concerned it could go on crutches. For a thousand zlotys I fixed those four tires so no cooper in the world could put 'em back together."

"Slashed?"

Yoyne gave a lash of his whip on one side to speed up the horse and turned around to face his passenger.

"So maybe you think, Panie Shifris, that I did this in secret? That I kept lookout? Come off it! Each one in the eye. The whole market saw, and the mayor was looking down from his window.

"And the mayor, nothing?" asked Shimen.

"Why not? The police had arrived. They took me to jail . . . so I went. It's not in my nature to argue with the police. So I was sitting in jail by the window, waiting till the mayor went to lunch. 'Panie burmistrzu,' I called to him.[1] He was not such a great nobleman as he approached. 'You remember, my dear lord,' I said, 'when someone had stolen your grey gelding and you came to Yoyne, crying, fainting, and Yoyne took care of it for you all neat and tidy? Do you remember?'

"But he didn't recognize me: 'If you keep carrying on like that,' he said, 'I'll send you off in chains.' So, I thought, hold on a second: 'Would you like,' I said, 'Panie burmistrzu, to see a trick? If I sit here in jail while your little chestnut horses get taken from their stable? Maybe you'd like to see that? You just have to say the word if you do . . .'"

---

1. *Panie burmistrzu* (Polish): Mr. Mayor.

"Well, and he?" Shimen asked.

"He . . . We should both live and be healthy, Panie Shifris, as he called the guard and ordered me released from jail. They knew that with Yoyne there are no tricks; what Yoyne says is as good as done."

"And what happened with the motorcar?"

"Sold, my good man, lost half its value."

The horn and noise of an approaching car could be heard. Yoyne suddenly interrupted their conversation and turned all his attention on his horse, taking the reins firmly in his hands: "*Giddyup! Giddyup, iddyup, iddyup!*"

He drove that horse over every hill and dale, all the while glancing behind him to see whether the car was catching up to him, and kept driving. The horse raced breezily, flew, never letting itself be overtaken by the car. Only after ten minutes at such a gallop did the horse throw its head back—stop!—he could not go on. A horse after all is not a machine! The car then passed them and the driver stuck his tongue out at Yoyne.

"Damn your mother!" Yoyne yelled back. "Wait!"

The car had already disappeared in a cloud of dust.

"And whose is that bus?" Shimen asked.

"That fat Meierbach's, a fire in his fat belly!"

"A car can still cruise about?"

Yoyne turned around to his passenger.

"You think, Panie Shifris," he said, "that I'm a fool? That I don't know you can't clog up the world with pea straw? There are motorcars everywhere, so they'll have to be in Godlbozhits as well. It just really annoys me: you ginger dog, an '*izvoshtshik*'[2] just like me—why do *you* get to leap out in front?"

"So the industrialist Meierbach is right?" Shimen said accusatorily.

"As far as I'm concerned cholera can take them both tonight: both the ginger bastard and the fat industrialist! But at least that one is a person, at least that one speaks to you like a person. So I go up to

2. *izvoshtshik* (Russian): coachman.

him: 'Panie Meierbach,' I said, 'is it right to deprive a coachman of his bit of bread? Are you not lacking, God forbid, enough for a good living?' 'You're right,' he said, 'we should both be healthy, Yoyne, you're right. How much,' he said, 'do you make at coach-driving? Twenty-five, thirty zlotys a week? I'll give you your thirty zlotys. Fair? You certainly won't,' he said, 'have to to work hard, you'll only,' he said, 'be selling tickets and standing by the wagon, pointing the passengers to their seats. You'll be rid of,' he said, 'all that headache with the horse and the stables.'"

"You mean a conductor? And what did you say?"

"I—I asked him for some time to think it over. I only know one thing, that the Russki has a cunning head on his shoulders. It's not for nothing that he's an industrialist and I'm a coachman. If I could make at least twenty zlotys a week from coach driving, I swear, or I could go and give it up: bread and water. You should be true to yourself; but what does one do, Panie Shifris, when you can't even work enough to buy oats for your horse."

"That's really not good," Shimen agreed.

"Not good's putting it mildly," Yoyne said. "Coach driving is buried ten cubits underground."

The horse, which till then had been going slowly, suddenly lifted its head, and with a horselike anticipation of rest began cheerfully clopping over the stones of the outskirts of the city. Among the greenery and the Polish cottages the first shop signs appeared. The city was visible just beyond.

✣ 14 ✦

The One Who Took Shmuel's Blood, and from Whom Shmuel Got It Back

Shimen came in. He nearly forgot to take off his crumpled student's cap. At the old nicked and moth-eaten table sat Uncle Melekh, Shmuel, and a strange young man with a rabbinical face behind large American glasses. The strange man was busily stroking his silky black goatee with two fingers while explaining something in a restrained Talmudic chant. Shimen entered quietly.

"Greetings. Who is this young man?" the strange man asked.

"One of ours," Uncle Melekh answered. "My wife's sister's son. You can speak."

"Have you ever heard of such a thing!" The strange rabbinical face lit up with excitement. "It was one of Reb Itshe-Volf's grandsons. That was not just some simple how-d'ya-do. It was from the nobility!"

And soon the strange man got back to the matter.

But Shimen should really tell it himself. He wasn't born yesterday, but was rather something of an enlightened young man. So he himself should tell it: They weren't talking about profaning the Sabbath, about the fact that among the soldiers it was impossible to guard against eating un-kosher food, God forbid. All of that was set aside. But Shmuel is a young man who works in a pharmacy, earns, no evil eye, good money. Is he going to just throw all that away? Let someone else go learn how to shoot, go learn how to jump over logs. Some business, eh? It's a story of going off for two years to the army, a loss, in sum, of twenty-four times fifteen dollars a month, which makes already three hundred and sixty dollars. And how much is it worth not to lose your humanity, not to be buried? And what do you do—may the hour never come, may my mouth cause no evil—if a war should break out? What excuse will you have? Play a part for a hundred dollars? You should be ashamed! And it's not worth two hundred? I tell you, Jews: undress down to your shirt and remain a Jew at home!

The pale rabbinical face flushed, turned red with self-sacrifice. It wasn't just some Jew, some "big shot," who was talking about getting out of the military; it was Reb Pinyele, a rabbi, brother-in-law of Rabbi Mayerl, and a grandson of the Nashilover Rabbi. The Nashilover Rabbi was a close personal friend of Itshe-Volf's, and Itshe-Volf, may he rest in peace, who knew three hundred pages of Talmud by heart, did not deserve to have his grandson fall into the hands of goyim, going off to be a soldier—no!

"Well, there it is, good-bye," said Pinye the rabbi on taking his leave. "But you know. I'm not going to make any money here."

⸺ ⸺

And in the backroom of the newly built pharmacy that had been constructed on the site of Uncle Melekh's ruin the pharmacist played cards with the fat doctor.

"So tell me, pharmacist, the little one has some money?" the doctor asked.

"Which little one?"

"You know, the one who works for you in the pharmacy. Zaydman his name is, I think."

The fat doctor took out a little notebook and checked it to make sure.

"Yes, Zaydman's his name."

"He has a hundred dollars," said the pharmacist. "Why do you ask?"

"You've heard of course that he doesn't want to go serve in the army."

"The devil take you, Heniekl! No, low, high, four kings . . . Are you sitting on committees again? You've just been denounced . . ."

"Don't get distracted, Itsikl, listen: queen, king, ace; and you'll have four kings when I lend you one . . . So listen, I don't give a damn about them, those 'informers,' they can all kiss my big, fat rump."

"Well," the pharmacist shuffled the deck. "Listen, Heniek, if you are indeed sitting on the draft committees and you don't release that little one, then you're no longer my mate. But understand, I don't want that priss—I mean the clerk—to catch wind of it. Give her a raise! Then she'll keep her mouth shut. 'You don't want to, then go break your neck.' She knows that I can manage well enough with the little one."

"So be it, you're a mate," said the fat doctor. "Thanks to you it'll cost fifty dollars."

"Heniekl you bastard! From this draft you're making a lousy mint? How do you not have thirty young people? Just listen, mate, you'll do it for me for no money."

It was already late. The fat doctor got up and started to leave.

"And when, you swine of a pharmacist," he said, "am I going to start losing to you at cards? And where will I get a woman? My wife is getting close to the end of her pregnancy. It's a principle with me: you show your rump—you pay!"

The next day the pharmacist called Shmuel in to see him. He, Shmuel, had to go serve in the army; that was something he had to say clearly so as not to lead him astray. He, the pharmacist, needed to know that, because he had to see "someone" while there was still time.

Shmuel was crushed. He had saved up his money penny by penny from hard work, never letting himself buy anything, and now he had to go give away the whole amount all at once. Like a beggar with bits of sugar, that's how he got the money together. Such a joy it was for him when for his first wages he'd earned five dollars. Those five dollars he invested on interest, and the next month added another five. It was supposed to grow on the interest. Not even when he made a little extra did he touch a penny. His ambition—fifty dollars! And finally there was fifty, and then it really started to leaven, to grow by leaps and bounds, till he brought the pharmacist a hundred dollars. Even though it was at a lower rate of interest he preferred to give his money to the pharmacist than entrusting it to unknown hands. They had all now gone bankrupt—Rabinovitsh and Leybele Pipe had gone bankrupt, the Meierbachs had, people said, secretly, also gone bankrupt—so he wanted to have it in safe hands.

And when Shmuel came to his boss to reclaim a part of the entrusted money, he didn't even ask him why he needed it. The pharmacist didn't let on that he knew who the money was going to. Business is business. The doctor didn't interfere in his business, so he didn't feel the need to interfere in his. Every business has its secrets.

And Shmuel, too, didn't give himself away. Pinye the rabbi gave him very strict instructions not to mention a word of it to anyone. "You're playing with fire," Pinye said and then counted out softly and clearly, like a prayer:

"Forty-six, forty-seven, forty-eight . . . fifty. So that's that, I'm going," he groaned and held the money cautiously in his hand (foreign money!). "And may the One whose Name I'm not worth mentioning help. Aside from money you should also have success. At any rate, one does one's part and helps with the money; but as for being freed from the goyim's hands, that's a stroke of luck. May one have some merit in heaven."

He left and came back with nothing. They didn't even want to hear about the fifty dollars. In any case, they did know that he didn't want to serve. If he was going to sacrifice his life, it was out of regard for Reb Itshe-Volf's, may he rest in peace, grandson and his holy grandfather, the Nashilover Rabbi, of blessed memory, who along with Reb Itshe-Volf, may he rest in peace, were Hasidim of the same rebbe and stayed good friends till the very end . . . What can I say? Maybe they would have gone for seventy-five dollars, but he, Pinye, didn't want to interfere; he knew it was a matter of blood, not money. Jewish blood . . . He didn't want to get involved.

Shmuel ran to the pharmacist and claimed another twenty-five dollars. Pinye the rabbi brought the money where it was supposed to go and warned Shmuel not to appear before the committee until he notified him. Oh, had Shmuel received a summons? He shouldn't worry about it, he would only be in jail for a few days. You can't die from sitting, right? You have to wait for a "good committee."

And when the news was announced that the "good committee" would be tomorrow, Pinye the rabbi still didn't want to risk it. His gentle rabbinical face was aflame with self-sacrifice, as he busily stroked his black goatee. Then he went to the captain.

And now he has just come from the captain. It was a good thing he had gone to find out, too. The captain had gotten angry, the captain wanted to throw him out; for such a thing he would take three hundred dollars and a kiss on the hand, and now they're haggling over a measly hundred?

Uncle Melekh couldn't take it; he would gladly have grabbed that bastard by his finely combed beard and smashed those American glasses into his sanctimonious face. But he restrained himself; blood cost so much . . .

"And what's the matter with going to serve?" yelled Uncle Melekh. "I also served and still came home. They didn't take me away again."

From then on Pinye the rabbi steered clear of Uncle Melekh and avoided talking with him. "Listen," he said to Shimen, "vulgar's vulgar. Can't be helped. You didn't know your grandfather Reb Itshe-Volf, may he rest in peace. Your uncle came to him as a son-in-law like a sack to a piece of satin."

And when Shmuel counted out the hundred to the rabbi in his house, the rabbi asked, "Your father shouldn't know about this. Your father, forgive me, is a person . . . not a modern person. He might let something slip. It's better if he didn't know about this."

Now since Shmuel admittedly remained a Jew at home, though a Jew without dollars, he looked around at the situation like a victor who alone is left standing on the battlefield—poverty and need all around. Uncle Melekh had lost all his money, Leybele Pipe had gone somewhat bankrupt, and his dear little son, Arele, curse his name, had swindled him out of the rest, gotten married, and left. So he, Shmuel, would now have to start building it up anew, but under much worse conditions: interest had become much cheaper, and at home they had to hold on to their zlotys. He regretted the wasted money, and he swore to earn back the sum many times over by economizing on food and working harder than ever.

In his way stood the pharmacy clerk, Panna Mina. When she was gone, Shmuel had been the perfect little clerk and could make twice the pay. But Panna Mina had no intention of losing her position. Panna Mina, an older girl with frightened black eyes and an ugly wart on her face, was supporting an elderly mother in some tiny shtetl along with two little sisters. And while she regularly sent twenty zlotys a week, the director of the gymnasium still sent the older sister home every Monday and Thursday. He, the director of the gymnasium, was within his rights: he could give a 50 percent reduction as a scholarship, but the rest still had to be paid, since the teachers had to eat. And the cobbler was also right: it was not often that they got everything on credit. If they paid him in kind he'd wait a week or two.

Her mother wrote that her little one sat at home barefoot, unable to go to school, and there wasn't a scrap of wood to be had. So she asked her, Mina, her dear child, her golden soul, not to cause her any grief; it was enough that her mother had a swollen liver from all of her sufferings and her heart was also bothering her. She didn't want to cause her any grief, but winter was approaching, the children were freezing, naked and barefoot. Perhaps she could get an advance from the principal? At least twenty or thirty zlotys, enough to keep body and soul together. She, her old mother, had heard it said that the Godlbozhits pharmacist was a rich man with a good heart; he certainly couldn't refuse her.

The pharmacist wondered why she, Panna Mina, a pharmacist's clerk who had worked at her job for ten years already, and always so skillfully, so diligently, had suddenly begun doing everything so phlegmatically. She went around as though possessed, kept making mistakes in measuring out the medicine and in reading the prescriptions. Sometimes little Shmuel would come to him, the pharmacist: it was either witness every prescription himself, or risk going to prison. Because he couldn't be sure that sooner or later she wouldn't poison someone with a prescription.

He, the pharmacist, told her all of this because he was a person who abhorred scheming. And when little Shmuel heard such frank talk he worked that much harder, taking a prescription right from a customer's hand, calculating and preparing it before Panna Mina managed to stammer out, "What would the gentleman like?"

If only the same could be said of the pharmacist himself. With his prescriptions he was responsible for people's lives and he couldn't trifle around with "feelings." But a woman feels with a woman's heart—as Pani Stefe said of herself. She, the pharmacist's wife, knew what it meant to be a girl getting up there in years going about unmarried. So if she, Panna Mina, wanted a husband, wanted to be reinvigorated, young and cheerful at work, there had to be something going on to account for why she rejected all the matches that the pharmacist's wife proposed to her. Maybe an unhappy love affair, or—who knows? Maybe someone really had seduced and abandoned her. Yes, obviously to you she seems such a modest girl; but as the saying goes, "Calm waters destroy the shore."

She, the pharmacist's wife, was responsible for a person who lived with her under one roof and ate the food she prepared. She could not allow a housemate of hers to bring such a demoralizing influence into her house. She was suddenly struck with an idea: "Maybe Isidore." Yes, yes, that's what you think men are like, not at all picky: beautiful, ugly, it doesn't matter as long as it's an unfamiliar female. And that quiet little lamb, that Minele, it seems to you that she is unable to speak one word to a man, even when you can see that man's gay! Ho, ho!

And she, the pharmacist's wife, decided on her own to find out, to learn what was going on.

So she, the pharmacist's wife, would anticipate Panna Mina's every move, even if it meant misleading her husband. But such a scandal, such a hue and cry—never. Once Mina did come running into the pharmacy screaming hysterically, "Who went searching through my drawers? Tell me at once!"

The pharmacist's wife, who just happened to be all alone in the pharmacy, remained calm, and asked in a dignified way, "Whom do you mean to be speaking to with your hysterical screaming, Panna Mina? Perhaps my husband? Perhaps me? Do you really think, Panna Mina, that your letters are that interesting? Your lo-o-o-ve letters?"

With comic disdain Pani Stefe burst out laughing; Panna Mina burst into tears. Her tears flowed like a fountain into her white handkerchief.

The pharmacist came in.

"What happened?" he asked.

"What should have happened?" Pani Stefe echoed her husband's question a note higher. "Is it not natural for an unmarried lady getting on in years to fall quite often into hysterics?"

Pan Isodore looked around for a while as though he did not understand, as though he were thinking about something else, and then all of a sudden he started pacing back and forth around the pharmacy, his hands thrust in his trouser pockets, spanning the length of the floorboards:

They shouldn't pester him with such tales! It wasn't *his* job to marry off every old maid. He owned a pharmacy, he did. Pharmacying was a business. Weighing and measuring with utter precision; one little drop too much and the patient is poisoned. He couldn't keep around any irresponsible people, or hysterical women. He wouldn't put lives at risk, he wasn't going to go to prison for anyone.

Still, maybe he wouldn't fire her just yet. The lecture had calmed Panna Mina a bit, and even though she went around like a stranger, not saying a word to anyone, she no longer made scenes with all the crying and hysterical outbursts.

However, it was then that something happened for which the pharmacist nearly went off in chains. The doctor at the hospital got involved, and the whole pharmacy was nearly ruined. Here's what happened:

Jan, the peasant from Rogów who worked at the Meierbachs's factory, his son took ill, gravely ill, so much so that they had to go see the barber surgeon. And when a peasant's child is grievously ill the barber surgeon writes an expensive prescription, the most expensive prescription, one that will overflow the largest bottle. Needless to say, the peasant Jan from Rogów did not have enough bread to eat. But for the sake of a sick child you would pawn everything you had because a pharmacist—as the whole world knows—won't fill a prescription if there's even one penny missing.

But after taking the medicine, the peasant's child only got worse, much worse. They had to take him to the hospital. The doctor demanded to see the prescription that the barber surgeon had written for the child. From the hospital Jan went straight back to the factory and told Pan Meierbach about his sick child and how the hospital doctor had demanded to see the prescription. "Surely there was too much poison," the peasant thought aloud.

Pan Meierbach dropped everything and ran pell-mell to see the pharmacist.

"Just listen, Isidore, it's like this, the lad was poisoned, and the hospital doctor said it came from that bottle."

The pharmacist smacked his hand.

"Will I never be rid of that bad luck?!" he pointed at the clerk. "I just knew she'd eventually poison somebody."

"Quiet! Don't yell!" Meierbach spread out a fat hand. "Just don't get cold feet. As long as Jan has that bottle with him, I'm still his boss."

He still had heart palpitations, the pharmacist did! Jan brought the prescription along with the bottle, wrapped in a bit of rag like a dead bastard child. From his bosses he received a gift of five zlotys and he thanked them, thanked them very much. The pharmacist tore the pharmacy label off of the bottle and hid it in his pocket.

"Phew," he spat with relief.

"What's wrong?" asked Iser Meierbach.

"Just had a bit of a scare," the pharmacist's piggish face flowed into a smile. "To hell! To hell with them! That the barber surgeon can prescribe poison. And two hundred grams of aqua destillata is not enough for a peasant?"

"So you've hidden the label?" the fat industrialist winked cunningly and suspiciously.

"Listen, obviously twelve zlotys for two hundred grams of aqua destillata is a little too expensive, a smidge expensive."

"So now I'm really seeing how people make money," the industrialist said with jealousy in his voice. "Twelve zlotys for a little water."

The pharmacist laughed, drooling with satisfaction.

"So my good friend," he said, "has sized me up . . . And you think the barber surgeon works for free? A full 40 percent I gave him, otherwise he wouldn't go for it."

"And if you're left with eight zlotys for a little bottle of water, is that not enough?" Jealousy was still eating at the industrialist. "Give me that kind of business in my factory and I'll fill the market with gold."

The whole story came out later, maybe three years later, right after Meierbach's second bankruptcy. And the industrialist described how the pharmacist was the biggest swine of them all. The Meierbachs had received a small debt at "interest," not—God forbid—capital, of maybe a thousand zlotys in total; he was the first to climb up the mortgage.

The fat industrialist became furious, his murderous little eyes burned.

"But that little bottle with the prescription Meierbach brought you, eh?! Fraud! Otherwise where would you be rotting today, eh?!"

But they could have talked to the pharmacist till the cows came home. He knew them well, those Meierbachs, those crooks. Every nine months they went bankrupt, and they'd feed their fat bellies on someone else's hard work. Just take a good crap into their hands. He, the pharmacist, you see, made a lot off the both of them—both off Moritz, who snorted with his mouth, and off the crude Russki, the Bolshevik.

This all came out, as was said, maybe three years later. But the poor pharmacy clerk could not wait that long for the whole thing to be cleared up. She did not even wait until she was fired. As soon as the pharmacist had charged her with the "poisoning," with being the "bad luck that he would never be rid of," she went up to her room in the house, shut herself in, anxiously wrote a note, and . . . That evening, when they forced open the door and turned on the lights, there hanging from a hook near the lamp was Panna Mina, her mocking blue tongue sticking out. When touched she spun on the rope, clumsily showing off the ugly wart on her face.

Till noon the next day, after the burial, her death caused some turmoil at the pharmacist's house. At first the pharmacist's wife could not stop crying, constantly wiping away the tears: such a quiet dove . . . such a decent child . . . Later, however, when people had stopped talking about it, and the hanged girl, despite all probabilities, had not come back from the grave to strangle her, the pharmacist's wife permitted herself to criticize: "A person who has obligations to an old, ailing mother and two little sisters, could that person do such a thing? You call that a daughter?! You call that a sister? *Pfui*! She couldn't have had a better death!"

And Shmuel—Shmuel, Uncle Melekh's boy—now felt that the whole business, the whole pharmacy "lay on him." At first the blue, stuck-out tongue and the wart on the dead girl's face pursued him throughout the evening hours. He kept remembering the wrongs he had secretly done the dead girl, the information about her work he had given to the pharmacist, the harassments, the pins he had placed in order to get rid of her. So he fearfully awaited the dead girl's vengeance. But as he got more and more immersed in work he forgot his coworker, toiling away for all he was worth.

He was going to work his way up, slowly but surely.

He had already even started fresh and saved up a little money again; he cobbled it together to lend on interest, though the joy in it for him was gone. Then all of a sudden he was examining an order from the military authorities: he was to report immediately to the twenty-fifth regiment.

And did that ever cause an uproar. It had cost all that money and for nothing? They ran to Pinye the rabbi. Pinye said that it was folderol, nonsense . . . So here he is going to see the captain—and here he is coming back from the captain: they'll soon rescind the order. Some pissant soldier there had made a mistake and issued an order. So he, Shmuel, could sleep soundly.

But neither the next day nor a week later was the order to go serve in the army rescinded, and so, after several days, Shmuel had to present himself, bitterly . . .

Again they ran off to see Pinye the rabbi. Pinye stroked his silky goatee, moistening his earlocks. So here he is running off to see the captain. And here he has just come back from the captain, his rabbinical face is a white as chalk: "Listen . . . it's bad. This is bad." The captain had been transferred to another regiment; his replacement had looked over all of his papers and reversed every decision.

The pharmacist learned of what happened and decided to consult the fat doctor.

"Listen here, what kind of a game are you playing at? You take a young man's last penny and then order him to go serve in the army?"

"You call twenty dollars the last penny?" said the fat doctor. "I shielded him for a year. Enough. What? For twenty dollars maybe he wanted to be completely free?"

"And how much did the captain get?" the pharmacist asked.

"What captain, which captain? What d'you mean, captain? I'm a captain."

"So why did the little one tell me that he gave a hundred dollars? Are you deceiving me? Samuel!" he yelled back into the pharmacy.

Shmuel entered in his white apron. The fat doctor looked at him for a moment; right away he grew light-headed. He turned bright red from anger, and stood up, which made his double chin and fat belly tremble.

"Just listen here you, stripling," he said confronting Shmuel. "If you don't want to go and serve, don't you know who to go to? And who did you come to to show your bare ass? Why didn't you go to Pinye the rabbi? What sounds fair, that I, the doctor, will take twenty dollars and that whorish Hasid takes eighty! And for twenty dollars you're going to trick the Russians in front of me?! Eh?! It won't, I think, do any harm for you to air your legs. Poland needs soldiers!"

Uncle Melekh didn't know any tricks. He went off to that sly bastard in order to tear his beard out, "You're going to give back that money at once!"

Pinye grew faint, "Reb Melekh is not at all speaking like a person . . . not at all like a Jew." Where could he get the money to give back when he had given the money away already: twenty dollars to the doctor and eighty to someone whose name he didn't dare mention. Hadn't he, the scoundrel, sworn an oath that he wouldn't reveal it? The Uncle didn't understand; after all, who needed to reveal it? Just give back the money and go to hell!

And Pinye went on, "Listen, you're not talking rationally, Reb Melekh. If you believe me, Pinye, that I couldn't reveal the name, then surely you could also believe that I have given the money away. That's a *kal-vekhoymer*.[1] What of it? Am I some little boy from the street?"

Uncle Melekh ground his teeth.

"Don't talk, because I'm going to *ki-i-i-ll* you! Either the money or tell who you gave it to."

Pinye was terrified and fled. It seems that despite everything he was most afraid of Uncle Melekh. That evening he sent for Shmuel.

So—he was ready to reveal the name, but only to the rabbi. He, Shmuel, had to understand—he was after all an educated young man—that Uncle Melekh was a little . . . how should one put it? Well, it wasn't from Shmuel's ancestry on his mother's side. All he, Uncle Melekh, had to do was let a word slip somewhere and then everyone would, God forbid, go to prison. That one, the one whose name he didn't dare mention, was a decent person, kindly, from an aristocratic family. "I don't know if he profited ten zlotys from the whole affair."

So they went to see the rabbi. The rabbi deliberated for a long time and issued his ruling that Pinye had to swear an oath that he had given the money to free Shmuel, and not, God forbid, for himself. However, given that an oath is a serious matter, the rabbi was not going to accept an oath even from a simple Jew let alone from a learned Jew like Pinye; therefore his ruling was . . . half. Pinye was to pay half.

Pinye accepted the judgment but he had no money. Everyone in the city knew that he was, heaven protect us, a Jew without any livelihood to speak of; but he could take out promissory notes against the judgment. Pinye the rabbi was certain that he could redeem them, the notes, on time.

---

1. *kal-vekhoymer* (Hebrew): a technical Rabbinic term indicating an a fortiori argument.

Now it appeared that Uncle Melekh was right: Pinye and Rabbi Mayerl were in cahoots. For his part he wouldn't be getting involved in any lawsuit with that sly bastard. He would catch him by the throat in the middle of the street and choke him till he squeezed out a couple of pennies.

And he would have done it too, Uncle Melekh would, but in the meantime once again, Shmuel didn't go off to serve. The fat doctor had received a new sum of money, and the whole thing was set in perfect order. And so it is: You should always go straight to the top, not—begging your pardon—to the "bottom."

✣ 15 ✣

The Painter Tykociński Makes Festive Portraits; Editor Eyges Puts God's Name under the Tongue; Zalmen Komashnmakher Drags It All through the Mud

One time Shimen unexpectedly bumped into Feygele in the middle of the Godlbozhits market, face-to-face. He greeted her courteously and politely. He, Shimen, was strong enough not to seek her out; but if by chance they happened to meet, please, it would have been strange for them not to talk. They really were the best of friends.

"Are you coming over for Sabbath?" Feygele asked again, this time impatiently. "Well, yes?"

"Maybe."

"No, tell me if you're coming, because I need to know whether to wait for you; otherwise, you won't find me at home."

He felt the need to turn her down, Shimen Shifris did, to cut her off, and have an end to it. *Where one can no longer love*, says Nietzsche, *there one should—pass by*.[1] But instead, he asked, "And what will I do there? I'll just bore you, Feygele."

"You'll see, it'll be festive," her eyes shone with encouragement. "Eyges will be there, and somebody else."

---

1. *Where one can no longer love, there one should—pass by*: "Wo man nicht mehr lieben kann, da soll man—*vorübergehen*!" (Friedrich Nietzsche, *Also Sprach Zarathustra*, "Vom Vorübergehen").

"Already somebody new?"

"You do know me." Feygele concealed half her face by turning it downward, as though embarrassed, while with the other half she flirted seductively. "You do know me, I cannot long . . ."

"Do I know him, this new one?" Shimen asked.

"You ought to know him. He comes here every year. Tykociński's his name."

"The painter?"

"Yes."

He had nothing left to ask; the words stuck in his throat. It really was a foolish thing on his part to go around with this delusion, this longing, this fantasy: Feygele . . . But he had felt for a long time, the intuition had whispered to him, that all of the women's gossip about Feygele, about her being a "tarnished woman," was raw jealousy. He knew from the start that she, Feygele, would be far out of reach. The painter Tykociński was known throughout Poland and even abroad, while as for him, Shimen, some fifty people in Godlbozhits knew who he was. The rivalry would doubtless not last long.

The last spark of hope went out. He didn't need to go to Feygele's party. How would he feel among those people with names like the painter Tykociński and the editor Eyges? And nevertheless he promised, "Good, I'll come."

He said these words softly, with feeling, and it seemed to him that Feygele answered him with a moist gleam in her eyes. Such they were, these sentimental hearts: just when you think it's the last drop, the final spark of hope, and all of a sudden you're pouring a fresh draught of lively, seductive fantasy. And after all, what did she mean, that Feygele, by cajoling him so intensely to come out, by looking into his eyes with her intimate glances? Perhaps she actually had convinced herself that all of them—Eyges, Kopsztyk, Tykociński, and whatever the rest of their names were—that all of them were only playing games, while he, Shimen, was the only one to devote himself body and soul?

No matter, he went. He could hardly wait for that Sabbath afternoon. He had made seven kilometers on the way to the Rogów estate in one breath, as if someone were chasing him. Uphill and downhill and uphill again. And then there appeared the peak of the red roof of the dilapidated, flayed little house on the estate. The Rogów estate. All the nobles who had purchased it had lost their shirts; that was its reputation.

He had just met the whole group—Eyges, Tykociński, and the young poet from Godlbozhits Shloyme Mandelboym—when there came peals of laughter. Feygele had laughingly, and without pause, introduced Shimen to her guests and again recounted the tale which had caused them to split their sides.

"So mother asks her partner, 'Leybele, what have you bought? Is it land?' Stones and bones. Grandfather can still recall how all of the nobles who owned the Rogów estate lost their shirts. So there he sits, Leybele, puffing on his little pipe and smiling to himself, 'You are,' he says, 'you should pardon me, a putz.' Ha-ha-ha! And he sees . . . oh! . . . how people are laughing. Ha-ha-ha! So he corrects himself, 'I mean,' he says, 'a *putzlette*.' Ha-ha-ha!"

That rickety house shook with laughter. In the other part of the house Reb Shmuel Rabinovitsh and his wife were sleeping their Sabbath postprandial sleep and either didn't hear or pretended not to.

"You've presented the story very nicely," said Tykociński laughing to Eyges. "Where do you get such foul language?"

"Heaven forbid!" Eyges swore. "I recounted Feygele's 'teachings' as my own originals in the union and they considered them the very best; that pack of scribblers couldn't get enough . . ."

"Wait, there's more," said Feygele, "that was in our house, in Godlbozhits, right after Leybele Pipe bought Rogów. Right away father saw that he had been deceived, and his brother-in-law—you know how he is—couldn't get a word out because of his anger. So he paces around the room, Leybele Pipe does, back and forth, raising his shoulder and humming a tune to himself. 'Shmuel,' he says to my father, 'you know what I've decided? On the river in Rogów a mill might be built, and that could be lucrative business'—'And what would you mill in this mill?' father asks, 'The grain that doesn't grow in Rogów?' Leybele was not amused and elaborated his plans. 'And by the mill,' he says, 'a sawmill could be built.' Now father is finally getting angry, 'You're mad,' he says, 'in all of Rogów there's not a stick of forest, so what'll you stick under the saws?' Here his brother-in-law at last couldn't bear the Pipe's bluff and his fantasies, 'He'll,' he says, 'stick under them and cut up . . . ten-ruble coins!' Ha! Ha! Ha! Ha-ha-ha! Ha! Ha!'"

Everyone laughed, getting carried away by Feygele's laughter, splitting their sides. Even Shimen laughed, though reservedly. Only Eyges asked stupidly, "What should he have stuck under them?"

"A finger," Feygele laughed, showing Eyges her tongue.

Suddenly Shimen began to feel unwell in that company. Feygele noticed, and took his hand.

"Come, Shimen," she said. "They'll just yak away, these foul-mouthed people. You've only got to nudge them and their speech will flow like water through a sack full of holes. Let's not keep them from unburdening their hearts."

"Why don't you tell the shikse?" Eyges said to Tykociński. "The way she talks would embarrass even a Cossack and then she heaps the whole blame on us."

At that Feygele stuck her tongue out at him again and walked off on Shimen's arm.

Once outside, however, they didn't have anything to talk about. But that's easily said, "nothing to talk about." From Shimen's mouth the tenderest words might have poured forth, like peas from a sack; but peas are immaterial in such a situation. He, Shimen, couldn't drain the noblest blood from his heart and then just pour it out into the middle of the street. And even if he could manage to get out his most ardent words, would they reach the heart of that frivolous girl?

They walked silently. The silence weighed heavily on Shimen. He would have preferred that she, Feygele, start speaking first. Every-thing depended on her. Shimen waited and could barely stand it. So he started in with a question, "Does he really please you, that Eyges, with his foul language?"

"You're so silly," Feygele said earnestly. "Eyges is a talented edi-tor and the most beautiful speaker I've ever heard. Girls fall in love with him at his lectures. He doesn't speak, he paints with words: about nature, art, theater . . . And what's more, he's a handsome man . . ."

"Handsome?" Shimen winced.

"Well," she said with that same earnestness, "you'd have to see him at the beach. In his white robe, with a towel wrapped around his head like a turban, with his black beard and smoldering eyes—a real Arab."

"So?" asked Shimen, his heart pounding.

"That's it," she said, "you know what I'm like. Everyone pleases me at the beginning. It doesn't last long."

A weight was lifted from Shimen.

"It's remarkable," he said, "a man like Eyges, not so young anymore, it's remarkable that he's not married."

"What? You don't know that he's got a wife?"

"A wife?"

"Apparently there may be a wife, or there may not be a wife. In any case he's got something."

"Really?" Shimen burst out, not without joy.

"Among them, those artists," she said, "many things are a wife. They're a bunch of gypsies."

Suddenly the tense muscle of his heart relaxed. He softened, like butter in the sun. He said, "Why do you like them, those artists? You see, Feygele . . ."

"They're so fun to be around." Feygele looked warmly into his eyes. And then, as though she were trying to avoid something, she started laughing and slapped his shoulder, "Well, come on now, come . . . We've got to get back. It's not right to abandon them for so long."

They encountered no one in the house. "They'll certainly be in Tykociński's garret," Feygele said.

They went up by a narrow staircase, like a ladder. Tykociński had rented the bright whitewashed garret as a workspace during the summer. The walls were covered in paintings, both oil paintings and watercolors. Following an old conservative practice Tykociński had covered his aquarelles with a shiny glaze. At first glance this made his paintings look cheap, but when one studied them a bit longer one observed the hand of a master. There were only a few landscapes—little houses, buckled, disorderly, with sagging roofs—everything in the color of decaying vegetation, of olive brown, parasitic mushrooms. There were

many more portraits, but one series stood out: an old Jewish woman
with thin, dry hands the color of earth, praying over the Sabbath candles; another old Jewish woman with a wrinkled parchment-like face,
praying over a pair of glasses into an open prayer book; and again, the
same woman in holiday clothes with a bonnet on her head and a wom-
en's prayer book under her arm, walking into synagogue; in another,
there was Moyshele, the aged eighty-year-old Godlbozhits porter,
with his hunched shoulder, painted in various ways. The shoulder as it
appeared from behind, the shoulder from the front, the shoulder from
the side. And then again that same Moyshele the porter, but now in a
tallis, one eye intensely absorbed in the book open before him, and the
other staring up to God above. Magnificent!

Tykociński had given his own interpretation of the paintings that he
showed to his guests. The naturally taciturn Tykociński was now whispering in an inspired, sentimental voice. Words flowed eloquently from
his mouth like water from a holy spring: He had painted that Moyshele
the porter so many times, but that one in the tallis, with one eye fixed
on the book and the other gazing into heaven, that is the crown of
his Moysheles, that is the true, Sabbath-souled, festive Moyshele. All of
those with the shoulder stooped under the sack of flour are the weekday
Moysheles, they are the busy, bustling, worldly Moysheles, they are an
antechamber, a vestibule to the true, Sabbath Moyshele, when he for-
gets his portering, when Moyshele and his soul find themselves somewhere high above! High! And no nobleman, no magnate is his equal.

Timidly, and begging his pardon fifteen times in case his opinion
sounded like someone not versed in matters of art, Shimen noted, "But
it seems to me that Moyshele the porter is a simple Jew, and that Talmud, and those staring, pious eyes are not authentic to a Moyshele the
porter, are not real."

A bitter smirk appeared on Eyges's lips. The poet Mandlboym
nearly burst out laughing. He bit his lip with significance and poked
Eyges in the shoulder like an equal. Shimen understood that he had
said something foolish and turned red from shame.

But Tykociński was a tactful person. Tykociński smoothed the
matter out.

"You must understand," he turned directly to Shimen, "Realism . . ."

"Expressionism," poet Mandlboym corrected.

"Realism," Tykociński did not let himself get distracted, "is an outdated form in art. To me it is immaterial to show what Moyshele the porter is on the outside, as he appears to us, namely a porter; there are many porters, and stronger, cruder ones at that. To me it is important to extract Moyshele the porter's soul, his substance . . ."

"Impressionism," Mandlboym corrected.

"His substance," Tykociński ignored the poet's terminology, "his interior, his innermost space, his hidden light, his Holy of Holies, and that's what I succeeded with in the painting with the book."

Calmly and in reverence for his own crowning work Tykociński stood to the side of the painting and pointed to another.

"Now," he said, "take that painting: a Jewish woman—her name is apparently Khane-Yente—a wrinkled face, hollow eyes, reciting *tkhines*.[2] All week long Khane-Yente is nothing more than a poor fruit seller who stands in the street with her little basket toiling herself weary, with great difficulty, for a dry piece of bread and some money for her grandchild's education. All week long she squabbles with the other saleswomen in the street, cursing, swearing, scolding. But when the Sabbath comes, Khane-Yente is a princess, Khane-Yente makes her arguments before God, speaking to Him with the choice *tkhine* language of a court Lady of the Father in heaven, with the language of Sore bas Toyvim."[3]

With a white silk handkerchief Tykociński wiped the dust from his second crowning work, from his Sabbath Khane-Yente. He did this with visible respect, like pious Christian women when they dust the image of holy mother.

2. *tkhines* (Yiddish): prayers, especially ones written in Yiddish and intended for women.

3. Sore bas Toyvim was a famous eighteenth-century writer of *tkhines* and other prayers for women.

Then Tykociński walked over to his landscapes. In passing, he expressed his displeasure with the new, postwar Godlbozhits, especially its construction of new houses—those tasteless red-brick houses, fit only to spit on.

But in case that new trite architecture doesn't satisfy you, a Jew still has a good head on his shoulders, and after all a Jew cannot go without some trick. So if such a Jew obtains for you a blueprint for a one-storey house, then at night, in the dark he will put up another story, rolling out a flat roof that's such an eyesore, blocking out your entire view of the landscape. And just go try to talk to him.

And what's more, even the pharmacist, seemingly an intelligent and educated person, who should have a sense of aesthetics, even he was deceived with his house. Apparently they made some turrets, some cornices, but it didn't come close to the old Godlbozhits style.

In any event, his, the pharmacist's, house at least had the appearance of a house: large, wide, with bright windows; but those other narrow, two-story houses of red brick: eyesores one and all. Something like thin flayed geese. Those aren't houses, they're factory chimneys.

But of course the repairs to the old roofs brought the painter Tykociński to despair. Just when a shingle roof, spotted with green moss like the nostrils of an old snuff-sniffer, begins to bow wearily under the weight of its years and the roof produces a little hump, a little gold hump, just then a Jew starts rolling out a spool of tar and cardboard and spoils the whole effect.

"Barbarians!" Tykociński cries. "Do you even know what you're destroying?"

"And when it's dripping into my bed, is it your concern?" the Jew answers, also with a question.

"Can't you fix it with shingles, like it was?" Tykociński screams.

"Today there aren't fools like there used to be," that petty bourgeois soul yells back down. "Shingles are not so durable, and are three times as expensive. It's money!"

"Money! Money!" These people would sell everything for money, even their grandfather's spice box, even their grandmother's head kerchief.

And again Tykociński complained. For him Godlbozhits was ruined and so were its people. Where can you find the prewar *shtraymls* and long coats? Where are the quiet, mysterious alleys, the overgrown paths and trails in Godlbozhits? Where is the restful Friday night with its touching Sabbath candles shining into the dark marketplace? Postwar Godlbozhits is heading with hurried steps toward banal Europeanization. Everywhere sidewalks, everywhere streetlamps. Already you've got nearly nowhere to escape to be by yourself; not for a million can you get a silk Sabbath cap, a woman's hat . . . Even a little round Jewish skullcap has become a rarity.

With that Tykociński finished his litany. Eyges took the floor: as a matter of fact he, basically, agrees with Tykociński. Although he, Eyges, still belongs to the old revolutionary school, and along with Y. L. Peretz he had in his day vigorously struggled against the *shtrayml*; but one must confess that progress in the Jewish street has adopted such wild forms that who knows whether one oughtn't take a step back. He, Eyges, was terrified by the loss of respect for art on the part of the younger generation. Take, for example, any boy from the lefty union, some Zalmen Komashnmakher, say, who'd hardly read a book, and he'll state his opinion with such certainty on literary questions as if he were at the very least a professor. He'll shatter everything for you, turning it all to ash. Bah! Even Peretz he'll critique.

He, Eyges, is therefore, basically, in agreement with Tykociński. But on one thing he cannot agree—one cannot so easily dismiss progress. Civilization and the rise of technology are facts one must reckon with. His, Eyges's, point is that one must find the synthesis of old and new.

But Tykociński held to his feelings on oldness.

"Believe me, Eyges," he said, "when I see an old, bowed roof, covered with mildew I am reinvigorated like a tree in springtime. I still remember the flavor of the old Godlbozhits with its polluted stream flowing through the marketplace. And under the water it teemed with mysterious life, and above it a greenish gold mold winding like a magnificent snake, like a kilometer-long colorful serpent through the shtetl. Even when the old-fashioned trash cans were cleared out and removed from the middle of the marketplace—even that I call cultural barbarism. Oldness must not be merely superficial; oldness must have a smell. When painting one must not merely see, but also feel what one's painting. Smell has a tone, a color . . ."

"But, Tykociński," editor Eyges extended his hand to him, "we're not contradicting each other at all; we're merely filling out, complementing each other. Painting presents life in its stable, in its plastic form, and literature in its dynamic one. I would say that literature is the Ineffable Name which we put under the tongue of a dead decapitated head, and we command that head to speak, to perform miracles. How much, I ask you, would this new generation, which knows nothing of the study house, which was brought up in the class unions, how much, I ask you, would it know about Hasidism, I mean, about the true, sublime spirit of Hasidism, about martyrdom, about Israel the eternal wanderer, the sower of light among the peoples. How much, I ask you, would today's generation of class struggles know about all of that if we don't remind it at every step of its ancestry, its Torah, its eternal book. We remind it of that every day in various ways: in the press, in hard science, and in belles lettres . . . We have taken dry bones, old, moldy lifeways, withered beliefs, and into them we have blown the modern Ineffable Name and have commanded: *Go, struggle, attack, and conquer the soul of the young materialist generation!*

"That's what I wanted to say," editor Eyges finished. "There's no disagreement between us at all. The difference between painting and literature is principally in the way in which it produces its effect. Painting is in its nature static art, while literature works primarily by its dynamism . . ."

"Bravo! Bravo!" clapped the poet Mandlboym, who had been standing back. "Quite right! I'll give you an example right here . . ."

And before anyone understood what he was talking about the young poet grabbed a slip of paper out of his pocket and began to read:

They've burst into song,
They've burst out ringing—
The bronze bells

On churches at night;
Like Sabbath braids
They swayed,
Swayed, swayed
On the chestnut-haired heads
Of maidenly Jewish daughters . . .

Having performed the poem with stuttering breath the young poet looked out over everyone's astonished faces with a look of success, gushing with triumph, "Do you feel the dynamism?!"

And before anyone could get a word out, he began talking like water through a sack full of holes:

"That poem I wrote especially for your paper, Mr. Editor. Perhaps you think I was worried about where to publish it? Please! My poems are published everywhere, even in Argentina. Here you've got a letter from the editor of the *Argentiner-Lebn.* He asks for, is dying for me to send him something; and money—honest to goodness—he's sending an advance. And I've just now received a fifteen dollar advance on five articles on Polish provincial life. So, what do you think, my things aren't published?"

He would gladly have listed all of the newspapers, journals, and anthologies featuring his work, but he didn't have any time, he had to take his leave hastily, shaking everyone's hand.

"Hallo, good-bye, colleague Eyges, good-bye friend Tykociński. I've got to be off home quickly. The proofs await me. I've got to send them off in the evening post. The editor's been sending telegrams that the next installment of my novel will be held up and the contract cancelled. Oh! And today I still have to write a poem. Hallo! Good-bye . . ."

He flipped up the collar of his coat, even though it was warm out, and disappeared into the corridor.

Only then did the crowd in the garret recover their senses. The first was Feygele who burst out laughing. Tykociński said, "The nerve of a young man! Well, there it is."

And Eyges corrected him, "The nerve, you say? The gigantic nerve? The colossal nerve! There's some kind of madness in that young man."

Finally Shimen too was able to put in a word.

"What's there to say," he said. "In Godlbozhits he's known as a scribbler, a braggart, and a fraud."

"A fraud? A thief more like it!" Eyges was serious, but his eyes were laughing. "That's the best quality of a contemporary poet. Tykociński! I bet you that in about a year. Well, two years at the latest, that dynamic scribbler will be a writer in full pomp."

"Or maybe an editor," laughed Tykociński.

"Don't laugh," said Eyges half-seriously. "Fraud, nerve—today those are the essential qualities of a literary man."

It had gotten late. Shimen started to take his leave.

"What's your hurry," Feygele said, quite casually. "Wait, if you'd like, and I'll walk you to the street, ok?"

Shimen thanked her with his eyes. Hand in hand they left the paint-soaked garret. He nearly carried her on his shoulders down the ladder-like stairway. And then they separated, walking apart toward the hilly field like two friends: he on one side, she on the other side, and dividing them in the middle was the sandy path for horses and carts.

"And whom do you side with, Feygele?" asked Shimen.

Feygele, who had gone on ahead, seemingly lost in thought, with her hands crossed behind her, suddenly came to a stop.

"Whom do you mean?" she asked. "Tykociński and Eyges? I will tell you the truth: when they start philosophizing, I start getting sleepy. I love everything, just not those conversations, not those philosophies."

"But," Shimen countered, "you can't just dismiss all of it."

He was about to say something important, something that was still not clear to him—his own idea about painting and literature, which did not accord with either Tykociński's or Eyges's idea. There in the garret, in the presence of official representatives of art, the dilettante Shimen Shifris did not dare do so. But here in front of Feygele he intended to display his expertise.

But Feygele had skillfully steered the conversation onto other topics: he, Shimen, should drop the philosophies, otherwise she'd start
yawning. Better he should talk about himself: What was it like in
Godlbozhits? What did he do? Did he enjoy it? But first he should
cross over to her and take her on his arm; it was not her habit to walk
in any other way. Was he really not so chivalrous, Shimen?! "Well
done! Hold me tight," Feygele laughed, "so I don't escape. And don't
hang your head so, as if a shipload of your sour milk had sunk. You're
young, Shimen, hold your head up; you don't need to ponder so much,
just live as much as you can. And most important—enjoy yourself,
because youth is fleeting and they don't erect golden tombstones after
you're dead."

Now came the moment for Shimen to speak. He longed to speak;
he trembled with such warmth for Feygele who was now so close to
him that he would gladly have taken his heart and waved it before
her like a sack so that she might be able to see the precious gifts it
held for her. But how to begin? His life now was so uninteresting and
grey. To enjoy himself? To have a good time? He could certainly enjoy
himself. He could certainly have a good time. But the question was
with whom and where could one have a good time in Godlbozhits?
He, for example, went to the Zionist Party. Would she, Feygele, start
going there? No? So what would her introduction be: the smokiness,
the floor trodden over with mud, piles of garbage, shells of pumpkin
seeds, cigarette butts, dirty walls . . . Everyone writes his name on
the walls as a memento, drawing charcoal caricatures, off-color jokes.
And the girls—that they should sit through this at the table, by the
lamp; at least they listen to a newspaper being read, if not taking the
trouble themselves to learn some Yiddish . . . Why? Everyone's drawn
to behind the stove, where it's dark, where the boys smoke Sabbath
cigarettes; and from behind the stove you hear a shriek, you'd think
it's a brothel.

He, Shimen, could do without that pleasure; there's no joy in that!
He would so devote himself to work that people would never catch a
glimpse of him. But the question remains: What work is there to do
in Godlbozhits? She, Feygele, might well believe him when he says

that, but for the fact that a man needs to live and one cannot pour out the impure for the pure, he, Shimen, would never work with Tsadok, even though Tsadok, as Feygele knew, was his flesh and blood. That whole factory, Tsadok's tannery, that is, was as big as a chicken coop, and for that there were two partners. They could, nevertheless, make a living with great difficulty if they themselves rolled up their sleeves and lent a hand. But that wouldn't do. How could that be? He, Tsadok, had devoted so much energy to becoming a manufacturer, would he now lace himself back into those large tanner's boots? And since those men had become such great industrialists, Tsadok's partner's wife had travelled to Warsaw and brought back a sealskin coat. When Mirele found out about it—the well-born Mirele, Tsadok's wife—she started tormenting her husband, "Your sweetie-pie partner bought a coat for his wife, and you haven't." Tsadok grew angry, yelling, "So why are you pestering me, go buy yourself a Karakul coat from me!" Mirele didn't take long to think about it and went off to Warsaw and bought herself a Karakul coat. That lasted till it came time to pay the bills for both coats, the sealskin and the Karakul. Then they started in at each other—where were they going to get the money to pay for such expensive furs when even the pelt in the soaking bucket wasn't their own? They argued and argued until they started stealing from each other. This went on until there wasn't a pelt left in the factory. So you'd like to work in such a place?

And in case a position in private industry was not enough, Shimen also had a public one—namely, he kept the books for *Shalvah ba-sadeh*. Feygele didn't know what that is? *Shalvah ba-sadeh* in Hebrew means rest, respite, as well as an inheritance, one's own bit of land. This was the name of the organization that Lozer Kohn had founded in order to purchase land in Palestine. In any event, the land was still both in God's hands and in those of the Arabs, but Lozer Kohn had already collected three pounds for a deposit on a dunam of land.[4] Dunams

4. A dunam is a unit of land area used in Ottoman territories—it is roughly equivalent to a quarter of an acre.

were being snatched up like hotcakes. Whoever wanted to get hold of a plot of land in the Land of Israel, Lozer Kohn said, let him have it; afterwards no one would be able to get any land no matter how much money.

So perhaps you think that Lozer himself had invested a penny into his business? God forbid! He wasn't an amateur when it came to such things. Yes, for dunams, you see, he was down for a full fifty, but money he demanded up front.

"And how much salary do you get for that work?" Feygele asked.

"Salary," Shimen laughed.

He, Lozer Kohn, demands a contribution. It is, he says, an honor for an exemplary young man like Shimen to be his secretary in the first Jewish colony of Godlbozhits Jews in the Land of Israel. And since he, Lozer, is president of the Mizrahi, president of the Talmud-Torah, president of that very *Shalvah ba-sadeh*, will he be asked to pay?

"So what is it worth to you to do such work," Feygele asked, "since as far as I can tell you don't even derive any moral satisfaction from it?"

"Feygele," Shimen said, "don't think that I'm a complete fool."

And he explained to her that Lozer Kohn was on intimate terms with Fayvele Shpilman, and Fayvele was president of the newly founded cooperative bank. Lozer Kohn was using his influence with Fayvele, and in time he could have a very good position.

That's what Fayvele Shpilman himself had already promised him, Shimen. Meanwhile, Fayvele said, one would have to work six months without pay because in the beginning the bank would have no revenue. After those six months, Fayvele reckoned, Shimen could count on fifty zlotys a month, and then more and more all the time. He, Shimen, could work his way to a position of a solid few hundred zlotys a month.

That's what Fayvele assured him, and meantime he gave him work to do at home—without pay. Interest, percentage, Fayvele said, this is a whole other way of bookkeeping. There are, he said, some quite good bookkeepers, but before they can calculate your interest the deadline on the note may have expired. In reckoning interest one must "massage" one's hand, and he, Shimen, should see to "massaging" thoroughly.

Fayvele gave him the job of computing the interest on his notes. Fayvele was a discounter. Fayvele had a lot of money, and on that discounting he made a fortune. Sometimes Fayvele discounted in partnership with the fat doctor. The fat doctor also had a lot of money, but Fayvele had maybe three times as much. The doctor enjoyed life, frittering his time in the club, on women, while Fayvele lived thriftily on ten zlotys a week.

"No!" Feygele could not accept that. The mistakes people make! It's certainly true that Fayvele has a lot of money, and that he is a userer, a fleecer. That Shylock had ruined her father, Shmuel Rabinovitsh, with his interest. Just imagine: 15 percent a month to pay on the dollar? Half a fortune's worth of his honest labor did Shmuel Rabinovitsh lose to Fayvele Shpilman. But that the doctor is a rogue, a playboy, as everyone thinks? That's a mistake.

He, Shimen, should apologize. She, Feygele, certainly knows the doctor better. True, she hadn't known him long—it was only a week or two since she had met him—but still she knew him more deeply than those others who considered themselves his colleagues. Behind a mask of cynicism and coarse words resides a soul yearning for the beautiful. Russia, the revolution, had made him somewhat wild, but it couldn't destroy his soul, his true nature.

Shimen had a thousand facts with which to demonstrate to Feygele her error. The fat doctor was a pig, a vulgar youth, and a crude soul. But on that blessed night when he was so close to Feygele, he didn't want to argue with her, to contradict her. He merely noted, "And what of his own wife whom he neglects?"

Feygele responded with an accusation, "And you, Shimen, do you also spout this nonsense? That's fine for those pious Godlbozhits goody-goodies. He, an educated man, do you think *you* could live with such a kosher calf as his wife, Mekhele Podreytshik's daughter? For what sin would you have him atone his whole life with that little hunchback?"

"So who made him marry her?" Shimen asked not so nonchalantly.

"Who?" Feygele repeated. "That's exactly the point, no one knows whom the shoe pinches. He had to, it was a duty of honor. Mekhele, you understand, supported the doctor through gymnasium, through university, so he had to . . . But," Feygele concluded, "just because he did that foolish thing and got married, should he sacrifice his whole life? Is he not allowed to lift his head? Can you say that, Shimen?"

Well, if she was so sure of herself then he, Shimen, wouldn't argue with her. But one thing did interest him: how had she happened to make the doctor's acquaintance?

Happen? He, Shimen, ought to know. She, Feygele, does not seek opportunities; they chance upon her. She was out for a walk when a beautiful freshly varnished car drove up. From a distance she had noticed that it was the doctor's blue car. Who in Godlbozhits didn't know his car? But no matter, she continued on her way. Suddenly, the car drove right up to her and came to a stop. The doctor got out. "If the miss would permit, he might give her a ride." She, Feygele, saw no reason to turn down the pleasure of taking a ride in a luxury automobile. She got in and sat down next to the doctor who was driving the car himself. "It must be such a terrific pleasure to drive a car!" she said. "It's alright," he said. If she wished, he would consider it a great pleasure to teach her. By all means, she should take the wheel in her hands. Please, put your right foot on that pedal there. It's not so difficult; and she should not be afraid as he was sitting next to her. She oughtn't constantly turn the wheel back and forth; the car should go smoothly, with fewer zigzags.

That's how they struck up a conversation and became familiar. On taking her leave he invited her out for a drive the following morning, and every day since she has attended her lessons on how to steer a car.

Shimen had stopped listening, staring off in the distance. In his mind he kept repeating: *Czeszniewski, Eyges, Tykociński, the fat doctor— they're all the same!* If there were more than two it wasn't worth the trouble of counting them since there wasn't a big difference between them, and it wouldn't cause much distress.

Coming toward them was a slender girl with short, fair hair and blue eyes. Feygele called out to her, "Bebi! Let me introduce you. This is Shifris, Shimen Shifris. This is my sister."

Bebi had a wide mouth. Bebi laughed with all her teeth. Usually a wide mouth is not attractive, but Bebi laughed attractively.

And when Bebi hastily made her good-byes—she was in a hurry—Shimen had to utter a few pleasantries, "You have a pretty sister, Feygele; I never knew you had such a pretty sister. Completely different than you."

"And you, Shimen," said Feygele, "have an interesting brother, a very interesting brother. Also completely different from you."

"You mean Shmuel? His name's not Shifris, it's Zaydman. He's not my brother; he's my cousin."

"I don't mean Shmuel. Shmuel I know well; after all, he's Bebi's admirer. I know what I'm saying. I mean Nosn."

Shimen was surprised, "Nosn? How do you know him?"

"I like the look of him," Feygele answered his question indirectly. "He has such interesting, sharp facial features. Your face, Shimen, is so smooth, ordinary, and his is so angular, energetic. Such austere, honest eyes, and hands, hands . . . Such long, laboring fingers. He's a tanner?"

"Yes."

"One senses that right away," Feygele said, "even though he keeps himself washed so clean. But he doesn't seem concerned about the smell. Just the opposite, it makes a stronger impression."

"But how do you know him?" Shimen was still surprised.

"You know," she said, "everything with me is by chance. We were traveling home once in a cart, Bebi and I. Bebi spurred on the horses. Suddenly someone came running up the path from the hill to the side and called out, 'Miss Rabinovitsh! Miss!'

"I didn't know him before, your brother. If not for the fact that he called me by name and in Yiddish I would have sworn it was a thief, such wild eyes he had. 'Listen, miss,' he said, 'you've got to save me, the police are after me. Take this package and burn it, throw it away, do whatever you want with it.' And he handed me a package," Feygele continued. "Burn it? Why? What a shame. He should climb up onto the cart and we'd set of at a gallop; somehow we'd work it out."

"It could have gone very badly for you," Shimen whispered with terror.

"It never goes badly for me," Feygele said. "We let him up into our garret, and put his package in the cellar. The police never even came by; after all, it's right to Shmuel Rabinovitsh one goes looking for communists."

"It was quite bold on your part," said Shimen.

"You think so?" she said, giving it some thought. "I was ready for anything then, even to go to prison, and Bebi even more than me. But God forbid my father should find out! Your brother is known here in the village; he palled around with the Rogów peasants, him and another one, a Christian. Since then the Christian says hello to me. '*Nash chlovyek*,' he said to me the other day."[5]

It had to have been getting late, since the sun was beginning to set in the west like a burning coal. Approaching them came a peasant with a beard. On his shoulders was a small sack, tied to his axe instead of a stick. It was Bartolomey, the woodcutter, who worked during the day in Godlbozhits. And when Bartolomey finally headed home carrying a sack on his shoulders, people knew that he had toiled an honest day's work, and that it was no exaggeration for him to say to them now, while it was still light out, "*Dobry wieczór Państwo*."[6]

Yes, it was already late, good evening good people. Bartolomey was carrying a bread roll in his sack. His children would devour it in an instant. Bartolomey earned his living by chopping wood in the city. Bartolomey was a poor peasant, sporting a faded beard because shaving cost a fortune and Bartolomey earned hardly enough for bread for his children.

"*Tak, tak*,[7] stones and sand, and from that you can't knock out bread. *Do widzenia Państwo*."[8]

That reminded Shimen that it was time to take his leave. He still had six kilometers to go to get back to the city. He wanted to accompany Feygele back, but she wouldn't hear of it. It was getting late, and

5. *nash chlovyek* (Russian): our mutual friend; literally, our man.

6. *dobry wieczór Państwo* (Polish): Good evening to you, sir and madam; the latter—*Państwo*—is a form of address to a married couple.

7. *tak, tak* (Polish): yes, yes; that's how it is.

8. *do widzenia Państwo* (Polish): good-bye to you, sir and madam.

he had to go through the forest, she said; there was no danger, she'd find her way back.

They said their good-byes. Shimen started walking with soldierly strides to the forest. He felt good and didn't regret having persuaded Feygele to come out with him. After all, Feygele was an intelligent girl one could carry on a conversation with. Such a pleasure he didn't have in Godlbozhits.

It was already pretty dark when he arrived in the city. Respectable middle-class Jews were walking with festive, well-rested steps into the study house for afternoon prayers and back out of the study house. Simple Jews were standing around in little groups in the middle of the marketplace chatting or telling jokes. In some of the groups young people were earnestly debating. The poet Mandlboym detached himself from one of the groups and pounced on Shimen, "So, what did they say? Did it make an impression?"

Shimen didn't understand what the dynamic poet wanted from him. Shimen was still lost in his thoughts about what had happened at the Rogów estate; his heart was gnawing at him with longing.

The poet Mandlboym didn't wait for an answer. He had already rejoined his group and had dragged Zalmen Komashnmakher with him, insisting he had a secret to tell him, a very important secret.

"They know, Zalmen, I'm telling you, I feel it. I have entered the shrines, into the very Holy of Holies of Yiddish literature."

Zalmen took on a serious air, "Really? When?"

The poet called his witness. "Go," he said, "ask Shimen Shifris what the painter Tykociński said about my works, what the editor Eyges said about my poems. They'll be published on the front page."

But Zalmen at once grew serious.

"Is Tykociński such an expert in literature?" he asked.

The poet grabbed his hand as though he had blasphemed God.

"What are you saying, Zalmen," he said, terrified. "Tykociński . . . Do you know who Tykociński is?"

"I know," Zalmen said firmly. "A painter, an idealizer of old, sniveling Jewish women, women reciting blessings over candles, reciters of *tkhines*."

"And editor Eyges?" His courage was failing him.

"Eyges," Zalmen said firmly and loudly enough for the whole marketplace to hear him, "Eyges is a bourgeois writer and a bootlick of the clergy, the capitalists, and the petty bourgeoisie."

"Do you know what you're saying?!" the poet fumed. "Eyges was one of the first fighters against the '*shtrayml*' on the Jewish street. Eyges is a sympathizer of the working class."

"A sympathizer you say?" Zalmen exclaimed loudly and cheerfully. "Once he had been an intelligent fellow traveler, an SR.[9] Now he is a clerical-fascist, a corrupter of labor."

"Ignorant lowlife!" shrieked the poet angrily and fled.

"Idiot!" Zalmen Komashnmakher yelled after him.

9. A member of the Socialist Revolutionary Party (SR).

⊹ 16 ⊰

Nearly Everything about Zalmen Komashnmakher and His Weaknesses; Something of Moritz Meierbach's Business; Also about the Fat Doctor's Soul

In the middle of the marketplace, like a thorn in the side of the supporters of a modern Godlbozhits, stood an old, crumbling brick house with a peaked, half-decayed shingle roof. From its small square windows protruded the tin smoke pipes of little iron stoves.

Had such a miserable house stood on some side street it certainly wouldn't have upset anyone. But here? It wasn't enough that that ramshackle house visibly stuck out and cut into the sidewalk, but growing out of it were two stone pillars, like a dog's paws. Those pillars seemed anxious about how long the wall would hold out. And in the meantime those shameless pillars have asked the hygienic Godlbozhits gutters if they might be so kind as to go around them into the marketplace.

Not one city planner had ever given any thought to how to conquer that fortress of agedness and degeneration, and so no progress could be made. It was all like talking to a brick wall since the house had no owner either. Somewhere abroad there were fifty or so questionable grandchildren and great-grandchildren who were aware of the inheritance. But traveling to Godlbozhits meant paying rent and getting hit with a bill for back taxes. All so that they could thank God just to be able to head home empty-handed.

Meanwhile, there were those who took advantage of the situation. For one there was the painter Tykociński who painted the house ten times or so from every angle. And for another there were the current tenants, who felt the house to be their well-established inheritance and lorded around as if over their own property. The house had only one large room which was now outfitted with alcoves and walkways, half walls, chintz curtains, and Spanish partitions. But all the inhabitants had one God in heaven and one ceiling over their heads.

And there was one other thing that all those neighbors shared: a grandfather. Shmuel Khayes was his name, and he lived by himself in that spacious room, for rent, stitching rustic coats and *sukmanas*. Nor did he do too badly for himself. He was a kindly man. When he married off a child he didn't do what other fathers did: "Take it and go!" No. Shmuel Khayes took in his new son-in-law and separated off an alcove for him. And even if that son-in-law already had some little children Shmuel Khayes still fed them. If only he'd still been alive and his children would never have known want.

But a man doesn't live forever, and the world doesn't stand still. After the old man's death his learned son-in-law had no other choice but to take up teaching. And from what he earned he was able, thank God, to marry off two daughters. He married them off and, in accordance with his father-in-law's practice, may he rest in peace, took them in. He separated off two beds with a Spanish partition. That is, as long as, God forbid, they didn't overstay their welcome.

And even though it was already quite cramped in that one room, none of the grandfather's children ever complained. Even the youngest daughter, Mirl—a not very attractive girl whose face was always smeared with snot—when her time came, they found a husband for her and divided off an alcove for her, a place of honor; no one begrudged her her bit of the inheritance.

At first they thought no children would emerge from that pairing, since Mirl was a misfortunate creature, and even right after the wedding they had to run around after her to wipe her nose lest she go around, you'll pardon me, snot-nosed. And her husband, Moyshe, even though crippled and deaf as a post, was still a lively young man with a formidable intellect.

It turned out just the opposite: the deaf Moyshe couldn't make a go of anything. No matter how many jobs he undertook nothing came of any of them. And now, since he had become a coachman, he devoted all his mental energy to various schemes to break horses of the need for oats. As opposed to Mirl, now an established Jewish woman, who bustled around among her seven moppets like a brood hen among the chickens. All you have to do is put a little something in her hand—a bit of buckwheat, a few potatoes, some flour—and she'll make for you some delicious browned groats.

Mirl's greatest tricks, however, came to light with regard to the economics of fuel. It's quite true that in order to cook dinner you needed half a bundle of wood for the stove. If, that is, you owned a forest of your own. But if you had to buy wood by the bundle, then the farmer was in the catbird seat. Mirl's solution was what she called "fire feet," which involved whittling a piece of wood into however many small chips you may want, those bits then get lit and are allowed to smolder so the fire doesn't catch right away.

It is what it is, but of course it's better to have your own forest so you don't need to resort to such tricks.

Take bread, for example. Go try and be efficient, take a half kilo of bread, divide it among nine mouths while setting aside some of it for "dessert" after the groats. Isn't it better to have your own mill?

And despite all of this, in that smoky little alcove there grew up an easygoing young person, small and solid like a cask of beer, good-natured and kind.

You could tease him day in day out—"Well, Zalmen, when's the social revolution coming?"—and he wouldn't get angry, Zalmen wouldn't, but would answer calmly, "Don't laugh, it's as ready to go as money in your pocket, certainly readier than what's in Fayvele Shpilman's bank. It just needs a little push and it'll come."

Zalmen felt sorry for his mother, but he couldn't stand his father. Once his mother had bought some little treats for the children—a herring tail, a bit of butter for the bread—and the old deaf man sniffed it out, snuck up and cut off the bigger portion, lickety-split! His mother yelled and cursed, while he, the deaf man—well, it couldn't be *him* they were talking about. "Huh?" he asked. "Huh? You're talking to me?" He heard nothing, he knew nothing; he just thought the whole world was trying to fool him. But, when they called to him that the *mikhe* was ready, oh he heard that![1]

And Zalmen pretended not to notice that he resembled his father in also being no slouch when it came to eating. When there was a good day at work, and an extra zloty had been earned, they'd go to the baker and get those genuine, warm flatcakes that crackle between your teeth. They'd also buy a half an ounce of butter and an egg at the shop and fry it in the frying pan in the mistress's kitchen. That was a real feast!

However, when he'd finally hold up the flatcake, ready to be spread with butter, he'd remember something. Then he'd separate out the larger portion of butter in reserve, and he'd remove a small slice from the fried egg. The rest he'd hide behind a paper on the board by the stove.

At one o'clock his pale little sister with the two thin braids would bring him lunch: some browned groats with potato, his mother's famous dish. Then he'd call the little girl into the master's alcove. The little girl knew very well that when Zalmen called you into the little alcove, you'd better get your teeth ready. It didn't take long; before Zalmen had even looked around, the little one had snarfed down the freshly browned dish, chewing greedily, her nose running.

Zalmen would beam with pride: "So you like fried food?"

The little one's eyes laughed and her cheeks glowed.

"Well, just you wipe your nose and you'll be a beautiful little girl," Zalmen would say. But why he said this wasn't clear, because he would then take his cobbler's apron and clean up the little girl's nose himself like the best governess.

But next to fresh flatcakes with butter and his little sister, Zalmen Komashnmakher, the solid cask, loved the union. But it was the kind of love that left no one unpestered:

"Comrades, spit in the spittoon!"

"Comrades, '*shapki daloi*'![2] This is not the study house."

---

1. *Mikhe* (Yiddish): a kind of porridge made of stale bread and water.
2. *shapki daloi* (Russian): hats off.

"Ladies, a little quieter, this is not the women's section of the synagogue."

"Comrades, calm down!"

Comrades this way and comrades that way . . .

Zalmen was master in the union. Zalmen the Tankard (that's what they called him because he was solid and round like a cask of beer) rolled up his sleeves, girded his loins with a sack, and cleaned the stovepipes. Comrade Zalmen needed no remuneration, and the union saved a few pennies. Comrade Zalmen could even whitewash the room if it was needed. Comrade Zalmen could set the female comrades to their work: red pennants and red frames around the portraits; the most important thing was that there be a lot of red, because red is blood, red is truth, and red is revolution.

And when someone was needed to graffiti walls in the middle of the night, again it was Zalmen. And when someone was needed to hang a red banner stealthily, who do you think would do that? Of course one didn't dare say so. Such things were packed away in the "hole."

The police knew him as a stooge. Caught red-handed? Never. But people knew who was doing everything. When they tried to put him in jail on the eve of May 1st a red banner still got hung on the post office at dawn. Zalmen teased the senior policeman, "Do you see some kind of trick, Panie senior policeman? I'm sitting in jail and hanging banners on the post office at the same time."

But the senior policeman surely understood that beside Zalmen Komashnmakher there were others who were hanging the banners. After all, don't select just any old senior policeman. And still, Zalmen was imprisoned regularly every May 1st and at every opportunity without either why or wherefore.

Then came the general meeting of the union and it was agreed that as long as he, Zalmen, was sitting in jail in city hall anyway, he should at least sit a little higher, among the fathers of the city council. Zalmen was to be a city councilman.

True, Zalmen would rather have cleaned the union's stovepipes sixteen times over than even once sticking his hands in the filth of that corrupt city hall. It was also true that in the union there were more educated forces for city councilman than Zalmen. But such thinking was futile; an order is an order. So he went.

As expressed in its resolution the executive committee believed that Zalmen Komashnmakher, a simple but politically aware worker who had learned some Marxist economics, possessed more sophistication in social questions than the greatest minds of the Godlbozhits bourgeoisie.

All agreed. Only one Khaykl the sexton's son could not agree. He stood up and said, "Comrades! I protest . . . One must send to city hall an educated and intelligent person. It seems that Zalmen cannot speak any Polish. He will simply make himself a laughingstock."

Khaykl was an ace at Polish. Khaykl was a guide for tourists who came to visit old Godlbozhits. Around his sleeve he wore a white and red band with the emblem of the city—a sailing ship—and prattled on to the foolish summertime punters and the chumps from Warsaw who were too clever by half:

"This house, *proszę jaśnie Panna*, is 1,652 years old; and here lived, proszę jaśnie Panna, the Polish king Jan Chrobry who slayed the dragon—that is, proszę jaśnie Panna, a kind of fire-breathing beast with a hundred heads . . ."[3]

But of course if you didn't believe him, Khaykl, you could ask all the directors and all the professor-doctors and all the painter-artists whether they knew him, Khaykl; whether he, Khaykl, wasn't written about in all the newspapers?

Comrade Nosn almost from the very beginning had protested against admitting Khaykl the sexton's son even as a common member of the union. "That one," Comrade Nosn said, "is not a proletarian element; he is a kind of domestic lackey who licks the boots of the bourgeoisie, celebrating their joys and mourning their misfortunes." He, Nosn, had the perfect example from Meierbach's factory where he worked. There was a servant there who went about in a short coat— one Yosl Pyekholde who earned a pittance from the Meierbachs,

3. *proszę jaśnie Panna* (Polish): the honorable miss, my dear miss.

perhaps even less than a simple worker. And nevertheless he repeatedly claimed:

"*I* can't sell . . . *I* don't want to sell . . . *I* am not in a hurry to sell . . . *I* don't need money . . ."

Or:

"*My* factory, *my* customers, *my* workers . . ."

The whole of Yosl Pyekholde wasn't worth a fig; you sent him out to a customer and he'd spoil the deal. The Meierbachs derided him, and the Russki in particular compared him to mud. And nevertheless he was kept on, and he was fed.

Apparently their compassion was running out—a person is with you for so many years. Even an old dog you don't kick out, but he, Nosn, didn't believe in their compassion. Industrialists surely had better sense than to send their compassion packing. In point of fact, they still needed him, that Pyckholde; and in point of fact they still made use of him.

There was one thing Yosl Pyekholde was useful for—namely keeping his ear discreetly to the ground to listen out for what the workers were talking about amongst themselves: who was agitating, who was in favor of a strike. He would pass all that along right away to the office, and then there would be whispering, interrogation, spying.

Recently the Russki told him, Nosn, quite candidly, "You, Nosn, won't be with me for long; you've got too big a mouth. You may be a big shot there in the union, but in my factory I'm boss."

"What's this about?" Was it because he, Nosn, had enlightened the workers as to who and what they were? Because he wanted to organize them? So what? Should that make him cautious? Could that be forbidden?

"Well," declared the Russki with his murderous little eyes, the anger making his throat flush, "you're too clever for me, Nosn, you'll not be agitating around me for long. Your union makes no noise worth listening to."

Nosn wasn't greatly bothered by the Russki, and he wasn't much worried about what he said. That's what an industrialist was and he had an industrialist's logic. If he ate his heart out at every little thing he wouldn't have a heart for very long. And a heart he had to have, Nosn did, a strong one. He had to work both physically, for his bread, as well as socially—work that was full of great responsibility.

However, those lackeys, the servants, the noblemen's lapdogs, to whom the master casts bones to lick—one had to keep an eye on them.

And he would not let such a Khaykl through the doorway of an honest professional class union, that is, unless the rest of the comrades on the executive committee defended him.

And the motives of those comrades were as follows:

Khaykl was a delegate from the domestic and hotel employees' section. Khaykl was what he was, but what with his smooth tongue and owing to his personal relationships in those circles, he had on his side the majority of those employees whom it was difficult to persuade by class-arguments. Thanks to personal trust, he had shown them how to navigate in the organization, in the union.

It is true that they, the comrades on the executive committee, understood quite well that it was ridiculous to base a professional class-movement on personal feelings for this or that gallant with sideburns and riding breeches. However, experience, especially Godlbozhits experience, teaches that some of the girls who were drawn in physically by Khaykl's influence, girls who at first thought that the purpose of a union was to dance or to flirt, girls who comically aped the manners of the grandes dames, those girls desired a cozy corner in the union like the *Bnot Zion*,[4] arguing: "Everything comes to them, the wealthy class? The poor class may also enjoy a little of life" . . . Such girls, once in the union and thanks to a systematic indoctrination, then became good and class-conscious comrades.

And here's the upshot: Khaykl was useful to the union as a member. And even if Nosn's premise, that the Khaykl type was not a proletarian element, were completely accurate, there were still no good reasons why the union should reject the tangible benefits which that one—though no proletarian—brought to the union.

4. *Bnot Zion:* Daughters of Zion: a girls' youth group.

Of course, Nosn as well as some other comrades did not agree; nor did they agree at all with the majority of the executive committee; and above all they did not agree with the non-proletarian mentality: Not only was it ridiculous but it was absolutely false and harmful to base a movement on the personal feelings of backward proletarian women for a kind of lackey servant with sideburns and riding-breeches. Not only were direct education and class arguments the only proper way of drawing even the most backward proletarians into the movement, but all other ways lead to an impairment of class-consciousness, to its demoralization. And finally: Khaykl as a kind of lackey servant was not merely a "non-proletarian"; Khaykl was comparable to the rabbis whose bags he had carried until not so long ago, comparable to the clergy and other servants and bootlicks of capitalism. He was a direct enemy of the proletariat.

Unfortunately, the majority of the executive committee did not share Comrade Nosn's opinion. They pointed out that Nosn exaggerated the danger; they made light of the matter, and history would show who was right.

Meanwhile, however, events in Godlbozhits displayed a small sample of the fruits of introducing tractability and opportunism into a professional class union. This took place during the city council elections.

The elections to the Godlbozhits city council provoked fierce arguments among the burghers' candidates, equally among the Christians and Jews. Ultimately they had agreed to an armistice, a plan, among themselves, occasioned by the first attempt on the part of the Godlbozhits proletariat and poor people to put their own spokesman on the city council instead of what had always been up until then respectable Jews.

One time the former Godlbozhits bailiff, Dubczak—a peasant who wore a fur cap summer and winter, and instead of a tie and collar had a shiny red button on the front of his shirt—one time this clever and cunning peasant came into Isidore vel Itsik Sonnenschein's pharmacy.

Years ago the semi-citified peasant Dubczak used to get on well with the Godlbozhits Jews, which was good for him because in the elections for bailiff he had all the Jews on his side. But then the great noblemen came to see him—the Bronickis, the Chajeckis, the Wiśnickis—and began to reason with him: "You, brother *chrześcijanin*,[5] why do you associate with these nonbelieving Jews when all of us Christians are on your side? Do you not know that Judas betrayed our Lord Jesus for thirty pieces of silver?"

It was admittedly a surprise to him that these great noblemen who always acted so haughtily—it was beneath their contempt that a peasant should be their bailiff—it was a surprise to him that these noblemen, these *szlachta*,[6] were suddenly coming to him, bowing before him like the three kings had once bowed before Jesus's manger. But when they stretched out a brotherly hand and spoke to him as they would to an equal he let them persuade him. So he broke with the Jews and put his name in with the circle of the "Catholic Fathers," subscribed to the *Great Poland Catholic*, and diligently read that newspaper from beginning to end. He read the paper every Sunday with great pleasure because it described the whole political situation, of Christians and Jews, and why it was so good for Jews in Poland, as opposed to the Christians for whom it was bad. Everything was laid out in black and white.

But the good times didn't last a year. The noblemen kept him under their thumb, gave him advice, governed with him. And meantime Godlbozhits was no longer a township; it had become a city. A city needs to have a mayor, and as mayor he, the peasant Dubczak, wouldn't do. But the nobleman Wiśnicki would.

So Dubczak asked: if it's right that a peasant is an equal *chrześcijanin* to a nobleman, then why had he been acceptable to nonbelieving Jews as the head of the city but now among his brother Christians he wasn't?

5. *chrześcijanin* (Polish): Christian.
6. *szlachta* (Polish): the Polish nobility.

It had been a full three years since Wiśnicki first became mayor, and he, Dubczak, went away like a cat from the cream. For three whole years he could find no solution to his question until one day—like a thunderbolt—he observed leaving the Jewish pharmacy none other than the implacable Jew-hater Wiśnicki, the one who never let a Jew through his doorway, and who, should he happen to shake hands with a Jew, would then wash his hands with soap for three hours.

Nosing around and investigating the matter, the cunning peasant learned that Mayor Wiśnicki came to the Jewish pharmacist for two things: first, for a private loan; and second, to make sure that the Jews would back him as mayor for his upcoming term.

With regard to the money, the cunning peasant couldn't find out exactly whether and how much the pharmacist had lent, and at what percent interest and on what terms. As to the votes of the Godlbozhits Jews, however, Dubczak knew for certain that the Jewish pharmacist had promised him all of them.

That was on a Sunday. Dubczak went straightaway to sit with a friend of his in an alehouse and read the *Great Poland Catholic*. He read and reflected gloomily: a nobleman will come to an agreement with a nobleman and a peasant will take it on his rear. Wiśnicki is a nobleman, and the pharmacist, even though a Jew, is also a nobleman. They might argue with one another, saying terrible things. But when it comes right down to it, they come to an agreement and show the peasant the back door . . . It was starting to get him upset, that clever peasant, how those gentlemen put one over on him! All of a sudden he noticed in the paper in front of him a notice from that very Godlbozhits. He read:

In Godlbozhits the Jews have greatly multiplied and spread out among us. It's not enough that they've seized all of the shops in the marketplace, but a group of Jews have devised a scheme—they are exchanging their names for pure Polish ones in order to fool the believing Christian customer. Thus, for example, the local Jewish pharmacist replaced his legal name Itsko with Isidore . . .

Having read it through, the peasant carefully folded up the newspaper, took his leave of his friend, and went straight over to the Jewish pharmacist.

There in the back storeroom, once they were alone, and with a mysterious air, he spread out the *Great Poland Catholic* before the eyes of the astonished pharmacist.

"The gentleman should read . . ."

The peasant cunningly noticed how the Jewish pharmacist turned red, then pale, and when he raised his head and asked with restrained anger, "Whose handiwork is this?!" the peasant shrugged his shoulders and answered craftily, "Surely someone local . . ."

"Wiśnicki?!" the pharmacist guessed.

"Do I look like I know?" the peasant smiled cunningly. "A local, a native . . ."

The pharmacist was really getting worked up.

"And you think that I'll let him be *burmistrz*, Wiśnicki?![7] He'll be a beggar! An old beggar! Money I should lend him? May he be stricken ill!"

He was so angry, the pharmacist was, that he didn't even notice how the peasant had carefully folded up the newspaper, set it aside, and left with a cunning peasant's humility, "*Do widzenia . . . moje uszanowanie dla Pana aptekarza . . .*"[8]

<hr>

The pharmacist was upset for a whole day after this happened, and when the pharmacy closed he thought about taking his revenge out on his good friends and letting them have it at that night's poker game.

At cards they were a sworn foursome: the pharmacist, the fat doctor, Moritz Meierbach, and the secretary of the municipal authority. Once in a while the little group fell to quarreling amongst themselves. The doctor's breeding would all of a sudden annoy Meierbach: "What can be so good about it? Berele the porter's son. Can anything be good? You can't make a silk purse out of a sow's ear . . ." The pharmacist in

7. *burmistrz*: (Polish): mayor.

8. *Do widzenia . . . moje uszanowanie dla Pana aptekarza* (Polish): Good day . . . my respect to Mr. Pharmacist.

turn was irritated that Meierbach kept taking cards and not discarding any. As for the doctor, he knew no tricks: "Panie Meierbach, as far as I'm concerned you can pass off to the lamp! If you don't have any money, you don't play." All three were annoyed at the city hall secretary with the large beer belly, seeing that from time to time he let slip a "Jew gypsy." Still, no game of cards was ever spoiled because of such nonsense.

That evening, however, the pharmacist was so agitated over the notice in the newspaper that he had decided to take his revenge out on his best card friends. He would put out the light in the back storeroom and head home: like hell they'd plop down on his upholstered chairs and drink his tea with three spoonfuls of sugar! In any event, Moritz Meierbach already owed him no less than a 187. He won that off one hand, Moritz Meierbach! Only to bet it over again. And as for the fat doctor—may he throw it all up!—if some preserves were put out he had a habit of gulping it down by the tablespoonfull. The goy at least didn't like preserves; but put a tankard of beer in front of him and you could pump him full.

That's how well the pharmacist thought of his good friends. So he decided to play the trick on them of shutting the door in their faces, as soon as someone showed up chomping at the bit then he'd invite him to sit down to a pack of cards.

But meanwhile it had turned nine o'clock and not one of his guests had shown up. The extraordinary possibility suddenly occurred to him, the pharmacist: perhaps they already knew about the article in the *Great Poland Catholic* and had agreed to forsake him, leaving him to worry all by himself? Who knows, maybe they had themselves actually had a hand in that notice?

But the pharmacist's suspicions were unfounded, at least as far as Moritz Meierbach was concerned. The pharmacist, who had a leisurely business routine, opened the pharmacy every day at eight o'clock in the morning and at eight o'clock in the evening raked up the remaining loose change. Such a small-time pharmacist could never have any idea what it meant to head a factory, with its staff, its workers, its merchants, its millions in business; what it meant to run things as successfully as Moritz Meierbach ran them; what it meant to arrive, however many years ago, possessing nothing but a stiff bowler on his head and the wind in his pockets, and now to own a factory complete with machines, stock, a hundred workers, automobiles, a mill, a saw-mill . . .

The whole world certainly knew that Moritz Meierbach was an important person, a very wealthy man. But he could show you a trick or two, Moritz Meierbach could, and if it all didn't suit him, then over-night he could turn into a poor man, a pauper, owning nothing but his black bowler and his pants with the empty pockets.

In any event, the two Germans who had come from Danzig with a small suitcase assessed Moritz Meierbach's contested notes, the ones for machines, for raw pelts, and for tannery chemicals.

You can count on a German. One of them studied the mortgage records and noticed that the factory belonged to Moritz's brother, Iser Meierbach; that the house was purchased out of Madame Celina Meierbach's dowry; and that the mill with all its furnishings was given as a birthday gift to Moritz's nine-year-old heir by a distant relative who had first bought everything in cash from his father, that is, from Moritz Meierbach. The bottom line was this: Mortiz Meierbach, the signatory of the notes, didn't own a button.

True, that German who looked at the books was also no novice, and threatened to set aside all the sales records as false. He, the German, had his own investigative offices, and he would show that Iser Meierbach, Moritz's brother, had come from Russia without a penny to his name, that he had worked for Moritz as a simple worker in the factory, and that his implication of his brother was done premeditat-edly in order to deprive the German firm of a portion of its legally acquired assets. But Moritz Meierbach, for his part, made assurances that if he had done anything he had certainly not done it deceitfully, having done so through an attorney. So they could go whistle him a waltz . . . As for his brother, all his work for the factory was just for show as was agreed upon between them, because at that time there was talk of big strikes, wage disputes and revolts, and he needed his own man among the workers so he could know about it all in advance. Of course he, Moritz, could produce those same workers from his factory as witnesses to testify that his brother had brought with him from Russia a treasure of gold, diamonds, and English pounds, and that he went around with pockets full of these the way one carries around pebbles and bits of paper.

What's more, he, Moritz, invited the gentlemen to lunch. First and foremost, they shouldn't go hungry; and when one isn't hungry business goes better. What? The gentlemen wished to go to a restaurant? But please . . . his wife had prepared lunch for the gentlemen, and did they not wish to meet madame?

So the Germans let themselves be persuaded, and he, Moritz Meierbach, did not speak to them at all like he did to his debtors, but rather the way he spoke to his good friends. True, he was not at all afraid of them, they could do absolutely nothing to him. But did he, Moritz Meierbach, want simply to deprive the factory of money? Did he not know that he was responsible? Did he no longer wish to do business with that firm? Good! They, the gentlemen, proposed an adjustment of 60 percent. He, Moritz Meierbach, said no—no. Conditions could improve. Meanwhile, he proposed 20 percent. At most he would give 25: 10 percent in cash and 15 in notes. Could they not agree? "Ah, please . . . Don't be embarrassed, make yourselves at home . . . Gentlemen, please enjoy these oranges . . . There's no pressing need to make the agreement right away . . . Please, perhaps the Bordeaux? Or maybe another liqueur?"

So Moritz Meierbach was a little late to the daily card game, arriving at a quarter of ten. By then he had finished with the Germans. But the pharmacist oughtn't think that knowing how to talk to a German is easy, that it's like weighing a hundred grams of aqua destillata. "There you go," the pharmacist said, "once the fat doctor gets here we can start a game of poker." He sent for the secretary, who was laying on the bed, dead drunk, with a broken hand and cursing his great-grandfather. Earlier the goy had drunk quite a bit, smacked his wife around, and then fallen down the stairs, breaking his hand. Go deal with a goy.

After filling Meierbach in on the details the pharmacist asked, "Where can he be wandering about, the fat doctor? For some reason ever since he bought that car, he's not seen for days at a time?"

"It seems," said Meierbach, "he's got a doxy and drives her around for whole days in his automobile. He doesn't give a damn about his wife! You see? He'll fast regularly for Mekhele the tailor's daughter . . ."

"And he himself, though, what's the matter?" said the pharmacist. "A rude man, a boor, Berele the porter's son . . ."

"You're bringing up Berele the porter's son!" Meierbach said. "Really? You should listen up: my Iser once had an acquaintance who traveled from Russia to Chelm. He described how he sat there in the 'Cheka' with that fatty. He said this about influence: that influence worked everywhere, even among the Bolsheviks. He sat there in prison, he said, with one Dr. Beyglman, a young doctor just recently graduated. The doctor, he said, had been a quartermaster in a field hospital for the Bolsheviks, and they suspected him of selling medicine, so the GPU imprisoned him. But in that same city he, the doctor, had an uncle, a Bolshevik commissar, one Shnaydman . . ."

"Shnaydman?" the pharmacist started. "That's certainly Mekhele's brother. Mekhele recently told me about him, showed me a picture . . ."

"Take it easy," Meierbach said. "If not for that brother of Mekhele's that rude pig might today be rotting in the ground somewhere. They, the Bolsheviks, don't stand on ceremony: it's against the wall and a bullet in the head! You think my Iser made it through by miracles? By luck they found nothing on him."

Right, so what was he trying to say? Once, his uncle, the commissar, came to see him in jail and delivered the following speech: "I wanted to make a man out of you, Heniekl, obtaining for you positions of responsibility in a hospital. Not because you're my brother's son-in-law, to hell with family feelings! . . . Rather because I remember you from home, and I remember your father, the hardworking porter. I thought: an intelligent young man, a medical doctor, and from a proletarian background at that, will be useful to us. Now I see that you are not worthy of your background; your father was an honest, hardworking man, and you're just a common thief. At least if you had sent the package of medicine to the White Guards, as they had first suspected of you, then you would have gotten a bullet in the head as befitting a serious adversary. But a petty thief, eager for a couple of pennies for his own pocket. I think it would be healthier for the proletarian republic if you were sent off to my brother in Poland who, according to what he wrote me, has 'saved up' a couple of pennies from the bloody war. Yes, you're meant for each other, like the lid to a pot."

That was the speech that his uncle, the commissar, delivered to him, and a short time later Dr. Beyglman left for Poland.

Now something became clear to the pharmacist:

"That's quite a story. The fat one told me something once, that he'd been there as a quartermaster for the Bolsheviks in a hospital, and that later he'd been arrested and was even almost shot because he was an SR."

"A fine SR, a fine socialist," Meierbach laughed, "a real extortionist, a fleecer—nothing other than 36 percent."

"Even to this day he considers himself a socialist," the pharmacist noted.

The two of them chatted like this, the pharmacist and the industrialist did, near the open doors and hardly noticed how Khaykl the sexton's son had quietly slipped into the pharmacy.

And perhaps they had noticed, but didn't pay it any heed. Respectable society in Godlbozhits were used to the fact that Khaykl the broker stuck his nose into their company. They tolerated him just as one tolerates a family dog that gets underfoot. Khaykl slipped his way into their company, told a couple of salty jokes, made some salacious comments, and left. Or rather, he hadn't quite left before Meierbach reminded him, "Say good-bye, Khaykl." Then Khaykl bowed extravagantly, coolly doffed his hat, and went on his way with proud dignity, "You see, I'm Khaykl, a person who has dealings with the greatest nobles, doctors, professors, artist painters. I, a person who is written about in all the newspapers."

This time Khaykl made an exception; he hadn't come to lift the spirits of the noblemen with an off-color joke.

"I heard you speaking, Panowie, about SR, socialism," said Khaykl seriously. "So I said to myself: I'll go in, I too can speak a word or two on that idea."

They, the noblemen, interrupted their conversation only for a moment, listening to Khaykl's strange words, and then picked up their conversation as though Khaykl weren't there:

"Do you know, Moritz, what the fat one said to me recently? He said that if the workers put him forward on their slate for the city council, then he was their man. He's known as a socialist."

Khaykl came out of the corner and without the least decorum interrupted their conversation, "That's what he said, the doctor? He really said that himself?"

"Go to hell," the pharmacist cursed. "Won't you let me carry on a conversation?"

But Khaykl was speaking in a hurry, feverishly, like a dog with his tongue hanging out: Did they know, the Panowie, that he, Khaykl, had insinuated himself there in the union among those scoundrels? They wanted to put forward Zalmen "the Tankard" for the city council. Did they know, the honorable Panowie, who that was? It was Zalmen Komashnmakher, deaf Moyshe's son. It would be a terrible disgrace . . .

"Deaf Moyshe's son? Good to know," said Moritz Meierbach. "That deaf man is my coachman. If I didn't give him something to earn he'd bloat from hunger."

And Khaykl for his part added, "Did he, the doctor, say that himself, Panie Pharmacist?" he turned to the pharmacist. "Said it himself? Where can he be?"

"What doctor? Who said?" the pharmacist said angrily. "Go to hell along with the fatty! Do I know where he is? Maybe he's playing in the club? Maybe he's with some whore? Do I know?"

Even then Khaykl didn't take his leave as he should have, didn't bow as was proper, nor did he doff his hat sufficiently far. Rather, he left the pharmacy as though being chased, running to find the doctor.

But from the doorway the pharmacist called him back, "Just listen, in case you find him, that fatty, tell him that we're waiting on him for poker."

And when Khaykl had left the pharmacy for the second time he ran into the city hall secretary in the doorway. With a bandage on his head and his left hand in a sling he said angrily, "Nasty Jew! Watch where you're going."

———————

The possibility that the poker game might actually take place started pecking out like a chick from an eggshell. That's the conclusion the pharmacist's wife came to when she peeked out stealthily from the back storeroom and quickly and discreetly closed the pantry with the preserves and other sweets. She was tired, she was going off to bed.

But the pharmacist's wife knew that there wasn't much she could do. Those card players, once they sat down, would sit there till dawn, and sweets were on offer at around midnight too. They were in very high spirits there in the pharmacy. If the secretary had managed to gather up his broken hand and come wounded, then the doctor would surely also come. After all, that one was always dying for a game of cards.

There in the pharmacy they evaluated the fat doctor materially. But they were mistaken in their judgment. They, those solid and materialistic burghers of Godlbozhits, Meierbach and the pharmacist, had no idea of what went on in the soul of a young doctor such as he. They only saw his exterior, overgrown with fat, with greed for money, and with all other kinds of base desires; they didn't look into his heart, which was full of love.

Often they didn't really understand him: when a man goes and buys himself a luxury car, and drives it around over the decrepit roads of Godlbozhits.

"What do you need that expensive car for?" the pharmacist asked him. "What does it give you?"

"And what do you need that house for?" the doctor asked back.

"What do you mean?" The pharmacist didn't understand. "I get rent from it and it's a secure investment . . ."

"And I'm telling you that in Russia I saw people with bigger houses, and what did they get out of that? They'd have done well to look to their own . . ."

"That means what, there's nothing anymore?"

"That means," the fat doctor continued slowly, "that you've got a little money, live a good life, drive a pretty car, eat well, visit a beautiful shikse. What do you reckon, that it'll take a good long time for the Bolsheviks to take over the whole world? I should know! I've seen what a revolution is . . ."

And the fat-laden doctor thought to himself that it was worth it to buy the expensive car even if only to get to meet such a sweet girl as that Feygele Rabinovitsh, that sugar-tasty girl.

On that beautiful autumn Sunday he quickly dispensed with his patients, ordering them to come tomorrow, or the day after, and straightaway hopped in the car and drove off on the narrow country road to Rogów. The slender Feygele was already waiting for him with her lovely head of light hair, combed in a part, and such sweet, laughing eyes.

"You know, doctor," she said with a honeyed little voice, "today we'll be able to drive around a bit longer. Tykociński has gone to Warsaw to prepare his exhibition."

It didn't matter that he, Dr. Beyglman, was not a punctual person, that he had patients in the afternoon, that he had to get back home. When Feygele spoke to him with her honeyed little voice he was ready to abandon not only his medical practice, not only his own pious wife with the hunched little shoulder, but also even the gentle shikse with the flaxen hair and calf's eyes who was studying with him to be a midwife—the shikse who was in his gynecological practice his right hand and his "left" wife.[9] All of that he was prepared to give up that very beautiful autumn day and go off wherever he might chance to go with that sweet girl who was sitting next to him, steering his luxury automobile with her slender little hands and long fingers.

9. "left" wife: an illicit partner.

"Are you really going to Paris, Feygele?" he asked her with longing in his voice.

"Tykociński tried very hard to persuade me to go with him," said Feygele. "But I still don't know . . . I don't want to tie myself down, and if I go with him then I can't really do otherwise."

"And you won't long for me at all?" he asked again.

"You know very well," she sighed, "I am unable to pine away. I always have so much going on around me. But I will mention you as the best man in Godlbozhits."

They drove into a village. The doctor put his hand on hers on the wheel, gave a push to one of the pedals with his foot, and the car came to a stop.

"I have to make a stop," he said. "I have an ill patient here. I won't be long, alright?"

"Alright."

The car had stopped next to a peasant cottage, whitewashed and already readied for winter with leaves and pine needles. Around the yard a flock of chickens and geese wandered around, and fat pigs wallowed in the mud. It was one of the wealthiest cottages in the village of Karczówka.

Feygele glanced occasionally at the rich black clay soil, which was for the most part already plowed over for the winter sowing, and compared that soil with the soil of her own village, Rogów—rocky and sandy, in the shadow of a mountain. She was overcome with pity for her father, Shmuel Rabinovitsh, whom Leybele Pipe had hoodwinked into that rotten Rogów business. The sawmills and the mills all came to nothing, and likewise nothing came of the brickyard that was supposed to be built. It turned out that nowhere in the whole village had any clay suitable for making bricks. The plan for a limekiln also fell through since the local stones only had a small percentage of lime. The whole deal wouldn't have sufficed for firewood, let alone a source of income.

As a result, her clever, industrious father turned grey before his time; as a result, money was scarce in their house.

This was the situation that Feygele felt she needed to escape, and to escape as quickly as possible since Bebele was growing up and pushing her out. Being successful really is a good thing. But from all of her success Feygele couldn't sew herself a new winter coat, and her miserable old coat, well, one might call it a rag.

So it was that she went off with Tykociński to Paris. She was under no illusion about him: Tykociński was a good-natured man, and an artist with a reputation besides. But for that reason Tykociński had to know that he had caught the eye and the attention of Shmuel Rabinovitsh's beautiful daughters. Feygele hated to boast, but that didn't mean she didn't know her value. Did she, and how! And she was young as well, compared to Tykociński's forty-two. It was just a little safer dealing with a man of Tykociński's years, if he did indeed have an artist's temperament. And if someone like that loved her, that too was no trifle. "It's better to take one who loves you than one you desire," her father said. A wise man, her father!

So she went off to Paris. But what was she going to do there in Paris? She would be lost in a sea of elegant ladies. Paris is not Godlbozhits where you are the center of everything. On the other hand, would such a Feygele Rabinovitsh want for anything were she to become *Pani Doktorowa* in Godlbozhits? A nod of the head and he, the doctor, would divorce his hunchbacked wife; he'd do it that instant.

But she, Feygele, was too lazy to make such a scandal. Now she was too lazy even to think about it any more, and when the doctor came out of the cottage she was right in the middle of a hearty yawn.

"Aaaahhhh," she yawned widely. "I almost fell asleep."

"Is that so?" the doctor laughed. "Asleep? In broad daylight? If you really are so sleepy you can rest your head on my shoulder and I'll drive the car slowly uphill."

Feygele obeyed. The doctor took hold of the wheel and, leaning down to the sweet head on his shoulder, he gave her a kiss, the first kiss.

"I was held up," he said, justifying himself. "It's a case of severe paralysis of the hands and feet."

And he, the doctor, described how the peasant confessed everything to him: even now he still hadn't wanted to call a doctor, but he
was ashamed for his sons to have to divide his estate which he had
worked so hard to build. Starting with three acres of land that he
received as a dowry for an ugly wife he had built it up into fifty-two.

"Oh, what darkness there still is among the peasants," said Feygele,
and the doctor took her comment as an opportunity to talk about his
own valor.

"If you want to talk about darkness," he said, "let's remember
my student years in Russia. Then the slogan was *Going to the people*.
Years! Years! Half a year you'd wander around some far-flung village.
A Rogów or a Karczówka was a Berlin compared to it, and a dozy
peasant, like that Wojciech Palka, is to that dumb lump like a civilized
European to a negro from Africa. And we lived and worked under such
conditions, were conspirators. So, what? Was there any gratitude? The
Tsarist police never did anything to me, but our workers, our government, put me in prison and sentenced me to the firing squad."

"Firing squad?" Feygele was frightened.

"Yes, firing squad," the fat doctor said heroically. "And do you
know for what sin? Because I didn't belong to their party, to the Bolsheviks, but rather to the SRs."

"What fanatics!" Feygele cried out. "Terrible! SRs were socialists
too, after all."

"Certainly socialists," the doctor said, "the true socialists. And
they were persecuted because they stood up to the injustices perpetrated against the abused peasants . . . And it was decreed humor-
lessly—a death sentence."

"And how did you escape from their hands?"

"By a stroke of luck," the doctor said, "a brother of my current
father-in-law was a Bolshevik commissar. He interceded on my behalf
and they allowed me to leave Russia. But don't think he did that for no
reason, for gratitude, or because he bore me any love. No, he bound
me by my word of honor that I would go to Poland and marry his
brother's daughter."

Despite the gravity and horror of the story Feygele couldn't keep herself from laughing out loud.

"Poor man!" she pitied him through her laughter. "You poor thing, you had to get married to a hunchback."

The fat doctor turned red. He felt he'd botched the finale to this heroic exploit of his. And Feygele was insufficiently naïve and insufficiently sentimental to be moved by such unfortunate situations.

Though it was already beyond hope, he was determined to play the hero to the end.

"Yes, Feygele," he said firmly, "I value my word of honor more highly than anything else in the world, and here it was a matter of more than my word of honor. You surely know, Feygele, that my father was a poor man, and my current father-in-law took me in, supported me through gymnasium and then through university. I became engaged to my current wife during those earliest years. My current father-in-law treated me like his own child. Oh! He was not then a wealthy man; he was a military tailor, sewing officers' coats for sixteen hours a day, and he gave me money, and housed and fed me, so that I could finish my studies. Could I have done any differently?"

She wasn't laughing any more, Feygele. This was truly a work of tragedy; but she would not have been able to live like that for any price in the world. Oh! She couldn't restrain her laughter at the mere thought of it. "Ha-ha-ha! To live with . . . a hunchback. That is so comical."

"And so Feygele thinks that he lives with her like a husband with his wife," the doctor asked bitingly. "So, he swears to her by what is holy, he can give her his most sacred word of honor that he still has not laid a hand on his wife, that she is still a virgin."

"So it is a double tragedy," Feygele said at last, seriously. "Both for your wife and for you. Well, then, don't worry, doctor! You're young, you should be able to rally. You should be able to get your life in order and really enjoy things all the more. They don't erect golden tombstones after you're dead."

And no doubt in order to get rid of the bad impression that she had made by laughing, when they took their leave Feygele let him kiss her on her cheek, on her mouth. She smoothed his hair and said "poor boy," and said it so lovely that after she had left the fat doctor found himself falling into melancholy.

In order to stave off depression he went for a while to the club, ordered a liqueur and something to nibble, and slowly started to drink. Then he went over to the billiard table, knocked a ball—and that's all. It lasted only, it seemed to him, a short while, but by the time he arrived home it was already good and dark. An autumn's day is short, very short.

And as soon as he stepped through the doorway of his house his wife, with her large, frightened dark eyes, and her hunched little shoulder, ran to meet him. She seemed like a child. He would never in his life believe that he would be able to touch this crippled girl, and yet . . .

She ran to meet him, whispering a secret in his ear—perhaps for the third time since they became man and wife—"Hcniu . . . do you know, Heniu . . ."

"Impossible!" he cried out, not drunk but not completely sober. "Impossible I say! You're lying!"

The hunchbacked creature was terrified. She shrank down and rolled into a ball at his feet, begging for mercy, "You don't remember, Heniu . . . Then . . . You were so kind . . . so cheerful . . ."

He grew gentler, serious, and smoked a cigarette, pacing back and forth in his study.

"You know for sure?" he asked. "Maybe it just seems that way to you?"

The hunchbacked creature was cheered by his calmness.

"For sure, Heniu! I'm going to have a child . . . I will play with it . . ."

"Don't talk nonsense!" the doctor yelled irritably. "You mustn't have a child, you . . . you might die!"

"But I want . . . I want . . ." she whispered like a child, stubbornly.

"What do you want?" he asked acidly.

"A child . . ."

"But understand," he said at last, cajoling calmly, "you don't have thighs suitable to being a mother. You would die in childbirth."

"But I want . . . I want . . ." the creature sobbed, beating her head with balled-up fists.

"Kasia!" he called into the next room.

A pale Gentile girl, still wet behind the ears, entered, the same one who was studying with him to be a midwife. She remained standing in the door, rolling her bright calf's eyes and waiting.

"Get everything ready!" he commanded curtly.

The girl disappeared for a while and soon returned with a small case of shining nickel instruments. The alcohol lamp was lit, sending off a steady, quiet flame. Rolled into a ball, with a hunched little shoulder jutting out, the child mother lay huddled on the floor, scratching the floor with her nails and howling with foreboding, "It'll hurt so much . . . It'll hurt . . ."

The fat doctor strode back and forth across the study, demanding his white apron be brought to him and put on. He remained calm, just smoking a few more cigarettes as usual. This wasn't the first time, so his hands didn't shake. He took the balled up creature by the hand like a little child and led her to the birthing chair.

In just a couple of minutes the girl carried away a white receptacle full of red blood.

Then he himself brought out the birthing chair on its rubber wheels, the wrinkled child upon it.

And then he finally went back. Washed his hands and dried them for a long time on the hand towel. Smoked a cigarette. Walked back and forth across the spacious study.

"I've put her to sleep," he said. "Go, Kasia, and bring in the cognac. It's in the credenza."

He poured a glass for himself, and one for the midwife who served him as his right hand and his "left" wife. Then he pulled the colored cord on the electric lamp, and the Philips' burner cast shadows on their faces.

"Well, come Kasia . . ."

And she repeated, perhaps for the hundredth time, the old refrain, "Not now . . . later . . ."

Of course, she didn't mean it seriously; nor did he at all intend to lose today's poker game.

At a quarter of eleven the company greeted him with a cheer in the pharmacist's back storeroom, everyone chatting and joking, but Moritz Meierbach was in a hurry.

"Gentlemen, let's play! In heaven it'll be reckoned a bet. Three nines."

"Three aces."

✢ 17 ✢

The Important Burghers Argue over Seats, God Cries; The Important Burghers Finally Make Up and Go to Sit Down—Not Before the Seats Slip Out from Under Them

The elections for the city council were set to take place in January, and already in October the important and respectable burghers of Godlbozhits—the Meierbachs, the Brodersons, the pharmacists—realized they were not alone at the trough. Aside from the youths in the union—Communists, Bolsheviks—about whom there was simply nothing to say, there appeared out of nowhere new providers for Godl-bozhits: Lozer Kohn, president of the Mizrahi on the one side, and the teacher Livshits, president of the Zionists on the other.

All Godlbozhits knew what Lozer Kohn was before Broderson had handed him that business with the American orphan relief com-mittee. Meaning what? A common boot maker, a cobbler prick . . . begging your pardon for the expression. As for the teacher Livshits, the Litvak with the little black mustache, it would have been only fair to know who he was, for one, where he came from, and who asked him to get involved in the city's business?

They, the new city providers, spoke and fumed in an affected newspaper language, which was, in the opinion of the Godlbozhits elite, not suited to such a small shtetl as Godlbozhits. Here old cus-toms still reigned among the Jews, thank God; here people knew that a Hasidic prayer house is a Hasidic prayer house and a city hall is a city hall. To city hall you had to send a distinguished person, not some Jewboy with a long kapote and a round hat, not some cobbler prick . . . begging your pardon for the expression.

So that cobbler prick came—that is, Lozer Kohn, who, even though he had been president of the Mizrahi innumerable times, and even though he had made a pretty penny off the American infant milk for the poor orphans, *still* wore a cloth kapote, and in winter a plush trimmed cap on his head—he came into the middle of the marketplace and with the nerve of a wealthy parvenu and an ungrateful soul cast a word into the void: "Meierbach has betrayed Jewish interests."

How so? Because five years ago, when the Christian community divvied up the forest among themselves, and thumbed their noses at the Jews, then, five years ago the respectable burghers, the assimilators who would never even glance at the study house suddenly entered the study house between afternoon and evening prayers and pounded on the lectern, "Jews! You should know that if you fall asleep and fail to elect Jewish members of the city council it will go badly. They will also divide up the market square!"

Who should they select as a city councilor? Obviously Pan Meierbach, obviously the pharmacist. Who else? A Jew with a beard?

And how did it turn out? The Christians, it is true, did not appropriate the market square. But the rest of the urban fields, squares, and meadows they did once again divide up amongst themselves. Silence; not even a rooster crowed. One might ask: Why when it came to the forest did they make such a ruckus, but when it came to the fields and squares was there total silence? It's quite simple: the two Jewish city councilors, the providers—Meierbach and the pharmacist—took that opportunity to buy substantial squares for themselves for pennies, and who could protest?

That being his game, Lozer Kohn went around among the market sellers and agitated against Meierbach, against the pharmacist, and even against Broderson. But didn't he know that in any case the matter of the urban squares was a hopeless venture? If the Christians had determined that those squares should be divided up amongst themselves—after all, they did have a majority in city hall—what did it matter that some of the squares fell into Jewish hands? And if Wiśnicki was the one buying and not Meierbach, would that have been any better?

But truth and fairness must come to the surface like oil on water, and that's what people evidently saw in Lozer Kohn.

A total of three months before, Lozer, the founder and president of *Shalve ba-sadeh*, had been the hero of the day, the real father-in-law at the wedding.

On that day the first party of emigrants, consisting of two families, left Godlbozhits for the Land of Israel.

The first ones to have the honor of being redeemed from Exile and of going to their own land, which *Shalve ba-sadeh* had prepared for them, were the dark Shmuel-Elye, a restless Jew and a desperado whose business deals had gone south, and one Shmuel-Khayim, a sickly Jew who stood at death's door and believed he could regain his health in the warm sunshine of the Holy Land.

All of Godlbozhits accompanied them off with music and blue and white banners. The horse-drawn droshkes on which they rode were literally carried aloft. It's no exaggeration to say that all of Godlbozhits joined in their journey morally and in spirit.

For maybe three months nothing was heard of the two emigrants, but then again, they were illiterate. Then all of a sudden Shmuel-Elye's mother-in-law in Godlbozhits received a long letter from her son-in-law and daughter. First, they informed her of their good health, and hoped to hear the same of her, the mother-in-law. Second, they, the writers of the letter, wished that their family and all of the Jews should know neither misfortune nor need any longer, but that misfortunes and plagues should be poured out on Lozer Komashnmakher's head and on every inch of his body. He should be ground up as he had ground them up, good God! Firstly, the land is not land at all, but sand and stones; and secondly, the Arabs live there and they won't leave the land as long as the organization still doesn't pay as much as it promised. And what's more, because everything is so very expensive the Jews buy it up, and if Jews are buying, of course it costs still more. In brief, they turned to the organization in Tel-Aviv where *Shalve ba-sadeh* bought the land

and made an angry scene in their offices protesting that they had been sent there, Jews with wives and children. In the Land of Israel, they said, one must have either Jews with truly large fortunes, or young men, pioneers, who were prepared to sacrifice their blood for the Land. Yet as for the unpaid money, it's true that they, Shmuel-Elye, Shmuel-Khayim, and others like them, had paid down to a penny, but members of an organization were guarantors for one another, and if, for example, Lozer Kohn and those of his ilk had purchased fifty, a hundred dunams at a time, and not paid a penny, it was the same as if they, Shmuel-Elye and Shmuel-Khayim, had not paid.

The letter went on to describe how Shmuel-Khayim got sick and had to be taken to the hospital. He at least was fortunate—wrote Shmuel-Elye—"I and both wives and the little ones wander the streets and there's not enough for a pound of bread."

And then he, Shmuel-Elye, asked his mother-in-law, the instant she received his letter to go see the bastard and smash all his windows. At least people should know what a murderer he is.

Her heart was full, Shmuel-Elye's mother-in-law, but she lacked the breath to cry, and as soon as she had broken the first window at Lozer's place she immediately grew frightened and didn't finish the job, especially since people started arriving from the area, fast becoming a crowd, a black wedding, and she, Shmuel-Elye's mother-in-law, was a respectable person.

That same day the job was finished by Aunt Mitshe. She knocked out the glass from all of Lozer Kohn's windows as well as from the glass-paneled door that led to his shop. Those who had reason to fawn on Lozer, to boost his respectability, shouted that Aunt Mitshe had gone raving mad. Mind you, up until then she wasn't completely well—talking a lot, not recognizing people—but now this disgrace was out in the street and she was running around crazy and breaking windows. This claim, though, was a bold-faced lie, because right after breaking Lozer Komashnmakher's windows, she, Aunt Mitshe, went right back to her kitchen, kept her fire going day and night, regularly feeding it with woodchips, and in the intervals distributed everything from her house to poor new mothers. That's how she lived till her final day. In her sorrowful mother's-heart she had her own reason for breaking Lozer Kohn's windows on that fateful day: she, Aunt Mitshe, could not watch indifferently as her child's nest was smashed apart. One needs to know that even though lame Moyshele was a crippled coachman and had a moll of a wife, he was still Aunt Mitshe's child, and her mother's-heart was swollen with miseries.

Here's what happened: Lozer Kohn's wife, the pious, thin Khane-Rekhl who prayed every day like a man, yielded her soul one night to her Maker, never again to retrieve it, and as was fitting for a pious woman, hers was an easy death without suffering. Lozer's cunning little eyes were covered with a veil of tears, and he gave a eulogy for his departed wife in the synagogue with such a plaintive voice that the whole women's section blew their nose like it was Yom Kippur, and the pious women wished for their own souls to be yielded so easily and for eulogies such as those. That was one thing.

Some weeks later Yosl Treger came to lame Moyshele:

"A tragedy has befallen you, my lame friend! Haven't I just met Tsipore leaving Lozer's back storeroom? Lame dog! You're a Cohen after all, why are you silent!"

The lame cripple grabbed his head angrily, abandoned his cart and horse in the street, and raced home, whip in hand, repeating to himself the whole way, "Damn the trollop! I'm a Cohen. Just let's go to the rabbi, you bitch! To the rabbi! To the rabbi!"

And she, the bitch, was utterly unimpressed. To the rabbi? To the rabbi! She, Tsipore, could make do without the property and the opulence which she enjoyed with him; but don't let that hapless "team" make up any despicable slander about her. She didn't give a damn about him, but she would still accept such lame goods, even though you would have to have seen what red cheeks she had at their wedding, and what a ruin she had become with that misfortunate cripple. Would he still bring such shame on her?!

"I'll crack your skull!" she cried. "You lame dog! Where's the broom?!"

And beating his breast he shouted, "I am a *cohen*! To the rabbi, nasty bitch!"

So she slapped on her ragged kerchief, not even bothering to straighten her disheveled wig, and turning past the marketplace with curses they went off to the rabbi.

"Rabbi, I am a Cohen. She'll make me unclean!" yelled the lame man.

"Sainted rabbi! This minute a divorce! Right away, this minute!" Tsipore agreed.

The rabbi stopped up his ears; the rabbi couldn't listen to such shrieking; the rabbi looked into his little book and read from it, "Do not think that separating a couple by divorce is a thing done lightly. The angels and God Himself cries when a sacred marriage is nullified. Do not think that a divorce is an easy matter. One will need to work hard."

The shouting couple remained quiet. They listened, wanting to get the gist of the rabbi's speech. But they didn't understand.

Tsipore boldly went first, "What does the sainted rabbi mean?"

The rabbi still didn't turn his head, saying into his little book, "Well, then leave thirty zlotys."

The rabbi's little office, which breathed the breath of maybe twenty rabbis, saints, and holy men; that little room that breathed the sanctified stuffiness of several hundred books, was suddenly filled with the evil thoughts of two simple people, a husband and a wife.

"Thirty zlotys, that's thirty breakfasts and thirty dinners for seven mouths, two pairs of shoes for the winter, an installment of rent to the landlord, a load of wood, a couple of bundles of straw for the horse."

And the rabbi, if he could have foreseen that they would start talking about horses in his office, horses and straw right in front of the armchair of his holy grandfather. The rabbi didn't let himself think about it.

"Well, meantime you can leave a deposit of ten zlotys. You'll pay the rest, before the divorce."

Lame Moyshele scraped some money out of his breast pocket and counted out coins worth tens and twenties, counted and recounted: seven zlotys and twenty groschen. He didn't have any more than that.

The rabbi turned around with his back facing the couple and spoke into the table:

"They think a divorce is a trifle. A divorce is not just any old thing; at a divorce the angels cry, and God Himself cries as well, for a divorce one needs to work hard."

Tsipore finally grasped what he meant and begged pardon at the sainted rabbi's back for the great headache which they had inflicted on the sainted rabbi's head. Then she would run straight home and go pawn the gold chain that she had received at her wedding so there could finally be an end to her miseries.

At last the rabbi turned around hastily and spoke to the ceiling:

Let him, Moyshe, meantime hand over the seven zlotys and the groschens. It's getting late and one must begin writing. A divorce is not just any old thing, it doesn't just happen on its own. Well then, let them go see the sexton and the scribe and send them over.

On their way out they sent the scribe over. But when the couple went in to see the old sexton Tsipore remembered something and said, "Moyshe, give me just a couple of groschens so I can buy something to cook. The little chicks are chirping from hunger."

The lame man had nary a groschen left, so he rushed out and somehow got hold of a loan for a ride—thirty groschen—and handed it to her.

The old sexton saw this. "Is such a thing possible? Where is it heard of Jews that they can so hurry and rush to get a divorce? And when it's said with such a fine how-d'ya-do, what is that?"

Then the old sexton's wife also got involved: a good word for this one, a good word for that one, and there'll be peace for the couple.

So they ran to the rabbi to get back the seven zlotys and the groschens. At their "begging-your-pardon" he turned around toward them, pulling his neck in between his shoulders like a goose. He wouldn't give back the money.

That touched Tsipore right to the very quick. "What does that mean, 'he's not giving back the money'? Seven zlotys and the groschens, that's seven breakfasts and eight dinners for seven mouths, that's a pair of shoes for the little one who goes barefoot to school, that's . . ."

Then she vented her bitter heart on her husband: "All because of you, you lame loser! My breadwinner! You can so easily earn tens of zlotys?!"

But he gave as good as he got: "All because of you, bitch carcass!"

She slapped him right in his ugly mug; he slapped the broom of hair on her head; she scratched his nose; he caught her by the throat; she shrieked at the top of her lungs. The rabbi's little study, the one that breathed the breath of maybe twenty rabbis, saints, and holy men, was now full of foul curses.

Tsiporah yelled, "In that case, let the rabbi have the divorce written." And at that she unbuttoned her bosom and pulled out the golden chain. That's what she had done when she went home. What else? Was she going to leave her jewelry at home so that lame team could squander it?

So let the rabbi have the divorce written!

The rabbi then again stretched out his long gooselike neck from between his shoulders and called into the next room, "Scribe, write!"

And that same day God, seated on the armchair of the rabbi's holy grandfather, and with the angel Gabriel on his right, washed with their tears the rainbow of book dust in that holy rabbinical office in Godlbozhits.

Lozer Komashnmakher had shattered windows, and Aunt Mitshe had bruised hands.

Several days later Tsipore left Godlbozhits. Soon thereafter Lozer Kohn followed her. Then both of them came back and Tsipore moved right in with him—right after the wedding.

To spite all his enemies, Lozer Kohn set up a large shoe factory. He made it clear to his comrades, "I've had enough of taking care of this community. Now it's time to take care of myself."

And indeed, ever since he had clothed the drowned in woven shrouds, ever since he had provided for their orphans with American infant milk and for the members of *Shalve ba-sadeh* with fields and orchards in the Land of Israel, and especially ever since he had lived with a pious wife for some thirty years, he might be permitted to start building something for himself as well and experience what a true Jewish woman is like.

That was completely appropriate as far as he was concerned. But Godlbozhits was not a city of well-wishers. They were mortified over the fact that Lozer Kohn, a common bootmaker before the war, was now such a wealthy man; over the fact that he, a man in his old age with married children, had such a youthful lust.

"So that's that," Lozer forced himself to say, knowing it was a waste of breath. "They won't elect me as city councilor."

That's how, quite easily and without even lifting a finger, the respectable burghers had gotten rid of one candidate for a seat in the city council. Despite that, however, the second candidate, the teacher Livshits, stuck like a bone in their throats—you could neither throw it up nor swallow it down.

"What do you want," Meierbach argued his just case, "do you also want to stand on the slate? Why not, stand. But it must be by age: first the pharmacist, then Meierbach, then . . ."

But Livshits hardly let him get a word out:

What do they think, he didn't know what elections are? First of all, elections were a blind affair and one couldn't be 100 percent certain that anyone but the first candidate would be elected. And even so, that certainly wouldn't happen on account of the assimilators, the sycophants who were isolated and had no block of voters behind them. Godlbozhits Jewry were Zionistically inclined and for this reason the Zionists would take their birthright. He, Livshits, was not a private individual, he was the Zionist organization.

Meierbach snorted and sprayed spit when he spoke, "This is not Palestine, this is Poland!"

Livshits did not get vexed, rather he laughed, and laughed heartily at that so-called intellectual. And that's who you want to be a representative of sensible Godlbozhits Jewry? With such political ignoramuses even a child could recognize that the Zionist organization with Grinboym at its head directed a coherent exilic political program.[1]

So he let them, those respectable burghers, vent their anger in the back storeroom of the pharmacy, and wherever else they wanted, while he, Livshits, would convene a great popular assembly in the Zionist Party—entrance free for members and sympathizers.

The respectable burghers heard that Livshits was calling for an assembly, so they sent Moshke Abishes to keep tabs on what was said.

Moshke Abishes arrived right at the very end of the presentation so he had to stop his ears against the chaos and din. Everyone was banging on the tables, clapping bravos, "Viva! Down with assimilation! Long live the Zionists! Hooray!"

Then Moshke Abishes returned to the back storeroom of the pharmacy. The pharmacist and Moritz Meierbach were waiting for him.

"Well?" asked Meierbach.

"Don't ask!" Moshke said. "Fire!"

The pharmacist's head sank.

But Moritz Meierbach lifted it back up.

"I'll show that Litvak scoundrel!"

"And I'm telling you," said Moshke calmingly, "you shouldn't provoke a quarrel; place Livshits on the slate."

"Are you listening?" Moritz Meierback softened. "He doesn't want it. It's beneath him, the Litvak."

Moshke Abishes rolled a cigarette, knocked it against his nail, and blew out the tip.

"Hot-tempered," said Moshke calmly. "It's not so bad. He wants it."

"What does he want?" Meierbach asked hurriedly.

"The first spot."

---

1. Isaac Grünbaum (1879–1970) was a Polish-Jewish political activist and a Polish Zionist leader and journalist.

"To hell with him! The Litvak swine!" said Meierbach spraying spit. "He won't agree to anything else? The gall of that young man! Well, I'll show you, Moshke, that he won't lead a city around by the nose. If I wanted, he'd be gone in twenty-four hours . . . If he goes around stirring things up I'll demand he show his Russian passport . . ."

"And I'm telling you," said Moshke, cool as a cucumber, "that you don't need to lose your temper, you need to come to an agreement. Don't let your enemies rejoice. Don't let those cobbler boys from their union go about with a full belly."

That argument helped. Moritz Meierbach calmed down at once.

"Better Livshits than Zalmen Komashnmakher."

They sent word to invite old Broderson:

The city requests that he come, that he might intervene to come to a peaceful settlement.

So the old man, as was his habit, consulted his wife, and she, as was her habit, answered, "If it's city business, Stasiu, if the city's requesting then go."

But when the old man had already put on his mink coat with the beaver collar (the only one he was able to rescue from the claws of the Bolsheviks) Sonia rushed in and said all in one breath, "Father dear, don't go . . . For my blessed peace of mind, don't go."

She explained, Sonia did:

When he, Yakob, came home from the city, very upset, he was heartsick and couldn't even eat lunch because of his grief. She felt, Sonia did, that he had given up. She put her hand to his forehead—she didn't need a thermometer. Exactly thirty-eight degrees. So she sent him right to bed, covered him with a blanket, and soothed him. Now—tell. So he told: up until now only the pharmacist and Meierbach were against him, but now his father-in-law was also against him.

The old man again removed his mink coat with the beaver collar.

"Do you hear, Maria, what people are saying?"

But Pani Maria did not understand.

"What does it mean that the city has sent for him?"

Sonia wanted to respond, but she didn't get a chance because the door was thrown open and the ill Livshits burst in.

"Who is the city?" he raved. "They are the city?! I am the city! The Zionists are the city!"

And right then he broke into a fit of coughing, fell into a chair, and set to agitating his weak heart.

If that was the case, if he, Yakob, was such a cruel man, then all of them had nothing to live for. They certainly didn't let him go home. Sonia took off his clothes and forced him to get into her father's bed. No one was going any more into the city.

But the city does not permit rest; the city comes into the home. Moshke Abishes was the matchmaker, running hither and thither. It wasn't long before he had brought Meierbach and the pharmacist together with Livshits in Broderson's house.

People made their arguments calmly, without tempers flaring.

"What does he want?" Meierbach asked. "He wants a spot? By all means, with the greatest pleasure. On the contrary, a young man, at the opportune moment, could be of use . . . But does such audacity really suit a young man, to want the first spot?"

But the young man with his audacity stood firm.

"Yes, he has such audacity, his party has such audacity!"

Once again they were getting nowhere. As luck would have it, there was Moshke Abishes. He edged up to Pani Broderson, whispering quietly in order not to disturb the negotiations, "Does the Pani have an idea of what is going on in the city? The youths from the 'red' union are sparing no effort. They are watching closely for the bourgeois class to tear itself apart. They want to install their people in city hall. Perhaps the Pani has heard of Zalmen Komashnmakher? The greatest Bolshevik. He has often said that as soon as he gets in there he's going to remove all of the bourgeois' guts . . ."

Pani Broderson clapped her hands, "Can you imagine, Stasiu? It must not be permitted, how wretched, my God!"

As Pani Broderson interfered in the deliberations, Sonia too helped out; but Livshits remained stubborn, taxing his heart, and holding firm as a wall: the first spot, and only the first.

The men had started to turn red from restraining their anger, and the women were wiping their tearful eyes with handkerchiefs, when all of a sudden Moshke Abishes loomed over them and threatened with his finger pointing into the space over everyone's heads, "Just remember! You're going to make sure that the 'reds' will get into city hall. The city will weep on account of no one but you!"

Perhaps Moshke's brandishing of the red specter helped, and perhaps Livshits with his weak human heart ultimately grew too tired to fight like a lion; at any rate, they came to an agreement: the pharmacist would be in the first spot, Livshits in the second, and Meierbach in the third.

And as soon as the city had come to their agreement, people could finally and calmly take stock: Godlbozhits needed to elect twelve city councilors. Jews were one third of the population—therefore, four city councilors. In the elections, the bourgeois class put up one slate; the fat doctor with the common masses and Khaykl the sexton's son as his assistant offered a second slate; and the "reds" a third slate. The fat doctor might attract a few votes from the common masses, but not a lot. Moreover, as for the "reds," the young men and women, the majority of them didn't even have the right to vote, and a sensible person, a Jew with a beard, certainly wouldn't vote for those scamps. Therefore, neither the fat doctor nor the "reds" had a chance for even half a seat. That left only the bourgeois class with its sure three seats, and maybe even all four.

Thus did Livshits reckon, and Meierbach had to admit, he was what he was, that Livshits—a teacher and a Litvak swine, sure—but he had quite a head for electoral calculations; he could figure out the results of the election before anyone had even placed a vote.

And if Livshits made a mistake in his calculations, it surely wasn't his fault. It was the doctor who was at least a little to blame, driving around in his own car and dragging ill and elderly people to the polling places. And more than anything the election agitators from the "red" union were to blame, who secretly did their underground work, agitating and persuading the poor, ignorant masses that once Nosn Garber and Zalmen Komashnmakher came to power the property of the wealthy would be taken and distributed among them. In any event, around midday on the day of the election Sonia Livshits, at the Broderson's home, took her husband's temperature—it read 37.5 degrees. Then, despite his protest, she put him back to bed and promised to go into the city and be on the lookout to make sure that Jews were taking out of their pockets the "sixes"—the number of the "reds, "and putting in "fours"—the number of the bourgeois slate.

Mrs. Livshits performed the mission she had taken upon herself with zeal, and following her example all of the young Zionist men and women spared no effort on the elections. Right at the last minute before the polling place closed two Zionist girls came racing up, leading Aunt Mitshe under their arms. In one breath they explained they were coming inside: "Mitshe, come with us—the pharmacist's orders." But she, Mitshe, said that she had ballots; Nosn had given them to her. They said that Nosn had sent them here, that he, Nosn, had made a mistake earlier and ordered them to give her a different ballot.

Not to worry, Livshits might be allowed to lie in bed like a lord on election day—his lady comrades had worked enough for his sake.

And now the votes were finally counted.

The fat doctor was the chairman of the electoral district, so the fat doctor stuck his long nose with his shortsighted eyes into every ballot. His fat neck flushed with blood every time the number of a called-out ballot was repeated.

"Three!" he called out loudly. That was the number of his own slate. And then, "Six . . . Six . . . Four . . . Three! . . . Six . . . Six . . . Four . . . Six . . . Six . . . Six . . ."

A flood of sixes. They pounded on the pale Moritz Meierbach's brain like hammers: Six . . . Six . . .

He was terribly angry at the city, his city, that had betrayed him. It's a good thing he was in a polling place so he couldn't vent his spleen and fume as was his way.

All counted. And as soon as the last ballot was called out, Comrade Moyshe, the one with the philosopher's mane, the librarian of the union, had the full election results at his fingertips. In the Christian election bureau the votes had already been counted for a long time.

They had eight seats. The workers—three. The bourgeois slate—one, the pharmacist.

Livshits and Meierbach and the fat doctor—all three of them were left high and dry.

At first the fat doctor was crestfallen, but when he looked at Moritz Meierbach, he cheered up.

"As long," he said, "as I'm not alone."

And Meierbach couldn't restrain himself any longer, spraying spit like a shower of foam.

"Boor," he said to the doctor.

The doctor didn't hold his tongue:

Were he not so hot-tempered, the great nobleman, were he not to spray so much spit, he'd sooner learn to sign his name.

This quarrel between the fat doctor and Moritz Meierbach lasted maybe a week, until the pharmacist made peace between them again with a game of cards.

"The sacred card dealer," said the pharmacist and shuffled the deck, "the sacred card dealer oughtn't suffer your quarrel."

✦ 18 ✦

What Can Happen When an
Earnest Bookkeeper Gets Bored

The second of April of that year was certainly a day to which Shimen Shifris attributed better than what one might normally ask from such a day, having as it did more mud than sunshine. By that time he had spent more than a year and a half back in Godlbozhits—two winters and a summer in between. By then he had deceived both himself and deceived others day in, day out: "I'm going to Warsaw to study," just like lame Moyshele with his "Go away, I'm going to drive." He kept traveling to study, and sitting in his spot. By then he had already little by little been giving up on his ardent love for Feygele Rabinovitsh. She lay somewhere in a corner of his heart like a little green leaf that gets placed between the pages of a book: it can neither blossom nor grow, but is preserved from rotting. Thus his idle and monotonous existence stretched on, day after day. So how was one to know that precisely that muddy day would be the day of crisis?

Shimen got to work half an hour late. Actually, you couldn't call that late because in Godlbozhits you still didn't work, thank God, by the clock—so you could never be late. At any rate, after coming into the bank and greeting the teller at the little window with a sleepy "Good morning," Shimen opened the oddly large ledger and set to writing.

He was now an earnest bookkeeper in Fayvele Shpilman's cooperative bank. And that's what it was called—Fayvele Shpilman's cooperative bank—in order to distinguish it from another, also so-called cooperative bank, which had opened as a rival shop and which wasn't worth a plug.

226

In point of fact, even now Shimen Shifris still wasn't earning a large salary. A hundred zlotys a month after a year of working for free and another half a year after that for fifty zlotys. God knows what kind of pay that was; but if you compared his, Shimen's, salary to the current salary of the teller, at forty zlotys a week, and to the pay of the other two clerks, who earned "four weeks to a month," Shimen's position clearly seemed important and serious. But Shimen still had a future: the bank kept developing, growing, and Shimen Shifris was growing along with it.

The director of the bank was Fayvele Shpilman himself: a Jew with a silken mien and a quiet muffled voice, if slightly hoarse, as was characteristic of usurers. However, Fayvele was no usurer. Fayvele traded discount notes: commercial discounts with fixed interest, with stipulations for damages, and five additional days for every note.

This was his world, and the cooperative bank was his spiritual joy. He loved it, his social cooperative bank, one might say, like his own child. He had created it, this institution, raised it up to be a great, beautiful bank where people had work and poor Jews came to get a loan. He was the first to invest his capital in the bank, and still kept investing and investing . . . He wasn't stingy because, as was said, he considered it his good deed, his place in the world to come. He wasn't on the synagogue board, he wasn't a city councilor—he was a cooperativist.

Fayvele Shpilman would not tolerate any of his employees coming to him with demands: I want thus-and-such a salary. Nevertheless, he himself remembered his employees, particularly those who were worth their hard work. And now he was coming to the board of directors with a proposal that the bookkeeper Shimen Shifris's salary be increased by 30 percent—that is, from 100 to 130 zlotys a month. It's true, no one was opposed to it, if there was money for it. But even if his whole board of directors were against it, he, Fayvele, would still get his way. The members of the board understood that well enough, so no one was opposed. On the contrary, someone stood up and proposed that if there was money for 30 percent, the director need not do worse than a bookkeeper, so the director ought to get a raise as well.

Since again no one was opposed, no one said no, but someone on the board who was good at math did a quick calculation on the corner of a newspaper that 30 percent of 600 zlotys a month was a 180, making altogether just shy of 800 zlotys a month. Fayvele put the cart before the horse: 800 zlotys a month is, true, a substantial salary, by Godlbozhits standards, but the board knew that for him, Fayvele, earning five hundred was not such a difficult matter. He needed only go about in the street, a sniff here, a whiff there, and he would earn three times as much as he did at the bank. His wife wouldn't leave him alone: "That bank'll be the end of me," she said, "day and night bank this, bank that . . ." Of course, if someone from the board of directors wished to undertake handling this business, he would hand it over lock, stock, and barrel, and add a nice drink of brandy to boot.

That was his nature after all, Fayvele's, unburdening himself impetuously even though no one had said a word. No one said anything, because what was there to be mistaken about? More than half of the bank's deposits were his own, Fayvele's, money. If he left the bank and took out all his money then they would be utterly ruined and they might as well go and close up shop. Let them think that he, Fayvele, wanted another percent from his money.

And when the board members had dispersed, Fayvele called Shimen in. He, Shimen, ought to know that Fayvele liked him and considered him like his own child. From now on he would receive 30 percent more in pay. They, the members of the board, would in no way permit him, Shimen, such an increase, but when Fayvele said to increase it, let them talk till the cows come home, let them bite the dust. True, 130 zlotys was still not the largest of salaries, but the bank kept growing and he, Shimen, was growing along with it. It was Fayvele's hope that Shimen would in time come into his own with him. "In a couple of years," said Fayvele, "in a couple of years, one doesn't get younger, but rather older; what use is it to me to work in a bank? Because the couple of zlotys a month that I make at the bank I can't bring in from my own business dealings? What I mean is: who will take over the bank when I've gone, if not you, Shimen? Who?" The teller, that little girl maybe will direct the bank? She got a ten zloty raise, but that was money wasted. For him, Fayvele, the most important thing was a person with a head on his shoulders, and that means, begging pardon, only derrière in the chair.

He was pleased, Shimen Shifris was, very pleased, and he himself didn't know whether it was because of the raise in his salary or because of the intimation that he would one day be director of the bank, or maybe really because of the fact that Fayvele considered him an serious bookkeeper. At any rate, when he closed the large ledger and strode merrily home the molten sun was laughing out to him from the little muddy streams. That's what one calls a good day: making gold out of mud.

And when Shimen's material concerns were satisfied, that satiety aroused spiritual desires; intellectual needs in turn fed on the crude material satisfaction. He remembered that it had been almost a year since he'd read a book. Would that be his purpose, his life's goal—to be a Fayvele Shpilman? A filthy usurer?

It was already Sabbath in the city. Not the soul-rejoicing Sabbath from before the war, booming with hymns after a meal of a large carp's head, with white challahs baked till shining, embraced by that warmth that radiates from white, lustrous stove tiles. No, since poverty had appeared and spread from Bath Street to aunt Mitshe's house, Uncle Melekh had sat on Friday night with his blue-brown nose stuck in a bowl stale groats, sullenly grumbling his hymns and stubbornly trying to warm himself, rubbing his shoulder on the cold unwhitewashed stove. He, Uncle Melekh, now no longer rebuked his children as he once did for not sitting together with him at his table Friday nights. It seemed that he himself would also not have been pleased with sitting down to a gloomy meal, and before he had finished the meal he had already taken off his boots and crept under the warm featherbed—the sole remaining pleasure from bygone days.

If Uncle Melekh didn't break into tears on such a Friday night, it was perhaps because of the fact that he was a simple, hardened man who didn't have the lyrical soul of a Shimen Shifris. The proof is that he, Shimen, who was not at all religious, and only a little nationally inclined, his heart bled with pain at the exiled, captive "Sabbath

Queen," for that sole joy, that one piece of the sublime that the little
Jewish shtetls were deprived of.

It is possible that that was not his own idea; it is possible that that
was the effect of a painting, "The Poor Sabbath," that Tykociński had
shown him. In any case, he, Shimen, felt that pain deep in his heart,
and as he strode over the muddy marketplace to the Zionist Party he
even bore a grudge at the anemic electric streetlamps for the way their
workaday, indifferent light diminished the little flames of the sincere,
soulful Sabbath candles shining from the Jewish windows.

There was almost nobody in the Zionist Party, but the floor was
covered with pumpkin seeds and cigarette butts, as though a quartered
regiment of soldiers had left just a moment before. Among the discol-
ored cigarette papers, thickly covered with flyspecks, a large oil lamp
with a mended blackened glass was smoking, filling the "hall" with the
suffocating smell of kerosene. Shimen was barely able to see the librarian by the little bookcase in the corner.

"I would like to request something by Sholem Aleichem," Shimen
addressed the librarian.

"We haven't any Sholem Aleichem," an icy nose answered with
visible regret. A large pince-nez trembled meaningfully on that especially intellectual nose, accompanying her in her distress.

"No Sholem Aleichem at all?" said Shimen with genuine surprise.

The icy intellectual nose instantly struck a pose of sympathy for
this earnest Godlbozhits bookkeeper. From her very first look at him
she had complete confidence in this non-partisan Shimen Shifris. She
lamented:

"You should take a look at a trade union. There there is order, there
people read, they treat books with respect and keep buying new ones.
They've got a beautiful library, so many scientific subjects, they buy
all the newest titles, people take an interest. But here, in the Zionist
Party, if someone eventually does borrow a book it's returned around
six months later, unread, with notes scribbled all over the covers and
margins—the lofty philosophical musings of the cultivated youth of
Godlbozhits. Even so, it's better if the book is brought back, because
most are kept so long that they get lost. Under such conditions buying

new books is obviously inconceivable. Nor does anyone really need them, those books. People only know about coming here to smoke a Sabbath cigarette, and that's all. What can one say? Even someone picking up a newspaper is a rarity. And there's nothing whatsoever to say about the girls. Were it not for some lad or another they would never come here at all; they're so shallow, these girls today . . . And the boys too are no better—they only want such . . ."

All of a sudden Shimen noticed that the icy-red intellectual nose had turned to him and had begun to captivate his attention. He not too courteously interrupted, "What do you mean? That there, in the trade union, I'll be able to get hold of Sholem Aleichem?"

Then he quickly added, as if to defend himself, "I've never been there, but it wouldn't bother me to go just for a book."

His trousers were thoroughly spattered from striding over the wet mud, the famous Godlbozhits "cream," by the time Shimen finally arrived at a bright glass door through which innumerable heads were visible. He entered the first room, where the library cases stood. The cases were still shut. A young man quietly informed him that Comrade Moyshe, the librarian, was just now in the other room where the executive committee was giving a report on its activities. Books could be borrowed first thing after the meeting.

He, Shimen Shifris, had not realized that his entrance might draw such attention from the audience of workers. His questions were quietly and courteously answered, and just as courteously a place was made for him to stand by the door that led to the other fully packed room. He asked the comrade on duty, "Might I listen?"

The comrade hesitated and answered, "Then where will you go crawling off to in the mud? I will go ask the chairman."

He wrote a couple of words on a slip of paper and sent it from hand to hand over people's heads to the presidium table. An unfamiliar girl with bright blonde hair done up simply in a peasant style, who was sitting at the presidium table, looked up with a pair of large, curious eyes at Comrade Nosn who was standing nearby. He nodded his head yes. Then the girl stood up and said cordially, "You can stay, Herr Shifris, if it interests you."

So he stayed—of course he stayed—and he asked about that unfamiliar girl.

"Not from around here," the comrade on duty informed him. "She directs the evening classes and the cultural section."

"Been here long?"

"Four months."

"Ah, so . . . That's why I don't know her." He said that, Shimen did, as if to defend himself, out of politeness, because in truth it wasn't really necessary for him, Shimen Shifris, to be familiar with the girls in the trade union.

And now finally he could, and needed to, hear a little. The delegate from the bakery workers, the short and solidly built Comrade Enzl, was speaking. He was constantly squinting his bleary eyes, and waves of blood flowed steadily to his pale, overheated face.

"In all of Godlbozhits there is at last not one single unorganized bakery worker!" Comrade Enzl proclaimed in triumph. "The eight-hour workday has been preserved. Our comrades verify that the working conditions outlined by the union have been put in place everywhere. A strike was declared at master baker Zucker's for trying to deprive his workers of their shares of bread. The strike ended with complete victory."

Then Comrade Golde spoke about the conditions among the domestic servants: "The boardinghouse owner and president of the Zionist Party Livshits appears to be waging a stubborn fight. To our demand he responded that 'on principle' he did not recognize trade unions. So just go argue with a person who has such golden principles. The upshot is that apparently the fear of being without service work right in the hot season has compelled that 'principled' opponent of class unions to recognize our union."

Then Comrade Nosn spoke:

"Unfortunately I cannot come with a similarly cheerful greetings from the leatherworkers. Despite all of our efforts, we were not successful in attracting the majority of those workers to the union. In that sector the majority of workers are Polish, Christians, and the opposition, though quiet, covertly maneuvered at just that psychological moment, when the trade union was composed almost completely of Jewish members. That situation was skillfully exploited by the factory owner, who is a familiar of the priest, and the priest spat fire and brimstone from the pulpit against Jews and communists, warning the Polish workers that they were to have no dealings with the 'Jewish-Bolshevik' union. But it is interesting that the young and unskilled workers, those who do the scut work, were inclined to organize, were ready for solidarity at every call, while at the same time the older, skilled workers stood like logs, like stones in the road, with their ever-present doubts about the usefulness of unions, with their constant fear of retaliation, with their continuous reliance on the benevolence of the factory owners. And that opposition was not just anybody. There was the old scraper Fisher, who in '05 had led a glorious strike at that same factory! And there was the master Russia-leather worker Gawenda who had also gone out at the same time with the red banner and in broad daylight tore down the Russian eagle from the city hall! Now those were heroes! Imprisoned!"

Then Comrade Nosn's speech turned to the work in city hall and described, in passing, episodes from the elections. All told the union could count on one seat. Its success was a happy surprise. It appeared that old Jews, craftsmen who went every day "at daybreak" with their tallis bags under their arms to the study house to pray—those same Jews, when it came down to electing their representative, delivered their votes to the heretics, to their brothers in work and want, and not to those fine and upstanding Godlbozhits burghers for whom those pious zealots were electioneering. True, some of those hardworking Jews did so in secret: they took all the number slips but took care to hold on only to the "sixes" and slip them into the election envelope. Shame and fear of those respectable Jews and important burghers was still deeply rooted in them. But it was a step forward for us, for the workers, affirming that we have a large following among the unorganized and even the ignorant masses. One need only educate them, doggedly educate them and put that following to positive use.

"Unfortunately," Nosn went on, "among our own comrades there have been found such . . ."

At that moment the collectively held breath of the audience was interrupted. Stretched above everyone's heads and leaning out toward the presidium table stood a head with hair combed to doll-like perfection and sideburns like a servant's. That freshly coiffed head was pointing its hand somewhere down at itself, probably toward its heart, and yelled, shrieked really, "Do you mean me?! Me? Comrades," he turned to those assembled, "when the doctor wanted to come to us, did we need to admit him or not?! Do we need intelligent and educated people or not?! Comrades!"

"Enough! Enough of that 'shmintelligence'!" came the yells from all around.

Then came the ring of a bell in the hand of that bright-haired girl seated at the presidium table, and everything went instantly quiet. Only Khaykl the sexton's son was still waving his hands, grumbling.

And she, the girl with the bright, simply styled hair, stood up. Her head didn't even reach the shoulders of those standing around her, but it seemed like she was rising and overtaking all of them, looming to the ceiling.

She only said a few words, "Comrade Khaykl, you can record this word for word."

She said nothing else, but remained standing with her large eyes fixed on Khaykl's doll-like face with the sideburns until he sat down. Then she turned to Nosn, "Comrade Nosn, you can go on."

And Nosn described some quite interesting things, straightforwardly, and sometimes even humorously, "Here they were sitting in the city council together with the respectable people—'pepper in the nose, salt in the eyes.' It quite upset them, those well-fed bellies. They especially had it in for Comrade Zalmen. Whenever he opened his mouth they interrupted him. He spoke very flawed Polish. So what? But he spoke to the point, and I assure you, he could learn Polish faster than those bourgeois ignoramuses could learn some political economics.

"Oh! Comrade Zalmen had become a scare word. Thanks to Comrade Zalmen, or rather in spite of him, the Zionist president had first formed a partnership with the assimilationist pharmacist and then even the Jewish pharmacist with the anti-Semitic mayor Wiśnicki. Everyone knew that for years Wiśnicki had been waging—and did so to this very day—a campaign of incitement and boycott against Jews in general and against the Jewish pharmacist in particular. But that didn't stop them from being kissy-kissy and from joining forces against Comrade Zalmen.

"Then the representative of the peasants from the outskirts of the city, Dubczak, put forward a proposal that a paved road be constructed connecting to the Rogów road, because almost a third of Godlbozhits lived along that road. All the city councilmen from the outskirts were in favor of that proposal. The pharmacist had spoken out against it. 'Enough taxes,' he said, 'we don't need a new tax.' The mayor himself and some of the Christian councilmen showed their solidarity with the pharmacist. Dumbfounding! We, the workers, were the lynchpin, and we voted for the proposition. We justified our position: 'As workers we are in favor of every enhancement of the public good, of public use, of giving work to the unemployed unskilled laborers.' The proposal passed. Then the pharmacist started shying abuse at us, cursing that since we don't pay any taxes it's easy for us to talk, since we want the whole burden laid on the poor shops that have already been so crushed.

"I took the floor to clarify: 'It is not true that we want everything put on the shoulders of the poor shopkeepers. Just the opposite: the poor must in general be free from taxes; taxes must be paid by the rich, the wealthy, and be paid heftily, in increasing proportion to their fat profits. The pharmacist's siding with the poor shopkeepers is not at all honest; it is an old, hackneyed means of inciting the poor merchant and craftsman, the poor petty bourgeois against the worker. Of course, we'll soon see whether the Herr pharmacist is so sincere about his paternal guardianship over the petty merchants. I propose that those craftsmen who work themselves, without the help of hired workers, and petty merchants of the last class be completely exempt from the road tax.'"

Nosn had not yet finished his second proposal when the pharmacist and mayor Wiśnicki started whispering amongst themselves in a corner. They spoke so closely into each other's ears that it seemed they were giving each other kisses. Then the mayor took the floor.

"Panowie," he said, "I was against the proposal because I know that the farmer as much as the merchant is burdened with too many taxes. But since your own yids have voted for the proposal, we shall undertake to divide up the road tax. I propose: fifty zlotys for every business license of the second class, thirty zlotys for the third class, and twenty zlotys for the last class and for craftsmen.

"Good, good," the pharmacist agreed.

Then Nosn took the floor, unpacking this provocation:

"Now here are some of them, these fine burghers, these providers for the petty merchants. One does not need to build any paved roads. But if one does so, let it be at the expense of the poor masses. These great wealthy men, of whom there are maybe ten or twenty in the shtetl, let them together give a thousand zlotys, and those few hundred poor merchants who earn hardly enough for a bit of bread, let them put up ten thousand zlotys? Is it not more fair for the poor to be freed completely from taxes and the rich to put up five hundred, a thousand zlotys each. There is really no need to fleece the poor for paved roads from which first and foremost the rich factory owners and merchants, the wealthy burghers, will so grossly profit, until— until the just order will come and the benefit of public institutions will belong to everyone."

The respected burghers of the city raised a hue and cry: "Bolshevik! Go to Russia!" And that fair proposal, naturally, was rejected. That, however, did not prevent them, Nosn and his comrades, from missing any opportunity of exposing the reactionary intentions, hostile to the public, in the good and pious proposals of the bourgeois councilmen.

Shimen breathed a sigh of relief when everything finally ended. Those simple words had spoken to him with such pure logic that it seemed to him he had already known it for a long time. He had heard it somewhere, or better yet, they were really his own ideas that someone had taken from him.

Comrade Moyshe, the one with the philosopher's mane, had mean-time opened the library case and started lending books. Small groups of people had formed and were discussing things. Curious, Shimen caught phrases from all around but pretended that he wasn't inter-ested. From the library desk he heard snippets of book titles: *Political Economics*, *Erfurt Program*, *Marx*, *Engels*. A happy thought occurred to him: he would read these various socialist books, clarifying their thought, their idea; and then here he would stand at last—he, Shi-men Shifris, an educated man—taller, so many heads taller, than those Comrade Zalmens, than those Comrade Goldes . . .

He walked over to the library desk and asked, "Something from socialist literature."

"Whose? What have you already read?" Comrade Moyshe asked.

Instead of answering the librarian's arrogant question Shimen named the work that had already struck his ears so many times, "Marx's *Kapital*."

Someone called out, "That's too hard to start off with. Give him *Theory of Historical Materialism*—you know the one."

Shimen looked around. It was her, the girl with the bright, plainly styled hair. Now he could just make out how those large eyes had the luster of a steel sickle; how her plainly styled hair ended in two chi-gnons behind her ears like among aristocratic village lasses; and her little nose—retroussé, comically retroussé, determinedly retroussé.

He was astonished, Shimen was: such a small village lass, and yet she spoke to you like a real expert with such self-assurance in her tone. Nevertheless, following her suggestion he borrowed the book. He did so graciously, as if obliging a lady's whim. They fell into conversation:

"First time here?"

"First time."

"I've heard of you, Nosn has told me."

And she quickly added, "Perhaps you're going home? I would like someone to accompany me, but I shouldn't like to impose on anyone in particular."

"With great pleasure," Shimen agreed.

"Who's left, comrades?" she called out to the group.

That did not at all please Shimen. The little one was already beginning to provoke.

They left arm in arm. Several other couples followed them out. Walking arm in arm was not altogether comfortable since she was a head shorter than him and Shimen had to bend over. Moreover, there were several mud puddles large enough to have required a child be carried over them. Apparently she sensed this and every now and then would tear herself away from his arm, nimbly jumping over the little muddy streams.

"What do you think, Shifris," she laughed, "you think I'm so helpless?"

"Oh, I don't think anything," he said seriously. "But jumping like that you could fall."

"You'll pick me up. Right? Of course, you're a gentleman after all?"

"That depends."

"Apparently, Panie Shifris. You haven't even introduced yourself to me."

"Better late than never. I'm Shifris, Shimen Shifris."

"Zosia Lerner."

"Zosia?" he asked with disbelief.

"Yes, Zosia. Why the surprise?"

"Officially?"

"Of course officially. Oh, how silly you are with your questions. Just like a grown-up and a little child at the same time. So tell me, do you like the group?"

"Of course I do," Shimen answered. "I'll tell you the truth: I didn't recognize that side of Nosn. A real politician! I talk with him very little about such things."

"You should. Who's stopping you? You're brothers after all."

"I'll talk with you," Shimen let slip out.

She looked into his eyes and drew his arm closer. Her large, steel-blue eyes seemed larger in the tepid light of the electric streetlamps. From the depths of those eyes he was struck by their passion, their spirit. Shimen felt pierced by that look, a look that sought to sneak its way craftily into him. She asked, "So tell me, did those speeches and reports really interest you? Because I don't believe . . . You are such a middle-class, ordinary young man."

He felt a little offended. Of course it interested him. He had thought about such things for a long time, and when Nosn told him about the council meeting and how the wealthy men wanted to foist the taxes onto the shoulders of the poor, he recalled a relevant fact:

She wants to hear? Let her hear. He, Shimen, was secretary of the merchants' union. It was an unpaid position, but he had to do the work because Shpilman, the president of the bank, was at the same time president of the merchants' union as well as delegate to the appraisal committee of the tax office. Sitting together with him on the appraisal committee was Moritz Meierbach. Perhaps they weren't to blame, but the fact was, the petty merchants were done a great injustice by having taxes determined based on sales volume. So they, the petty merchants, came running to Meierbach, to Shpilman: "How can this be? A Jew, whose whole business hardly amounts to a hundred zlotys, has to pay several hundred zlotys in tax?" They ran from pillar to post, but the bottom line was that Shpilman was barely able to persuade the chief of the tax office that a list of the most injured taxpayers be submitted and the chief would consider the matter. He, Shimen, was tasked with drawing up the list. So he wrote and wrote and there was no end to it. Everyone was wronged; no one didn't have to pay. People were barely able to live, barely able to breathe. And what if the list was finally closed and at the last minute someone else came running in with a grievance? He would have to start all over again. It was all so much that Shimen grew sick of it. "The chief won't even read such a long *megile*," he said to Shpilman. But Shpilman gave a wink: "Write!" So be it, he kept writing. And he had barely survived to calculate the total when the great men with their great shares arrived. Are you listening? Here's a Jew crying, having been levied a tax of a hundred, two hundred zlotys, and what does a pharmacist with his several thousand zlotys have to say? What do the Meierbachs with their tens of thousands have to say? Iser Meierbach stuck his hands into his trouser pockets and said the same thing as Shimen: "Such a swamp? The whole city? One person has to pay fifty zlotys and he's also called wronged? Dear me!" Iser Meierbach nearly got a headache—"The chief is obviously going to grab his head! And he'd have a point!"

And what was the upshot? To our great shame the largest portion, the truly wronged petty merchants, were stricken from the list, leaving hardly more than ten big shots, first and foremost the real bigwigs: Meierbach, the pharmacist, Dimantshteyn, and Lozer Kohn. Lozer the Sly greased over that grievance with a verse from the Bible, "Between a sure thing and an unsure one, the sure thing is preferable." And "sure" it was, in Lozer's opinion, that Meierbach's, the pharmacist's, and his own taxes would be lowered, decreased, as opposed to so many people with small sums whom the chief would not take into consideration at all. So how much should he, the chief, ultimately levy?—asked Lozer Kohn—nothing?

Shimen suddenly realized that his story was too long.

"Oh, this can't really interest you at all," he said. "You'll have to forgive me. I'm so stuck in that grim settlement, I see so much, that it's just such a delight when I have someone to unburden my heart to."

But the little lass protested:

He should talk, it really does interest her. Everything that happens in Godlbozhits interests her.

If so, then he can tell her of the city's informer, who was a real plague on the poor merchants and craftsmen. He, the informer, first squeezes money out of the merchants and then goes and informs on them right away. One could get rid of him—there is a lot of evidence against him—but the mayor and the police support him to the hilt. "The only honest Jew in Godlbozhits," they say of him; nor do the great men want to pick on him because he doesn't do them, those great men, any harm. On the contrary, he occasionally does them a favor when needed. This is a tacit agreement between the respectable burghers and the informer: to his face they pretend to curse him, and behind their backs they thumb their noses at the poor, suffering Jews. He, the informer, certainly knows the great men's language; he's skillful with a wink. But he knows that, nevertheless, were he one day to

pick a quarrel with one of them, he'd say good-bye both to his livelihood as an informer and to his trusteeship.

Zosia stopped, and asked, "Who are you talking about? Oh! Of
course you mean Moshke Abishes."

"You know him?" Shimen asked.

"I don't know him well," she said. "But he has taken rather a strong
interest in me. He asks after me."

Then she asked abruptly, "Who is that lovely girl one often sees
him with? His daughter?"

"What daughter? That's his wife."

"A wife?" Zosia was truly astonished. "And she wanted *him*? She,
such a beautiful woman, and such an old man?"

Shimen laughed.

"Quite a match," he said. "Him a respectable man and her a modest
woman." And Shimen went on to explain: "She—Leah 'Stänglmeier'
they call her, because the former Austrian commander Stänglmeier
obtained a permit for a restaurant for her. Stänglmeier certainly didn't
take any money from her. From pretty girls the Austrians much preferred to take 'nature's' payment. He in turn, Moshke Abishes, often
used to come with the gendarmes into the restaurant. He, Moshke,
even then still had a wife, but couldn't give a fig about her—I mean
that wife of his—while she was alive. He would always stay in the
beautiful Leah's room waiting for Stänglmeier to leave."

"And still he married her," Zosia said. "I guess, when one's in
love . . ."

Shimen interrupted her, "She still made good use of his recources.
Were it not for the fact that he was a respectable man, a trustee, and
that he lost a lot of business, she would have spent a great deal."

"I like that stubbornness of his," Zosia said. "It shows that he has
a strong will."

"A fine, strong will," Shimen laughed. "She already has a new lover,
Yoynele Roytman, the one with the busses."

"And he, Moshke, says nothing about it?"

"What should he say? He knows she's close to Roytman. Once,
people say, he even found them together in their house."

"Interesting characters," Zosia said. At that moment she pressed closer to Shimen, turned back around, and forced him to spin around with her.

"Look," she said. "Just look how far our comrades have stayed behind us. You know, Shifris? I really love them, our people. They are so discrete . . . eh? You have nothing to say?"

Something moved in him where his heart was supposed to be. With one hand he stroked the hair over her ear and lightly touched her cheek. She radiated a velvety warmth.

Then, since he knew that he really couldn't develop feelings for this girl-child, but that there where his heart lay something was nevertheless stirring, he began speaking in a lyrical, sentimental tone about what he had been reflecting on that evening: about the celebratory nature that the Sabbath had lost for Jews; about the silver candlesticks that no longer sparkled with the radiance of Sabbath joy; about the emptiness of Godlbozhits' middle-class youth; and about still other things that he had seen through the lens of an earnest bookkeeper in Fayvele Shpilman's cooperative bank.

None of that was at all interesting. It reeked of small-town bourgeois-intellectual psychology. But Zosia didn't want to debate with him. He was so naïve and silly, that handsome, ordinary young man!

"Come on now, don't worry so much! Do you hear? I like you just as calm and satisfied as you are. Don't worry, Shifris. Good night!"

✣ 19 ✣

And What a Bookkeeper Can
and Will Not Understand

He, Shimen Shifris, had nothing to reproach himself for. He defended himself against his newfound love for that little, clever, and sensible woman with the full toolkit of the independent man who knows from his own experience that love is a dream, a mirage, a matter for teenagers. He, Shimen, had already lived through all of that. One can build nothing with that. A person who wants to secure a position for himself dare not fritter away any energy on love affairs and longings.

Nevertheless, he did not manage to maintain his composure, and all of the blame, or credit, for that state of affairs fell on the narrow shoulders of that little woman with the little retroussé nose. She, Zosia, or the little Zenia—as Shimen in a moment of sentimental uplift called her—she made no secret of her love for the petty bourgeois, rangy, and round-faced young man. Day after day she pursued him, spending all of her time with him, speaking to him in delicious, enthusiastic language about people and nature, until finally she no longer needed to seek him out—he came on his own.

Shimen remembered the precise moment when he realized he loved her. It happened not as one might have imagined, in a moment of sincere apology, eye to eye with that little woman, in the twilight darkness. Rather, it happened, despite all expectations, on a bright snowy day, sitting in the bank behind a typewriter.

The day before, she had said, "You're speaking so stiffly, so rigidly today. Shimen, you are afraid, you are running away from love." And he bucked up, answering with a joke, "Love is afraid, it's running away from me." This was on the riverbank, facing the golden sunset, among the low bushes covered with blindingly white snow. It was when he was warming her little hand in his own and could have pressed his cheek unhindered to hers, so velvety and warm. But he did not do that. He took his leave in an old-fashioned philosophical style, "Such, fräulein, such is life . . ."

That was yesterday. But today, sitting behind his typewriter and tapping out an urgent letter on an important matter concerning monies collected for Fayvele Shpilman's bank which another institution in a foreign city had permitted itself, despite the obligatory rules, to hold up; hammering the keys so quickly and irritated by the nerve of that institution Shimen Shifris stopped at that particularly hurried passage with a finger raised, and the keys fell: one . . . two . . . Then it was as though he woke up, forcefully pressed a letter, one of the typewriter's buttons, and again stopped; and before he had finished writing the letter he leaned his head on the edge of the typewriter.

On the frame of the typewriter, where the copy was attached, there appeared, completely transparent, the plainly styled hair with the two chignons behind the ears, like an aristocratic village lass—the head of the little Zenia. Those large steel-blue eyes, so cloudy and sad, that little nose, stubbornly but not pretentiously retroussé. "Yesterday I did you an injustice," he whispered, Shimen Shifris did. "I made you sad, dear girl."

He was so lost in thought that he hadn't noticed the director approaching when he asked with fatherly concern, "Is something the matter, Shifris?"

"I don't feel all that well," Shimen replied, relieved.

"So go home then," the director said. "Once you've slept you'll feel better."

At home a new joy awaited him, a fluttering little note: *Eight o'clock by the little sleds.* The note had been brought, as always, by Simkhe "Revolution," who gave it to Shimen gravely, the way one carries out an important assignment, and went on his way. A good chap that Simkhele! Though still a child, he spoke with a piercing rooster's voice, with the conviction of a well-thought-out idea: "Not today, but tomorrow the revolution must come." And because he often repeated this in his discussions, and because he believed it unfailingly and with the force of a stubbornly naïve youth, his party rivals jokingly called him "Revolution." That's how that name stuck. There was nothing more comical than watching that "Revolution" in a pair of men's trousers and a jacket, with a bucket of paint in one hand, and a brush in the other, spattered from head to toe, with his hair in his face so you could hardly see his eyes. That little rooster, who was already earning a zloty a day from his boss, was absolutely certain that the revolution was just behind the door and was but waiting for him, for Simkhele, to throw that door open with all his might.

But he was no fanatic, no hidden saint, Simkhele. His messiah didn't require him to fast and mortify his flesh. For the time being, one should enjoy this world. When a downy, refreshing snow was falling, as it was today, Simkhele was one of the first to get out on the road. And then, when the road was smooth and shiny, like a polished table, Simkhele's narrow little sled was among the first to zip down swift as an arrow from the peak of the highest hill along the twisting path into the valley and further still—until just a little ways onto the paved road.

Today he won it out for Comrade Zosia. There were always older comrades of better pedigree who got to take the comrade teacher on their sleds. Today, however, he was in luck, the comrade teacher had picked *him*: "I want to have a go with you, Simkhele."

But she hadn't come alone. Accompanying her was that Shifris from the bank who was a "fellow traveler" of the union.

"No harm," said Simkhele, "there can be two people."

He, Simkhele, had only a little space in front as long as he pressed himself down and held his feet in front of him like two oars.

"Of course," Simkhele assured, "this sled goes better and smoother."

The little one persuaded them, doing his best to get them to fit. The comrade teacher visibly agreed. She said nothing but watched Shifris's mouth to see what he would say. Truth be told, Simkhele didn't have a lot of confidence in Shifris. He was clearly embarrassed, that great nobleman, to go riding sleds with that whole group, and instead of admitting as much he kept looking for faults in his, Simkhele's, proven sled: it was too short, too little room, it could flip over.

But Simkhele just watched the comrade teacher's eyes to see what she would say. And when the comrade teacher thanked him, took Shifris's arm, and the two of them strolled off, Simkhele wasn't going to sit shivah for them. On the contrary, he stuck two fingers in his mouth and gave a whistle, which was the signal, and ordered, "OK guys! All sleds in a row! One . . . two . . . three . . ." And, incidentally, he was also really whistling, Simkhele was, at all those white-collar proletarians for whom it was beneath them to associate with working-class children. He whistled at them and at their toffee-noses.

Of course, he was annoyed, Simkhele was; even at the comrade teacher he was annoyed. And they, Shifris and the teacher, strolling arm in arm—a black stain on the white snow—didn't even think about Simkhele. He was a foolish, inexperienced child, that Simkhele, if he thought that a whole world of pleasure and passion revolved around a sled. Neither the comrade teacher, nor all the more so Shifris, were giving any thought now to sleds. They had to be making love, gnawing, aching, and then kissing.

"Why didn't you want to go sledding?" she asked.

"And why," he asked in return, "did you want to? I need you, not the 'gang.'"

She swallowed a word and finished, "After all, it's so enjoyable to speed down a hill on a sled."

"And to be two alone together is not enjoyable?"

"Yes, Shimen," she leaned her head on his shoulder and he cuddled up to her, touching two fingers to the soft skin of her cheek which sent a velvety, electric warmth into his fingers.

"Tell the truth, Shimen," she suddenly straightened her head and looked him right in the eyes. "Were you afraid to ride the sled, that someone might see you?"

"I'm not afraid," he answered. "Who do I have to be afraid of?"

"You're embarrassed."

"Yes, I'm embarrassed," he interrupted, as though out of spite.

"Ah, I understand," she said with irony. "You, a bookkeeper at the biggest bank in Godlbozhits. Perhaps I might be undermining you. Go! I can't, you're insulting me."

She tore her arm away from his hand.

Shimen felt wretched. "Zenia, what are you saying? I cherish you . . . I just hate a gang. I would like us always to be like this, a couple."

They were standing right by a snow-covered bench in the tree-lined avenue called *The Love Allée*. Shimen scraped off the crumbling snow from the bench. They sat down. Zenia had already thoroughly apologized, resting her head on his breast and playing with his hands.

"A couple . . ." she looked up at him with shining, beguiling eyes. Slowly their eyelashes drooped, their eyelids closed, and her narrow lips opened. Shimen leaned his head down, clinging to her lush, dewy lips.

"You know, Shimen," she said to him after a while, "I don't want to live any longer as a subletter at the tailoress'. I am going to rent my own small room. If you want, will you visit me?"

"Yes, Zenia."

"And when people, friends, come to visit me, you won't be jealous!"

"No, after all I know that you work socially."

"You won't interfere with my work! Right? You know, Shimen, if you ever set a condition that I must choose between you and my work, I won't give it a minute's thought—I'd choose the latter."

"I know that," he said in a hushed voice. "I understand that."

"And that I love you, you know that too?"

He was silent.

"Why are you silent?" she searched his sad eyes.

"But you know . . . I have already experienced . . ."

"Go on, child! You cruel boy!" she kissed his mouth, his eyes. "Go on, you handsome one of mine! I am not Feygele Rabinovitsh; I can love, really love . . . sacrifice myself . . ."

And then, with her lush, enthusiastic voice she recounted some of her experiences, but only some, because she was actually a veritable bundle of experiences, and one evening, even a whole week, would not have been enough to tell everything about herself. For Shimen, the serious bookkeeper at Fayvele Shpilman's cooperative bank, every one of her topics was like a sensation. All of the people, feelings, and passions that Zenia talked about with her melodic, charming speech were beyond the limits of Shimen's provincial middle-class experience. Like an adventure tale for children about heroic hunters who do battle with a whole tribe of wild, man-eating Indians, that's how captivated Shimen was by that heroic struggle of the weary workers against the profit-hungry factory owner and his lawful defenders. He envied Zenia's intelligent comrades who sacrificed themselves completely for the workers' cause, who went off to prison and torture, persecutions and hunger for the pure and simple truth that speaks from the books of Karl Marx and his disciples.

In light of such hard, steel will, of such heroic deeds, Shimen cried out as one who had grown small, shattered, "It seems to me that we, petty bourgeois, will always be crushed between those two aggressive forces: the capitalists on the one side and the workers on the other. The former consider our work and our ideas inferior, and the latter don't trust us, they look at us like little parasites."

"You express yourself quite beautifully, Shimen," Zosia said. "Not clearly, but your own way. Did you read those books I gave you?"

But it was as though Shimen hadn't heard the question. Instead of relying on books that he had read he was trotting out his own, Shimen-Shifrisy ideas. He didn't want to be inferior.

"No!" he cried out. "We petty bourgeois are not between the hammer and the anvil. We are a great, great class! We are a great multitude, we are the axle on which the wheel spins. Here are the capitalists above, and here are the workers below, and we, middlemen, spin along by momentum and still always remain the axle . . ." Shimen was charmed by his own words, by his new thought. After all, being a young petty bourgeois man hadn't been a gloomy existence for him. She, however, Zenia, was not, it seemed, swept along by his improvisation. His original words made no impression on her.

"You know what, Shimen," she said indifferently, "you still need to learn so, so much, and above all: to see, to observe reality. You switch too often from one mood to another. That's the whole psychology of the petty bourgeois class. That is hysteria. You have no consciousness of certainty. Every petty bourgeois has at one time been inclined to fantasize about a brilliant capitalist career, and then another time in turn about becoming a resigned proletarian. A capitalist becomes one of maybe ten thousand; but before our eyes tens of thousands are pro-letarianized. So the question is: if indeed a proletarian, then why not a conscious one, a proud one?"

"But we, the petty bourgeois, are nevertheless the axle," Shimen insisted. Zenia smiled.

"How," she asked, "can one speak about a disoriented, confused petty bourgeois as an axle? One has to lean on an axle, an axle has to carry a load, and the petty bourgeoisie are physically and mentally in the process of decline and disintegration. That is, after all, its visible, scientifically founded, almost biological, fate."

"And things are better in the Soviet Union?" he asked abruptly.

"Why the Soviet Union all of a sudden? What do you mean by that?"

"I mean," he said, "Iser Meierbach today showed me a letter from a cousin of his who is in Russia. In his letter he said that he could not write very much, that he was afraid, because letters were being censored, but he did write one thing, that the other day they made a search of his neighbor's place and found a couple of dollars. Well, he's been sitting in prison for three months and they're torturing him there: he must deliver up his associates, the ones he never had."

"You know," she said, "the whole cock-and-bull story of that Jew, who is trembling over the fact that his letters are being censored but who still writes, is suspicious enough for me. But what is interesting to me is why you've taken that speculator's story right to heart, that enemy of the workers' cause?"

"There it is!" Shimen shot back. "Immediately an enemy, immedi-ately to shoot! And when someone hides a couple of dollars, right away the death sentence? Give him a month, two . . . But torture? Shooting?!

She looked straight ahead, and asked, "Have you read yesterday's paper?"

"Yes, what about?"

"You didn't notice anything?"

"What?"

"Think."

"What are you talking about? I don't remember anything."

"Then I'll remind you: on Dzika Street a little sixteen-year-old boy hung a red banner on a streetcar wire."[1]

"Ah . . . Do you mean?" he interrupted. "Oh! I remember—the boy fled and an agent called out 'Stop.' The boy didn't obey, so the agent fired at him and left a corpse."

"Hold on," Zosia interrupted him, grabbing him by the hands. "Wait, Shimen . . . 'Stop!' otherwise a bullet in your back. 'Stop!' otherwise death. Well, that sixteen-year-old boy from Dzika Street after all was not Meierbach's relative with some dollars. How can he interest you? Really Shimen? And how can it interest you that people are sent away for long, hard years in prison for the littlest trifle: for a meeting, for an illegal leaflet? How can all of that interest Shimen Shifris?"

Shimen didn't respond. Zenia lowered her head into her hands and lost herself stubbornly in thought. That lasted too long, to the point that he grew concerned. He delicately took her hands and looked into her eyes veiled in sadness.

"Zenia, dear, what are you thinking about?"

Lightly, with the tips of her fingers, she touched his face, his hands, and said quietly, "I would like to get inside of you, to know, exactly, what that ordinary, dear young man thinks about the girl Zenia? I know you love me, but to follow me? No. For certain you would insist that I cut myself off from everything and everyone, that we get married and live like two little doves, right Shimen? I know you through and through, you middle-class boy of mine! You handsome one of mine!"

She cuddled up to him, clinging to him; and he suddenly realized that he didn't know what to do. He soothed her with fervent kisses, caressing her like a child.

---

1. Dzika Street is a street in Warsaw.

"You know," she said at last, calm and confident, "I am sometimes afraid to tell you much about myself. It has such a grave effect on you. I feel that you want, that you are making such an effort to understand me, but there is a wall between us . . . Do you know," she added suddenly, "that I was in prison for two years?"

"Really? When? Why?"

"An illegal meeting. They found nothing. Otherwise it would have been four years, six years . . ."

They sat for a while in silence, each one absorbed in their own thoughts. All of a sudden Shimen lowered his head into her hands and their lips touched. He did this with a certain respect, almost reverence. She didn't stop him, but after a while she said, "Come, Shimen, it's getting cold; well, that's enough for today."

He walked her home. He held her hand a long time on parting, and left her with visible regret, and still, returning all alone he, to his surprise, detected in himself something of relief. She, the little, weightless Zenia, had grown larger that evening, had become weighty and burdened him with her authoritative knowledge, with her simple intelligence. He, Shimen, had dreamt that he might enclose that girl whom he had come to love within a protective wall of his masculine reason and masculine solidity. But everything was different. He went forth, he was elevated, but not by his own strength—he was pushed forward like a ball. "It's not going well for you, Shimen," he thought about himself, "you've become confused, so go rub your burning forehead with some frosty snow. Rub hard! You're not going to make a hole . . . You need to be calm, you need to be serious. You, a solid bookkeeper, do not need to be an enthusiast."

With such thoughts Shimen turned from River Street right into the marketplace. In the corner by the pharmacist's house he ran into Iser Meierbach who was walking back and forth on the sidewalk.

"Good evening," Shimen said.

"Good evening. Where are you coming from? From a stroll?"

"Yes," answered Shimen.

"Alone?" the fat belly asked.

"Alone," said Shimen, lying. "It's getting so boring in Godlbozhits."

"Don't you know, I'm like that," the industrialist leaned his protruberant belly against Shimen, "Don't you know, I'm the same way: when the long winter nights come you might as well go and bury yourself merrily in your house . . . There's not even anywhere to play a game of cards. At the pharmacist's? That one's hurting for a penny. If he loses he's ready to kill someone, and if you drink a glass of tea with him you can be sure he'll begrudge you it."

"Perhaps you know how late it is?" Shimen asked.

"My watch has just stopped."

"I'll go look in at Aba the watchmaker's."

"Wait, I'll go as well."

The two of them strode over the filthy snow of the marketplace, which, after a market day, was covered with garbage and mud. All of the stores were already closed, shut tight; but from one, Aba the watchmaker's little shop, a small lamp was letting some smoke out into the marketplace.

The fat industrialist barely made his way through the narrow half a door that was open, and swept along with him the chain of the other closed half.

"I don't know," his crafty little eyes laughed out from a face full of pouches of fat, "I don't know. Aba, your door seems to have gotten narrower."

Shimen and Aba burst out laughing at the joke. Without being asked, the industrialist sat down on a chair. The chair groaned.

"Take a look, Aba," said the industrialist. "Something's not right with my watch. It's stopped."

Aba took the watch in his hand and pushed it right up to his nose and shortsighted eyes.

"Alright, let's take a look," he said.

"When can I have it back?"

"Tomorrow."

"Good," he agreed, but he didn't at all feel like getting up from the chair. After all, that was his nature, Iser Meierbach's: as long as he wasn't sitting, it didn't bother him, but as soon as he sat down it was difficult for him to stand back up again. Nor could he just sit idly, Iser Meierbach. He pushed the chair closer to the table and took down off the workbench the first, nicest watch.

"This is a 'Moser,'" he read on the face. "Real trash, first-rate rubbish. There is a 'Pavel Moser,' and that costs ten times as much as this."

"It seems that 'Cyma' is among the best watches," Shimen added.

"'Cyma,'" said Meierbach, "is the best of the ordinary."

"Honestly," smiled Aba, "you're experienced like a trained watchmaker, not like a leather-factory owner."

"Blimey!" Meierbach exclaimed. "You haven't got as many hairs on your head as I've torn out. And now you're talking about watches! Perhaps you want me to appraise a jewel for you? Gold? Platinum? Stupid man! God forbid all of Godlbozhits possessed what's in my little vest pocket . . ."

"And what's become of all that?" asked Aba.

The pouches of fat on the industrialist's face made a grimace from distaste, offended.

"Go ask the Bolsheviks, the scoundrels," he said, as though it were very unpleasant for him to speak about it.

Nevertheless he continued unsolicited:

Go on . . . He should begin recounting from the beginning to the end? Their mouths would gape, their hair would stand on end. Sixteen times in one day a new emperor: Now the White Guards, now Kerensky, now this hetman, now the other one, now the devil alone knows who. And each one looking, searching, plundering. Here they talk about a pogrom, there on the other hand about a tax. And still it wasn't as bad as with the Bolsheviks. Can one say that war is a good thing? Of course it's better to live in peace, without fear. But after all, one could still do business with all those gangs, buy and sell. And as soon as the Bolsheviks came in it all went as bitter as gall. It's not enough that they took everything from you, looted, confiscated. But they set up a "court," if you could call it that: Zaynvl the lorimer and Ivan the peasant, and they pronounce sentence—*Fire!* Is that not murderous? Would it ever have occurred to someone that trading in valuables would result in a firing squad?

How did this all start? Right, next door to him, to Meierbach, lived an elderly Jew, a wealthy currency trader. A respectable Jew, a bourgeois Jew, a noble person, where nobility means kindheartedness. So of course they arrive at that merchant's house in the middle of the night and find the real mess. So they seized him. Why? For what reason? No one said. They only interrogated him about his acquaintances. At that time it still wasn't so draconian. They seized, they confiscated, but they left your life alone. That Jew in turn thought that he was suspected of being a counterrevolutionary and in league with the White Guards; so he gave up his acquaintances: by all means let them inquire if he was involved in such matters.

Well, what were they looking to eat? They arrested, cleared them out to a man. And wherever they found currency, gold, diamonds there was no delay, just to "court" and a bullet in the head. They also searched his, Meierbach's, place, but he was ready for them—sick with a stomach ailment. Nevertheless for the mere suspicion they exiled him as far as the Urals as forced labor. They barely permitted him to bring along his wife.

Having come with his group to the Urals, they were sent to sort old clothes. So let it be old clothes . . . Then they gathered together everything that they could, removing expensive coats, furs, suits, and divided them among the population. He sorted in that way for one day, maybe two, before his talents were recognized and he was made something of an arithmetician.

So, becoming the foreman made things a little easier, and taking stock it became clear: Was that going to be the end of him, to work for a "ration" of half of a black roll and a pound of kasha? So the man looked around: gold was simply lying around in the streets. Here you could buy up expensive diamond and pearl necklaces for next to nothing, and in Moscow they would fetch three times as much. So he hustles. You can't just sit still.

They started to catch wind: fleeing wasn't an option. They were everywhere, the Bolsheviks, and everywhere you were asked: "What is your name? What's your occupation?" You were constantly thinking up ways of getting sent on official business to Moscow. Then you

travel completely free with a document in your hand and no one both-
ers you. Yes, but among the Bolsheviks it was no easy matter. If you
confide in someone and things go cockeyed then you're lost.

And so it happened that lodging with him and his wife was an
old woman who worked in the office there. So she, Meierbach's wife,
confided in her that she had left behind a son in Moscow and didn't
know what had happened to him. As it happened that woman was also
the mother of a child. One thing led to another—and thanks to the
influence of that woman he received a *przepustka* for several days in
Moscow.[2] Naturally they didn't go empty-handed . . .

On returning from Moscow he, Iser Meierbach, was as dejected as
before. The little that he had brought along had sold quite well, but
what meaning could it have that there in Moscow people were raking
gold in the streets. Here they were arresting people, here they were
shooting people—and there they were making a fortune. The trip had
agitated him all the more. He, Iser Meierbach, could not sit idly on his
you-know-what. What could be done here? What solution could he
come up with?

All of a sudden he came to learn that they were going to ship several wagonloads of clothes to Moscow. He, Iser Meierbach, right away
knew what to do. First and foremost he worked hard, took great pains,
worked more than was needed, was everywhere at once, helped out in
the warehouse, with the bookkeeping. Work was for the devil and less
so for people. Iser Meierbach, when he wanted to, worked harder, more
than the best Bolshevik, and the upshot was he received an assignment
to accompany those several wagonloads of old clothes to Moscow.

Of course, in the end he didn't return. He thought to himself, "To
hell with 'rations' and with 'Comrade.'" As long as the pass was still
valid he would stay in Moscow, constantly on the move and living in a
different place. They, Aba the watchmaker and Shimen Shifris, might
own one hundredth of what those things cost that he sent to the Urals
and back. For the most part it was watches that were sent there and

2. *przepustka* (Polish): permit, pass.

what came back were expensive things: pearls, diamonds, gold. The most expensive things were sent by someone dressed as a Red Army soldier. He took a genuine peasant, bought him a military coat, a cap, a knapsack, provided him with a pass, and—*forward march*! He went off as assured as an iron bridge.

However, a boor is always a boor! It happened that bags were being searched at the train station, so that peasant goes and abandons his knapsack, up and runs away. May Shimen own what was in it, but for him, for Meierbach, it was as much as finishing a cigarette.

Then he suffered another setback. This time it was on account of a woman. She was caught and he, Iser Meierbach, was afraid she would give him up. There was no choice—he had to flee, so long as his head was still attached to his shoulders.

And now there was the problem of getting across the border. And obviously he was also bringing a little something with him . . .

At last he stood up, Iser Meierbach did. He still had to get home, it was getting late, but if he had time their mouths would gape! Hard times were endured before the other side of the border was seen.

"One thing one has to admit," the fat industrialist said, already standing in the door, "one could earn a ruble only from the Russians. Never you worry: I didn't have Nosn Garber and Zalmen Komashn-makher as breadwinners. It was just a misfortune with the Bolsheviks, the scoundrels. But remember what I've said: it can't last and it won't last! People won't stand for it!"

✢ 20 ✢

Why It Was Difficult for the Pharmacist to Recover from His Nervous Stomach

After the snow came the frost. The old Jews of Godlbozhits couldn't remember such a cruel winter: water froze in kitchens; in the street people went about with frostbitten noses and ears bundled up; the schools were closed and the children stayed home all day in bed with their clothes on. There were the beginnings of a coal shortage.

That's how the situation seemed in the marketplace. And as for what was going on in Bath Street, in River Street, there in the rotting huts without floors, without windows, the poor people living there with their naked, barefoot, and frostbitten children—as for that, it was too awful to consider. A fear of hearing all those miseries took hold, and the Godlbozhits burghers were generally not so heroic as to be able to listen to such grief and suffering. Any little grief and a bourgeois Godlbozhits Jew gets stricken, God preserve you from it, with colic, and constantly has to apply compresses to his belly. The doctors, naturally, laugh at such folk remedies. Their advice is: eat delicate foods, stay warm at home, and the main thing is absolutely don't worry.

And the Godlbozhits burghers might well have gotten away without terror or grief, because at first the city seemed deserted. The little bit of poverty was hidden away there in some hole and was too lazy to stick its nose out. But some mischief-maker spread word that city hall was allocating half a pood of coal and a quarter pood of potatoes per family, and at the city hall gate a line of ragged and tattered poor people immediately showed up: little old men with frozen beards and children with little brown-blue faces. In their frozen hands some held sacks and some held rags, all patiently waiting in the crisp new frost.

Due to the severe cold, standing in one place in that way was simply impossible. So someone in the line devised a solution and began to stamp his feet in place: one foot up one foot down; another knew a way of rubbing his nose and ears so that they wouldn't freeze; the others imitated the first two, and a moment later as if on command the whole line had started simultaneously stamping their feet and rubbing their ears.

That strange image drew the attention of all of the idlers and curious onlookers. From every corner emerged the porters who went about with their ropes around their hips, without a stitch of work, and from the gates there appeared the woodcutters and sawyers who waited in vain for a load of wood to chop.

They, the bearded and shaggy Rogów woodcutters, sawyers, and carvers employed a proven peasant method for warming themselves. This involved a way of beating the arms together, hopping in the process, and all the while emitting a loud *Hup!*, as they usually did to buck themselves up when hoisting a heavy beam onto a wall or a log onto the sawhorse.

This stampede of people in front of city hall kept getting larger and larger. Someone had let them know about it at the police station. Two policemen, with bayonets fixed to their rifles, arrived at the marketplace and began at first pushing the crowd away from the city hall gate and then driving them into the marketplace. Many people fell down as a result of that pushing; women stumbled over their own ragged kerchiefs, yelling loudly. And all the while on the sides the porters and woodcutters in their patched jackets kept shuffling cheerfully, as if on command, like chopping wood, they crossed their arms with a bang, their feet hopping, their healthy peasant lungs panting with hot breath: *Hup! Hup! Hup!* . . .

It was enough to make the two earnest policemen break easily into smiles. On the one hand, like men who knew their duty, like policemen, they drove the crowd, and on the other, like hometown folk, like sons of peasants, they took in the show.

The crowd had started to disperse. Children were running off in the direction of their homes, hopping on one foot every couple of steps from the cold like chickens on a frost; mothers hurried to their little chicks whom they'd left unsupervised with a rag to suck on; and old people with heavy steps and even heavier boots set their loud footsteps on the frost-glazed cobbles of the market pavement. The last ones to start to disperse were the porters and woodcutters, who weren't in a hurry to scatter for no reason from one end of the market to the other.

But suddenly the frosty marketplace was riven by a loud whistle. Dancing his zigzag way downhill came mad Tevl. Barefoot, in worn and tattered knee breeches and a torn and ragged shirt up to his belt, it was as if he didn't feel the crisp frost. As always he was dragging a fully stuffed bag behind him and a heavy basket in front of him, loaded with goodies: moldy bread, raw rotten meat, broken pottery, old cans, and dead cats.

The loud whistle was his signal: "I, mad Tevl, am here." Nothing more was needed. The crowd which had already half dispersed returned to the marketplace. Children began to run back, yelling to one another: "The loony, the loony!" In the span of a minute a thick circle of young and old people had formed around mad Tevl the way you would around a street performer. People knew that mad Tevl always had some crazy new idea.

Tevl meanwhile laid down his stuffed bag, set his basket down on the ground, and began running around with his crazy eyes ranging over the crowd, looking for his victim.

"You want meat?" and he stuffed a rotten piece of lung into the curious person's mouth.

"Who still wants some meat?" he said, holding a dead mouse in his hand and spinning in a circle, ready to give someone the honor.

"Give him some bread! A potato," a timid voice called out from the crowd. "A potato . . ." The crazy man considered this for a while, dropped the dead mouse, and picked up the bag and the basket. The crowd made way for him, and with a stooped back and tiny little steps he wended his way to the city hall, winking to the crowd that they should follow. Immediately the whole crowd surged in his direction.

The crazy man meantime had entered the city hall courtyard and started banging on the cellar door.

"Wiśnicki! Wiśnicki!" he banged on the cellar door and called in a comradely way for the absent mayor. "Give a potato!"

The crowd laughed, clamored, and applauded the crazy man's joke.

In the midst of the din a ragged boy snatched a roll from a breadseller's stall. The poor seller raised a cry and ran after the scamp with the roll in his mouth. A policeman set out after the boy, while the crowd encouraged the little one, warning: "Run away!"

Meantime a voice called out that the lock had been torn off of the pharmacist's cellar, and people were looting coal, potatoes, and cabbage. The shopkeepers hurriedly closed their stores; in the confusion the bakers overturned the brazier and with their long skirts behind them, were busy piling the baked goods into their baskets. In their haste the rolls fell out and started rolling over the slippery marketplace. The women screamed that they were being robbed. At that merest hint the fine Godlbozhits burghers, the ones who didn't have open stores but who lived on the first floor and lived on interest, were taken ill with diarrhea, hiding behind the stove and clutching their aching bellies to the hot tiles—how refreshing.

In the meantime the crowd in the street had grown larger. Unidentified persons had gotten everyone going, exciting the frozen people. The frozen and hungry crowd had begun to digest the crazy man's joke. Nearby, the mayor's dry cellar smelled of floury, satisfying potatoes and pickled cabbage. The mayor's maid had just left by the side door, carrying a basket full of shiny black coal. The crowd starter murmuring louder and louder: "Potatoes, coal!"

A third policeman arrived. All of them were stationed at the ready in front of the gate to city hall. It was quite likely that the incited mob would get into the building and destroy the place.

But all of a sudden a window up above was thrown upon. The crowd quieted down and turned their gaze upward. In the window, at the window ledge, stood the mayor.

"Citizens!" he called out. "Tomorrow coal will be distributed!"

For a moment it was quiet, and then someone from the crowd yelled out, "It's a lie! They're fooling you! Don't let them!"

"A lie! A lie!" came the cry from every side.

The mayor raised his hand, putting it to his heart.

"Upon my word of honor!" he yelled down. "Tomorrow coal will be distributed!"

"And potatoes?" someone screamed up from below. "We're hungry!"

"And potatoes!" the mayor yelled back down with difficulty. "Upon my word of honor!"

And with that the window slammed shut.

The crowd in the street was still somewhat noisy, loud, but gradually started to disperse. The promise and the word of honor had calmed tempers.

And if the next morning those two staple products still had not been distributed, it wasn't completely the mayor's fault. It seemed that such items—coal and potatoes for poor people—were not in the budget, and for things that were not included in the budget the mayor was not himself permitted to authorize the expenditure. Such a thing required special approval of the full city council, and then it still had to be approved by the oversight authority.

It was therefore neither the next morning nor the one after that Pan Wiśnicki's word of honor could be fulfilled. He got a great deal of grief from this fact. He longed for the next city council meeting, and at that meeting the mayor racked his brains, calling for the proposal of the workers' councilmen and himself to put forward "Support for the Poor."

Large sheets of paper had already been cut into sixteenths, ready for balloting on the proposal, when someone asked a stupid question, "Good, let's distribute the aid! But where are we to get the money for this?"

Zalmen Komashnmakher responded to the upstart, "There's money for everything, but for aid for the unemployed there's nothing? After all there's a budget for that, there are taxes . . ."

"Now you listen here," responded councilman Litwiński, a real brute, "do you pay a lot in tax?"

"Lay them on me, take from me whatever taxes you want, just don't let anyone freeze from the cold! Don't let anyone die of hunger!"

Zalmen said this with all his heart and with sincere emotion, but the burghers led by the brute Litwiński merely antagonized him.

"Beggar!" they yelled at him. "If you own so much then shall they take it from you?"

The corners of Zalmen's mouth turned up in a smile.

"I've really got nothing to take. But you," Zalmen turned grave. "Houses! Estates!"

The brute jumped up and banged on the table, "So you've worked so much for my house, you bum!? You scoundrel!? And for the Pan pharmacist's house you've worked so much?"

Instead of losing his temper Zalmen burst out laughing. He was really enjoying this house solidarity between the anti-Semitic brute and the pharmacist.

His laughter put the brute in a murderous rage. He grabbed a chair and threatened Zalmen with it.

From the sidelines people started interfering. Some encouraged the brute, while others got between them to avert a fight. The peasant Dubczak was thoroughly confused. He was running hither and thither across the half-empty meeting hall, stomping his boots and growling, "That Zalmen is a rebel! He's inciting all the yids to rebel!"

The brute finally put the chair back as he suddenly remembered something. His neck flushed with blood.

"And whose face do you think you're sticking your ugly mug in, you filthy Jew?!" he roared at Zalmen.

There was almost another uproar. The mayor's bell, instead of calming things down, sounded like an alarm.

But in the midst of it all a weak, woman's voice echoed from the gallery. Delicate, like the silver tone of the priest's bell when he goes to visit a dying person, this soulful woman's voice broke in among the shouts of the city fathers, calling for calm, quelling the anger.

The voice came from the priest's wife—a genteel woman with smooth, shiny little cheeks, wearing a pince-nez and a black veil on her hat.

"Might I have the floor?" her little voice echoed sweetly.

Though it was generally not permitted for someone from the gallery to take the floor at a city council meeting, this time an exception was made for the esteemed lady.

She thanked them beautifully, that lady with the shiny little cheeks and the mourning veil on her hat:

She had a plan for the honored and esteemed fathers of the city council: why should another burden be placed on the shoulders of a city hall which was already burdened with so many general city matters. After all, in Godlbozhits the circle of charitable Christian-Catholic women was already active; and what's more, that circle of which she, the lady with the shiny little cheeks, was president, did much, so very much for the poor, needy Christian population. She believed that the Jewish community also took care of the Jews and the Pan rabbi helped the poor Jews. Why, therefore, burden city hall with needless hassles and introduce further disorder into the distribution of charity?

She finished, the lady did, and the mayor thanked her—thanked her in the name of the whole city council and city hall.

Zalmen Komashnmakher rose suddenly from his seat:

"The Herr mayor does not have the right to speak in the name of the whole city council. The workers' faction asks that the proposal be put to a vote, that immediate aid to the unemployed and needy be given by city hall out of the municipal coffers. The unemployed do not want alms from charitable ladies! The workers are against philanthropy!"

His proposal failed, just as all his other proposals failed. But the striking and incomprehensible thing about the whole affair was the following fact: the pharmacist Isidore Sonnenschein voted *for* the proposal of the workers' faction.

A stranger might think that the pharmacist was taking revenge on the Gentiles for the brute's "filthy Jew" crack, which very well may have offended the pharmacist. But the Godlbozhits Jews knew that when it came to national honor, in all of Godlbozhits there was only one Jew who was especially pedantic, and that was the teacher Livshits; the rest would have sold all their Jewish pride at the least injury. The pharmacist for his part was certain that if someone said "filthy Jew," he probably meant all Godlbozhits Jews, the fat doctor and Moritz Meierbach included, but not him, the Pan Isidore Sonnenschein who maintained his household in pure Polish spirit.

The real reason for the aforementioned incomprehensible move on the part of the pharmacist was not the result of some monumental effect, but rather it was done deliberately, with very specific political intentions—namely, the pharmacist suffered from an illness common to almost all the fine Godlbozhits burghers, pious and freethinking alike. It came from the time the Cossacks had sought to hang him for his Jewishness. Then on the spot he was stricken with diarrhea. And since then his stomach ailments hadn't let up. Every remedy was utterly ineffective, and the doctor had but one piece of advice: no excitement, no aggravation.

On the face of it the pharmacist Isidore Sonnenschein might have permitted himself such a small luxury, to live a peaceful life. His pharmacy in Godlbozhits had, thank God, secured a franchise which no one could take away from him, a franchise which would pass as an inheritance to his descendents. For as long as he lived there was no worry about livelihood.

The hard winter and the simultaneous economic crisis that had begun to be widespread in the country were certainly not to be counted among pleasant things, but even so, that was no cause for distress for the pharmacist. Before the frosty winter there had been a mild autumn with its flus, colds, diphtherias, scarlet fevers, typhoid fevers—all illnesses with medicines that had firmly fixed prices in the pharmaceutical tax. No, neither on account of need, God forbid, nor cold, would the pharmacist ever awaken his old illness. Even if water were freezing in the kitchens of poor people's houses butter would be melting on plates in the pharmacist's house and there would be no frost coating his windows. Not to worry—the pharmacist's maid hadn't sold any coal on the box.

If he had to remember precisely, he, the pharmacist, still felt a chill in his belly the previous morning when he got the newspaper. There it was in capital letters: "Strike of the glassworkers in '*Hortensja*'"—"The eve of a general strike of the streetcar-employees in Warsaw"—"Bloody demonstrations of the unemployed in Radom." Had he actually read the article he would certainly have been reassured. He, the pharmacist, an educated man, had to know that a newspaper must print its sensational headlines in large type in order to sell. For all that, however, the articles themselves, both those with the editor's italics and those set in normal type for the rest of the writers—the articles themselves were written by judicious people, professionals, who assessed the situation calmly and collectedly: everything for, everything against, and the bottom line—"The walkouts are spontaneous, the demonstrations are led by people from the underworld, the initial intervention of the authorities will put an end to all of the unrest."

Had he, the pharmacist, read the articles calmly, he would have spared himself a good deal of grief and worry. However, he had no patience for reading (since, truth be told, he had patience only for doing the prescriptions and counting the till), because for two days nonstop the poor man was holding his pants up—his guts, God preserve you, were running out of him.

After that morning paper came the demonstration of the hungry and frozen in front of city hall, which took place right before his eyes. Soon they came to inform him cheerfully that the rebellious mob was taking the coal and potatoes from his cellar. The danger had taken actual form. Hunger wasn't to be trifled with. In truth, the whole affair started with mad Tevl, but when a fool throws a stone into the water—as the saying goes—ten wise men can't get it out again.

He gave some serious consideration, the pharmacist did, to the situation, and as a councilor on the city council he decided that he needed to see to taking some kind of action. Perhaps some public work: repair the roads, dredge the river, or some other kind of work to keep the unemployed occupied? But now it was right in the middle of winter, the ground was frozen and as hard as rock, so how could one talk about undertaking works with such frost outside?

In any event, already being part of city hall he could still not free himself from the nightmare, and that situation persuaded him to vote for Zalmen Komashnmakher's proposal. "The devil's got hold of them," the pharmacist thought to himself about Zalmen Komashnmakher and his ilk, "so let me throw them a bone, let me stop up their mouths. One needn't pick a fight."

The pharmacist's familiars knew that he loved a game of cards, a pert woman, and the kind of ribald joke that makes you slobber with laughter. That's how it was, however, among his close associates, among his peers; with people from the lower class, the pharmacist was as stiff as a top hat. She, Stefe, constantly pestered him that he had to be able to keep the riffraff at a distance. But he had already gotten used to it, "Respect, scoundrels! From a distance they tell you, violence!"

There was really no one but her, his wife Stefe, to thank for his fine manners and aristocratic bearing, so she herself had to witness with her own eyes how her Isidore discussed things with those shoemaker boys in the corridor of city hall as though with his peers.

"Pan Sonnenschein—a regular Joe," Zalmen winked with one of his little eyes.

"What?" the pharmacist asked as though he hadn't understood, and a satisfied smile spread over his fat piggish face. "What? Voted for you? Pleased?"

"Of course," Zalmen said. "Truly pleased—one of us."

And for the first time in a number of years the pharmacist began to speak in a public place with people not of his station. Around him stood Comrade Zalmen, Comrade Enzl, and several other workers' city councilmen, and he opened his heart to them. They oughtn't think to be jealous of him. In the pharmacy too it wasn't today as it used to be. Time was, when the peasant got a good price for his grain, when the worker earned good money, when one needed care, one went to doctors and paid for medicine. But today you come across people in the pharmacy who haggle like they're in a food stall. Just try and make them understand that this is a pharmacy with a fixed rate—just try and make them understand.

Finally, after such a comradely diversion it would have been unseemly for Isidore to do anything but extend his hand, by way of farewell, to those two scruffy men.

Almost instantaneously Isidore noticed his wife who came right up to his face.

"Stefe? Where did you come from? Were you in the gallery?" he asked.

"Put your hat on this instant," she said angrily. "What a disgrace! So you notice me then? You've got some new friends. Fine friends! There's nothing to say. The communists are against philanthropy, and Master Sonnenschein is with them. Fine!"

"Who's against philanthropy? I am only saying that city hall . . ."

"Don't interrupt me," Stefe lifted her head haughtily. "How much courtesy can I still ask of you that you let me speak . . ."

"Haven't you already begun to say your piece?!"

"When I've begun," Stefe drew nearer to her husband, nearly shoving her arm under his, "When I've begun . . . Take my arm, it's such a disgrace! To spite you, today they're setting up a charity committee. I'm going to go myself. Yes! To spite you!"

As to her benevolence, the pharmacist's wife certainly overdid the spite. If the pharmacist's wife went to bring help to the needy, it wasn't in order to spite her husband, but rather because helping those nearby was her innermost desire. She was, one might say, a born compassionate nurse, and perhaps she got married only because there was no such thing as a Jewish convent. Even in her mother's belly she was an alms worker. That, in fact, is what they, her dear, distinguished friends, the ladies of Godlbozhits, claimed, spitefully and meanspiritedly.

First of all she had to drum up the committee, and how difficult and painful that was for her! Madame Broderson was undoubtedly inspired by the beautiful, true Christian act of helping the poor. She had never in her life, however, gone begging, and she didn't know where the doors opened. She was herself accustomed to giving and not to speaking of it. Oh! What had become of those times! Her husband didn't wait to be spoken to: How much is needed? A hundred rubles, two hundred? Said and done . . ." So it is, dear Pani Stefe—those times are gone. The Bolsheviks have ruined everything. Five houses in Moscow, a forest outside of Kiev. So it is, dear Pani, there would be no shortage of wood in the poor people's houses."

Madame Meierbach, too, tried to conjure an excuse:

She, Madame Meierbach, certainly would not refuse, but she could not do anything contrary to her husband. He would take offense, and rightly so. Everyone knew how many people lived off of her husband's factory, but only a few were aware of how many poor people he supported. Perhaps Pani Stefe was also aware? First there were those who were indebted to her, Madame Meierbach: this one for a shirt, sad as it is to say; this one for a skirt; this one for a hand-me-down petticoat; this one for a brand-new pair of shoes. She didn't need to boast, she wasn't God forbid talking about it, and she didn't ask for thanks from anyone. All well and good! But still—you charity cases, not to sin by grousing, you know how it works. When it comes to the city council elections, it didn't matter to Moritz Meierbach, but it did to some wretch, to some tannery boy. Is it then a matter of honor, dear Pani Stefe? Pani Stefe may believe that she thanks God that Moritz didn't get to be a city councilman—after all, he wouldn't have any time even to eat—but it was a slight: to Moritz Meierbach they come for another lovely donation; for a shirt, sad as it is to say, to Meierbach; for a pair of shoes—to Meierbach. And as city councilman they choose some tannery boy, some, forgive me for the expression, shoemaker lad? So go to Nosn Garber! Let him give you coal, let him give you potatoes, let him give you a shirt, sad as it is to say, let him give you . . .

And still they kept wheedling each other, the two ladies did. Whether it was because basically they were women with polite, sensitive hearts, or because Stefe was a real alms worker—either way, Madame Maria Broderson consulted her husband, "What do you think, Stasiu?"

And old Broderson answered solemnly, "If, my dear, it's to help the hungry you can't refuse!"

She went, Madame Broderson did, and so did Madame Meierbach. Her fear of Moritz's reproof turned out to be unfounded. He
responded like a true generous man:

"I'm giving three bushels of potatoes on account. At such a time
when people are hungry and freezing they needn't reckon with their
own pride. Hunger is not to be trifled with. Do you know what's going
on? Do you know how many people once worked for me and how
many do today? Believe you me, when I see a fired worker my heart
sinks. Just yesterday I met Jan Polka from Rogów in the street, with
a bundle of wood, and I swear to you that I couldn't eat lunch from
grief. Just imagine: a Gentile works for me for thirty years, and just
two weeks ago I had to fire him from his job. And how, I ask you, am I
responsible for the fact that he got a crippled leg? At the machines one
has to walk constantly back and forth; at the machines one has to have
young, healthy people, not cripples. At any rate, the Gentile, when he
saw me, took his cap far down off his head, but in my heart I knew he
was my enemy. And why, I ask you, should he be my enemy? What am
I guilty of? I'm in a position to give a person food free for a day, two
days . . . But to give food continually to a person that I don't need to?"

Yes, he did give his speech, Moritz Meierbach did. What did he
want to say about it? A certain amount of the collected money would
need to be reserved for the respectable indigent. Here, for example,
he already had one in mind. That one would quietly die of hunger and
not raise a hand, nor turn to the city for help. God forbid anyone be
allowed to know about it because that would be a great humiliation
for him. He would speak to you, Pani Stefe, but for God's sake not
even Isidore should know about it. He is Yosl Pyekholde, his former
employee.

Is she astonished, Pani Stefe? A person in the Meierbachs's business, she says? She shouldn't be surprised, the Pani. The sturdy Yosl
Pyekholde with his lovely beard was, he should forgive my saying so,
never good for anything. However, he walked the walk with them, as
she, the Pani, knew; he was still someone one could rely on. But today
he couldn't, he wasn't the same Moritz Meierbach, he simply couldn't.

His brother in Russia had to be sent money, he was supporting a sister, he couldn't provide for an entire city.

"Yes, the times, the times," agreed Pani Stefe with sorrow in her voice.

And considering the difficult times that loomed over the important Godlbozhits burghers after the seven fat postwar years, Isidore Sonnenschein began to taste the delicious flavor of his wife's spite—of her aid committee. It was just like a sour dough from which a capable woman magically produces a tasty bread. Since the aid committee, under Stefe's supervision, had begun to collect potatoes, barley flour, and pieces of wood in the pharmacist's back storeroom, Isidore got the distinct feeling of relief in the pit of his stomach, his loose bowels had stopped, as though cured instantly, and were it not for the gloomy, withered faces that rather cheekily snatched the donated bit of food from their hands, without even a thanks, as though it was their right by inheritance, Isidore would now have spat upon the terror he had experienced:

"*Pfui*! What? Pipe dreams, useless! What? To hell with it!"

However, about eight days later, when that donated bit of food had been completely exhausted in the houses of the poor and the crowd once again grew restless: "Food! Coal!" When Stefe had finally had enough of the banging of the alms can. Incidentally, she had to travel to Warsaw to get herself a dress for carnival. When the well-off people had, thanks to the frosty weather, stopped being sick, but the poor people, even though they were given prescriptions free of charge. The pharmacist's nervous stomach again started to torment him. He flew into a rage at everything and everyone. Not even his wife was immune. He cursed the maid and upbraided the clerk for his own livelihood.

"So with what," he argued, "can I support a person? I can't make these two or three prescriptions myself?"

Shmuel, who was standing right by his chair mixing some medicine, didn't respond. To himself he thought that it was unjust for the pharmacist to upbraid him for his livelihood. He, Shmuel, stood at his post in the pharmacy from early in the morning till ten, eleven o'clock at night; summertime he worked like a dog. He, the pharmacist, certainly wasn't serious about firing him, he just liked to blow off steam from time to time.

To buck himself up, Shmuel touched his wallet. There rested the notes for the money he lent. For another year or two he would save up, interest would accrue, and he, Shmuel, had this position where . . . He would open his own pharmaceutical warehouse and be his own man. And meanwhile he, the pharmacist, couldn't get angry. One was not so quick to chide a *person*. In the worst case there was still a union. Shmuel wanted to be an honest person, he didn't want to deal with any unions, but when the pharmacist went about with such power.

Isidore Sonnenschein himself knew nothing of how many enemies he had hanging around his own house. He was rearing vipers at his breast, and even his own wife was just waiting for the moment when she could let him have it and plague him.

For such an opportunity she, Stefe, didn't have to wait long. Let him be brought around to the fact that when one pals around with those not of one's station it turns out one's shaking hands with a scoundrel, a who knows what.

That evening Comrade Zalmen came into the pharmacy accompanied by someone else. Comrade Zalmen delivered a note to the pharmacist and said, "We request a reply in two days."

Said good-bye and left.

The note contained a demand: recognize the trade union; neither hire nor fire anyone without the consent of the union; and do not alter working conditions for the worse without the agreement of the union.

"Now *those* are your colleagues!" Stefe fired off with visible satisfaction.

And he, Isidore, instead of expressing remorse and admitting that his wife was right, completely let loose, yelling and hollering so that he could be heard all the way outside. She, Stefe, was used to his nerves, but she had never before heard the likes of that day.

And perhaps you know who was responsible for Zalmen Komashnmakher's audacity in bringing demands into the pharmacy? Maybe she, Stefe, was responsible, or maybe the one who palled around with those scruffy men?

But go look for logic in a man gone wild, who speaks like a deranged person:

Because he works day and night, suffers, squanders his health, while she, Stefe, nags him relentlessly, cuts him down for nothing.

It was half an hour later when Iser Meierbach came in, and Stefe opened up to him. You see, being wild, Isidore had spoken such words to her that she was embarrassed to repeat.

The pharmacist sat, with his head in his hands, his face white with rage, and said nothing. Iser Meierbach picked up the note, the "demand," and one could plainly see how, while reading the note, his murderous little eyes ignited and the little pouches of fat on his face flushed with blood. Finally, he flung the note away and vented all his rage not on Zalmen Komashnmakher and Nosn Garber, nor on the trade union that was ruining the city, but entirely on the pharmacist.

"You," he said to him, "such a fine man, I really thought you were clever. Now I see that you're only fit for your little bottles and nothing more. You, foolish—you'll forgive me—clod! Just look, just look at that!"

Iser Meierbach picked up the note, pointing at it, "He's frightened of such louse squashers, such snot-nosed boys! Look! If it were me I'd give him a kick in the ass and 'scram'! I'm going to be afraid of Nosn Garber?! They'll get nothing but curses from me!"

Sitting the whole time with his head in his hands the pharmacist added with stubborn resignation, "If it was also like this in Russia, why were you then not so clever?"

Iser Meierbach as good as choked, "You, foolish—you'll forgive me—clod! Don't I have time to think? So I will think . . . And meantime, because you can—d'ya hear? Pay the exorbitant price! Ignoramus! Meantime isn't there still Bolshevism! And when their time comes they're not going to treat you respectfully at any rate. To hell with you! So just listen, just listen up. I'm going to go take it on myself! Foolish—I'll say it to your face—pharmacist! Gonna knock their teeth in! A waste of a good moment's thought!"

Iser Meierbach grabbed the gloomy pharmacist by the shoulders and shook him good-naturedly, "A waste of a moment. Take the deck. To hell and Hades with them!"

The pharmacist came back to life.

"What? What'd you say? Spades? To Hades? Ha! Ha! Ha!"

His piggish face spread with comic enjoyment, a little drool running down his chin.

"Ha! Ha! Ha! To Hades! Spades: eight, nine, below."

→ 21 ←

Shmuel, Uncle Melekh's Son, Met with an Obstacle

Shmuel, Uncle Melekh's son, met with an obstacle. In barely a blink of an eye he'd left his straight pharmacist's path, and then had a very difficult time of it, not being able to extricate himself. Here's what happened:

The trade union had organized a large recruitment campaign under the slogan: "All Godlbozhits physical and intellectual workers belong to the union." To that end a large propaganda meeting was organized to which lecturers from Warsaw were invited.

The success was enormous. Right after the lectures the majority of the assembled but still not organized workingmen signed a declaration with the secretariat of the union. Among those who were enthusiastically carried away and declared their membership in the union was Shmuel Zaydman, the pharmacy clerk. Early the next morning the union for its part sent announcements to the relevant employers that their workplaces from that day forward fell under the authority of the union and it demanded, as was the practice in such cases, that the eight-hour workday, social security, vacation and leave, and so forth, all be observed. It must be said that whatever anyone else did Shmuel Zaydman didn't need to play around with such nonsense as signing declarations. First of all, he was a middle-class child and so in principle didn't need to join their union, which was rather beneath the dignity of a young man of that sort, namely an independent pharmacy clerk. And secondly, in another two or three years he intended to open his own pharmaceutical warehouse, and all of his exemplary behavior there was meant for the time being. Incidentally, all of his meager savings he had entrusted to the pharmacist, so he could crush him like a bedbug.

Moreover, Shmuel didn't, God forbid, mean any ill by registering with the union. The next morning he had already forgotten the whole thing, and the day after that, the crucial day, like every other day of the year, he was far too lazy to get out of bed. Just when the clock turned ten to eight he wrested himself from under the blanket like someone set for martyrdom, pinned on the sleeves of his filthy, torn shirt (begging pardon) somehow attached his white cuffs and his white collar, poured water over his nails and the tip of his nose, sprinkled himself with some cologne (pilfered from the pharmacy), smeared his head with some kind of grease to make it shine, put something to eat in his pocket, and set off to work at full tilt.

Till around midday nothing happened. The pharmacist was still a little vexed and distracted. But nothing particular came up about it in conversation with Shmuel. But it all came gushing out when the fat doctor arrived. The pharmacist turned to him, "You know, doctor, I'm going to be finished as owner of the pharmacy!"

The doctor stared at him, "What do you mean?"

"I mean the union; Zalmen Komashnmakher's getting rid of me."

And with that he handed the doctor the note from the union, the "demand."

Shmuel was as good as innocent in the whole matter. He had at first forgotten about the declaration which he had signed and hadn't made the connection with the signature on the note that the pharmacist was showing the doctor. He was simply curious to know what kind of a note it was, and while grinding a prescription in the stone mortar he looked over the doctor's arm at the note. It seems that that bit of cheek on Shmuel's part utterly infuriated the pharmacist. Quite unceremoniously he tore the document out of the doctor's hand and shoved it right under Shmuel's nose.

"There you go, you can go off to the union, let *it* pay you, let *it* give you work!"

Shmuel immediately understood. He turned bright red and started mumbling an excuse:

He . . . He didn't want to, they forced him to sign the declaration. They said that it was an empty formality. If the Herr wished he could at least go and remove his name.

The pharmacist softened:

Had he done Shmuel some wrong that he would cause him such a disgrace with the unions? Because Shmuel had to know that he paid neither of them any attention: neither Shmuel nor the union. He need only say the word. He was merely wondering, who had made him, Shmuel, a respectable person: the union, or him, the pharmacist? Shmuel should just give a thought to what state he had taken him out of and then made a person out of him, a pharmacy clerk. What would have become of him were it not for him, the pharmacist? At best a tannery boy, like Nosn.

Shmuel took a half-hour break and ran to the union. The secretary gave him a tongue-lashing, "What do you think, this is some children's game? The union should be discredited by making demands and then rescinding them right away?"

So Shmuel ran off to see Nosn who was at the factory. He went in and found the workers at lunch. Nosn was gnawing on some black bread with a fresh onion and drinking from some kind of bottle. Shmuel spoke with him imploringly, tears in his eyes.

He, Nosn, should understand: a pharmacy was not a cobbler's workshop. The pharmacist was going to fire him, he'd be finished, and not even a hundred unions would be able to help him. A pharmacy is a licensed business, a pharmacy had to stay open even on Sundays, a pharmacy was no trifle, in a pharmacy one is not allowed to strike.

Nosn reassured him:

Shmuel should calmly go back to his work. He, Nosn, would see to getting him out of the union. He had said quite recently that such splendid people, pharmacy clerks, needn't be snatched by the union. For such stiff collars one could wait till they came on their own— and they would come! With tears in their eyes they would come! He believed that, Nosn did, just as he believed what he was eating right then was whole-grain bread. Meantime, however, Shmuel needn't suffer any grief. As far as he was concerned, no declaration had been taken from Shmuel. Regrettably he lived with him under the same roof, and was all too familiar with the psychology of the Shmuel Zaydmans and the Shimen Shifrises of this world . . . Oh, did he know them! Shmuel oughtn't worry. He'd be released from the union. He would take care of it for him today.

They had to spend a moment on the question of expelling Shmuel Zaydman at the meeting of the executive committee, and it lasted for over an hour. Nosn took the opportunity to expound his philosophical speculations. Even though no one argued with him he kept trying to convince them.

"Such irresolute, lily-livered members, like Shmuel Zaydman, are only liable to weaken the union's readiness to fight, to dullen its will and perseverance to push through the just demands of those working in the struggle with the capitalists and employers. No!" Nosn cried out. "It is in no way the task of the physical proletarian to persuade the so-called intellectual workers to convert to the union. Those ones always come with demands for immediate and specific gains, mumbling quietly about the 'barbaric' methods of class struggle . . ."

"In a word," Zalmen interrupted, "ripped at the seams."

Spirits were getting high among those assembled, and Nosn, as if it had nothing to do with him, kept speaking:

"Among themselves those people certainly think that they are doing us a favor by belonging with us to a single organization, that they illuminate us with their 'intellectuality,' when in truth it's exactly the other way around. For nearly all of the campaigns that are successfully carried out by employees in Godlbozhits they have only the assistance of the physical workers to thank, but rare it is that during a strike of physical workers we would have recourse to the assistance of the intellectual workers . . ."

"White-collar proletariat," Zalmen completed the thought. "Perhaps, Nosn, we've finally had enough of your pharmacy clerk?"

Comrade Zalmen intended his remark completely in earnest. The union had other concerns than Shmuel Zaydman. The crisis and the unemployment that had begun to be rampant in town had provoked considerable anxiety in the responsible leaders of the union. Shmuel Zaydman was the least link in the chain.

And yet, in a very short time the union had to return once again to deal with the "Shmuel Zaydman" matter, and deal with it very severely. That's what the strict principles of the union demanded.

Shmuel Zaydman had indeed retracted, but the pharmacist's advisers and his own finely tuned senses didn't permit him to believe his worker. According to the fat doctor's advice, he should hire another person at the pharmacy, a girl apprentice—Bebele Rabinovitsh. In principle, Shmuel would even be glad to have back his former good-will. Beneath the pharmacy clerk's filthy torn shirt beat an innocent sentimental heart that throbbed at Bebele's merest approach. Poor indeed was the way he expressed in words his love for the girl with the blue eyes and the wide mouth, and he did so through his pharmacy clerk's knowledge—he began to serve as an eager teacher and friend by explaining the secrets of mixing prescriptions.

He himself did not at all perceive the great harm he was causing himself with his sentimental effusion. After about two months people were already talking about how Bebele Rabinovitsh was making pre-scriptions as well as Shmuel did. And if pharmacy clerking was a pro-fession one could learn in a matter of a few months, then among the marriageable girls of Godlbozhits a pharmacy clerk would not be such an impressive profession, and the value of Shmuel Zaydman's dowry would soon have fallen by half. Of further concern to the owner of the pharmacy: in such a situation he oughtn't pay a man so much money especially in a time of crisis such as this. Naturally the result would be that he, the owner of the franchise, would have to share with Shmuel Zaydman. For two hundred zlotys a month he could today have two people like Shmuel, clerks . . . Nonsense! Today such salaries are pro-hibitive! If Shmuel agreed to give up a hundred zlotys a month, he could keep working, and if not—so be it, meantime he'd have to man-age with that Rabinovitsh girl.

Shmuel didn't felt at all well when he learned of this proposal. Not only did this mean a 50 percent decrease in his salary, but at the same time it also meant a sharp blow, a hammer strike to the head of the rising pharmacy clerk. He felt as though the wings of his pharmacy career had suddenly been clipped. Finished was his steady uphill journey, step by step; finished was his own pharmaceutical warehouse. And what was the consolation if Bebele squeezed his hand in a friendly way: "Don't be afraid, Shmuel, don't have a go at him. If he fires you, I'll go too; I won't work for your bread!"

That was really lovely of her, but Shmuel shook his head in despair. "The pharmacist, he'll find a reason!"

Khaykl the sexton's son was perhaps not the most appropriate person for Shmuel to spill his heart to. Had he given it any thought at all he certainly wouldn't have done so, but Khaykl happened to be the first person to come into the pharmacy right after the pharmacist informed him of the good news. And had the first one to come in been the chimneysweep Shmuel would have unburdened his soul to him as well.

As it happens Shmuel was in luck:

He, Khaykl, held all the important people on a leash. 'Quite right,' they should say, the pharmacist and the fat doctor. And he didn't want to list who else: was there not one dark little piece of business of theirs that Khaykl didn't know about? Did they not have one woman who didn't first have to be registered with Khaykl? Quite right, he, Shmuel, should ask, let them say themselves. What's more, he, Khaykl, he had the whole union in his pocket. And if he led a strike against the pharmacist, he'd have to go and close his pharmacy for now and for ever. "Are you in the union?" Khaykl asked.

"Not any more," Shmuel sighed. "I've removed myself. I'm ruined . . ."

"Don't worry, my friend, Khaykl can register you back in."

"Nosn won't allow it . . ."

"Nosn?" Khaykl thumbed his nose with his brisk little hand. "He's not the boss of me."

And with that he brushed his rings slyly over his palm. That is, one only drinks water for free, my friend.

Shmuel gestured his refusal, "Uh, er . . . Brother, I can't pay much. Honestly, I can't . . ."

Then Khaykl waved his hand, spinning round on his heel:
He hated talking with a poseur. "Good-bye."

Shmuel begged his pardon, snatching out a banknote, and word of
honor he'd get him the rest.

Shmuel was certain that he would be saved by Khaykl's efforts.
And he was still further confirmed in that certainty when the union
had taken on themselves the initiative for a strike. In truth, however, this had very little to do with Khaykl's intervention. In general
recently he had very little influence on the activities of the union. As
a result of that business of the city council elections the whole of the
working class of Godlbozhits saw him as a real servant of the rich and
the nobleman's bootlick. Most especially he lost his reputation among
the housemaids for the fact that his wife, Blimtshe—the one who was
a waitress at the boardinghouse at the Brodersons—he had cheated
his wife of her dowry with his girlish "honor" and mischievously spun
round his checkered hat with a "You're only wasting your breath."

If the white-collar proletarian Shmuel Zaydman deserved for the
working class of Godlbozhits to undertake a hard struggle on his behalf
it was only because a victory for the union at the pharmacy meant
strengthening the position of the organized Godlbozhits proletariat.
At that time in the city a series of interventions, wage campaigns, and
strikes had begun, including the strike in the tile factory, the bakers'
strike, and the strike of the shoe-factory workers. Shmuel Zaydman
was only one small, insignificant pawn on the chessboard of the trade
union, where there were to be found far more weighty and important
figures. At that same time the adversary, the class of employers and
capitalists, had quietly made common cause and had fiercely attacked
the positions conquered by the Godlbozhits proletariat. The central
directives taught that at a time of fierce attack the least significant
pawn, the worst position, can have an influence on the entire front.

But it was nevertheless a sad truth that in connection with the
strike in the pharmacy Khaykl the sexton's son had connived his way
back to the top of the union. He had so yelled his lungs out, had so
intensely needled and bloviated to both sides that an outsider might
well have thought, "That Khaykl the sexton's son is running the whole

show." Incidentally, the striking clerk himself spared no effort to get Khaykl into the delegation sent to negotiate with the pharmacist.

"Khaykl," Shmuel Zaydman assured them, "has a certain influence with the pharmacist."

Indeed, no one from the union administration knew anything of the matter of the bribe that Khaykl received from Shmuel, nor that he, Khaykl, was the chief supplier of women to the pharmacist, the fat doctor, and someone else whose name Khaykl hadn't wished to divulge.

In any event, ultimately nothing came of the delegation, and Khaykl then banged his fist on a table in the union, "The axe will fall; blood will flow!"

And just in case someone didn't believe his words Khaykl grabbed the switchblade from his pocket and opened it, "Guts from the belly!"

The whole time he had meant the pharmacist. But that came as a surprise to a number of quiet comrades since outside of the union Khaykl and the pharmacist were known to be as thick as thieves. He would go into the pharmacy as if it were nothing, and they had even been seen whispering to one another.

Just as the pharmacist promised, the strike didn't bother him in the least. His man, Shmuel Zaydman, had merely spared him the trouble of firing him, because he had wanted to get rid of him for a long time anyway. First, Shmuel was a slovenly slug, sleeping till ten in the morning and always having a load of dirt behind his ears. Second, he, the pharmacist, knew that Shmuel was intending to open a pharmaceutical warehouse in Godlbozhits, and if so—to hell with him! He was only annoyed at that snot-nosed girl, that Rabinovitsh. A girl is really his concern? He should be concerned about some peasant's disease—ten for one! But you, hussy, could become a person, someone respectable; at home you haven't got a piece of bread, so why are you going off to strike? Who put you up to it?

"But they came in, the rogues, didn't even have time to say a word. I'm still figuring it out—I've got no Rabinovitsh."

That's how the pharmacist complained to Khaykl. Hearing this, Khaykl grabbed his head, "Just you say the word! Just give me a signal!

The fat doctor knows a lot? She's the real comrade of 'those' comrades. A real big shot in the union, a real "boss," as true as I'm standing here. I'm telling you, Panie Master, Khaykl's telling you, that the fat doctor himself is caught up in this business. I know a little of what he was busy with in Russia, but not all of it. Khaykl is still a boy!"

He put a finger to his nose and couldn't keep quiet, "That the fat one makes a living with the little one, I've got no doubt. But if you just give me a signal, is getting a girl a problem for me? First-rate, primo, Warsaw girls with the real education, the real 'twist.' Real dolls for sure with great racks, little mouths, 'hot lips' . . . Not that bit of junk with the wide 'yap' and a chest, you'll pardon the expression, sunken like a trough . . ."

The pharmacist went so far as to smack his lips and drool with pleasure, hardly able to breathe from laughing, and swore, "You're going to hell, Khaykele you sly dog!"

But when the day of the market fair came and there was no one to accept and prepare prescriptions for customers the pharmacist stopped laughing. He even suffered some intense grief when he saw how his most loyal customers, who couldn't wait for him, went off to the pharmacy across the street. Isidore Sonnenschein came to the precise realization that every penny of profit that he didn't make—that is, a cash loss from his pocket—no one would make it up to him. And all of his advisers, his buddies, who told him to do without an employee, merely wanted to see how someone else might fare. What harm did it do them that he, Isidore, was arguing with the scoundrels while they were enjoying it?

Those buddies, however, did offer a bit of advice:

He should bring in someone from Warsaw, someone with a degree in pharmacy. What's wrong with that? When it'll cost him another three hundred zlotys a month, is he too sick to be ill? Stubbornness is a tasty morsel, and I'd like to give a dose to those scoundrels . . .

Such were the arguments of Moritz Meierbach, assisted by Stefe. They so importuned the exhausted pharmacist that he paid for travel arrangements to Warsaw, wasting a whole day. And the next morning looking out from the pharmacy's glass door onto the muddy marketplace there appeared an unfamiliar smoothly coiffed woman's head. When someone opened the door the tall young lady withdrew with a dancing gait in soft, blue slippers behind the counter, from the little pocket of her white apron she took out a shiny silver pencil and asked in the genial way of a big-city salesclerk, "What might the gentleman wish?"

This time the one who had been so inquired of was certainly no gentleman. It was Comrade Enzl, a determined, solidly built bakery lad with a pale, bloodless face, and small eyes damaged from working many nights by lamplight. Comrade Enzl was certainly no gentleman; he didn't even answer the question of the courteous young lady, but instead yelled outside, "Moyshe! Come in, what are you waiting for!"

And when Comrade Moyshe, the "philosopher," entered, taking off his cap as his thick black mane fell uncontrolled over his forehead, the young lady, apparently an experienced pharmacy clerk, got right down to business, "We also have in stock Gentleman and Venus, but Olla are the best, superior . . ."

The young lady didn't even blush, because a big-city pharmacy clerk knew nothing professionally of small-town shyness. Comrade Enzl and Comrade Moyshe, however, did turn red and after a while even grew befuddled.

"No, *Proszę Pani*," Comrade Enzl said after a moment, "we've come about you."

"Me?" young lady said surprised.

Comrade Enzl explained, "We are from the union, we are, from the trade union. This position, your position, is out on strike, and you need to leave it immediately. You certainly wouldn't want to be a scab."

Now she started to blush a little.

"I understand, I understand," she said in a hurry. "I myself also belong to a union—in Warsaw, that is. Give me, gentlemen, some time, I have to inform the owner."

The delegation gave her the requested time. She used it not to inform the owner about leaving her position, but to consult with him. Iser Meierbach happened to be there for the consultations.

"What do you think," he said to the young lady, "that this is a union? Employees? Well now, a Warsaw union of pharmacists, intelligent, educated people? They are—forgive the expression—a group of louse squashers, filth. Surely you've seen who their representatives are . . ."

The young lady, moreover, gave her own testimony:

"One comes in with a black head of black hair and another one with such tiny little eyes, like a Kalmyk. God in heaven! Those are the representatives of the pharmacists? God in heaven! I would have sworn they were . . . I thought they wanted to buy prophylactics."

And early the next morning she again appeared like a doll in the glass door, powdering her nose, putting on lipstick, and withdrawing with silent steps in her soft, blue slippers when someone approached the entrance.

That morning, the first one to notice was Comrade Itsikl, the little hunchback and "vice-minister for economic affairs," as he was called, because, after Comrade Zalmen, he was the second chief of the union: he cleaned up, heated the stove, hung placards, distributed leaflets, and all of it done with such joy, with such zest, as if his hump had been created to bear that burden.

And when Itsikl noticed the clerk he immediately notified the comrade delegates, and they went straightaway to the pharmacy.

"Miss, please pack your bags and leave in good health. You, Miss, are too weak to be a scab in Godlbozhits . . ."

Just then the pharmacist came in, and seeing the union members he called out, "Janie!"

It seemed that Jan, the guard at the pharmacist's house, had been prepared in advance because right at that first call he was already in the pharmacy.

"Throw these scoundrels out!" the pharmacist ordered.

"Get out!" Jan repeated and set on the comrades like a wild ox.

The comrades didn't move from their spot. An altercation ensued between them and the pharmacist's guard. Jan tore the lapel off of Moyshe's jacket, Enzl's teeth were bloodied, and Jan got a black eye. The young lady raised a cry, and the pharmacist fled with the till.

Suddenly the little hunchback threw open the outside door and yelled in, "Comrades, run away!"

The comrades did not run away. The police arrived, questioned the young lady, wrote a report, and took the comrades into custody.

The next morning they were taken from detention to the investigating magistrate. The pharmacy clerk was also called as a witness, but she didn't appear; she was already no longer in Godlbozhits. The same day as the event in the pharmacy she had packed her bags and fled to Warsaw. Whether or not it was out of scruples that she fled and left her meal ticket without an employee, she really couldn't have done otherwise. After all, she couldn't have stayed in a city of beasts and bandits.

↣ 22 ↢

Moshke Abishes was leaning on a table in the pharmacist's back storeroom, gently rolling a cigarette, knocking the tobacco with his nail, just smoking and talking as blithely as you please:

They're obviously quite clever, those Meierbachs, those pharmacists, and he, Moshke, is a fool. Certainly he was a fool when he warned: "Remember! Nothing good will come of the union!" When he begged: "Hand over five hundred, and I'll make it so that the whole union, the whole cockamamie thing of theirs, will be shut down." How would he do that? That's not their concern. They just need to know Moshke: What Moshke says, gets done . . .

The pharmacist was standing there, his hands in his trouser pockets, and looking right at Moshke's mouth. It was apparent that he was listening to Moshke only with one ear, while at the same time thinking about something else. Moshke Abishes knew him well, the pharmacist: At any little thing he'd get in a tizzy and lose his head.

"I don't want any shenanigans," the pharmacist said.

Moshke smiled, "Shenanigans . . . Heh, heh . . . When they grab you by the throat: 'Your money or your life!' When those ones go around like bandits . . ."

"That'll end up costing me hundreds," the pharmacist was writhing like a worm.

"In your place I would've let it cost me thousands for them to get nothing out of it!"

"You're being loose with your thousands, beggar!" the pharmacist laughed.

"That you're finally laughing," said Moshke contentedly, "makes me glad."

Moshke leisurely licked shut another cigarette.

"Meantime let's keep to one piece of business. God forbid that he be left even the cigarette ash of five hundred. If he's getting mixed up in the matter it's only because it concerns the whole city. One must not allow a gang of ruffians to govern a city. It's a matter of affection, for the upper crust at any rate, and here one need only lift a finger, grease the wheels. 'When one greases, one drives.'"

"Let them be a matter for other hands," the pharmacist let out.

Moshke blew out the tip of the cigarette.

"That's that," he said, "you don't have to. But is it you who's boss of your business, or Zalmen Komashnmakher? Is it your say, or Zalmen Komashnmakher's?"

"Do you really think," the pharmacist thrust his hands into his trouser pockets authoritatively, "do you really think that I care what the union says? If only I could get a respectable employee, how they'd hold their tongues. Of course, when that Warsaw *pisher* grabbed her bags and ran away."

Moshke cleaned out the tip of his cigarette with a bit of straw.

"I've got someone for you," he said after a moment's deliberation. "Someone who can get the job done!"

"From here?"

"From here."

"A pharmacy clerk from here? With a diploma?"

"With a diploma."

"Who could that be?" the pharmacist wondered. "A Jew? A Christian?"

"I'll tell you who, you see him every day: Śledziński."

"The lame drunk?!"

"He doesn't hate a glass," Moshke agreed, "but he'll fit the bill perfectly: a proper Russian."

"And that anti-Semite will work for a Jew?" the pharmacist said astonished.

"For a drink I'll bring him round to the whole thing."

"Is he really so hard up? Surely he could have opened a pharmacy?"

"The trousers he's wearing are not his . . ."

288   Leyb Rashkin

That information of Moshke's about Śledziński's trousers was more than sufficiently graphic. Apart from his weekday suit of faded green material, Śledziński still owned a khaki-colored holiday outfit, a soldier's cap with a peacock feather, and a chest full of medals. As a fee for finding this position he gave Moshke a promise of a cut of his future salary, and meantime he dragged him off to Moshke's own wife, to Leah in the shop, forcing the dark-haired Moshke to drink with him in brotherhood.

"You're a lovely little Jewboy, as God is dear to me! One lovely little Jewboy in all of Godlbozhits, and your wife Leahle, one beautiful little Esther. The rest—mangy rats, Bolsheviks, and German spies."

The lame Gentile gave Moshke a drunken kiss, and was ready to pawn a medal just for another brandy. He stayed in the shop till well after midnight.

And nevertheless, early the next morning there he was, standing stiffly in the glass door of the pharmacy, his soldierly chest full of medals thrust forward at attention.

A commotion among the workers, and the joy of vengeance among the bourgeois employers. Just let them try to pick a fight.

And when a delegation from the union did try to come into the pharmacy, the lame man hopped out from behind the counter and drew a revolver from his pocket, "I'll shoot you like dogs!"

He didn't have to say another word.

In the union all hell was breaking loose. No one, it seemed, had convened a meeting and nevertheless the hall was full of workers. There was quite a din:

"Why have we been called?! Where's the executive committee?"

Khaykl got up on the table.

"Comrades! The executive committee has hidden! The executive committee has been stricken with fear! The strike committee has handled this action incompetently! Let us express our no-confidence!"

"Why no-confidence?" someone else replied. "They've cooked up this problem, let them eat it!"

"Comrades, calm!" Zalmen called out from a corner. "Comrade Nosn is coming from the factory, we'll consider the question and adopt a position . . ."

"What position?!" Simkhele "Revolution" jumped up. "When they're going at us with their fist, with a revolver, will we be parliamentarians? Playing around with positions? Are you revolutionaries or not? Comrades!"

"Bravo, Simkhele! Bravo!" Khaykl broke into applause. "Bravo!"

Zalmen raised a hand, wanting to say something, but at that same moment there was some jostling from outside, with people pushing through the door and making way with a racket. All eyes were turned to the entrance. Someone who had come in was talking loudly and with his hands, "He gave 'im one punch, then another punch. Blood started flowing."

Through the door two comrades were bringing the hunchback Itsikl in under their arms. His face was pale, like chalk, two pieces of cotton wadding in his nose, and around his mouth and on his little jacket—dried blood. Itsikl had large, terrified eyes and was unable to utter a word.

"Lay him on the bench with his head down," a comrade said.

"Move back a bit, it won't help, it's coming from his nose."

Comrade Zosia arrived. She was carrying a clean towel and some liquid in a little bottle. Someone brought some water. Swiftly, with a practiced hand, she washed the little hunchback's face, then waved the liquid under his nose.

"Comrades, make a little room," she asked.

The hunchback's color returned. His voice weak and nasal from the wadding in his nose he explained:

"I was looking into the pharmacy through the display window. All the boys were looking, so I looked too. Then Moshke Abishes comes over: 'What are you doing here?' he asks. 'What's it your business?' I ask him back. 'You've come from the union to spy,' he says. 'And that matters to you why?' I say. So he calls to the lame guy: 'Look,' he says, 'that's Itsikl from the union, give him a flick on the nose for me' . . ."

Itsikl heard nothing more because the lame one had grabbed his head from behind with his paw and gave it a whack with the handle of the display window, once and then again.

But if the lame man hadn't come from behind but rather from the front, Itsikl wouldn't have let him off. He'd have shown him. He'd have bitten his hands, clawed his face, that would have made the goy remember.

Comrade Zosia smiled. Comrade Zosia completely agreed with the little hunchback; she knew that even though Itsikl was small and weak, he was still a brave young man, and with bravery one can manage quite a bit. But Itsikl shouldn't talk so much, because the blood might start running afresh from his nose.

A moment later Comrade Zosia looked around and asked into the other room, "Where are the comrades? Where has Khaykl gone off to?"

Comrade Zalmen replied, "Khaykl noticed you so he slipped out. But only out of respect for you, comrade. You should have seen the hubbub he was brewing."

"Order a meeting of the full strike committee for five o'clock."

"Alright, Comrade Zosia."

At five o'clock sharp the full strike committee met in the hall. Only Khaykl was missing.

"We'll go on without him," said Comrade Zosia. "Let's begin the deliberations."

But unbeknownst to those leaders the initiative had slipped out of their hands. Khaykl had gotten hold of a revolver and pushed it into Simkhele's hand. Simkhele was as worked up as a young rooster.

Accompanying him was the tall Asher, a young man with a pair of mitts well capable of delivering a blow, but who didn't quite know the right time to use them. Khaykl assured him that the time had come.

They stood behind the closed shutters on the windows of the pharmacist's back storeroom. Tall Asher lifted Itsikl up. Now both of them could see in between the gaps of the shutters: the pharmacist was distractedly pacing back and forth over the whole length of the back storeroom. He was scolding his wife . . . No, he was explaining something to her, completely upset:

"That lame goy—he's going to end up poisoning someone and that'll be it. Twice he confused prescription bottles. Onto a salve he

stuck a label for cough medicine. How nice can you look! This afternoon he came in, that lame one, dead drunk and cursing. No! No!
This can't go on. Maybe send for Shmuel Zaydman?"

The pharmacist's wife bit her nails, and hissed, "And let those
scoundrels win? And let that snot-nosed hussy with the gaping maw,
the fat doctor's favorite, put on airs? Otherwise that's what she'll do!
Wait a little, Isidore, let's just think of something."

And then she added, "I'm going, Isidore. Will you be coming to
supper soon?"

What the pharmacist answered Itsikl didn't hear. Someone had
given him a shove from behind. It was Khaykl.

"Well, what's cooking here," said Khaykl with annoyance.

At that same moment a doorknob was heard opening. All three
moved away from the shutter. Khaykl turned around and disappeared
into the marketplace. The pharmacist's wife, not looking around,
walked right past without noticing them.

"So, going in?" said Simkhele impatiently.

The two of them felt their way along the dark hallway till they
found where light shone through a keyhole and knocked.

"Come in," came the answer from inside.

They went in. The pharmacist, who was seated at the office desk
writing, turned around, "What did you want?"

Tall Asher cleared his throat, "We're from the union, we are, a
delegation . . ."

"Union shmunion, delegations," the pharmacist spat. "I've got no
business with the union. Tell him, Shmuel, if he wants a hundred zlotys he can come back to work tomorrow. For the period of the strike I
won't pay; I pay for work, not for striking."

"You can tell him that yourself," Simkhele answered. "We're not
your messengers. We've come to you on behalf of the union."

The pharmacist jumped up from his armchair, pushed up his
glasses, and looked at the insolent pipsqueak who was challenging him.

"What do you think," he yelled, "we've got Bolshevism here? Snot-
nosed brats!"

"Think about what you're saying!" Simkhele warned.

"Think about what you're saying!" tall Asher said, bounding over.

"Scram! Beat it!" the pharmacist pointed to the door and slyly grabbed his suspenders through the arm holes of his waistcoat.

And just in case the two union men were in no hurry and didn't move from their spot, the pharmacist pushed open a little cover on the office desk, took out a small, shiny pistol, and slipped it discreetly into his trouser pocket with his right hand while his left hand he pointed to the door, "Scram! Beat it!"

Like an echo of his "scram, beat it," a bang sounded in the air, and onto the pharmacist's shiny bald pate there fell a piece of plaster from the ceiling. The pharmacist blanched with terror, and at the same time his stomach churned, as though someone were turning a crank inside it. From pain he tried to sit down, but stood right back up again and looked around to see if there was something sticking to his backside. A moment later he had fainted down into his soft armchair.

It was in that condition that his wife found him. The union men had disappeared.

"Supper's nearly cold," she said reproachfully as she entered, and right away held her nose. "Something . . . Something . . . It's like a garbage can's being cleaned out."

Pani Stefe, it seemed, had more sensitivity to the stench than for her husband. Otherwise she would certainly have noticed right away that Isidore had fainted.

It was only when he turned his chalk-white head around behind him that she cried out and ran straight into the pharmacy for some valerian.

The maid and the governess came running down from the house. They sprinkled him with water and rubbed his temples. Stefe sobbed spasmodically, "Isidore! Isek! Izho!"

They'd barely managed to rouse him. And when he opened his eyes they held two large tears, like kidney beans. Heavy beads of sweat stood out on his forehead.

"What's the matter, dear?" asked Stefe with a tender voice, as she drew close to him, ready to sacrifice . . .

The tears slid down his saggy cheeks, "I'm not well . . . not well . . ."

He hiccupped.

"Oh! Bring me . . . Bring me . . ."

"What, dear? Maybe an orange?"

He held his breath, waved "no" with his hand, and tried with great effort to get up out of his chair but immediately grew weak and lowered himself back down.

"Bring me . . ."

"A lemon?" Stefe offered with sympathy in her voice.

He fixed on her two deadly serious, nasty eyes, and gasped:

"Clean underwear."

✦ 23 ✦

When Yoyne Roytman Is Strong and When He Is Weak

There was such dense steam in the kitchen you could truly cut it with a knife. Turned with her shoulders to the door, fat Malke stood over a well-used frying pan, intensely absorbed in her work: one turn with the spoon, and then licking off its greasy foam. It was not for nothing that she, Malke, had such fat red cheeks and such a plump beg your pardon.

Khaykl had quietly closed the door with his fingertips; he snuck in and gave her a tickle under her arm. The maid let out a choked scream, nearly pouring the fry grease all over herself. But when she looked around and saw the rascal her cheeks turned flame red. She hurriedly buttoned up her overflowing bosom and flirted, "Khaykele, a pain in the hands, Khaykele . . ."

Khaykl put a finger to his mouth.

"Shhh, quiet . . . Didn't you hear me come in?" he asked.

"How could I hear?" the fat maid flirted. "When you walk with such aristocratic little footsteps, you've become quite a Panie Noble-man, you . . ."

"I don't please you anymore?"

The maid blushed to her ears and said evasively, "You never have any time. You only pal around with noblemen."

"If I don't please you," Khaykl said, feigning offense, "then I'll go where I *do* please . . ."

"Oh! He's offended so quickly, the Panie Nobleman!"

Khaykl held her round the waist, "You're going?"

294

"Now? Later . . . I'm just going to give them their sup and lead them to bed."

"You're still not done," Khaykl was annoyed. "It's already ten o'clock."

"Don't ask, what a hell it's been in the house today. Three kinds of lunch: one for the old witch, one for the missus, and one for the gentleman: he's still shitting liquid."

"Sick?"

"Sick!" the maid burst out laughing. "Don't you remember when he shat his pants . . . Since then he eats only kasha with butter."

"Do they know what was the matter?" Khaykl asked.

"Who knows them? At the baker's I heard that he was poisoned on account of that pharmacy clerk, Bebele Rabinovitsh, that he'd fallen in love with . . . When his wife found out she wanted to take her life. She also ate away at him like rust. A real piece of rust, I tell you. Otherwise, could a person really live out a year with her? I should be so lucky that he's preferable to her. At least he'd say something sensible to a person once in a while. I tell you, it was so pitiful to see him coming up with his trousers in his hand. Ha-ha-ha! And the governess was cursing her years that she had to wash them in the bathtub. Ha-ha-ha! . . . Ha-ha-ha-ha-ha! . . . Oh! Khaykl . . . Don' . . . don't tickle . . . Let go . . . Cu . . . curse you . . . Khay-kl . . ."

As luck would have it footsteps were heard coming from inside, otherwise the maid would have cracked up from laughter. One could get a hernia when Khaykl starts in tickling . . . a hernia . . .

And Khaykele, as though it were nothing, smoothed his mane. "Now," he said with importance, "I shall go in to see the pharmacist. He's in need of a favor from me."

In the central room sat the old lady, the pharmacist's mother. She answered Khaykl's greeting with evident disgust. The clever old woman well knew, or intuited, who it was who supplied prostitutes for her son.

In the bedroom the pharmacist lay stretched out on a small sofa. At Khaykl's entrance he didn't react at all uneasily. His trousers were unbuttoned, and he was clutching a hot-water bottle tightly to his belly with both hands, groaning from time to time.

In between groans Khaykl learned that there was absolutely no way that he, the pharmacist, could manage with the lame goy. He was going to have to let him go. That a goy should come into the pharmacy drunk and stand behind the counter. Such a swine—scram! And here he was himself, sick, while his business was faltering, collapsing.

For him, the pharmacist, a couple of zlotys a week was no matter. But when such a slug, such an idle good-for-nothing, comes to him, to Isidore Sonnenschein, and says, "Panie, such and such . . . I can't make it on the hundred zlotys a week." He, Isidore Sonnenschein, was certainly no Tatar, no quack doctor. Just think: You deserve my paying you with a stick, serves you right. Take another fifty zlotys a month! But grabbing him, the pharmacist, by the throat: "Give me money, or else I'll kill you"?! That's roguery, that's banditry . . . Of course, let Khaykl himself explain.

Khaykl shrugged his shoulders: What should he say? He, Khaykl, certainly didn't know what to say. Once upon a time we were rascals too; it had a flavor, an odor to it. Then came the conscription, and we went to see the fine upstanding burghers, to Reb Leybish, to Reb Ayzik, to Yankl Shenker: "Reb So-and-So, poor youths are going off to be soldiers, they need a three-ruble note." Well . . . They gave their thanks. Since the impudent brats made a scene at the tavern they broke their bones so they wouldn't do that again. When one cheeky kid picked a fight with Reb Ayzik's only son, the gang joined in, and in a trice that kid was awash in red soup. That was all some time ago. Today, however, who are the rascals? Brats, snot-nosed kids, who can't even wipe their noses, who don't know how to deal with a person. No decency, no manners—big shots, of course!

"Quite so," thought the pharmacist. "Banditry! What else, I ask you, what would you call it when someone comes to see a person, 'Give me thus and so much or else I'll shoot . . .'"

"Did they really shoot?" Khaykl said, agitated.

"They made to shoot at the ceiling," the pharmacist reassured him. "But what a question, when I've been made sick by the whole thing and to this very day I haven't recovered."

"And there've been no police?" Khaykl couldn't believe it.

The pharmacist held his belly with his hands, grimacing. The pain was clearly bothering him.

"Just listen . . ." He was going to tell Khaykl the truth. He'd finally had enough troubles from the whole business, and all the while the pharmacy was going to hell. Let them go to somebody else! He was a sick, broken man. There was only one thing he wanted to do: however much money the business was going to cost him, better Khaykl should earn it and those people there in the union not get a thing. Or even better: he was prepared to pay that little one a bonus of fifty zlotys a month, perhaps something more. Better all his money and—done! Khaykl, too, would be quite satisfied, as long as he shouldn't have to speak with those scoundrels in the union, as long as it shouldn't go through their hands. Well? What did Khaykl have to say?

Khaykl rubbed one hand over the other, "Don't worry, Panie Master, it'll all be in perfect order. My name's Khaykl . . ."

On the other hand, it wasn't such an easy thing. A pack of youngsters was stubborn. They'd run you through fire just to be stubborn. But it was no matter—he was Khaykl after all, Khaykele the Scoundrel.

Taking his leave of the pharmacist Khaykl went out through the main entrance. He intentionally avoided the kitchen and fat Malke. He didn't have any time now to start flirting, she'd have to wait, the maid. The more he left them waiting, those maids, the more they'd be impatient for his footsteps.

He was already at the union, looking in through the window in search of Shmuel, wanting to go in. But then he thought better of it: One doesn't just dump one's bag of bones any old place.

He went back out into the street, and found Moshke Abishes, "Moshke, are you interested in making an easy couple of zlotys?"

"Make some money," Moshke said, "why not?"

But when he heard what was involved, he calmly advised, "Listen to me, Khaykl, for this you need Yoyne; they've got their eye on me, the 'reds' do."

"Bless you, Moshke, well said. Yoyne will do nicely . . ."

He rubbed his hands together with glee, "It'll be a couple of zlotys, Moshke."

"Will it at least be worth it," Moshke asked, "even though it's a piddling amount?"

"The pharmacist is paying a hundred, and the little one, doesn't he know he's got some money?"

"What a question, if he's got! But I'm afraid he's stingy, pinches a penny."

"Don't worry, Moshke, he'll weep and pay."

They waited till Yoyne had come with his bus from the train, and when he had arrived and the passengers had all left they darkened the bus and sat down to conclude their business.

A little later Yoyne left the darkened bus, stretching his hands to buck himself up, "Bah, it's absolutely necessary! It's got to go!"

From the open door Moshke advised him, "Listen to me, just do it calmly, he mustn't be frightened . . ."

Yoyne went off by a back street. Under his boots the empty market bridge trembled.

"Where is the union?"

"Just there, on the right."

At the entrance stood Itsikl.

"Hey, buddy!" Yoyne called out to him. "Just send out the pharmacy clerk to me."

"You couldn't speak more cultivatedly," Itsikl said offended.

Nevertheless, he sent him out the clerk. Itsikl knew that Yoyne Roytman didn't mean to offend with such an uncultured expression. Yoyne was merely one of the benighted, politically unengaged "masses."

Shmuel Zaydman came out.

"Ah! *Moje uszanowanie, Panie prowizorze!*"[1] Yoyne greeted him.

Standing in the light of the electric streetlamp Shmuel Zaydman, the once self-assured pharmacy clerk, looked like a wet cat with frightened eyes.

"Roytman?" he asked with surprise, and shivering from the cold.

---

1. *Moje uszanowanie, Panie prowizorze* (Polish): My respects, Mr. Pharmacy Clerk.

"*Tak totshno*,"[2] said Yoyne Roytman. "Just come out a little further, I've got something to talk with you about."

"With me?" Shmuel wondered.

They went off into the dark alley.

"Look," Yoyne turned around and pointed at the window of the union, "there they can help you like a bandage for a cough."

Shmuel's face wrinkled and his eyes bulged. It was as if he had only been waiting for someone to tell him that terrible truth. It was supposed to last only a day, maybe two, and here the strike was dragging on for seven weeks. The speeches at the meetings were already growing tiresome, the struggle "till victory" was of no interest to him. He didn't want to be victorious, he just wanted to stay in the pharmacy, mixing prescriptions and safe in the delusion that however little he was paid there was still something to set by. Politics made him jumpy, he didn't want to get involved, and now he came to realize that eventually any day now they would imprison him for some strange transgression. Just the other day a policeman approached him: Why had he abandoned work? How long had he already been on strike and who had instigated him to do so? And what's more, he, the policeman, warned him against acts of violence, and he would hold him personally responsible if the pharmacist were terrorized. May good times come to the hard-working pharmacy clerk! He'd lived off savings for less than two months and still he was having problems with the police.

"What's going on?" Shmuel threatened with his hands. "Yoyne, what's going on?"

Yoyne took offense, "Y'had to go to the union, to those derelicts, did you? Couldn't've come to Yoyne? Who's held in greater esteem: me, or Zalmen Komashnmakher? There's more grease in one word of mine than all of them together. And with the pharmacist I'm closer than you. Studied in the same *kheyder*, gone to the same broads. Whoring pharmacist. So I say to him not to speak to you, he's a relative of

2. *tak totshno* (Russian): the very same.

mine, and he shouldn't make any trouble for me. Otherwise he'd suffer a seizure and he shouldn't bother!"

Shmuel's heart was pounding, "You've spoken with the pharmacist?"

"Words have been exchanged. 'Itsikl,' I say—I don't call him Isidore—'Itsikl,' I say, 'Shmuel Zaydman's a cousin of mine on my mother-in-law's side, I'm responsible for him, *ya ruchayu!*[3] But he won't get out of this for nothing. Two hundred zlotys a month for an educated pharmacy clerk is not a lot. That's what an ordinary driver makes from me.' So he says, 'But he's gone to the union.' So I say, 'None of your business, *ya ruchayu!'"*

They arrived at the marketplace. Coming toward them with a cigarette in his mouth was Moshke Abishes.

"Believe me," Moshke said to Shmuel, "I really don't want to interfere, but it won't do, it just won't do for Melekh Zaydman's son to go around with shoemakers and tailors . . ."

"Don't interfere," Yoyne said and pulled Shmuel aside.

And then when they were alone he stopped and stuck his hands into his trouser pockets, "Just listen, what am I getting out of this business?"

"Well . . . You'll earn," said Shmuel.

"It's no 'well,' it's three hundreds. And Moshke's also getting something."

Shmuel took a stab, "A hundred zlotys, I swear, that's everything I own. After all, when one hasn't earned for so many weeks . . ."

Yoyne interrupted him, "Don't lie down in the box. I can make that in a year."

"Maybe a hundred and fifty . . ."

"Now listen, you," Yoyne was getting angry, "don't be like that vicious cur who cries and shits . . . The three hundreds might be missing a penny . . ."

"And the union?" Shmuel groaned. "It'll be dangerous . . ."

"I shit on the whole union! I'll whip them heaps and Nosn to boot."

3. *ya ruchayu* (Russian): I vouch for him.

The next morning, at exactly eight o'clock, Shmuel was standing in his white apron behind the pharmacy counter biting his nails: three hundred in fresh, crisp money, Moshke Abishes won't get annoyed—when he protects someone, God forbid. But what was Nosn going to say? And what was the union going to say?

The union was asleep, the union it seemed had not anticipated such a thing. Just then Shmuel Rabinovitsh arrived home from synagogue with his tallis bag under his arm, which woke Bebele up.

"Sleep, sleep daughter. So you've got your union! Justice . . . Honesty . . ."

"What's happened, papa?"

"Well, you'll see: Shmuel works in the pharmacy, and you they've left in the lurch . . . Did you have to strike? Well, was your papa right?"

Bebele didn't respond. She quickly threw on her dress, smoothing here and there, flattening an eyebrow with a moistened finger—ready.

The union was closed. Nosn? Nosn was in the factory. Zosia? She knew nothing. Zalmen? He didn't begin to understand.

Then the small group was called together. It was buzzing like a beehive. A delegation was sent to gather information. Correct: Shmuel *was* working. He answered all their questions: The pharmacist sent for him and paid him his full salary. "And Miss Rabinovitsh?" He knew nothing. "Are you deceiving the union?" No answer.

A second delegation with a directive: Cease work immediately.

Children ran after him. A mob of porters, drivers, and onlookers. "Shmuel Zaydman, the union demands of you: quit work this instant."

Shmuel didn't respond. Shmuel stood like a golem. The pharmacist came out from the back storeroom; Yoyne entered from the front.

Yoyne started pushing the crowd away from the door, both hands working, "Is the Pan pharmacist asking for them to be there? No? Well then, march! Quick time!"

A confrontation with the delegation from the union was imminent. The crowd outside was burning with curiosity. It wasn't simply going to fizzle out.

All of a sudden—a policeman:

"Disperse! Disperse!"

A little note in pencil. The Pan Master would be so good as to give in:

Came—signed in, worked calmly—good, attacked . . . again. Threatened? Yes. Beaten? No, just threatened, terrorized . . .

"Disperse!"

In the union they were holding a meeting. Comrades! Calm down please! When everyone wants to speak at the same time we'll get nowhere. White-collar proletarians are also proletarians, and traitors are everywhere. Com-rades! Order! Don't give the police any opportunity to get involved. Answer each attack with dignity. Simkhele! Simkhe . . . Enough of the phraseology . . . Demonstration in front of the pharmacy! General strike! Drivers' strike! The bell is ringing. Com-rades calm!

And in the street Yoyne Roytman started using his hands. All the while he was nearing the pharmacy and pushing aside the boys who were gathering in front of the store window, looking and yelling inside, taunting Shmuel.

"What a black wedding you've got?" Moshke Abishes couldn't understand.

Suddenly the maid at the pharmacy threw open the outside door and poured out the contents of a chamber pot. The boys scattered with a shriek. On the battlefield only Itsikl was left standing, the hunchback, awash from head to toe. He stood, his eyes goggling at the large window of the pharmacy door, as though he was taking offense at it, at that bourgeois door.

"Give it a push," Moshke Abishes laughed, and winked to Yoyne.

Yoyne steeled himself and *wham!* with the toe of his boot between those little feet, then with his knee in the hunched shoulder . . .

Itsikl let out a cry like a slaughtered chicken and lay in a ball on the sidewalk.

"Comrades! You've got blood! He's killed him!"

The young ones ran together, sniffed around Itsikl, and cried into the pharmacy, "Mur-dered!"

"Call for the doctor, right away!"

People ran out of all the shops, from every corner of the market-place. The little group of people waited. One said, "A murderer of a young man, that Yoyne!" Another said, "Oh no! How pitiful, a poor cripple . . ." A third said off to the side, "That'll teach him! Tit for tat . . ."

In the union people were informed. Comrades ran around pale as chalk: Itsikl! Itsikl . . . A kind soul, wouldn't hurt a fly . . .

And there the murderer stood casually by his car and gave the signal—drive! The passing car kicked up a cloud of dust, covering the crowd in front of the pharmacy. The fat doctor choked, coughed, and wiped his glasses, "Carry him delicately, it's a hemorrhage. Hopefully it'll pass."

Itsikl was carried home by two comradely pairs of hands. He looked like a tiny child. He was as white as a corpse.

Dusk. The bus arrived with the blare of its horn. Yoyne jumped down from the cab, his cap pushed down so he could hardly see. A mate whispered something in his ear. Yoyne shoved his hands into his trouser pockets, planted his feet firmly, and spat five meters away: Just let 'em try! He'd thrash the lot of 'em!

It was already getting dark. From every lane, from every house children suddenly streamed out, youths with sticks, iron rods, and shoemaker's knives. There was a din: "Murderer! You've killed a comrade of ours! Bandit!"

Yoyne turned pale, pressing his back firmly against the bus. A circle had formed around him, a wall of youths. Not one of the adults he'd had his eye on.

Suddenly a rock hit him in the cheek. He lurched forward. The circle was getting larger but stayed closed tight. In their little hands were sticks, iron rods, and knives.

Yoyne snatched out a revolver, "I'll shoot!"

The circle drew tighter, "Shoot! Go ahead, bandit, shoot!"

The gang around grew thicker, bolder, drawing closer. Yoyne leaned firmly against the wall of the bus. In front of the menacing muzzle of the revolver stood a forest of sticks, iron rods, and knives.

At the very last minute Yoyne put away the revolver. With a quick jump backwards and he was already on the roof of the bus. The gang surrounded the bus. Hup! Yoyne leaped overhead, swift as an arrow. The gang ran after him with yells and whistles. Yoyne went into his house—the gang pursued him; Yoyne went up the stairs—the gang pursued him; Yoyne went into the bathroom—the door was forced open . . .

"Not here!"

"Where's he gone?"

"Dropped down by the garbage can and disappeared unnoticed."

A day passed, then two. It was a stroke of luck for him, Yoyne Roytman, that Itsikl recovered; it was also lucky for him that the pharmacist gave in to all the demands, and that Shmuel Zaydman submitted himself to the judgment of the party's tribunal. Nevertheless, Yoyne was still lying low hidden in some hole, afraid to show himself in the marketplace.

On the third day there came to Godlbozhits a bus, packed full with Yoyne's "brethren." From the surrounding shtetls they came, alerted by Yoyne's wife. Among them were only two actual brothers of Yoyne's: the big Moyshe, a broad-shouldered coachman with a close-cropped stubbly beard, and the blind Hertske with a closely shaven chin and blind in one eye. They were both Yoyne's "*przyjaciele*," his chums.

Each one of his brothers could have held his own in a fight with ten healthy peasants, but rumor had it that blind Hertske surpassed all of them, could thrash them all.

And it was unknown how the youths found out, but Hertske was a comrade.

The brothers came for a "trial," and as they were well versed in such things they first summoned opposing counsel.

"Who is the prosecutor?"

"Nosn Garber."

But the reply came from Nosn: He knew nothing, he demanded nothing, he was not going to any trials.

"So it's for Zalmen Komashnmakher."

But Zalmen wouldn't interrupt his machine stitches: "Let him wring his hands and feet! No one's got any grievance."

"So what's bothering you so much, Yoyne?" blind Hertske asked.

"The adults—nothing," said Yoyne. "But the youths. Just look!"

Through a hole in his garret room he showed his brother how groups of little children were gathering.

Hertske squinted his blind eye and burst out laughing, "You've had quite a misfortune! So you're afraid of lice?! You need to have us against them? Who are these fleas?"

"Reds."

Hertske's blind eye popped open, the smile disappeared, "Reds you say? Come, friends, there's nothing more to do here."

"And the trial?" big Moyshe asked.

"What trial? Which trial? You think you're involved with an underworld gang? You can just buy them off with a glass of brandy? With them you've picked a fight? Well, I'm not jealous of you, Yoyne . . ."

"To hell with them," said Yoyne, steeling himself.

"And I'm telling you," Hertske warned, his blind eye squinting up and down, "Let me give you a piece of advice: recite your confession and leave your wife a will. You're a goner . . . ho, ho! So you've gone and picked a fight with them? With the reds?"

"Dead is dead," Yoyne said with resolve.

And yet he didn't want to die. Quite the opposite, when his brothers had gone away and he remained all alone hidden in his hole, he was seized with a desire to live. He hardly waited till night had fallen when he stole down into the house, slipped out from underneath his wife's pillow a gold watch and chain, felt the revolver in his pocket, and went back out silently, like a thief, by the back alleys. Unnoticed by anyone he stealthily approached the union, peering through the illuminated window. Inside deliberations were under way.

Yoyne hastily flung open the door and threw himself with some vehemence at the table and those sitting around it, "Here's everything I own! Here's my revolver! Take it, shoot me, hang me, just let my wife and children be fed."

The conferees jumped up from their seats, looking at him as if he'd gone insane. He kept repeating, "It's all the same to me, *vsyo ravno*![4] But my wife and children . . ."

The first to come round was Simkhele. He approached him, threatening with a lean little fist, "You're lucky Itsikl lived! You're lucky the strike was won! Just take your watches and go! We don't need your money! You're a kulak! You've a feeble class-consciousness! Will you still interfere with a strike?! Will you still be a scab?!"

"*Yey bogu*, no!"[5] Yoyne swore, his head bowed.

And then he slowly raised it, "Can I go then?"

"You can have gone for a while now," someone answered.

"Yoyne, take the watch and the revolver and go, don't stop," someone else said more gently.

Yoyne nimbly scooped the objects from the table, and dropped them unnoticed into his trouser pocket, "Thank you very much, comrades, *do svidaniya*."[6]

---

4. *vsyo ravno* (Russian): it's all the same, it's no matter.

5. *yey bogu* (Russian): by God.

6. *do svidaniya* (Russian): good-bye.

⁕ 24 ⁕

The Lost Strike

After the strike at the pharmacy, which was a complete success, came the strike at Meierbach's tannery, and that strike to a large extent was lost. It was tragic, but in that campaign the failure itself was not as appalling as waging a struggle under conditions that condemned that struggle to failure from the very start. Winning the workers from Meierbach's factory over to the union was actually the ambition of the young, spirited leaders of the Godlbozhits professional class union. Unfortunately, there were many internal missteps along the way, and the lousiest of the obstacles in that particularly stagnant provincial atmosphere of Godlbozhits lay simply like a heavy stone in the path of the struggling proletariat: namely, the majority of workers in Meierbach's tannery were Christians. The Jewish industrialist on one side, and the *jaśnie Panas* of the shtetl Godlbozhits on the other side, did all they could to emphasize the difference between Jew and Christian among the workingmen—that was understandable.[1] It was just sad that the older, experienced workers, among whom were such standard-bearers and strikers from 1905 like Fisher and Gawenda, had not once managed to organize even the circle of their own factory, and then they hadn't had the courage to entrust their cause to the hands of the class union whose membership consisted 95 percent of Jews: what would the *jaśnie Panas* say?

Moreover, those two older workers, Fisher and Gawenda, if not being suspected of something worse, had generally lost their good

---

1. *jaśnie Panas* (Polish): fine, honorable gentlemen.

sense and courage. In Godlbozhits, where the mechanization of tannery work had been introduced not that long ago, they, those oldtimers, were the last "golden artisans," the ones who knew the art of scraping a hide with a millimeter's precision. They still had their apprentices whose ears they'd chew off, but the old masters' efforts to train their replacements were in vain: from abroad Meierbach had brought in a shaving machine to give the tanned leather a uniform thickness. For the most part Fisher had to agree that the machine worked as precisely as their artistic hands did and about twenty times faster. This was easy to understand: while they, Fisher and Gawenda, had to feel the precise thickness with their fingers, almost intuitively, with the shaving machine you only needed to set the degree of thickness with the needle, and then you didn't even need to watch—the frame scraped on its own.

"*Mut verloren—alles verloren*," said the German, and Fisher was considered a German.[2] Pondering the nature and consequences of the shaving machine Fisher came to the conclusion that, first of all, the industrialist would have no more use for him, since if for just standing there and doing the monotonous work of dragging the beam of the shaving machine back and forth the industrialist could make due with some common peasant for two zlotys a day, why would he need to pay him, Fisher, five zlotys for the same work? Secondly, that machine was to blame for all their woes, something that he had already told to that Jewish hothead Nosn Shifris more than once in a discussion, and that one, like a true stubborn Jew, didn't want to accept his opinion.

With regard to the first sad consequence that Fisher had mentioned, the industrialist had found a way out of that uncomfortable situation: he, Fisher, could either hang around in the street swallowing spit, or he could just work at the machine. Better still: how much did a peasant make? Two zlotys a day? To him, Fisher, "because of their old acquaintance," he would give two zlotys fifty. Fair?

2. "*Mut verloren—alles verloren*": "When courage is lost—then all is lost" (Goethe).

In point of fact, though, gone were the days when Fisher had done piecework and earned now five, now ten, now fifteen zlotys a day. But for the industrialist's part, for Meierbach's part, it was still nice to make a distinction, to treat a qualified worker better than the peasant below at the soaking bucket.

One of Fisher's resentments was over and done with. He tightened his belt. Instead of cold cuts for breakfast, he now ate hard black bread, and instead of meat for lunch—a small bottle of dark chicory. Aside from that, every Sabbath, after getting paid, he had a substantial drink to buck up his courage, and the injustice of his lowered wages somehow grew more blurry. But the second anger remained—hatred of the machine.

On the one hand, there was the clever wall of fifty groschens more in daily wages that the industrialist had erected between the two old masters, Fisher and Gawenda, and the rest of the workers. And on the other hand there was the fame of the old revolutionaries, the strikers of 1905, on the laurels on which they rested. Such was the honor that the factory workers accorded them as old veterans of the proletarian struggle, while they, the fighters, the heroes, instead of going further on the path of their historical mission, kept creeping backwards to the ruins of their bygone glory days, dragging along with them the non-politically aware workingmen.

All of this meant no small disruption in organizing the workers at the factory to revolutionary acts. Another hitch in the organizing work of the union was the fact that the way work was conducted in Meierbach's factory was far from consistent. Alongside the work at the soaking buckets on the ground floor and at the machines, which was paid at a day rate, the finishing of the Russia leather in Meierbach's factory—at which a total of four men worked, three Jews and one Christian—still remained a matter of handicraft, and it was paid by the piece. Moreover, since Tsadok, uncle Melekh's son, had gone bankrupt for the second time at his pitiful factory, and since he had spent half a year loafing about the marketplace, twirling his mustache and repeating: "He, Meierbach, should be sick for as long as I work for him"—that Tsadok, uncle Melekh's son, with rolled-up sleeves and with hands just as filthy as before the war, again led the finishing at Meierbach's factory. And he did so under the same conditions as before the war—that is, Meierbach paid him by the pair, and he, Tsadok, maintained apprentices on his own account, did the manual labor with them, and worked them to the bone. One therefore needn't be surprised at Meierbach who right after Tsadok had heaped such vile abuse on him gave in to all his conditions. He, Tsadok, was what he was: loose-lipped, a tanner's ass—you'll forgive the expression—who wasn't fit to polish the Meierbachs' boots; but there was no one in the entire province who could match Tsadok at finishing a piece of leather. Customers salivated to get some bit of merchandise that came from the hands of Tsadok the finisher, and in business that's everything.

Working in the Russia-leather section was the Christian Jaworczik, the owner of a small house, which he rented out profitably in the summer, and of a wife who fattened pigs on nothing and sold them for a very high price. Furthermore, Jaworczik also owned several acres of land worked by a farmhand. He subscribed to *The Knight of the Immaculate* to read on Sundays, carried the guild banner in religious processions, hated Jews with every fiber of his being, and generally, despite his tanner's profession, considered himself among the finest Christian burghers in the city.[3]

The other two Jews who worked at Russia leather, aside from Nosn, were a father and son: Yankev-Arn and Mayer Kandltsuker. To look at him Yankev-Arn was a sickly man, but he could still outpray you at dawn. Starting work when it was still dark out and finishing at nine, ten o'clock at night. Rising at midnight, observing all the rituals of hand-washing, reciting Psalms every day, studying *Ein-Ya'akov*,[4] going to the ritual bath every Monday and Thursday, Friday to the

---

3. *The Knight of the Immaculate* (*Rycerz Niepokalanej*) was a Polish Catholic magazine founded in 1920s.

4. *Ein-Ya'akov*: a popular collection of the narrative texts in the Talmud, first published in the sixteenth century.

bathhouse in honor of the Sabbath, the third meal of the Sabbath with the rabbi; basically this was a Jew who loved to toil hard equally for the Meierbachs, for the rabbi, and for God in heaven. No, you couldn't speak ill of Yankev-Arn. Despite his heavy toil, he could ill afford a decent kapote for the Sabbath, and had to make due with a cloth robe.

His son, Mayer, was a friend of Nosn's, a politically aware and educated comrade. Cautious and stooped, like someone who frequents the synagogue, he was ill-suited for the practical work of the union. Always brimming with books and quotations, he said of himself that he still knew so little, that he still had not gotten down to the bottom of Marxism, and that he therefore still had to read so, so much more.

He loved discussing things at work, sharpening his mind. Heedless of the fact that Nosn answered one word for every ten of his, he was constantly developing some idea or other, for however long and however deeply, until he had verged on smacking of outright heresy, and then his father would interrupt him, "It's just about time for you to shut your yap, it's just about time!"

After such a careful intervention by his pious father it usually quietened down.

Four pairs of hands at four tables harmoniously rolling the cork over the Russia-leather hides, making them soft as butter, producing on the shiny, stiff fold a fine "little pea."

With such an assemblage of people and occupations it truly was a difficult thing to organize the workers at Meierbach's factory, especially when Iser Meierbach didn't just sit around on his hands. He was constantly praising this or that worker, inciting one against another, sowing discord among the workers. Helping him in his work was Yosl Pyekholde, that arrogant Jew, who was now going about collecting alms, and who earlier, when things were hunky-dory at Meierbach's factory, served the industrialist like a mangy dog. Since he wasn't good for anything whatsoever the industrialists themselves loathed him; but at conning and spying on the workers he was a real genius.

As for the trade union, it was certainly a mistake on its part that in trying to attract the tannery workers to the union it regularly sought the involvement of the older workers who in their time, in '05, had

gone forth under the red banner. In practice, that method of organizing workers from the top down instead of from the bottom up turned
out to be the wrong way of going about it. And for that misstep the
workers of Meierbach's factory paid dearly, just as other Godlbozhits
workers had more than once paid dearly for learning from their leaders the proper way of dealing with the various ruthless petty industrialists and burghers.

And why did it happen that way? Was it due to some negligence
on the part of the union leaders? Was it a lack of responsibility? Or
perhaps the management of the union was not in the right hands? The
earnest Comrade Nosn was certainly the right person in the right
place, and the jovial Comrade Zalmen as well; and if someone were
to reproach Comrade Moyshe for anything it would be for his gentle
nature, but never any negligence or lack of responsibility.

However, errors . . .

One could therefore blame the leaders of the union for the following: At the time when Meierbach's factory was working at full
steam they showed less stubbornness in organizing first of all the
unskilled workers, the ones who worked at the soaking buckets, at the
"drums," in the drying room, with the lime; the poorest of the poor,
whose lungs were consumed by various corrosive acids, whose blood
curdled in their faces, and the needle-pricking rheumatism twinged
in the joints of their feet. Ultimately, by the appropriate propaganda
and perseverance they would succeed in organizing for the struggle
for their interests only the seasonal workers at the sawmill—all two
of the cheap day laborers. The later union executive committee also
indicated in its report the notable fact in the history of the development of the Godlbozhits union that at the time when the union had
been a model of organization and discipline for all of the surrounding
towns, at the time when in Godlbozhits itself there could hardly be
found a single smaller workshop whose workers weren't organized by
the union, at that same time there still wasn't sufficient energy and
drive to infiltrate Meierbach's factory.

Be that as it may, however, the fact remained that the union didn't
aim only at easy victories—even in its first stage of development—seeing

how it had taken upon itself to conduct the strike in Meierbach's factory, as if almost anticipating the inevitable failure.

Because, in point of fact, this was no ordinary strike. The fate of the largest tannery in Godlbozhits had at that time already been sealed for ruin by the will of its burghers, the industrialists. For the union it was simply a matter of wresting from the predatory, bestial hands of the industrialist Iser Meierbach a portion of the plundered blood and toil which the benevolent law allowed the worker to enjoy.

And here is what happened:

One Monday in the beginning of February Nosn came to work quite early, as usual. It was already light outside, but on the ground floor of the tannery the little factory windows let in very little light. By the glow of the nightlights, which flickered constantly due to the haze of steam, sulphuric acid, lime, lead acetate, and other chemicals, in the half-shadow by the soaking buckets and cemented pits stood sackclothed workers, pulling out white-scalded hides with their tongs. Throwing one hide onto the cement floor, they simultaneously bent right back over and searched the pit with the tongs to extract another piece of leather. That sinister wet work, performed by silent, gloomy men in that basement room, as damp and dark as a grave, gave Nosn the impression of the members of a burial society, fussing over the ritual purification of a corpse. He wanted to say a warm comradely good-morning, and what came out was a kind of a mumble that no one heard. Nosn quickly ran up the steps and went in to his department.

Yankev-Arn was already there, working. His son Mayer rolled up his sleeves. Nosn reached out his hand to him and asked, "What's this? The motor is still silent?"

Mayer shrugged his shoulders. Then Nosn posed the same question to Jaworczik. He responded gruffly, *"A bo ja wiem?"*[5]

The matter was soon cleared up. Old Fisher came in and explained, "The motor broke down, so the mechanic fiddled with it; he'll probably leave the machine soon."

---

5. *A bo ja wiem?* (Polish): Do I know?

Meantime, however, before they quit the machine, Fisher had nothing to do. He perched himself on the middlemost empty table, between Yankev-Arn and Nosn, crossing his hands one over the other, and, like a Jewish mother who's finished washing the dishes, married off her daughters, and has nothing left to worry about, he broke out in a wide, bourgeois yawn.

He allowed himself to indulge that pleasure, old Fisher did: the industrialists wouldn't be coming till around ten. Besides, it was all the same, one way or another there wouldn't be more than a month's work left in the factory. The factory was closing.

"And you've let yourself be convinced that they're going to close the factory?" Nosn said. "An industrialist needs a profit."

"He'll close it," Fisher reaffirmed his position. "Of course he'll close it. The young Meierbach told me so himself. He's losing serious money."

"So that's it!" Nosn stood up straight. "Hard times . . . Crisis . . . A good opportunity to cut back on workers, lengthen the workday, push down wages. You, workers, toiling away, eating straw, that's alright, but the factory he won't close. The industrialist will have his profits."

"And I'm telling you that he will indeed close it. It'll be closed for him."

Fisher leaned in close and said more quietly, "Twice already they've gone bankrupt, now for a third time. Once—fine, twice—fine, three times and all their teeth'll get knocked out."

Nosn interrupted his work, crossing his hands.

"Oh, what naïve people you are!" he exclaimed. "Meierbach went bankrupt once and he saved his beautiful house by putting it in his wife's name. He went bankrupt a second time and here you've got all of the calamities: a beautifully outfitted factory, a sawmill, two buses. And you, Fisher, what'll you be left with if they fire you tomorrow? You might as well tie a stone around your neck and jump in the river."

From the neighboring room Tsadok stuck out his head. He was busy stretching an upper over the form and was plainly listening carefully to the conversation. If it was a matter of bankruptcy, he was something of an expert, so he too had something to say:

"My enemies should own what's left after a bankruptcy. After all, don't you see what I've got left . . . What Leybele Pipe and Shmuel Rabinovitsh have got left. *Melokhe-melukhe.*[6] Believe me, it's harder for them to earn a zloty today than me."

Nosn was getting upset, "Heartbreaking! So, go sew yourself a bindle and gather them together at the city!"

And then a little more calmly, "Who is talking about such beggars like you? You call that a bankrupt! To go bankrupt you need to know a little something and have something to lose! When one loses three hundred thousand in a bankruptcy and adjusts it by a quarter there's still something left for breakfast and dinner as well."

"And who's to blame for all of that?" Jaworczik asked suddenly. And right away he answered himself, "People have grown undisciplined. Today a peasant wants to live like a lord, a worker wants to give his children an education like the greatest industrialist, whether or not he's in a position to do so, he doesn't want to think about that."

He wanted to say something more, Jaworczik did. He knew the true causes and their remedy as well. Here's the proof: he, Jaworczik, really did have a bourgeois wife, she really did fatten pigs that sold for real money, and they really did sleep in the cowshed while renting their little house to summertime visitors for good money. He wanted to tell them all of this, but Fisher interrupted him, "And I'm telling you, my gentlemen, the machine is to blame for all of it."

"So what do you suggest doing about it?" Nosn pushed back.

"Oh! When all the workers join together like it was in '05, that'll be a solution. You don't need much, ten nails or so, and you can disable the best cylinders, the best machine-knives. Short of any advice now?"

"Old stories," said Nosn dismissively. "No politically aware worker would say that today; that's what the industrialists say."

Nosn waved his hand and went back to work. Every time he got into polemics with these people, with these oldtimers, he got annoyed at himself. Their ideas wandered off on wild paths where the guardians

---

6. *melokhe-melukhe* (Hebrew): a trade is a kingdom.

of the decaying capitalist authority lie in wait with stinking torches and seduce them into the labyrinth of an industrialist's petty ideas. If one could just take all those workers and bring them into the union at least for one evening, seat them on the benches and start teaching them the basic principles of proletarian thought, that's the way to go about it with the children of the Godlbozhits working class!

But it always worked out quite the opposite:

He, Nosn, at every such opportunity had to pursue the obscure train of thought of those enslaved, degraded working men; and after such a conversation he himself felt degraded. He felt like a good chess-player playing against a laughable opponent, helter-skelter so you also start making flawed and ludicrous moves.

All of a sudden the shrill whistle of the factory siren sounded. The motor started shaking the building. Fisher jumped up and went off into the machine department. Here at the Russia leather, too, they took up their work with redoubled energy to the rhythm of the motor's movements.

Ten, fifteen minutes before noon the mailman came into the factory building. He came in and started distributing letters for the workers to sign for. When he arrived up in the machine department they already knew what the letters meant. The "wet" workers ran up to those who knew how to read and there they read in all of the letters one and the same theme: the Meierbach tannery was notifying them that on the 20th of February all workers were to be let go; due to the crisis the factory was closing.

Fisher might even have spared himself the trouble of taking the letter and reading it. After all, he had actually known everything beforehand and could have lorded it over Nosn with bitterness. But for order's sake he extended his left hand to the mailman and, not inter-rupting his work, with his right hand lowered the weight on the shav-ing machine, and then with the same hand slid the leather under. But the one hand was not used to doing the work of both so swiftly. The weight fell at full force and smashed all the fingers of his right hand.

The old man didn't even let out a groan, just turned as white as chalk, trembled, and fainted. Someone ran over and lifted the weight.

A battered rag of flesh and blood began frothing before his eyes, swelling. His blood flowed. They tried to revive the old man. He let out his first groans of pain. The blood kept flowing. Someone ran to ring for a doctor. Iser Meierbach had disappeared somewhere. Moritz Meierbach generally didn't come to the factory. The news over the telephone so rattled him and made him so sick that he couldn't move at all. In soft felt slippers and a warm floral dressing gown he stood at the telephone and let himself be informed about how the misfortune unfolded.

A barber surgeon was brought to the factory. He bandaged Fisher's hand. Soon a doctor arrived hurriedly by taxi and ordered the wounded man be taken immediately to the hospital.

Meantime wives had started to arrive with lunch for their husbands. In their little baskets were clay pots covered with sackcloth and rags so that the food wouldn't go cold on the way. Fisher's old wife dropped her clay pot on the doorstep of the factory. Potatoes, cabbage borscht, and shards of clay mixed with the mud in the doorway. The old woman stood there, beating her head against the wall, tearing her grey hair and repeating in a single breath, *"Jezus Maryja! Jezus Maryja!"*

Seeing how she didn't move her crazed eyes from the smashed shards, an outsider might have thought: "Look how a stingy peasant woman pities the loss of a clay pot and a lunch of cabbage and potatoes."

The rest of the wives broke into sobs, so much so that it began to try their husbands' patience. Their moaning and groaning grated on their ears. When the car with the wounded man had driven off, with great effort they urged their wives on home and they themselves gathered in the spacious Russia-leather hall.

No one had called them; they came on their own. They turned their heads guiltily from one to another and didn't talk. A dull fear, like that of a frightened flock of sheep, drove them together. There was still no Meierbach. At the shaving machine in the empty machine hall someone had stealthily, and very quickly, washed off the bloodstains from the iron countertop and the floor.

And in the Russia-leather hall people were still gathering. With the heavy tread of tanners' boots they arrived, wiping cold sweat and bloody dust from their faces with shabby sackcloth aprons. The hall was packed. A quiet murmuring started. Then someone climbed up on the table, stretching out a hand, "Com-rades!"

It grew quiet. Nosn spoke. In simple words he described the life and labor of the tannery workers—their own lives of hard toil and need, of the hydrochloric acid that ate away at their lungs, burning the skin of their hands and faces, of the thick extractive steam that seeped into their knuckles and joints, pinching like pins and needles; of knives and needles that every moment threatened amputated hands and mutilated limbs. He spoke about the starvation wages that the industrialists paid their slaves for their hard labor, about the pain of a hungry family, about decaying rags instead of clothes for one's body, about the bare blue-brown feet of little children slapping around outside in the snow. And he compared all that to the wealthy children in warm fur coats, the ladies in Karakul and sealskin, the industrialists with tender hearts who couldn't watch a worker of theirs covered in blood at the machine, but was rather informed by telephone, probably not even interrupting his breakfast.

Then Nosn went over to where the non-organized workers were generally found. He spoke to them in a leisurely way, with the kind of calm in which compressed air felt ready at any moment to explode. One would have to be a heroic person to be able to govern that jumble of revolutionary ideas and appalling injustices, to keep to that one straightforward thread: what to do now?

After him, others spoke. Actually they didn't so much speak as pour out their heavy hearts. Old Gawenda told how Jan Palka, who had been fired from the factory some time ago, had received no aid from the social security office. Moritz Meierbach had been informed that according to the people in the social security office the matter of Jan's crippled feet was a congenital flaw—his father Maciej Palka from Karczówka also suffered from crippled feet. But that wasn't true. Everyone remembered that Jan got those wounds after being hit by a pole from the polishing machine, and earlier still he'd developed his severe rheumatism from the wet work of guiding the hides.

Lips were loosened. Someone said something to someone else and then everyone was talking at once. This one had been chiseled on the price, that one on his break time. Even Yankev-Arn had something to say. In tones of incredulity, he tore into Nosn:

"Fifty groschens per Russia-leather hide—let it be fifty groschens. Sure, there's troubles in the world, but pay the fifty groschens! No, d'you hear? For a debt of a whole month he just gives me a promissory note. 'If you don't want it,' he says, 'then don't work. I,' he says, 'am not gonna break my neck for your sake, I'll get notes too.' 'But why don't you give the goyim notes?' I ask. 'So you're a goy now too?' he says. 'At any rate a goy, a yokel,' he says, 'doesn't understand what's going on, but you, a Jew, ought to understand a bit of business . . . It's not going well, not going well at all.'

"That tricksy note for a month's pay ended up a formal protest. So the industrialist converted it into a new note for a further three months. So that's what he, Yankev-Arn, was owed for four months' work; the girl sits at home without shoes, there's not a stick of wood, and if it gets so bad you can't bear it, and you gird yourself and go to the fat one to make an accounting of the debt, he berates you: 'What d'you want, Yankev-Arn? You want me to go thieving for your sake? I give up! The devil take me, I'm worse off than you. My head's more broken than yours.'"

And when he, Yankev-Arn, got to talking, he could have recounted from beginning to end every wrong since he had started working in the factory. All of the blows and ear-lashings of the master craftsmen, the injustices of the industrialist. Not a single day would have been missed. But Nosn didn't have time now to hear him out. He was already in the other corner of the hall talking about something with Gawenda. A small sheet of paper was produced. It was written in large, crude letters in pencil.

A resolution was unanimously adopted: they called upon the factory owner immediately to pay all owed wages, all break time, and to promise appropriate compensation. They gave a deadline of ten o'clock the next morning. If by that time the industrialist had not given a positive response a strike would break out immediately in the entire factory.

The initiative for communicating the demands and leading the strike was entrusted to the hands of the trade union, and it understood its duty, despite the difficult conditions which accompanied undertaking its task. Nosn's supposition that Meierbach's closing the factory was only a ruse proved to be false. Quite the contrary, it was confirmed that already for two weeks not one raw hide had come into Meierbach's factory; people were only pressed to finish the hides that were already there. In town they were also aware that Meierbach had purchased a large tannery in Białystok, a factory with the most up-to-date machines.

In view of its pitiful situation the union made only modest demands: to pay all owed wages in cash, to promise just compensation, and to pay back all fees illegally levied on the workers and deposit them in the health insurance fund and the social security office so that the fired workers would be able to benefit from the unemployment assistance.

Nosn and Zalmen went off with the demands. Iser Meierbach was eating lunch. They waited. After lunch he showed them into his office. He was completely full and calm, "What would you like to say?"

They handed him the paper. He cast a mere glance at it and set it aside on his desk.

"What business do you and your union have with me?" the industrialist asked without anger. "Do I owe you something? Are you entitled to something from me?"

"We have come in the name of the workers," Nosn said.

"Then let the workers, who are making demands of me, come themselves," said the industrialist, still calm, but with restrained anger. "Nosn, from me you've got coming to you, for the eighty Russia-leather hides, fifty zlotys. Here, take it, and that's good-bye." He laid out three banknotes on the table. "And the rest is of no concern to you. What business do you have with me?"

The delegation stood and waited. It seemed to them that the industrialist still had something to say. Iser Meierbach handed Nosn the three banknotes, "Here, take them . . ."

Nosn whipped the little pieces of paper back at him, "You'll pay me together with all of the workers. In the factory office. We have come with these demands in the name of the union, in the name of the workers. So answer: yes or no."

Iser Meierbach did not respond right away. His little eyes burned with murderous rage, the little pouches of fat on his face flushed with blood. But he restrained himself and turned to Zalmen, "Would you be so good, young man, and go inside for a moment, I need to discuss something with Shifris."

"Don't go!" Nosn said to Zalmen, and then to Meierbach, "There are no secrets between us, I've got no secrets with you. You can speak freely."

Meierbach leaned his hands on the desk, looking right into Nosn's eyes, thought for a while and said, "Freely is freely. Why, I ask you, when you've got there your unions and your deals, why do I not just go there to meddle with you? Why is that not my affair? And is it your damned business whether I pay my workers or not, whether I notify the health insurance fund or not? Such an intimate you are with my business?!"

The industrialist was fairly trembling with rage. Nosn looked him right in the eyes, "Today?"

"Today, I warn you, you'll be sitting in prison if you don't want to go sit somewhere else . . ."

Nosn turned pale and said nothing in response. Zalmen made a pretense of bursting out laughing, "Ha-ha! Into the 'clink.' Pan Meierbach's threatening us with the 'clink.' Well, well . . . We'll just see who does what to whom . . ."

"What'd you say?"

"That's what I said: We'll just see who does what to whom."

And pointing with a little finger, "You're not such a big shot, Panie Meierbach!"

Instinctively Meierbach grabbed at his trouser pockets, putting his right hand in his wallet. Zalmen again burst out laughing, "Don't be frightened, Panie Meierbach, we're not carrying any bombs, you can search us. But I'm telling you, you're not such a big shot, Panie Meierbach."

"Good-bye, Panie Meierbach."

The next morning the strike was declared. In the course of the strike the union was also in charge of the legal situation of the fired workers. Many abuses on the part of the ruthless industrialist came to light. Nearly half of the workers weren't enrolled in the health insurance fund. Iser Meierbach simply called each one of them in separately and said, "If you want to work, you have to refuse the health insurance fund. I don't have free money to waste." In one case an inspector from the health insurance fund put together an official report, and then the worker in question himself had to go and ask the inspector not to make a big deal out of it. The inspector didn't understand the request, and the worker returned with that answer to the industrialist.

"So go work for the health insurance fund. I'm not running a hospital," said the industrialist as he sent him away.

Then the desperate worker ran back to the inspector.

"Panie," he warned him, "you're risking my livelihood, my life you're risking. You should know I've got only one solution: it's either kill me or kill you!"

That's when the inspector grew frightened and ripped up the report.

In other cases they did enroll in the health insurance fund, but the entire sum was deducted from the workers' pay. And then that first week it came to light that Fisher, who as a result of his misfortune had to have his hand amputated, had not been enrolled at the social security office, like so many other workers. The hospital doctor wrote up a report for the starosta's office and the starosta punished Meierbach with a two-hundred-zloty fine. Apart from that, in the starosta's office they explained to Fisher's wife that she had the right to demand compensation from the industrialist for what she should have received from the social security office. But as subsequent investigation determined, after listening to the witnesses, including the mailman and Jaworczik, with whom Fisher had spoken on that fateful day, it seemed most likely that Fisher got his hand crushed intentionally in order to be able to benefit from that compensation. He did this—the investigation determined—after having learned that he was losing his job. In general— the report went on to note—Fisher had been spreading anarchistic ideas for a long time, inciting the rest of the workers to stick nails in the cylinders and countertops of the machines so as to disable them.

Relying on that report Meierbach put in an appeal against the punitive measures of the starosta's office to the higher authority. The higher authority considered the motives of the industrialist, dismissing every charge against him and overturning the punishment. But Fisher's family wasn't assuaged. One of Fisher's sons, a worker in a metalwork factory, showed up from Warsaw. He threatened to take revenge for his father on all of the industrialists; he'd shoot Meierbach like a dog. The police got involved—the young man was arrested and later packed off to Warsaw as part of a prison convoy.

Meantime, events in the factory were unfolding one after another. Rumor spread among the striking workers that Meierbach was going to remove the merchandise from the factory, unfinished.

The news proved to be well-founded.

One rainy night, when the striking workers were least expecting it, heavy wagons from the big city pulled up in front of the factory building.

Someone knocked on the gate. It seems that the watchman had been appropriately informed and prepared, since as soon as he heard the first knock he was right there with a bunch of keys and threw the gate wide open. Quietly, as if carrying out a major robbery, the raw and half-finished hides were taken out of the vats; quietly the bales of creaking shoe-soles were packed in the storage containers and carried down to the yard. Quieter still and with held breath all of it was loaded onto the wagons and spirited away on the road into the dark of the night. When at dawn the workers grasped what had happened there wasn't a single hide left in the factory, and on the road no trace of the wagons.

✧ 25 ✧

Uncle Melekh Eats Heavenly Preserves

Shmuel Rabinovitsh really was something of a swindler and a cheat, but the difference between him and Uncle Melekh, he should forgive me, was like fine satin to coarse sackcloth. First of all, Shmuel Rabinovitsh was a person who knew how to hold a pencil in his hand, and secondly, he was simply a clever Jew.

"So what's the matter," he argued, "if they don't pay their notes? Take it to the notary. And what do you think the notary'll do? He'll eat it. But no thank you: it's already protested, it's already been taken to court, and the bailiff's already arrived. What will he take from me? My soul? What do you see: I've got it, and I won't give up?"

"You don't buy property for foreign money!" Uncle Melekh banged on the table. "For my toil you bastards'll buy yourselves property?! Robbers! Bankrupts!"

Shmuel Rabinovitsh turned as white as chalk.

"So what's the matter," he asked quietly, "if one goes bankrupt? Meierbach's gone more bankrupt than I have, but still he's not been eaten up."

Anger was so choking Uncle Melekh that he could hardly speak.

"Shmuel!" he threatened with a finger. "You just think it over well: it's only dead that you'll surrender my debt!"

Shmuel Rabinovitsh's wife rarely interfered in her husband's business, but she couldn't allow anyone cursing at the father of her children. With the well-used frying pan in her hand she came out of the kitchen and yelled into the other room, "You're a little older, Reb Melekh! No one knows whose future it is. My husband has girls to marry off!"

She was right about one thing: Uncle Melekh didn't need cursing. But her husband didn't gain much out of his wife's pious wish. It
certainly didn't matter to the dotardly Melekh Mitshes. It had been a
long time since Shmuel Rabinovitsh had been afraid of Uncle Melekh.
If there was any fear it was of the uncle's dull-witted sons: Reb Tsad-
okl, Reb Moyshele the lame, Reb Arele, and the rest of the children of
Melekh. Like true boorish youths they bled him day in day out. Still,
no one wanted to believe the former timber merchant, that he was left
without a penny to his name, that it was said simply: a pound of bread's
a pretty penny.

He was still thought of as a hero, and he had his partner, Leybele
Pipe, to thank for that reputation. That Leybele had quite the gift of
gab. Property in Rogów—he boasted to people—was a gold mine for
one's descendents. But one needed to have several thousands to get
a brickyard up and going, and then there would be no worry, thank
God, about making a living. There would still be something left over
beyond what one needed to live off of too. Eh? What do you think?

Pleased with the new project, the brickyard, Leybele took a bigger
puff on his pipe, and lifted a little shoulder: "Eh? What do you think,
Shmuel?"

What should he think, Shmuel Rabinovitsh? Of course he thought
that a little cheating was a good thing for business. One might actually
say that business without a little cheating is like fish without pepper,
like soup without parsley. But he, Leybele Pipe, had a knack for building a business *only* on cheating. So, I put it to you: just try and eat a
dish of only pepper.

It was admittedly a nice arrangement: He, Shmuel Rabinovitsh,
was ostensibly the brains, and Leybele Pipe was a fool, a braggart, and
a good-for-nothing. Nevertheless, Leybele had got hold of a piece of
land in the city and sent him, Shmuel, to live among the Rogów stones.
But that's easily said—"sent"—because, in point of fact, he himself
longed for the village, and dragged his wife and child along with him.

As much earlier, when he was sitting pretty, as later, Shmuel Rabinovitsh loved to calculate with his pencil, "Milk is so much, potatoes are
so much, bread gets baked . . ."

He grabbed his beard, pushed his cap far back on his head, and chastised himself, "And you know, it's fine for the Karczówka nobleman to live in the village, but not the big muckety-muck Shmuel Rabinovitsh, no?!"

But when he finally got to the village and got a sense of how his fortunes would fare there that same bit of pencil soon set out a different set of calculations, "Kerosene costs twice as much as electricity, for a pound of meat you have to send someone into town special, and even for an egg the peasant charges more than in town. That's the way of that peasant: if he can't fill his little basket, he sees no point in selling."

So he beat a retreat back to the city.

And when he finally got back to the city he ran to make a small exchange with Fayvele Shpilman in the bank, saw him with his fattened belly, and once again poured out his wrath upon Leybele Pipe.

"What a mangy rat! You call that bankrupt?! Melekh Mitshes's lousy few hundred dollars are still owed, and that lame Moyshele is chasing me around like a faithless wife? That's what I call, you'll pardon me, shitting yourself!"

"Why aren't you complaining that they shouldn't chase you around?" the Pipe asked trickily.

But instead of answering the wise man's inquiry, especially as the Pipe insisted, Shmuel Rabinovitsh explained the whole affair at length:

"Look at that Meierbach! He's already defrauded ten people, and who knows? A German may come, someone may invite him to lunch, and he'll get whacked in the side, and hush-hush . . . When I owed Fayvele Shpilman three thousand dollars who rushed to help me out? Get drunk on less of my blood? Ten percent and 8 percent a month. What was the hurry? Widows and orphans needed to chase me around? Melekh Mitshes has got to curse and swear at me? Who needs to owe money to such lice?"

From his vest pocket he took out a tiny nub of a pencil, sat down next to the table calculating for maybe half an hour, until finally he stood up all of a sudden and slapped the piece of paper as a witness, "Say what you like, my wife, but in the village it will cost half our income. And not having Melekh Mitshes by my side every day is worth something too."

———◆———

And Shmuel Rabinovitsh was finally ready again to head off to Rogów, as long as he didn't have to look at Uncle Melekh's face. But Uncle Melekh had gotten up earlier and gone on ahead, and he went, poor thing, with a heavy bag on his shoulders.

When all is said and done, Uncle Melekh had to have fared quite badly to have been persuaded to go from stone-house-owning burgher down to the level of a village produce seller. He certainly didn't do it with any pleasure.

After the strike in Meierbach's factory real hardship was felt in Uncle Melekh's house. The only thing Shmuel and the house shared was the fact that he came home every night, very late, to sleep. Even in good times extracting a penny from him for household expenses was out of the question—Uncle Melekh didn't even try. He, the uncle, was generally averse to making such demands of someone, even if he was owed. Shmuel Rabinovitsh really did complain to people that Uncle Melekh was bleeding him. But a heartache of grief was the uncle's lot, not Shmuel Rabinovitsh's.

Indeed, if the uncle approached Shimen and told him, "Shimen, give me a few zlotys," Shimen certainly wouldn't have refused. Shimen was not such a miser as Shmuel, Uncle Melekh's son. But again the same thing: if a month ago Shimen had left the house and didn't find it necessary to drop in once in a while to see whether the uncle was still alive or whether the fire had been lit in the uncle's stove . . . the uncle certainly still wouldn't have gone to him.

But Nosn, the one who brought his meager earnings home, remained loyal to the last moment, and when he needed a zloty for the union, or for something else, he came and said, "Uncle, give me a zloty, or fifty groschens."

But when Nosn also lost his livelihood, Uncle Melekh finally had to start doing something. He couldn't do a lot, he was an old man without a groschen to his name. But sitting around with his arms crossed was no plan either. But he couldn't go sticking his hand out begging, God forbid.

"It's hopeless," said Uncle Melekh, his mind made up. He was going to be a village produce seller. A few notions, a piece of soap, a needle and thread, a box of matches, and on the return trip: a few eggs, a hen—whatever God sent his way.

He tried to persuade Nosn to go with him, but he didn't follow him. Uncle Melekh understood him and in his heart agreed with him, "A young man, a craftsman—it would be beneath him, after all, to carry the baskets."

But one evening, two weeks before Purim, Nosn came home from the union and declared, "I'm going with you."

"If so," the uncle had become very excited, "then we might be able to bring along a little fabric too."

"And money?" Nosn asked.

"I plan on borrowing some, perhaps Yitskhok will lend some . . ."

"I'm not going to go talk to him," Nosn said.

"I'll go."

He went, the uncle did, but it seemed he was not at all pleased to go. At first he spent a long time stubbornly scratching under his beard. Yitskhok was at that time one of the big dry-goods dealers. Didn't even have his own shop, but still took in more than the other shop owners. A whole week he would drive around to the fairs with a rack of dry goods: down off of one cart and up onto another. Every week he'd go to Warsaw for fresh merchandise, and not infrequently even twice a week. He worked like a dog. Got up at four in the morning, froze in the marketplace, and came home on the cart at twelve at night. Hardly ate, hardly slept, hardly measured—he should pardon me for saying so—the goods for the peasant women. But all that—knock on wood it should be so for all Jewish children—just to "make a little extra"! In the marketplace and in the synagogue people talked with gusto about how Yitskhok was going to buy Reb Leybishl's ramshackle house and build his own place there. God help him! Business is business after all. What else is there to do with one's ten fingers? And he had a mother-in-law as well, a capable Jewish woman. Milke the village produce seller still carried two heavy baskets: one in front and the other behind. And to this day Yitskhok didn't know how it could be that she bought a chicken or a fish for the Sabbath. His mother-in-law always brought such things home; and from time to time even a little sack of flour, some peas, a little kasha.

It turned out that Uncle Melekh thought Yitskhok was worse than he actually was. In fact, learning that the uncle wanted to do some business, Yitskhok didn't say another word and cut what the uncle had wanted: a few pieces of floral linen for some aprons, several yards of white linen for a head scarf, a shawl; and for all of it he charged exact prices, as long as there would be some kind of profit. In fact, Uncle Melekh himself didn't expect any.

And at dawn there they both were, the uncle and Nosn, laden with baskets in the front and behind, heading out in the direction of Rogów, and from there they were supposed to take the road to Karczówka.

The day dawned beautifully. The snow was sparkling on the fields like diamonds. On the way they chanced upon a cart, which made things a little easier. The peasant was an old acquaintance of Uncle Melekh's from the good old days and regretted that he had to spend his old age working hard for his food.

That beautiful sun that suddenly began to shine, startling them, disconcerted Uncle Melekh.

"There'll be a frost tonight," he said.

And though that evening it was still bearable—by the by, it was plenty warm in the peasant's house—by the next morning the frost had come on strong. They were intending to head on to Karczówka, but just then it grew difficult for Uncle Melekh to catch his breath. Uncle Melekh was walking a couple of steps behind Nosn and soon declared without warning, "Nosn, I won't make it: my breathing's bothering me."

So they decided that the uncle should go home and wait till the weather turned milder. Nosn had actually wanted the uncle to stay and rest in Rogów, but the uncle was stubborn: the few kilometers from Rogów home he'd manage slowly enough.

They lowered the baskets and transferred more than half of what was in the uncle's into Nosn's baskets. Now the uncle's baskets were light enough that a child could carry them. They took their leave of one another.

"Good-bye."

"Good-bye, and God give you success."

With a firmly measured step under the load of the two heavy baskets Nosn set out on the road to the distant village. Just once he looked behind him and saw Uncle Melekh walking with a slow but steady step uphill on the road to Godlbozhits.

But after the uncle had passed the first hill things started to go badly for him. He sat down on the dry snow at the side of the road, taking off the baskets and loosening his collar. The scarf around his neck was choking him a little.

He was seized by fatigue. The air smelled refreshing and sharp. He leaned an elbow on one of the baskets, with his head on that elbow, and tried to take a nap.

He slept heartily. He was embraced by the sweet pleasure of a nap after a Sabbath lunch, like so many years ago. Grandmother Feygele, may she rest in peace, in her holiday bonnet appeared to him. In a little golden cup she brought him ethrog preserves, and in the cup was a little golden spoon, "Here, Melekhl, try some, it's the flavor of paradise."

He tried some, Melekhl did, and then a peasant alerted the people of the city, "A frozen Jew in the middle of the road!"

They brought the frozen man into the city. The burial society gave him a proper burial, his three sons said Kaddish, and lame Moyshele cursed, "May a calamity befall them! They didn't even want to spring for the arrangements. So let them suffer! Strokes for all of them!"

He meant his curse for Uncle Melekh's debtors: Leybele Pipe and Shmuel Rabinovitsh. Uncle Melekh's children had gone to them, handing over a note for fifteen hundred zlotys, and begged, wept, for at least a hundred for the arrangements. And even that they didn't want to pay, nor did they respond, like a brick wall. Alas, they didn't have it.

"They shouldn't even be alive, by God! They should be buried in an old shirt like Uncle Melekh!"

As he finished, lame Moyshele wrung his hands and lamented, "A catastrophe! From the whole estate there's not even enough left for a headstone."

Someone approached him from behind and tapped him on his winter cap. The cap fell down over his eyes. That one, behind, waited till the lame man righted his cap and then stretched out his hand, pointing at the pharmacist's house, "An ugly headstone? Eh?"

✧ 26 ✧

How Moshke Abishes Wanted to Wean the Rabbi Off of Oats

Moshke Abishes had gradually become so important in his own esti-mation that you couldn't even approach him. With the police he was hand in glove, in the tax office what he said was written down, and the secretary in the starosta's office was completely his.

So he strutted around the marketplace like an influential person. From one side he collected hush money from the store owners and from the other he denounced people in the tax office, fleecing the community head to toe while still mocking the burghers—each one individually and all of them together.

"Just hand over what you owe," someone asked him.

"Wait," Moshke laughed, "when I sell a couple of burghers I'll have some money."

"Don't go picking too many fights, Moshke," people warned him. "Were it not for the burghers you wouldn't be on the community council."

"I shit on the burghers! I shit on the whole community!"

Moshke spoke so arrogantly with regard to the Jewish community of Godlbozhits. And why not? When everything was his business.

Gradually he sold off all of the community positions and depos-ited the money in his own pocket, overcharging the community tax; he swindled, may it never happen, a funeral, and showed no one a bill. Ultimately he had taken charge of all of the taxes on kosher slaughtering and the butchers broke their feet running to him for a penny.

The city had its fine rabbi to thank for all of this. He, Mayerl, had designated Moshke a president of the community; earlier still, with the Austrians, he had given him control of the committee. It was his handiwork raising the slaughtering taxes, overcharging the burghers, selling the community positions. He, the rabbi, had gotten his cut from Moshke every time, and for his part let him be over and done with the whole community.

As to the claim that he was an accomplice to the thievery, he denied it categorically. It's true that Godlbozhits was a city full of brazen people; they scratched the rabbi's eyes out, they had no respect for a man of learning and the town's rabbi. It's true that because of our many sins the world had turned wanton and dissolute, that a rabbi got no "respect" from the bourgeois Jews. After all, what could a clean-shaven Jew, a freethinker say? After all, what could a young person from the union say? Did a rabbi today have any influence? Certainly not. The rabbinate today was held in very low esteem, worse than a chimney sweep or a water carrier.

In one thing, however, the rabbi conceded that the burghers were right: he had indeed made Moshke Abishes a person, had given him control of the committee along with the slaughtering receipts . . . "*But Jeshurun waxed fat and kicked.*"[1] Moshke, that is, had grown fat, he kicked, he said, "*Kulo sheli*"[2]—everything, that is, was his, nothing ever came to the rabbi.

Moshke Abishes started treating the rabbi like lame Moyshele did his nag. Every day he gave it a pound less of oats until he started giving it only straw. Until it had become "*the waters are come in unto my soul,*"[3] until it was no longer tolerable.

So Rabbi Mayerl put on his *spodek* and went over to the starosta's. "Your Honor the Starosta! In the holy community of Godlbozhits ignoble things are being perpetrated, the community's funds and its property are being robbed and stolen and plundered."

1. Deuteronomy 32:15.
2. "All of it is mine" (Tractate Bava Metsi'a 2a).
3. Psalm 69:2.

The starosta asked, "Who is the man who is perpetrating these dishonorable things?"

Rabbi Mayerl said, "The man—why, it's Moshke Abishes, the one whom you, your Honor the Starosta, by your grace approved as president of the holy community."

The starosta then asked, "What did he do, this president?"

And Rabbi Mayerl enumerated, so to speak, "This and such."

So the starosta summoned the secretary, "Panie Secretary, so-and-so."

The secretary said, "I myself have inspected the books and have found everything in perfect order."

So the starosta gave the rabbi a stare. "The rabbi's matter," he said, "is wishful thinking, and don't come here with your denunciations!"

The secretary, who was buddy-buddy with Moshke, went right away and told all of this to Moshke, who said, "If he's gonna go inform on me, that little rabbi, then I'll give him the disease, painfully, right in the gut!"

Everything was going smoothly for him, Moshke, until it came time for the elections to the Sejm. Moshke Abishes had had a keen sense of political smell right up to the gates of Godlbozhits. Sejm? What difference was it to him who would be in the Sejm? He, Moshke, chose the chief of the burial society, the magistrate, the president of the craftsmen. They could all even stand on their head and he'd still have his way. But the Sejm? "Let that silly little teacher Livshits tear up his *spodek* over it with his 'eighteen.' What, it's a matter of livelihood?"

However, when the *spodek* gave a sermon in the synagogue and ordered people to vote for the 'one,' Moshke said, "Cholera take his bones, that little bastard, that traitor! Since he wants a 'one,' then I want an 'eighteen,' and let's just see who'll win."

Out from under a mountain of dust, from under a prewar bowler, emerged—Stänglmeier. That former Austrian gendarme, then president of the association for the war wounded, ardent card-player and charge of the pockmarked lady dentist. Stänglmeier had been reborn, brimming with energy, founded a club for Jewish military reservists, a lodge of the B'nai Brith, campaigned for 'one,' nullified the reports on the antisanitary conditions, collected registration fees, threatened the owners of various franchise permits, of buses. "Hey! You, Zionist, big shot! I'm warning you, you'll serve time! Your father, it seems, had a license for brandy. Sold? Who's sold?! *I'm* sold?! Think about what you're saying, young man! I am B'nai Brith!"

Moshke sniffed with his nose, "Why does Stänglmeier always slink off to the rabbi, and what's all this running back and forth to the *starosta*'s?"

Moshke hurried off to see the secretary, but the secretary ran right into him, very angry, "Moshke, I need five hundred zlotys right away. There's to be an audit of the treasury. Moshke doesn't have it? From under the ground for all I care, just get it and bring it! Otherwise, there's another way: a bullet in the head!"

Moshke stood there perplexed. He had already lost the account containing what he had borrowed from everyone, owed all the treasuries, extorted from all the "frightened" Jews for the nobleman's sake. Where could one get new money?

"So I'll run," he said to himself, "I'll really exert myself, I don't know . . ." And considering it he thought, "It's hopeless, when they're already taking a bath. One has to rescue the goy. It's business. When one deposits, one withdraws."

Moshke scrabbled together three hundred zlotys. The nobleman laughed maliciously, "Three hundred? Two thousand three hundred! Do you understand?! Two thousand three hundred is missing! Well, what are you standing around for?! Go to your Jews, surely they've got hundreds of thousands! Save me, Jew! Otherwise I'm lost! Well, what are you standing around for, to hell with you! Jew! You can't? You don't have it?" The secretary's face was contorted with sneering desperation. "Well, good . . . Go . . . Take it home to my wife."

Moshke, he did what the nobleman ordered him to. He took the three hundred zlotys to the nobleman's wife. But when he returned to the *starosta*'s office he already saw from far away a crowd of people around the red building. Moshke started to run, his heart pounding, he had a bad feeling.

"What's happened?!"

"Dead?"

"Dead!"

"Eh? What?"

"The secretary has shot himself."

———•———

So the story goes: When Moshke Abishes married the beautiful Leah "Stänglmeier" he was no longer at all a young man. Here and there were already some grey hairs. But he so enjoyed getting married that the grey hair disappeared and the wrinkles on his face were smoothed away. That is, until that business with the secretary who shot himself, and in the matter of an hour Moshke's hair had turned white like an old man's. His face was sunken, his head drooped, and his shoulders stooped. Only his mouth still worked, cursing and swearing like never before. But who was interested in his curses anymore? It was like the barking of a toothless dog.

A few days later, after the secretary had shot himself, the bailiff arrived and ordered Moshke's household goods seized as well as the tables and chairs of his wife's restaurant. It turns out it wasn't enough that Moshke had laid hold of his own money and foreign monies for the profligate secretary, but he had also been his guarantor for thousands of zlotys in notes. Before, no one ever bothered Moshke; they were afraid to pick a fight with him. But now they couldn't give a fig about him:

"That informer—his guts'll get it!"

What more could he do now than curse and swear? He wasn't allowed to show his bones at the starosta's office. And people also learned that the officials in the tax office were giving him the cold shoulder, were embarrassed to speak with him, and didn't let him through the doorway.

"Serves him right!"

So the story goes: Recently Moshke went to the starosta's office. He had some kind of business to take care of. "Off with you, disgusting Jew," they politely hinted to him.

So the story goes: Recently Moshke went to the director of the tax office and started firing off his denunciations—"Moyshe Kats bought two wagonloads of wheat; Abish Anker brought a hundred barrels of herring on the Vistula; Melekhl Finklkroyt was purchasing at the fair without a license; Moyshe Vidak slaughtered three calves in a room . . ." The director held his head down and noted it all down, very quickly, with his pencil. Everything Moshke said he noted down. And when he finally stopped the director suddenly turned around toward him and said, "Finished? Now go, and may my eyes not see you again!"

But he was after all an informer, impure blood, so he remembered, "For Mayer Shnayderman, a shoemaker, there's an apprentice working . . ."

The director noted it in the margin of a piece of paper and said to Moshke, "Perhaps you've done, crablouse?!"

Then he, the director, informed his attendant, "That annoying Jew is not to be allowed in again."

But the time for assessing the sales tax was fast approaching, and it seemed to Moshke that they wouldn't be able to manage at all without him. Inside, the commission was consulting with the director of the tax office, and on the other side of the door stood Moshke Abishes. The attendant chased him away, saying, "The director has banned you!" But he, Moshke, kept coming back, putting his ear to the door. Finally the attendant left him alone. He still remembered Moshke's cigarettes and small change. The lowly certainly remember a favor longer than the lofty do.

At one particular moment Moshke heard the director's voice, "Tsirl Rotnberg, purchase and sale of flour, fifteen thousand!" That infuriated Moshke: "Ah! The bastard. He was the first one who stopped paying his weekly payment. Let cholera seize him!" Slowly he opened the door and went right in.

"High commission!" Moshke yelled. "His name's not Tsirl Rotnberg, his name's Ayzik Kalushiner, and he signed the franchise over to a cousin, he took in at least two hundred thousand in sales . . . Under pain of excommunication!"

And when he saw the astonished faces of those seated there, in order to add weight to his words he put his cap on, pulled out his *tsitsis*,[4] kissed them, and raised two fingers, "Under pain of excommunication—two hundred thousand! Whole wagonloads of flour, kasha, oats. I can swear on the ten commandments, on a black candle, on whatever you want!"

The only Jewish member of the commission, Fayvele Shpilman, a Jew with strong nerves—a person with weak nerves can't be a usurer—even he couldn't stay calm for long after that story. He, Fayvele, understood about a Jewish informer. The rabbinic tales were full of Jewish informers who were set back on the straight and narrow by Hasidic saints. At any rate, an informer was nothing new in Jewish history. But can a person go so far, and before every nation and community, before the goyim, make up a story that never happened?! Well . . . *Mne* . . .

Having kissed his *tsitsis* and sworn his oath, Moshke was ordered thrown out by the director, but his suggestion of Tsirl Rotnberg's two hundred thousand was raised.

"But you know, Panowie," he said, "that when a Jew swears 'under pain of excommunication,' it's a sacred thing."

Fayvele Shpilman was always a firm believer in the precept that you don't call the wolf from the forest. An informer? So be it, an informer. All of Jewish history was full of Jewish informers, and still the Jews had the money, and the noblemen had to come to them to borrow with interest. But this story moved him. He stood up and said, "Begging your pardon, Panowie. In our holy Torah it says that an informer loses both worlds, and his oath is no oath. And it also says in our holy Torah . . ."

The director gently interrupted him, "Panie Shpilman . . . Panie Shpilman . . . These gentlemen perhaps don't know, but I know quite well, I was raised among Jews from my earliest childhood. Panowie,

---

4. *tsitsis*: fringes worn under the clothes by religious Jews.

when a Jew swears an oath 'under pain of excommunication' and kisses his *tsitsis* it is—Amen!"

And despite the personal risk he took, Fayvele could achieve nothing. Moshke had ruined the flour merchant.

But ultimately that was Moshke's swan song, and not only in the tax office. The next morning a new misfortune befell him.

A delegate from the starosta's office arrived unexpectedly, a lame little man with a squinting eye. The little man introduced himself very courteously to Moshke, "Zamorski, delegate of the *starosta*." And then he requested a trifle: to show him the community's books.

Books? Of course. He wouldn't find anything there, the Pan delegate. Everything was in perfect order.

"And now I'll ask for the documents," the little man then said, just as courteously, and it seemed to Moshke that with his squinting eye he was looking right through him.

He handed him the documents.

"And now," the little man said, again pleasant and polite, "I will ask for just a little something more: leave me alone for an hour or two. At six o'clock this evening there will be convened a meeting of the board."

Leaving the nobleman alone in the community office Moshke felt a chill in every limb. At first he wanted to run to the rabbi's and break all his windows, but on the way his mind became clearer: Stänglmeier.

But instead of going to Stänglmeier, he went off to see the pockmarked lady dentist.

"But *proszę Pana*," said the pockmarked thing, "I am certainly not Stänglmeier."

"Am I approaching him in the street? Am I interfering in his business?" argued Moshke. "What has he got against me?"

"But, my dear sir, am I responsible for him?"

"The Pani can persuade him of anything; when the Pani says no— it's no. It's well known in the city that the Pani's word is sacred to him."

The pockmarked lady dentist blushed at the compliment, and sighed, "My good man. I cannot, I dare not get involved in his affairs."

Moshke stooped lower.

"Otherwise, Pani, may I have nothing left; otherwise, Pani, may I suffer a stroke, if I had today but one bite of all the community's good fortune! Otherwise, may I not live out the year if yesterday my wife and I hadn't gone to bed hungry . . ."

And suddenly he grabbed a knife from the table, handed it to the bewildered lady dentist, and stretched out his neck, "Slaughter me, Pani, and be done with it!"

Right then someone rang the bell. Stänglmeier had arrived. He took off his hat and looked with astonishment first at Moshke and then at the lady dentist. She bid him come with her into the other room, and said something quietly to him. He struggled angrily like a dog at its chain, trembling and yelling through the open door, "This cannot go on! The representative of the Jewish community must be an intelligent person. I'm telling you frankly, it's a disgrace for the community to have as its representative such an uneducated and ignorant man as you are."

The lady dentist's heart ached at that, "Hans, how can you say such a thing to a person?"

But soon she had moved away, doubled over and turned red. Stänglmeier gave her a look of contempt, of ridicule, and hissed a German curse.

Moshke snuck away.

———◆———

That evening he attended the meeting of the community board.

The squint-eyed little man was smoking one cigarette after another. To his right sat the rabbi in a new satin coat. His little head, wearing a skullcap, was drawn in deeply between his shoulders. Around the table sat the rest of the synagogue council members.

The little squinting eye made a brief opening statement:

"Gentlemen, don't interrupt! What I'm going to tell you now is in the name of the starosta. You must hear me out and not engage in any pointless debates. Debates lead nowhere. Moyshe will say this and Berl will say that. Gentlemen, that may be fine for a Zionist Party, the Bund, the Labor Zionists, a burial society. But a Jewish community,

gentlemen, is an agency. Pay it your full attention, gentlemen: an official agency! In the matter of a mere two hours I've already found"—he
pointed to a certain sheet of paper—"almost ten thousand zlotys mis-
appropriated: neither reimbursed nor recorded. We'll need to look for
who took this money. Perhaps it was me? Perhaps some stranger came
and took it? Or perhaps it was someone local, someone sitting right
here? Nonsense! The investigating magistrate will deal with that, and
I don't need to deprive him of his livelihood. Here we're dealing with
something else: the revenues from ritual slaughtering are being stolen
week in, week out on the order of 20 to 40 percent. This must not
continue."

Moshke stood up and pointed at the rabbi, "He is an accomplice
to the theft!"

Like a gander, the rabbi stretched his little head out from between
his shoulders, ready to respond. The little squinting eye calmed him
down. Then addressing Moshke, "I will not allow any insult to the
clergy here! Do you hear?!"

Then the little squinting eye went on with his monologue:

"I will ask you not to interrupt me. It doesn't matter to me who
stole it; to me he might as well be anonymous. I am merely explaining:
It will not continue! This is not the Bund! Not the Labor Zionists! Not
a burial society! Who has been monitoring matters till now?"

Someone among the council members replied, "The rabbi!"

The little head rose from between the satin shoulders, the gander-
like neck stretched up, up . . .

The little squinting eye calmed him down. Then addressing the
council members:

"You should be ashamed! That I, a goy, must take your rabbi into
custody. What is he to me? A cleric from a different faith. And to you?
Everything! Your defender before God, your representative to the
government. Who performs your marriages? Who records your new-
born children? Who permits your dead to be buried? Who koshers
meat for you? Who sells your leavening for Passover? And that is why
I say it's fine for communists, it's fine for the Bund, the Labor Zionists
to struggle with religion, with the government. But for Jews—with

such beards—*pfui*! You have been appointed to care for the synagogue, for the ritual bath, and first and foremost, for the rabbi: to pay him his salary, his appropriate salary . . ."

"He took it himself," interjected the tall Lozer.

"Silence!" the lame little man banged on the table, his squinting little eye casting sparks.

And then all was calm and quiet.

"But you see, gentlemen, the government grants you full autonomy to manage your own affairs, and you go and choose a president who steals . . ."

"In cahoots with the rabbi!" the lanky Lozer couldn't contain himself.

"Silence!" the little squinting eye was furious. "Respect for the rabbi! Respect for the *starosta*! Respect, dammit! This is a community board?! A house of disgrace!"

The members of the synagogue council sat utterly perplexed. The rabbi withdrew his pious little neck deeper between his satin shoulders, sitting like a hen on her eggs.

And the little squinting eye smoothed things out, ending hoarsely, "What is this? A Bund? The Labor Zionists? Or a community board?"

And when the members of the synagogue council left the community office the crowd assailed them with catcalls.

One yelled, "Council members are you? Your heads should be cracked! If I were a council member I'd . . ."

And another yelled over him, "Just grab the rabbi by his little neck and squeeze! Squeeze!"

But Moshke, the president, was forgotten, as though he had never existed.

But in the *starosta*'s office they didn't forget. Stänglmeier made sure of that. The very next morning he, the Austrian, came into the community office with a paper from the starosta: "Pursuant to article such and such. I nominate Herr Stänglmeier as commissioner of the Jewish community in Godlbozhits."

⇥ 27 ⇤

On Love and Passion

Those days things were not going well for Shimen. It was as if he'd been knocked off-kilter. He had become restless, shaken on the bronze pedestal of the greatest Godlbozhits bookkeeper, living hurriedly, in a fever, sometimes two heads taller, and other times a head shorter, depending on his mood. Some kind of tiny, insignificant worm had overtaken him. And at still other times he rose, surpassing all of them, looking with disdain, with pity, at a shtetl of creeping worms.

At all of Godlbozhits with its moneybags, usurers, synagogue council members, presidents, war profiteers; those who didn't get involved and those who made things run: voting blocks, Passover, craftsmen, charitable fund, ritual bath . . .

The self-satisfied young man had become dissatisfied, the full cheeks now sunken, the calm, lush eyes now darting and insolent.

"It's all because of Zosia Lerner," he thought he heard behind his back.

"She was a powerful influence on him. He got, I think, more attractive, more interesting."

"And I'm telling you, she sees in him a good match."

"Ha-ha-ha!" Shimen laughed inside. "Zosia and . . . A match. Ha-ha-ha! Stupid cows . . ."

"She really loves him."

"He's not her first."

"How she's gotten hold of him!"

"He'll realize it."

"After all, that's how it was supposed to be with Lola Tsiglman. Two thousand dollars . . ."

"Why are you comparing them? Zosia is an intelligent girl."

"Lola is tall, beautiful."

"But a bit of an idiot."

"And Zosia is a tiny thing, a half pint."

"She has beautiful eyes."

"Lola has money to go with her beautiful eyes."

Everywhere he, Shimen, went conversations came to a halt mid-sentence. People felt sorry for him behind his back, while flattering him to his face. And Lola—out of spite she grew more beautiful every day, wearing red, tight, and tempting blouses, holding her head up arrogantly, hardly acknowledging his greeting.

"And good riddance to her," thought Shimen with satisfaction.

All of this happened later, after he had come to know Zosia Lerner. Earlier, however, it was quite different.

The cold, tedious winter nights had come to stay. Shimen sat at the ledger and worked over the balance sheet. That's when Lola Tsiglman entered, flushed from the frost, and asked with all of her little white teeth, "Is father not here?"

Her father, Reb Elye Tsiglman, a wholesale grocery merchant, was president of the council. A Jew with a cigar always in his mouth and wadding in his ears; a man who laughed with great pleasure at his own boring stories.

The door and the shutters were closed. There was no one in the bank. Her eyes sparkled, her little white teeth laughed—and Shimen melted. Where is it written that love must come only on the fifty-sixth try?

The ground rules were laid down: a kiss on the tip of the nose, a gentle embrace around the waist, but on the bosom—hands off!

The next evening she returned, "Is father not here?"

Perhaps just then Reb Elye Tsiglman took the wadding out of his ears and was reciting his evening prayers, or perhaps he had already been asleep for a while.

"Why are people in such a hurry to escape?"

This time Shimen knew for certain: you could kiss both cheeks, a neck, under the chin, but not on the mouth. You could look, search; you could try to stick your hand into the bosom—let go at once! But at last! At last!

Otherwise she got angry, truly angry.

On the third day, since Shimen was waiting with an inner certainty, she didn't come. So he went to see her at home, asking, "Is your father not here?"

One evening earlier Shimen had brought Reb Elye Tsiglman a check for a large sum. But Reb Elye was sitting on the bus, wearing his holiday fur coat.

"Dummy!" Lola laughed. "But you've seen him yourself driving off to Warsaw."

"I completely forgot. And your mother?"

"At a neighbor's. What do you need?"

"Shpilman sent me, some money by check."

"Just wait a bit, mother will be back soon."

He sat down respectably at the table, Lola opposite him. What was there to talk about?

Lola walked over to a side table and started up the phonograph.

"Come on! Turn it off, it grates on my ears."

"Ho, ho! You're grumpy."

He went over to her, wanting to embrace her. She turned her back. The tip of her nose was angrily facing the phonograph.

Shimen looked at the clock: it was late. The evening was lost, he thought.

All of a sudden her mother entered. She was very pleased to see him, "Oh, a guest!"

She chatted with him genially and at length, asking his advice about a fur for Lola. Shimen didn't catch the full significance that this advice-seeking had for him. He was not very perceptive regarding the simple heart of a mother who wants to have both a son and a daughter, instead of an only daughter.

"A son-in-law would be like my own child," her mother said, but Shimen thought she was philosophizing a bit.

The deeper meaning of her words had hardly sunk in, when Fay-vele Shpilman, his director, asked him to stay to have a couple of words about closing the bank.

He, Fayvele, Shimen knew, was no matchmaker and didn't desire, God forbid, any matchmaking, but he knew Shimen and wished for him what he would for his own son. What's more, a good friend of his had asked him for a favor. But on the other hand, he, Shimen, perhaps didn't really need a matchmaker. However, he, Shimen, still ought to remember: one needed to have money. "And why, I ask you, oughtn't Elye Tsiglman give some? What I really mean is: he has only one child. Who was he keeping her for?"

Shimen blushed, hemmed and hawed and didn't answer directly.

That same evening at Lola's house. Her parents were snoring con-tentedly in the adjoining bedroom. He was sitting with Lola on the little sofa. Pillows were strewn about on the sofa. And he, the simple-ton, was sitting and reading aloud from a book. Was she, Lola, very busy? Had she well understood the deeper meaning? Lola sat calmly, understanding, but dispassionate, listening without blinking her eyes.

"Maybe it's enough reading?" he asked.

She agreed, "It's enough."

"So come here."

"But aren't I sitting right here?"

"Closer."

"I'm fine sitting like this."

"I'll turn off the lamp . . ."

"Turn it back on!"

But he succeeded: with one hand he reached over to her, stretch-ing it across the back of the sofa, kissing her passionately, and with the other he turned off the lamp. She made no more protests. He went mad, kissing and fumbling around her neck, undoing her pin.

Suddenly she whispered, "Let go! Let go, I tell you!"

He turned on the lamp as she collected herself, in a huff.

He didn't understand. "Lolu, what did I do? Lolu, don't be mad."

She made no reply. The tip of her nose was cold as ice . . .

"Lolu . . . Loltshu . . . What's the matter?"

"I've forbidden . . ."

He had another bit of luck: when saying good-bye she allowed him to kiss her hand.

Because of what happened he didn't go to see her for three days. Shimen was a stubborn person. Well . . . "Let her find out what I'm made of." On the fourth day—it happened to be Friday evening, so there was no work at the bank—a long, frosty night for him, he couldn't take it anymore.

He knocked on the door. The shutters had already been closed. It was Reb Elye's usual habit after supper to smoke a cigar, prattle on a bit about something or other, tell stories till around eleven, twelve o'clock, and then go to sleep. Friday evenings, however, he forewent the smoking. He just finished his meal and went straight to bed.

"Who's knocking out there?" he asked his wife Gitele who was sitting by the stove, warming herself. "They're getting together, I see, to go visiting."

Gitele listened as the maid opened the door and answered him, "Why can't you permit it?"

"Hmm . . . In my day people didn't behave like this."

"In your day," Gitele thought for a while, "it was pointless," she said.

"Seventeen times better than today. And what then? Anything goes. Boys and girls together?"

"Believe me, people are sinning less today than they used to."

"You're trying to tell me that people are getting together to recite Psalms?"

"Why Psalms of all things? They read a book, a newspaper."

"They read, they read."

Gitele was ready to defend progress, "Say what you will, but still, these days you don't hear of a girl having to go make a bris. So what's the matter with falling in love and giving a kiss once in a while?"

"Love, shmove. Here's a penny for all of love."

"You belittle everything."

"I'll show you a little trick," her husband said, "Shimen's obviously 'besotted,' right? But before you count a couple of zlotys, love's gone."

"What do I know," his wife said ironically. "You would like to save on a dowry."

"Why not?"

"So wait a little while. They haven't fallen in love for your sake."

"For your sake either."

Reb Elye turned to his wife, and gave her a caress under her chin.

"Well, go on now, go," she pushed him away. "You wanted to go to sleep after all."

"Are you angry, mother?"

Reb Elye took off his clothes while sitting on the bed, recited his evening prayers, patted down the feathers in the comforter, smoothed the pillows, and tried to lure himself into the bedding. In the midst of it all he reconsidered, went back to the stove and from behind gave his wife a little slap on the knee, "Are you angry, mother?"

"Well, go on now, go, you old fool, you wanted to go to sleep," Gitele said wearily.

"Am I annoying you, mother? Come on."

Gitele got up, yawned widely, and said, "It's a shame, the lamp is burning. I'll ask the goy to put it out."

She went into the kitchen and pointed at her daughter's room, "He's here?"

"The young gentleman," the goy laughed contentedly through two large horsey teeth.

"Go, put out the lamp in the bedroom, then you can also go to bed," the mistress said.

"And who'll shut the door?" the little goy said beaming with pleasure.

"The Panna."

The whole house was as quiet as the grave. Shimen was sitting in Lola's small room, engrossed in a newspaper, reading the political news. Separately, behind a folding screen, Lola was combing her hair. She wrapped it in a willow-green hair net, and soon came out wearing a red, floral robe, intoxicating the air with scented soap.

"You are beautiful," Shimen said. It was undeniable. He set the newspaper aside.

"Really?"

"And that red robe."

"Oh!" she said flirtatiously. "You like it?"

"And you as well. Even more so."

"Go on, read something," she flashed her white teeth and sat down respectably at the table.

He read. Across from him lay the girl's bare arms, grabbing his eyes away from the paper.

He broke off his reading, "You have beautiful hands, Lolu."

"Why have you stopped reading?" she asked.

"So it interests you then? Even though it's politics?"

She was a little miffed, "You think only you are interested in politics?"

He took her gently by the waist, guided his lips over her naked arm, and laid his head on her shoulder.

"Your head's hurting me," she complained.

"Perhaps you'd like to lie down on the sofa?"

She straightened out the pile of cushions, and sat down next to them.

"You please me today," he began.

"And not other times?"

"Then too. Come now, dearest."

"Lunatic! You'll suffocate me!"

The light switch was above the sofa. A twist and—pitch black.

"Boooooo . . . Are you afraid?" The robe had one bow—a silly bow.

"Oh, it's so hot. Let me catch my breath . . . lunatic . . ."

And those ribbons with the buttons. One could go mad fumbling about with them, when a naked body was burning underneath, caressing the hot velvet.

"Do you love me?"

"Yes." Seductive silk tights, a system of buttons and loops . . . "Why do you ask?"

"You've never said so."

"And now you know? Something's knotted up, tangled . . ."

"I know you love me . . . physically. But morally? Don't touch me! You mustn't . . ."

"You mean spiritually?! Loltshu . . ."

"I don't want to! You mustn't . . ."

"But what then?"

"So . . ."

"Hold me . . . like that . . . tight! Give me a kiss . . ."

"Don't touch me! Let go!"

"Kitten . . ."

"Enough! Let go!"

This time Shimen snuck home through the dead streets. A stabbing pain in his loins. His one satisfaction was that he was headed forward, prospering. Shimen was no uncompromising Don Juan. He believed in emotional evolution. So, for example, bit by bit he was awakening the shy wife in the beautiful Lola, slowly, slowly reaching his goal.

Another evening. The prologue was proceeding more rapidly: ten lines of a book aloud. Uninteresting. A whole day pressing laundry and her head was aching. Tired. The pleasure of the sofa. "Are you mad?! Make it dark. Wait, you'll tear it . . . I'll take out the pin . . . Lunatic! You'll rip the armband!"

Slippery, murderously cold tights over a flaming hot body. A system of buttons and loops.

"Have you barricaded yourself?"

"No, but you mustn't . . . I don't want to . . ."

"What then do you want?"

"So . . ."

"Are you afraid?"

"Yes."

"Don't be afraid. It'll be nothing."

"You'll forget yourself."

"I give you my word."

"You're all alike."

A pause.

"Kitten . . . Give me a kiss . . . I love you so . . . Hold me, tighter!"

"Shimen! I don't want to . . ."

"Come on, kitten! You'll see . . ."

"I don't want to!"

"Come on . . ."

"No. Not now."

"But?"

"After the wedding."

A bucket of cold water on his fiery head. Shimen tried, "And if we're in love?"

"After the wedding."

"It seems . . ." Shimen had finally returned to full consciousness. A formidable, powerful argument: "It seems you'll go right to being a prostitute. That's what you want?"

"No! That's disgusting. It makes me ill."

"So hold me! Give me a kiss. Like this, kitten . . . Tighter! Tight!"

"No! I'm afraid . . ."

"Don't be afraid. Word of honor."

"Your word of honor. I don't believe it."

"Then what do you want?"

"After the wedding."

⎯⎯◆⎯⎯

No, he wasn't upset, Shimen wasn't, not the least bit. Holding his head between his hands. In his loins such a stabbing pain. He felt like throwing up.

Angry? Was he angry with Lola Tsiglman? Absolutely! Who said that? Of course, people got together, they talked.

The filthy mouths of the good people of Godlbozhits! Everything was their business, they interfered everywhere, they stuck their noses in everywhere. Whether he was going with Lola Tsiglman or not. Whose business was it?

Two months later he met Zosia. He wasn't going to that love affair willingly. That little girl—she didn't merely love him, she mastered him.

He defended himself, "You say there are two hostile classes, and I'm telling you there's a third—the middle class."

"It's ground up, milled between the other two."

"It's durable, rock solid, easily adapted."

"The latter is quite logical; the former less erudite . . . Why aren't you reading?"

"What?"

"Political economy."

"Your approach is well known: material is everything; spirit—nothing."

"Don't babble such nonsense," Zosia was a little agitated. "You know nothing. You, a gymnasium graduate, know less than, let's say, a simple worker who has read a few good pamphlets, or who has gone to a few meetings."

"Well, I won't come to your union to learn anything. I'm already attending a higher class." Shimen said ironically.

"So the union will come to you," she answered with the same irony.

But soon she threw herself on him, embracing his head, clinging to his lips.

"I'm suffering, my little boy. I am wicked. They speak well of you in Godlbozhits. You're a talented bookkeeper, and in time you'll become director of the bank. And me? I love you, you solid, good young man of mine. You're so calm. You need some kind of intense experience that will unsettle you, sweep you away; some kind of misfortune, an earthquake that will throw you down a floor, into the basement. Of course you won't go there."

Shimen had his head in her lap, between her little hands. He listened, drew it all in, absorbed it.

"One day, the sun shone into the basements on Wolińska Street, and a child climbed up to the window, on crooked little stick-like legs: 'Sun, yum yum! Mamma, I eat sun!' The sidewalk was covered with mud, the iron bars over him were hard, grimy. The child burst into tears: 'Mamma, ba! Ba sun! Eat! E-at!'

"Another time—a strike at a factory. Oh, no! It's wrong, completely wrong, the idea that workers strike out of jealousy of the factory owner who buys himself diamonds, expensive furs, spends his leisure time abroad. A strike in a factory, my little boy, happens sometimes for the sake of a sunny apartment, sometimes for the sake of a child's school notebook, but mostly for the sake of a simple piece of bread.

"And when one strikes for the sake of a piece of bread, it makes one bitter, and when one brings down into the factory poor, ignorant people who show up to work instead of the strikers perhaps that is not completely those people's fault—and nevertheless they are scabs.

"It does happen from time to time that common people, or underworld characters, fight it out among themselves. You sometimes see it in Godlbozhits among the teamsters, on the buses. Knives flash, blood flows . . . Then a policeman comes and puts the brawlers in jail for a day, for twenty-four hours. But when striking workers won't let the food be snatched from their mouths, it is the right of the factory owner to hire scabs, or to close the factory as he pleases. Not infrequently it also happens that the strikers occupy their workplace, eating and sleeping there, and waiting patiently for the flexibility of the stubborn factory owner.

"But flexibility is not in the nature of factory owners.

"That's enough, Shimen. Why am I telling you all of this?"

Shimen felt as though he were experiencing everything Zosia had talked about. The little girl with the steel-blue eyes was getting inside him, becoming his conscience, his heart. Something inside of him was being shaken and built anew. Complicated philosophies and brain-teasing arguments disappeared. Two times two is four: everything came from the earth. *Bereishit*, in the beginning was the earth, and the plants, and the animals. Then came the stone, the axe, the spear. Then people used their hands, lifting the stone over the mouth of the well. Then the strong stole the well from the weak. Later men built houses, ships, and worked the soil; and the shares were distributed fairly: the clever ones who understood how to trade and govern the land—to them belonged the wealth of the earth, the ships, and the people who worked upon them; and the working people—to them belonged the work, the favor of being slaves of the masters and the lash of the canny whip."

"And the revolutions?"

"A good question, Shimen. This is what dialectics teaches us. It is actually not as primitive as I've just explained. You have to go with Marx's works in your hands. You must study."

"Will you help me, Zosia?"

"With great pleasure, Shimen."

They became good friends: a teacher with a student.

✦ 28 ✦

Why an Earnest Bookkeeper Needn't Waste His Time in Vain on Love

Meantime worms had snuck into Shimen Shifris's granary. Here he was dreaming up a palace of love and a mouse had begun nibbling away and undermining his existence, his position at the Godlbozhits bank. He hardly noticed it.

It was a little boy, one Getsele with a large head. This little boy came one day, accompanied by his little father with a flatterer's submissive little smile. Fayvele Shpilman mentioned it offhandedly, "I've hired a boy for the receipts, errands, and whatnot. And why not? Let him get apprenticed with some writing."

Shimen didn't understand. Even without him there were enough people for all the pointless work. They already had someone for the receipts, a Jew and a father of seven children. What else was there?

He quietly incited the Jew, the receipt-carrier, "Don't let them take food out of your mouth!"

The Jew, the children-laden father, merely put his fingers to his mouth. In his sign language that meant: "A Jew, a poor man with seven children, mustn't speak."

So was he, Shimen, going to get worked up over it? As far as he was concerned there could be two receipt-carriers.

"What's your name?" Shimen asked the little one.

"Getsele."

"How old are you?"

"Twenty years old."

Shimen's jaw dropped in astonishment. Twenty years old—in short pants, a tiny little person in an adult's jacket. But his head—an old head with sly, submissive little eyes.

And the little Getsele said, "Perhaps the *Pan* bookkeeper would like some soda water? Perhaps I can bring you something from the store? And how does one enter the figures, the number first or the sum?"

Several days later Shimen was visited by Getsele's little father. Two little fingertips graciously removed a stiff, round cap.

"Good morning, Pan bookkeeper! A . . . No matter, I knew your mother, may she rest in peace, we played together in the sand. The bookkeeper is praised in the city. Keenly praised. Fayvele might have to close the bank if he didn't have such a bookkeeper. It's well known that everything rests on the shoulders of the Pan bookkeeper. And how is my Getsele acquitting himself? The little one is running himself ragged for the Pan bookkeeper. Such a man with such an education, with such refinement as the Pan bookkeeper, there's nothing like him. He works hard, the Pan bookkeeper does. Till eleven, twelve o'clock at night he works. And why should the Pan bookkeeper work so hard? Not to worry, you should give some of it to the little one to do. The little one has young shoulders. The little one has nothing but praise for the Pan bookkeeper . . ."

"Excuse me," Shimen interrupted, "did you want something?"

"One little moment, one little minute, Panie bookkeeper." He'd be leaving momentarily. He didn't want, God forbid, to disturb the Pan bookkeeper. With lovely, girlish gracefulness he put his stiff, round cap on his balding head: He knew that everything depended on the Pan bookkeeper, and however the Pan bookkeeper wanted it, so it would be. He, the father, didn't, God forbid, want something for free. His Getsele was a lovely child, a polite child, body and soul. What could he do, become a craftsman? Or what, a tailor? A shoemaker? Is it possible for a Jew to become a government official, or in the city administration? I mean, why delude oneself? He was not asking, God forbid, for something for free, and however much the Pan bookkeeper said, he was ready to pay. He should just teach him the books a little . . .

Shimen apologized:

He was, in point of fact, rather busy, and had no time to spare. And why did he, the father, find bookkeeping so attractive? There was truly no worse occupation.

With little running steps he followed Shimen's large strides.

"True, true . . . Every professional hates his profession. But the Pan bookkeeper oughtn't say it. Bookkeeping is a fine occupation, an excellent occupation. He, the Pan bookkeeper, should take a page out of his book—he should find a suitable match today at three thousand, five thousand. But the Pan bookkeeper should let himself be matched according to how he would match: a bridegroom with two mills, with a sawmill, and with whatever else . . ."

Shimen was growing impatient, "Excuse me . . ."

"So do you promise me, Panie bookkeeper?"

"Promise what?"

"To allow the little one at the books."

"What, already at the ledger?" Shimen laughed.

"At that big book?" the little father looked at him flatteringly. "The Pan bookkeeper is making fun? The Pan bookkeeper must be joking? Is that something for the little one's head? For his ken? What shall I say. I would like . . . ah, at any book whatsoever."

Shimen promised. The little Getsele bowed subserviently. His small, glinting eyes flattered with their servility, and the top of his little head rummaged eagerly, like a pig's snout, in the complexities of double-entry bookkeeping. At ten thirty that night Shimen left him at the book, and when he returned to the bank the next morning the little Getsele had done quite some work. And what's more he had not forgotten to organize the Pan bookkeeper's desk and to add a "good morning" with his glinting, servile little eyes.

Even the director, Fayvele Shpilman, noticed Getsele's industriousness, "He ought to be given something. The boy's wearing out his shoes for nothing."

A month went by, then two, and the little father was once again at Shimen's.

Those days Shimen had begun living a double life: his hands entered sums, calculating swiftly, and his mouth argued with customers while his head, his heart blossomed tenderly with sentimental flowers, with beauty, with life, with Zosia Lerner.

And the little father of little Getsele made a nuisance of himself with all his flattery.

"My little one cannot stop praising the Pan bookkeeper. He's eternally grateful to you, and I would go through fire for the Pan bookkeeper! Today I spoke up for the Pan bookkeeper in a group of people. Ah, what people they were! On their way to some kind of general meeting."

"They're of little interest to me," Shimen said with self-assurance.

"That's just, bless me, what I told them. At any rate, Fayvele Shpilman—*You should pick him, but the* Pan *bookkeeper . . . He'd only need to make a peep, the* Pan *bookkeeper, and he could have fifteen other jobs, and better ones. You've got to kiss his hand for his work!* That's what he told them, that rabble."

That time the little father didn't ask for anything specific from Shimen. Just asked a little how he was doing, out of friendship, and asked him to watch out for Getsele, to support him, for which he thanked him, thanked him very much. He'd let nothing ill be said of the Pan bookkeeper! Graciously lifted his stiff cap, "Good day to the Pan bookkeeper, *do widzenia*. A beautiful bride with a large dowry! Hee, hee, hee!"

From the street Fayvele Shpilman entered in a very agitated state:

Bah, people, people! As though one were trying to rip a piece of bread out of that one's mouth. Shimen might at least work for nothing . . . for twenty zlotys a week. Bookkeepers wandering around in the streets. But I shut their mouths: "When they make you director, then you can make the decisions; but today I'm in charge."

That's how he answered them, those pot-stirrers, and then he repeated it loudly so that Shimen, who was sitting in the next room, could hear.

How it was all sweetness and light working for a director who was an influential person in his sphere, one who stuck up for his people, who knocked everyone's teeth out!

And as for Shimen, it still didn't alarm him. He was sitting in the next room at the ledger, biting his nails, and content that he was being left alone.

From time to time the work went very quickly, and today while working on a page of sums in the ledger he had to go over the figures three or four times, and the fifth time he made a mistake; he had absentmindedly transposed the entries in the accounts, which resulted in long hours racking his brains searching for the problem. He even decided to leave it for Getsele, telling him, "Try calculating the sums, and if they don't equal out, then go entry by entry. The same sum must be in both the 'debit' and the 'credit,' and the totals must be the same." Of course the little Getsele would throw himself at the ledger like a mouse at a hard nut, gnawing, biting, and chewing through; and he, Shimen, could sit at another desk, pretending to be poring over some chart, spinning his pencil in his hand and daydreaming sweetly, "Zoszka . . . Zenia . . . Child . . ."

Gradually he became very useful, Getsele did. Like the debt-ridden big-time merchant to the miserly usurer, like a drunken high official to the purveyor on credit of a filthy glass . . . he became useful, and Shimen took a strong dislike to him. He was sure that if that little one wasn't to be found everywhere under foot, he, Shimen, would have done his own work himself, would have had to do it. Now, however, his laziness had gone so far that he no longer had any patience at all for calculating a sum, he refused to transfer entries or to recheck them. All of that he left for the little one.

Getsele undertook all of this additional work eagerly, with passion and with his cunning flatterer's eyes. If the day was short, he still came in at night, even late at night, so that he could write out the receipts for payment. To transfer entries . . . But one time Shimen caught him late one evening at the ledger. The little one was holding the annual balance sheet in his hand, checking it, and when Shimen entered he unsuccessfully tried to hide it.

"What do you think you're doing all of a sudden with the annual balance sheet?" said Shimen choked with anger.

The little one turned red, stammering something incomprehensible. Shimen took the balance sheet out of his hand, pushed away the ledger, and locked everything up in a drawer. A kind of a suspicion was born in him, but he immediately buried it, concealing it within himself. The fleeting comparison with Getsele was contrary to his own ambition.

He wanted to say something, to scold him, but couldn't get a single word out. Gradually his anger abated. Scolding that little creature because he wanted to learn? That was not at all becoming of Shimen Shifris, nor in keeping with his open view of the bookkeeping profession.

And his anger? His discontent? That had nothing to do with Getsele. That Shimen should even think about him was so much dignity for such a small fry. He truly didn't pay him any heed; he simply didn't enter into his intellectual world.

He left the bank to see Zosia, but Zosia wasn't at home. A note had been left for him: "A comrade, an old acquaintance, has come unexpectedly. I have to be away for two days. Don't be angry, Shimen, don't be jealous. Your little girl with the retroussé nose."

He went off to his rooms. The landlady was frightened, "What is wrong, Panie Shimen?"

"A little out of sorts."

"Perhaps you have a fever?"

"Possibly, my side hurts."

"So there's nothing to think about: right into bed with you. I'll put medicinal cups on your shoulders, rub you down with liniment—the best medicine."

Shimen was not altogether pleased at his confinement; the morning after a cupping one wasn't likely to rise all that early. And it wasn't worth going in to the bank on the later side. One day not having to look at Reb Fayvele's mug and the little Getsele's face also was worth something.

Early in the evening he went to Zosia's. Again Zosia wasn't at home. "Where is she?"

"In the union of course," was the answer.

So he went off to the union. The two rooms were packed full. Some stranger was giving a lecture, speaking with flintily chiseled words. The crowd was listening attentively.

It seemed that someone among the comrades notified Zosia of the news of Shimen's arrival; Shimen was seldom a guest in the union. Zosia made her way through the crowd to him, "You've come to hear the lecture?"

"I've come for you."

She answered him with her eyes, squeezing his hand.

And in the air the speaker's words reverberated stiffly:

"It is more sensible, more certain, and more advantageous to teach an illiterate worker the alphabet than to waste time uselessly on making a 'conscious' intellectual politically aware. The former drinks in what's taught like the natural knowledge of his class, like his simple bread. Right away, from his very first day, the former contributes to the worker's cause with small, but self-sacrificing deeds; he is ready for the greatest dangers, to risk his life. As for the latter: first pad the way for him with soft cushions, and adorn him with flowers, then debate him till dawn, let yourselves be dragged by him through his muddy and muddled train of thought, and then finally you'll get your reward: His full sympathy, but he cannot 'commit himself'."

"Do you like it?" Zosia asked.

"Yes, but . . ."

"Do you want to go?"

"If you can."

"Wait."

She walked over to the speaker's dais, exchanged a few words with the stranger, and soon returned to Shimen, "Come."

They left. Shimen held her fast by the arm, like something precious, and was silent.

"You're not asking anything, Shimen?"

"What should I ask?"

"You're not interested in where I was?"

"I'm not your investigating magistrate, I don't feel I'm entitled to know."

"So I will tell you. Do you know where I was?"

"With that stranger."

"He's no stranger; he's an old acquaintance of mine, quite a close one."

Shimen was silent.

"Why are you silent? Today you are close to me, Shimen. I feel the need to explain everything to you."

He wrapped her in his arms, pulling her to him, enclosing her lips with his own. They were in a dark avenue. Below, a torrent rushed.

Zosia explained, "He left his home; I was the reason. He didn't regret it. Now he is completely mature, one of the most responsible activists. He was in Germany, Latvia, Lithuania . . ."

"How did you get to know him?" Shimen asked.

She went on:

"He was a student in his first year, it seems, in mathematics. I was in the sixth class. A rich boy. An only child. I visited their home. Prominent people. His father was an industrialist with two houses in Vilne. Their home was a Jewish one. Do you know what it means in Vilne, a middle-class Jewish home? People were rather nice to me there, in Vilne. They treated me earnestly there, like a bride. I enjoyed myself, I liked the game."

"And?"

"That is, it so happened he was then a serious young man, and he proposed—nothing other than we get married. It all blew up! Me a bride? Me, marriage? To be your little housewife? To nurse your little children? Grisha! An only son."

"Grisha's his name?" Shimen asked.

"Yes, Grisha. You like that name?"

"Yes. And he?"

"He? He quit his studies, went off to an iron factory to work as a simple laborer. Then he studied in a polytechnic, went to the first meetings and left home."

"And his parents?"

"They knew it was because of me that Grisha went off to work in a factory, left home, and still they've acted very properly toward me.

His father in particular. Not once has he run into me without greeting me very politely. Later, when I was in prison in Vilne, his sister, a thoroughly civil, middle-class girl, brought me packages."

"It was probably at his request," Shimen remarked.

"Possibly," she said, "but it was, for their part, decent."

"And today they're still rich?"

"Probably. Why do you ask?"

"Well . . . It's just I've got nothing."

"What a child you are! What do you mean? What do you think of Zosia Lerner?"

"Nothing," Shimen wormed his way out of answering. "And before your arrest you would meet?"

"Of course we met. We often worked together, had things to talk about. He is a very politically aware young man. But once, we were alone, he took me gently in his arms and asked for a kiss. I didn't refuse, but released my hands from his, so small and so bony they were. He felt the slight and from then on he didn't try to come near me, even though I admit I never once wanted a kiss from him later."

"And now?" Shimen asked suddenly.

"Now," turning back round she nestled into him, "But now I've got you."

They had finally reached the union. Zosia needed to go back in, but Shimen could go to her home in about an hour, an hour and a half.

And later, when he arrived, he found the stranger at her place. Zosia introduced them. There was no conversation to connect them. The stranger, it seemed, listened intently to what Shimen had to say and didn't react to his story with more than a few words. No. No interesting conversation, as Shimen had wanted, could in any way connect them. But given what Shimen had heard about him, he would have pronounced his judgment on the stranger: that man is incapable of opening his mouth. But it was still worse—that is, the guest was acting with disdain for Shimen's polished ideas. That vexed Shimen. And perhaps more than the stranger's indifference, Zosia's neutrality hurt him. This beloved girl was just sitting there, tepidly responding to his words, words which at any other time she would normally have reacted to most enthusiastically.

The stranger was becoming more alien to him, more hostile. Shimen was waiting for him to leave. That didn't happen. It seemed that what upset Shimen pleased the stranger. The gloomy man felt quite at ease sitting in silence.

It was already midnight and the stranger hadn't so much as moved from his spot. It looked as though he had decided to outwait Shimen. It looked as though he felt more entitled than Shimen to be the last one, the last one to say good-bye to Zosia. But one thing really bothered him: Zosia didn't seem at all angry that the stranger was staying put; Zosia seemed unconcerned about his, Shimen's, agitation.

Ultimately Shimen decided to spite Zosia and leave just as the stranger stood up unexpectedly, "I have to go . . ."

Zosia went to him, "You will spend the night here, Grisha. Where will you go this late?"

But the stranger responded coldly and forcefully, "I'll find someplace. Good night."

Shimen remained standing in the middle of the room. Zosia walked the stranger to the door then she came back to Shimen. Her face was lost in thought and morose.

He took her, yielding, into his arms. She was unusually beautiful and interesting to him at that moment.

"Zenia . . ."

And she thought aloud, "He'll be wandering around outside all night. I know him well."

Shimen felt guilty. Guilty?!

"Listen, it's a struggle between two of a kind; one must yield and suffer."

"You're an egotist, Shimen. He is a comrade, of the best people."

A moment later she had once again nestled into him, was once again completely his. She set the warm velvet of her cheek to his lips. Another moment passed and he noticed a shadow cross her brow.

"What are you thinking about, Zenia?"

"I'm comparing."

"What are you comparing?"

"He's so much taller than you."

She gently freed herself from his arms and lifted her right hand over his head, as far as she could reach.

"So much taller."

And then she returned to him, burying herself into him.

He remained cold, politely kissing her little hand, "Good night, Zenia."

She didn't stop him, and with a trembling, stifled voice answered, "Good night, Shimen . . ."

———

He tossed and turned in bed until dawn, unable to fall asleep. Dream and reality were taking him by the hand, dancing a circle dance in his feverish head. He was clinging to an idea, wanting to make a clear spiritual reckoning; but he couldn't think it all through, as if a wave of dream had overwhelmed him.

And he dreamt of a better world, a more beautiful, more just world in which he, Shimen Shifris, might also have his own corner with a little girl who had clever steel-blue eyes and a little retroussé nose like a shepherdess.

For a moment he was covered in sweat. "Did you, you self-satisfied bookkeeper, finally snap your fingers to bring that beautiful and just world closer?" For a moment he managed to get out of his own skin, to stand before himself, scolding, "You, Shimen Shifris, why are you standing so far away while others are sacrificing their lives? Perhaps you think, you splendid bookkeeper, that your well-fed body is more valuable than the rawboned bodies of the tens and hundreds of thousands who suffer hunger and need?"

But that only lasted a moment. Soon his dream had begun to revolve around two little things: a calm, secure livelihood, and an intelligent, interesting girl. Zosia was good, and Feygele Rabinovitsh was better still. If so—and he held firm to this precise line of reasoning—if so, you must give up this dream of just worlds. You, Shimen Shifris, must direct all of your energy toward the struggle for these two desiderata, and not futilely waste your time on indulgent reveries. You, Shimen Shifris, with all of your sympathies, will be of no use, not even a pinch of snuff's worth, to the matter of Zosia Lerner and her comrades. You will only bring harm to yourself: you will lose the best Godlbozhits society; the director will become mindful of your left sympathies; and meantime a little Getsele will mount your shoulders, snuffling about with his little head shaped like a pig's snout in your now shoddy ledger entries. Shimen, you're carrying out your duties as a bookkeeper poorly. You often make writing mistakes, not remembering as well as you used to. And now this Getsele's standing there at the ready with his submissiveness, with his flattery, filling the gaps, beating you to it, circling round, snatching it all right out of your hands. Remember! Don't let him, Shimen!

He fell asleep at dawn, and woke up well into the day. The landlady asked, "Maybe we should send for the doctor?"

He put his hands to his forehead, unable to determine whether in fact he had a cold forehead or a hot hand.

He lay there for two days, coughing and drinking the doctor's medicines. Neither hide nor hair of any of his acquaintances was seen. In the evening of the second day he was visited by someone from the bank—the Jew who carried the receipts, "How are you, Shimen?"

"Thank you, Reb Sholem. Tomorrow I'll be up and about. What news at the bank?"

"Don't ask. A total revolution. Next week we're having a general meeting."

"So why on some random Wednesday?"

"Don't ask, Shimen. World's gone upside down. I don't even know where to begin."

Shimen sat up.

"Tell me, please."

Reb Sholem smiled modestly, but knowingly, into his beard. That is: "A poor man is like a corpse, a poor man must not get involved, just listen and keep quiet."

"Well, you're insulting me, Reb Sholem. After all, I'm not Getsele."

So Reb Sholem recounted:

"Moritz Meierbach came to the bank yesterday. Some kind of freight bound for Białystok. Hadn't Shimen heard? People were saying that the Meierbachs were moving their factory to Białystok. Fayvele didn't want to send the freight. 'Enough trouble,' he said, 'I've had from your objections.' Well, don't ask. Meierbach! 'You stingy bastard! Since when,' he said, 'did you get to be a person? Since Meierbach made you one?! You beggar, you don't own,' he said, 'even what my garbage is worth.' Fayvele didn't spare him either: 'Don't get yourself in such a tizzy, Panie Meierbach!' he said. 'Stop spraying me with your spit! I'm not really interested in such great noblemen! Just hand over what you owe, then you can talk!' The two of them were appropriately matched, as befitting rich men. But then again, Meierbach is Meierbach, so in the evening a meeting of the board was called and they set a general meeting, for about a week from now. They're going to get rid of Fayvele."

And then Reb Sholem concluded, "But we'll just see what'll happen."

The next morning Shimen got himself up out of bed. Outside had been seized by an early but mild spring frost. Shimen wrapped his neck warmly in a scarf. He coughed dryly.

Out of a shop came Getsele's little father running toward him.

"It's cold, Panie bookkeeper," he said, cheerfully rubbing his hands together. "I'm jealous of you functionaries: you work where it's warm. So how's my Getsele getting on? He told me, he did. You've already shown him the big book. The little one thinks he can get the whole Torah standing on one foot. So I tell him: my child, my little fool, if only let's shoot for about three years from now, then you'll be able to put together a balance sheet like Pan Shifris!"

The little father rubbed his hands with evident pleasure, flattering with a saucy chuckle. It seemed to Shimen that someone was uncovering his naked body and slapping him chummily.

At the bank he only encountered Getsele. The little one as always flatteringly set his glinting little eyes on him. This time there was a tiny dose of insolence in them.

Shimen went over to his desk, opened the ledger, and blanched with alarm. Three pages of the book had been covered with the little one's round handwriting.

"Who permitted you to write in the ledger?"

The little one didn't answer.

"Who permitted you, I'm asking you?!"

Shimen was trembling with agitation. The little one took on a pathetic look, "The Pan director . . . ordered . . ."

Right then Fayvele came in. He noticed Shimen's agitated face as though it were nothing, inquired after Shimen's health and the symptoms of his illness, and advised that it wasn't necessary to get out of bed so hastily; after a cold one needs to get warmed up, a cold is nothing to play around with. And if Shimen was still feeling under the weather he should make sure to go immediately back to bed.

Shimen didn't respond. Reb Fayvele took off his galoshes and removed his fur coat:

And Shimen should go over what the little one had scribbled in the books. He, the director, had no confidence in the little one's scribblings, he didn't want to know. He had made Shimen responsible for all of the bookkeeping.

Shimen held his head in his hands, gritting his teeth. A fresh sunbeam fell across the wide-open book, ridiculing Fayvele's hypocrisy. It caught in his, Shimen's, throat:

"I won't dare ever again touch that ledger! You hear?!"

The little one huddled up at his desk. Fayvele went over bills of exchange—he wasn't listening.

"I am responsible!" Shimen yelled.

"Responsible shmesponsible," grumbled Reb Fayvele.

"By what law?!"

"Law shmaw."

"I will not tolerate it!"

Reb Fayvele laughed to himself, "Everyone's threatening me: Meierbach's threatening, Shimen Shifris is threatening. Some picture!"

"Such a fine Jew as yourself, Reb Fayvele!"

For a moment it was eerily quiet. He, Reb Fayvele, didn't respond to him, Shimen. He spoke to the others, "By night one can go into a union and one can come into a bank by day, one can. If one's healthy enough for the union one's healthy enough for the bank . . . So being ill doesn't bother one, doesn't bother one at all."

And he went on:

He, Fayvele, loved everything on earth, except unions. A person he thought of as his own child, he wouldn't have done anything before making sure that person was provided for, but you've gone off with those ones over there, you're palling around with "reds." "I'm done with you, my man! Go to the union. Scram, beat it!"

Shimen jumped up from his seat, "Who are you driving out, who?! Who are you telling 'scram, beat it?!'"

And then more calmly, "Do you think the bank is your own private farm?"

People were coming in from outside. Reb Fayvele was embarrassed; Reb Fayvele fell silent. Someone asked what all the yelling was about. Reb Fayvele explained:

He hated unioneers and strikers like spies. Were he in the pharmacist's place he would have known the pharmacy was sunk, and he wouldn't have given in to that man, wouldn't have given one inch!

And he went on:

"You'll see, among all those kids of Melekh's there's not one good egg. Meierbach had a Nosn Garber, the pharmacist had a Shmuel pharmacy clerk, and I've got a Shimen Shifris."

But in the street people slapped Shimen on the shoulder, "Ah! Shimen, a guy who knows what's what! He really got him good! He gave him what for, that God-fearing Fayvele!"

The pharmacist sent for him. Moritz Meierbach, Iser Meierbach, the fat doctor—the whole group had gathered at the pharmacist's.

He, the pharmacist, heard said that Shimen wanted to quit his position. Who did he think he was, that sneaky Hasid, I'd quit my own position! Fayvele was just watching, just standing alone with the little snot-nose and all the while swindling, getting things done. A cholera!

A pain in his side, that filthy loan shark! That devout lout! Now he's going to quit, Shimen is? What does he, Shimen, think, that Fayvele was still going to be director? May his hair grow back! How he doesn't see his own ears!

He, Shimen, needn't be a fool. Just calm down. Let them find out how to liquidate half an estate, and Fayvele wouldn't be director any longer. Enough! He, Shimen, is a young man, he has opportunities. What, a director necessarily has to be a filthy Jew with a beard?

The next morning Fayvele didn't allow him back to work.

"If he really is thick as thieves with the big noblemen and wants to become director—then let him be so kind as to wait until after the general meeting."

Shimen didn't come to grief over it. He clung, tightly, to the Meier-bachs' and the pharmacist's coattails. It wasn't long until the meeting.

One thing did worry him: the little small fry was making himself at home in his books.

And another thing was distressing him: he had heard nothing from Zosia. She neither sent for him nor asked after him.

So he asked after her. "Zosia left with the one from Vilne," a comrade informed him. "Important work."

He didn't hear the "important work"; he only heard "left with the one from Vilne."

He clenched his lips. For three days he went around distraught, hiding from people's sight. On the fourth day, in the evening, he went into a gourmet food shop.

He asked for a glass of soda water, and the waitress turned on the phonograph, praising a new kind of chocolate.

The door opened. Lola Tsiglman entered. She was wearing a white sweater that went up to her neck. She was accompanied by a young one-star officer. Right after them a group of young people came in, mostly girls with a few boys. They drank soda water, cracking pumpkin seeds, sucking toffees, and making a lot of noise. You didn't need to be an expert to understand that they came to watch Lola Tsiglman. But she, Lola, played a nasty little trick on them—she didn't drink the water, just wrinkled her nose, turned back around and, without a word of good-bye, her head held aloft, left the shop. Her companion put a hand to the visor of his cap and followed her out.

From a corner they said to Shimen, "At least you I would have thought she'd say good-bye to."

Shimen looked around; he noticed her right away, the bespectacled Zionist librarian with the icy red nose.

"What have you got to say to me?"

"I'd bet that it was because of you that Lola came here in the first place," said the red nose.

"Thank you for the compliment," Shimen bowed. "Lola is still the most beautiful girl in Godlbozhits."

"A girl? Ha-ha!" said some young cutup, slurping on a candy. "When you go around with a soldier. A girl, ha-ha!" He didn't develop his lewd thought to its conclusion, that young, merry wag, it wasn't necessary. The whole crowd started to giggle.

The red-nosed librarian came closer to Shimen, speaking to him confidentially, "That's what we call a small-town upbringing!" She grew angry, "What's it to them who strolls with whom? What concern is it of theirs? I should be as lucky as Lola Tsiglman with her beauty. But of course Feygele Rabinovitsh is more beautiful than Lola, and undoubtedly Zosia Lerner is a little smarter than Lola."

Shimen blushed. How was she getting to him, that red nose? What was she digging away at?

However, before he had a chance to react she had poured out on him a flood of sympathetic commiseration:

How a little shtetl thinks. The whole shtetl is already abuzz: Zosia has thrown over Shimen Shifris, gone off with someone else. How is that anyone's business? Why are they racking their brains over it? Maybe it's just the opposite? Maybe Shimen told her "good-bye"?

She, the red-nosed librarian, should have as much luck as a year ago when she said that Shimen Shifris would break it off with Zosia. That was easy to understand. Zosia was not for him. Today this one, tomorrow another. It's true, Zosia was a clever girl, an intelligent girl, but what's to be gained from that? A man wants a wife for himself, not for someone else.

Besides, she worried a great deal about Shimen. Even though Lola strolled about with others, he should just pipe up, he should just say the word: *yes*. Only the other day Lola's mother herself had told her, "Just give me that young man, and I won't spare any money."

And nevertheless, those last words were not completely disagreeable to Shimen. It reminded him that for all of his internal disorientation—to people, to the people of Godlbozhits—he was still the self-assured, earnest bookkeeper.

Bookkeeper? And perhaps in a few days he really would be the director.

That evening a matchmaker came calling at the red-nose's father, not an official matchmaker, but an intimate of Reb Elye Tsiglman's and a close friend of his, Shimen's.

"Shall I get myself dirty? Three thousand dollars done and done!"

"Let's just wait for the meeting," Shimen said smilingly, and he himself didn't know whether he meant it seriously or in jest.

But on the eve of the meeting Shimen learned that he was not to be the director.

"People need to have someone with some standing," Meierbach said.

And he looked around and knocked the dust off the old, doddery Broderson with the Polish mustache, "from sea to sea."

"Maria, what do you think?"

"If the city's requesting, you can't refuse," his faithful advisor agreed.

And he put on his mink coat with the beaver collar (the same one that he had saved from the clutches of the Bolsheviks) and went down to the meeting.

But old Broderson with his authentic Polish aristocratic mustaches was not destined to understand the Jewish bank. At the same time that the result of the meeting became known, namely that Reb Fayvele was out and Broderson was to take his place, it also became known that Fayvele had in the course of the week withdrawn all of his capital from the bank, removed the better bills of exchange, and left the bank with an empty treasury and contested rags.

There was an uproar in the city. People started making a run on their deposits. Fiancées, widows, orphans, maids—they all went running into the bank for their deposited savings.

The cash reserves were empty.

The aggrieved raised a hue and cry, and people smashed the bank's windows, looking to destroy the building.

Fayvele calmed the crowd, "Shhhh . . . They'll give it back . . . Quiet . . . They'll give it back . . . Bit by bit . . ."

But after one of those common debtors cursed him and another one threw in a couple of blows, Reb Fayvele cast off his sense of shame, "It's not my problem! And when still larger banks are going bankrupt! When the Danat-Bank has gone bankrupt!"

⇥ 29 ⇤

Behind the Lowered Shades of the Fat Doctor's Venetian Windows

Only a few days had passed since Fayvele Shpilman's cooperative bank had stopped paying out, and Shimen Shifris, its longtime book-keeper, was already wandering the streets of Godlbozhits like a "beaten willow twig."[1] But as if that still wasn't enough, the embittered own-ers of the lost savings simply accused him of being in cahoots with the thieving Fayvele, and not infrequently some Jewish woman accosted him in the street with curses, "Bandit! Thief! Give me back my money! My hard work! My orphan's toil!"

If only in all of Godlbozhits there could be found at least one person to whom Shimen could unburden his heart. Someone who would listen to him, who would understand. There were so many details and causes of the catastrophe at the bank that Shimen could tell. Most guilty was Fayvele with the "angel maker," the bigwig. Guilty, too, were the Mei-erbachs with their mountains of contested bills of exchange. Wads of thousands had been pocketed legally: discounted notes, checks with-out backing, bills of lading without goods, acceptances of signatories long in the next world, and the acceptances of children still waiting to be born; accounts without underwriting, accounts muddled this way and that. So, so many such facts could Shimen now tell, but all of it, all

---

1. On Hoshana Rabbah, at the conclusion of certain prayers in the synagogue, willow branches are beaten on the ground in a symbolic act of supplication and rid-dance of sin.

of these excuses, were a waste of time. He would just be asked a simple question, "Where were you till now?"

And he might as well open up, cut open his heart for each and every one.

Perhaps in the circle of his own family they did believe that he hadn't stolen anything in cahoots with Fayvele and instead that a misfortune had befallen him with his cousin Shmuel Zaydman whom he had dragged by the hand into the bank, persuaded him to deposit his savings there and in that way laundered his hard-earned few thousand zlotys. They, his little family, were not particularly fond of the miserly pharmacist's clerk; they may well have secretly delighted at his misfortune. But people ate away at Shimen like rust, cursing him together with the mud:

He, the bookkeeper, ought to have stayed at the bank, to have figured out what was going on and not gone wandering all over the place with a girl who's been around the block, paying all of his attention to her, and passing off all of his work and responsibility onto that little smallfry, Getsele. He, Shimen, should have learned his lesson from Feygele Rabinovitsh. Splendid marriage matches were proposed to him, Shimen, and maybe Lola Tsiglman was a bad match. A young man like that goes and gets his head all turned around with a thin flounder, a young pup, an experienced featherbrain. You might at least have said some kind of *person*?! No. None other than a socialist does he have to have!

Mostly he was pestered by Tsadok, uncle Melekh's son, but the rest of Melekh's children didn't spare him either, sticking the pins in right to the quick.

Someone, a good friend of Melekh's household, took pity on him and without Shimen's knowledge sounded out Reb Elye Tsiglman about taking Shimen into the store as a son-in-law. Reb Elye should have answered, "I've got, thank God, nothing but splendid matches. My daughter doesn't need to take what someone else has cast aside."

Someone ought to have suggested that the police commander be consulted, "What's the bank's bookkeeper doing wandering about day and night with the 'boss' of the union?"

And again Tsadok came with news, "Fayvele Shpilman is opening a new bank, a private bank, and he's making that little Getsele his chief bookkeeper."

Girls, on the other hand, those sensitive young women of marriageable age, did indeed take pity on Shimen, feeling sorry for him, fretting over him and taking him into their care. In a line like a long whip they hung onto him, dragging him off for walks, lingering on the paths, and politely, in a discrete way, they endeavored to extract from him the details of his sad experience of love. Especially, and disarmingly, the Zionist librarian had attached herself to him, sticking her red nose right under his skin, spoiling him with flattering little comments, "Don't listen to them, Panie Shifris. Don't listen to them, those fake, petty little people of Godlbozhits. Please . . ."

This "please" came from devotion, right from the heart.

And it meant that Shimen didn't need to listen to the comments of all of the people whose only goal was a little gossip, a little slander, because she, the bespectacled nose, knew Shimen's soul, could appreciate him as he deserved. And so it was no surprise to her that such a girl as Feygele Rabinovitsh, who no doubt was hardly lacking in success there in Paris, couldn't forget him, Shimen, to this very day.

He sensed things, he felt things, Shimen did! Here Feygele's name was not mentioned in vain; there was something of a significance to it. But he wouldn't oblige her. And she, the red-nosed girl, wouldn't let go, "Did you know, Panie Shifris, that Feygele's coming back from Paris?"

"I didn't know," Shimen didn't flinch a shoulder. The red-nosed girl smiled, "And *I* know who it is she's coming back for."

He pricked up his ears and kept quiet. He wasn't going to ask again, even if he was bursting with curiosity.

"Eyges, Tykociński, Paris, and after all that it's back to Shimen Shifris," the red nose bore into Shimen's face with her short-sighted eyes, not missing a speck. Shimen, even though his heart was pounding, shrugged his shoulders as though it were nothing, as though it were of no interest, as though it were all the same to him.

"Is it true that the fat doctor loves Feygele? Is he, the doctor, really going to divorce his hunchback? Is it true that the doctor isn't living with his wife?"

The red-nosed girl was disappointed in Shimen:

He, Shimen, gives the impression that he's not a local. He doesn't know, as far as she can see, what's going on around him.

Having passed through this fire, Shimen's love-weary heart could rest a bit. The whetted tongues of Godlbozhits had abandoned the exhausted ex-bookkeeper and had set upon the fat doctor. Those piercing little eyes began to drill through the lowered yellow blinds in front of the doctor's sizeable window; tongues began to wag around the doctor's place day and night.

However, the fat doctor's love affairs were not approached in similar fashion. For as candid and cynical as the doctor was in his medical practice, he was equally secretive about his intimate relations. But it wasn't for nothing that Godlbozhits was known all around as a shtetl of wise and cunning men. When you ask someone about the mind of the inhabitants of Godlbozhits, straightaway he'll answer you meaningfully, "Godlbozhits scoundrels—ho ho!" And from such a comment one was supposed to infer that Godlbozhits was not Chelm, that there they hadn't fallen off the turnip truck, that there in the city of Godlbozhits it was enough to give a wink or a crooked look and some person or event will be painted out for you in every littlest detail.

And in order to get to the fat doctor, first they had to set their sights on Feygele Rabinovitsh. Or to put it better, they had to stick her into some deep mud, into an abyss from which the fat one could go and pull her out, all the while trampling the heart and life of his own wife, a poor hunchback and a sickly woman.

Feygele therefore went off with the painter Tykociński to Paris and there they got married, or lived on faith. (Who knew them there, artists and easy women?) Then a musician friend of Feygele's fell in love with her, and when Tykociński found out about their relationship he broke things off with her.

Meantime an actor from a theater troupe had taken to hanging around Feygele, and in her he discovered talents as a ballet dancer. It didn't last long; the actor went off with someone else, but Feygele kept dancing. Feygele passed from hand to hand. Here she is dancing completely naked, like Mother Eve, in a cabaret, and here she's been hired during the day as a model for a painter, and at night . . . Oh, at night in Paris one doesn't recite Psalms, and in Godlbozhits one is still not so heartless to take a daughter of Shmuel Rabinovitsh and send her right onto the street corners.

But aside from pure human kindness, there were other significant motives that prevented Feygele Rabinovitsh from being instantly hauled over the coals. If Godlbozhits were to make a novel out of Feygele, she, that chaste young woman, might take the trouble to return form Paris so that the whole shtetl might see and be convinced of what becomes of someone who submits to a freewheeling lifestyle. And whether to derive a little pleasure and boost the spirits of the confirmed Godlbozhits maidens, or as a moral lesson—Godlbozhits needed her desperately.

As a partner for such naked dancing with that lewd debauchee over the glowing hot iron floors of hell the city chose the fat doctor.

He, the fat man, used to go about with Feygele in his luxury car; he, the doctor, spoke of Feygele glowingly, singing her praises. But with regard to his wife he ought to have demonstrated that they were "just good friends," that they even had separate bedrooms. Obviously it was worth it to Mekhele Podreytshik to toil day and night and show off a doctor for Shmuel Rabinovitsh's sake. But that's already another matter. What's important at that moment was the fact that he and his hunchbacked wife were "good friends"; that the little hunchback never left their house; that the fat one had hired a shikse with a pure white face and large calf's eyes, and that shikse, so people said, served him as his right hand in his forbidden gynecological practice, and as his "left" wife alongside a real hunchback who lay hidden there somewhere in the inner recesses and was embarrassed to show her face for shame.

There was a girl who had a fiancé in the big city. Unable to wait for his ardently loved letters to be delivered at home she would go every day to the post office and wait for the mailman to come out. It wasn't every day that she received a letter, but on those occasions that she did she was able to rifle through the long, narrow envelopes in the mailman's briefcase. And so once a green-marbled envelope especially caught her eye, its stamp—a woman in a long dress—was French, and its address was "Dr. B . . ." But she couldn't manage to read any more of it because just then the mailman shut the flap of his briefcase and strode off with a smile, "Buddy, you're not fooling anyone." That fact was enough for the pining bride of the big-city fiancé to whisper it about to her girlfriends, "The doctor's corresponding with Feygele."

And Godlbozhits began earnestly preparing on the one hand for the doctor to divorce his wife, and on the other hand for him to bring back Feygele from Paris for his own sake, to give her the beautiful houses that Mekhele Podreytshik had built for some foreign devil, and the fine son-in-law that he showed off as a doctor for Shmuel Rabinovitsh's sake. Shmuel Rabinovitsh had even managed to learn of this match and cursed him, people said, like a rotten apple . . . ut all of a sudden the straight thread of the Parisian novel that Godlbozhits was spinning got tangled, knotted up, and snipped in two . . .

The fat doctor's wife, so it came to light, was sick, and naturally she was sick from her miseries. Good friends visited Mekhele Podreytshik's wife to console her, to moan and lament. It turned out that the mother really was crying, but crying with tears of joy, "God be praised, after so many years, pregnant."

A thunderbolt struck Godlbozhits. That is—over and done with that business with Feygele Rabinovitsh; that is—the doctor loved the little hunchback and decided to have children with her; that is—Mekhele Podreytshik's got the luck of the devil; that is—with money you can buy the world . . .

People consumed him, Mekhele Podreytshik, with their eyes till he was completely devoured. The good people of Godlbozhits had quite some eyes. They should only be burned with vitriol!

One evening the fat doctor was summoned home from the club; his wife was not well. But there's not well, and then there's not well.

He ran up hill and down dale, the fat one did, losing his glasses along the way, and nearly killed himself on the concrete steps of his own home. Not even taking off his coat he went in to see the sick woman, examining here up and down, and then the crumpled little creature fainted in his hands, turning white as chalk and balling herself up in pain. Not thinking it over a moment he ran over to the telephone and called in several colleagues; and he also sent for the Warsaw Professor Michałowski. He wanted a consultation.

The old professor took only a quick look, taking the sick woman's hand. And hardly consulting his colleagues he advised authoritatively, "Don't wait. The operation must be undertaken at once."

He shrugged his shoulders, the old professor with the pointy grey goatee, he didn't understand why they were waiting so long.

"How is it," he gently chided, "that you, my colleague, a gynecologist, don't know what's coming? Is this your first time with an ectopic pregnancy?"

The fat doctor and husband asked astonished, "An ectopic pregnancy? How? From what?"

The old professor smiled sadly, sighing, "From what? For our sins, my colleague, for the frequent abortions, for the abnormal sex life."

Then the weary husband lowered his head, like a guilty boy. And later, when the little hunchback was covered with blood on the operating table, he collapsed into a chair, took a handkerchief to his eyes and loudly, so unlike a doctor, so unlike a man, cried. His colleagues led by the professor said their good-byes, leaving him alone in his grief with his beloved departed.

And people described something frightful, terrible:

It was midnight. The old devastated father had barely persuaded his distraught son-in-law to lie down for a bit. The old man had barely persuaded him to do this. The fat doctor went down the dark hallway and into his room. The shades had been lowered for several days. He turned on the light and pressed a button. In the doorway appeared the Gentile girl with the pure white face and the large calf's eyes.

"Bring me the cognac from the credenza."

The girl disappeared and a moment later returned, placing the bottle on the table and withdrew back into the doorway.

The fat doctor poured a glass, drank it down, then poured another glass.

"Drink!" he commanded.

The girl goggled her calf's eyes. In them were both fear and terror.

"Drink!"

She approached the table as though being pulled by an invisible cord, and with a trembling hand took the glass. Then she slowly drained it.

The fat one kept his hands on the bottle, training his eyes on her grimly.

"Drink, you're being told!"

And when she drank the glass the fat one let go of the bottle and stretched out both hands, "Come, Kasia."

She shuddered with terror, her calf's eyes nearly rolling back in their sockets, "Not now . . . I'm afraid . . ."

"Come."

"Afraid . . . The dead . . ."

"Come!"

The light went out. Someone cried quietly, someone wheezed.

———•—•———

And people described something still more terrible, more cynical:

In a soft, felt coat the fat doctor slunk off to the room where the dead woman lay. He put an eye to a hole in the curtain: candles, so many candles on both sides, six straws underneath the body and above it a gleaming white sheet gathered in folds over the bony, protruding limbs. Here and there the sheet was dampened with blood—blood from his wife and from his unborn child.

On a chair nearby sat her old father, a devastated father. He appeared to be sleeping, but just then he lowered his hand and covered the face of the dead woman. His head was bowed, bowed so it seemed like it was about to fall to the ground. But then he let go the sheet again, turning his head away, and the doctor met his eyes:

"Murderer! You killed my child!"

Terrified, the doctor backed away from the door, distancing himself from the nightmare. After all, he was particularly anxious lest he imagine such hallucinations.

With quiet footsteps he slunk away in his soft coat to the next room, the study, and turned on every light. That's it, let it be bright! He closed the door behind him, looking somewhat fearfully into every corner, then sidled to the writing desk. Pulling open a little lid he took out a piece of fine linen paper, an envelope, a fountain pen:

"Dear Feygele . . .

Perhaps you remember our drives in my car?

And now I am finally free and can say to you: Come, my bird, into my nest . . .

Come, come by car, come, Feygele."

✣ 30 ✤

Concerning the Necessary Qualifications for Inspectors, Representatives, and Presidents of the Community

All of a sudden the whole fantastic horror surrounding the tragic death of the doctor's little hunchback burst like a soap bubble, and along with it Shimen's deeply hidden hope that somehow he would get to see Feygele again and stretch out his masculine arm to her, "You've gone astray, Feygele, but now take my hand, lean on your faithful friend who never stopped loving you."

In the middle of April the painter Tykociński came back from Paris. He had let his sideburns grow, the way lackeys used to wear them. He was sporting an overall tunic of blue material with shiny buttons, the kind of outerwear that the chauffeurs of wealthy burghers customarily wore, and in which idle artist painters paraded around in the streets of picturesque provincial shtetls.

Tykociński sent for Shimen, "For you I have a personal greeting, can you guess from whom?"

"Well . . . from Feygele Rabinovitsh," Shimen blushed up to his ears.

"You guessed it. But of course you already know that Feygele got married?"

"No . . . of course . . . that is . . . I heard," lied Shimen. "To whom in fact?"

"Apparently an engineer, or some industrialist—the point is—a wealthy man."

"From Paris?"

"Naturally from Paris, Paris and how! That girl could never have dreamed such good luck. Her husband is a millionaire, one of the largest furniture manufacturers."

And whom did that girl have to thank for her good fortune? Obviously him, Tykociński.

They met at his exhibition in Paris, the very first day. Only invited guests were in attendance, distinguished patrons. He, Tykociński, led Feygele around, showing her his paintings. The just-mentioned gentleman, by appearance a respected older bachelor, came over and in a very courteous way asked about the meaning of one of the paintings. A conversation ensued, then an acquaintanceship. Well, at any rate, about four weeks later Tykociński received an invitation to their wedding.

"Ah, what a Feygele, that Rabinovitsh!" Tykociński quipped.

His breezy summary of that dramatic event annoyed Shimen. And perhaps he also envied the painter: if only to be an artist and take life so lightly.

It interested Tykociński, "And so how is Khane-Yente the *tkhine*-reciter?"

"Still a sprightly Jewess, selling fruit in the street."

"And old Moyshele the porter?"

"Dead."

"Dead?!" Tykociński couldn't believe it. "Really dead? Ah, what a shame! What a quaint subject he was, that old man with the crooked little shoulder! A little shoulder, gold and diamonds! Can you believe it, Shifris? That picture that you saw at my place of Moyshele the porter I sold in London for fifty pounds and a kiss on the hand. Ah, that little old man had a splendid little shoulder! A shame! A great shame!"

They went off in the direction of the hotel. Tykociński invited Shimen out onto the veranda of the restaurant. They could have a cup of coffee while Shimen told a little of the news of Godlbozhits. Alright?

"Alright."

Nearing the hotel both of them suddenly noticed the dark Eyges. Well, actually it was his head with its shovel-like beard jutting out over the wooden railing of the veranda. Eyges was chewing with gusto; he smiled at the two of them and greeted them with a raised hand.

"You here? How's that?" Tykociński was genuinely delighted.

The editor extended his hand to Shimen, "I'm Dovid Eyges."

"But, Herr Editor, we know each other," Shimen said, embarrassed.

"Ah! Really . . . Indeed . . . You are . . . Now I remember . . . Feygele Rabinovitsh . . . Right, almost got it . . ."

"Shifris," the painter prompted.

"Yes, right—Shifris."

Shimen felt pathetic, humiliated; he blushed like a girl. The editor hurriedly stuffed one spoonful of strawberries and cream after another into his open mouth and said something, rolling his tongue.

All of a sudden Shloyme Mandelboym came running over out of the marketplace. The young poet was running without a jacket and with his chest unbuttoned, as if it was who knows how hot outside.

"Halloa, Eyges! Halloa, Tykociński!" he bellowed as though the whole street were his, as though he wanted to surprise the dozing Godlbozhits marketplace.

From the neighboring tables people looked around, and the Polish proprietress of the restaurant came out, watching astonished, aghast. The sound of yelling in that staid restaurant shocked everyone.

The young poet roamed back and forth for a while, up and down the veranda, his hands in his trouser pockets, and suddenly he remembered, "I'm in a hurry, I have an interview with Representative Wojdisławski."

"*Pan-brat*," Tykociński shrugged his shoulder after the poet had left.[1]

"Ho, ho!" the editor said. "You think it's the old Mandelboym? The old scribbler? He's now a poet of great breadth, with verve, and most importantly . . . with vitality. And why only a poet? A playwright, a critic, an essayist, an interviewer, a talk-your-ear-offer. God forbid I envy what he manages to get his hands on."

---

1. *Pan-brat* (Polish): dear brother, my brother, indicating hail-fellow-well-met.

"That's the one," the painter laughed, "the one with the 'ringing bells on virginal, maidenly heads'?"

Shimen cleared his throat and asked politely, "Representative Wojdisławski is here? He's come on a trip?"

"Yes," said the editor. "Came in his own car. I actually came with him, and Inspector Rafalkes was also with us. Wait! You work here in a bank, right? If so, Rafalkes has come to see you. He told me something about irregularities, misappropriations at a bank."

Shimen stood up, thanking him for the information: Yes, he certainly does need to know that, he's somewhat connected to it. Though naturally not to the misappropriations. Shimen laughed.

That was just the right time for Shimen to leave, since the two representatives of literature and art had begun speaking in their professional jargon and Shimen was afraid lest he say something dilettantish. The sentimental painter lamented, "How the municipal authorities of Godlbozhits have botched things with their paving the streets, with their removing the lavatories and ramshackle, rotting little rooms. How Godlbozhits has lost its quaint character of old mildew, the particular hues of the Godlbozhits reek."

He took his leave, Shimen did, and with hurried steps ran off to the bank, leaping all the steps at one go, knocking, "Let me in."

At the table sat Inspector Rafalkes. He was wearing a bright, freshly pressed summer suit. Shimen recognized him, especially the ever courteous little smile on his round face, that polite little smile that lied to people about his sincerity, that fooled his own wife about his fidelity, and young inexperienced girls about his love. He did have one good quality, Inspector Rafalkes did: as an inspector he was a good confidant. But he also had a significant defect: as a confidant he was too lazy to work and not especially diligent.

He composed himself right away, but he didn't have any time so he hastily said to little Getsele, "Make up the list and send it to me in Warsaw. The rest of the report I'll put together at home."

"I wanted to talk to you about something, Herr Inspector," said Shimen.

"Please, please, but quickly if at all possible, as I'm in a hurry."

"In private."

"Ah, so. You'll excuse us," the inspector spoke to little Getsele. "You'll please excuse us."

The little man scurried out. The inspector stretched leisurely in the armchair, making a serious, strained face, "I'm listening."

"I didn't know," Shimen began, "I knew nothing of the inspection and believed that in no time."

"Ah! I'm a great magician," Rafalkes smiled, "an hour or two and now I know everything, even what's not written. It's possible that you can add something. That would be most desirable."

"I can add," said Shimen hastily, "that Fayvele Shpilman ruined the bank."

"Well," Rafalkes hiccupped. "One can't say that. I, from my objective standpoint, would say, for example, that Meierbach ruined it no less."

"Certainly, certainly," Shimen's eyes lit up. "Meierbach, the pharmacist, Goldshteyn—all the bigwigs, they all destroyed the institution, defrauded it. But Fayvele, the director, is most responsible.

"The Herr Inspector should consider: Shpilman was in control of everything, he created the bank, seemingly for the public good, but actually to use it to conduct his own private discount business. The Herr Inspector needs to understand: a usurer does not like to have money lying around gathering dust. An industrialist needs a profit, and a usurer needs interest. More than half of the deposits were Fayvele Shpilman's capital, and the other half, the petty savings of poor people, served to underwrite the director's capital in case of any losses. Then the fat bellies, the industrialists, came, threatening Fayvele to 'look in the bowl,' so he threw them a bone—he wrote them promissory notes, sureties, checks. What did it matter to him, to Fayvele? He kept his money partly in cash and partly in sound notes with numerous endorsers. And for his bad debts there were, after all, the poor people's deposits, pennies scraped together by the toil of housemaids, meager dowries, money set aside. 'You're owed money? Please, here, take Meierbach's protests, will you' . . . But why didn't Shpilman take his money with protests?"

Shimen spoke passionately, he needed to move a stone. The Inspector heard him out patiently, one might even say he listened quite attentively, and asked again, "So you also maintain, Panie Shifris, that Shpilman withdrew nothing more than his own money from the bank?"

"What?" Shimen fumed. "Strangers' money he'd have to have taken? It's not enough to have robbed and swindled the institution?"

"Well, quite, but you'll forgive me, that's not robbery. What was owed him he took. Formally he was in his rights."

"Formally."

"Quite so: formally. Morally, it's another matter. But that's not what we're talking about now, that's off on a separate path. But formally . . ."

"So what is your advice, Herr Inspector?"

"My advice. There is no other advice—the members need to pay in addition to the shares."

It was a shock to Shimen.

"Who will pay extra? Are they idiots?"

"They'll be forced to!" Inspector Rafalkes said severely. "According to the law, anticipated in the bylaws."

Shimen was seething, "So those poor, miserable Jews—it's not enough that Shpilman and Meierbach robbed them of their labor, but they still need to be fleeced of additional payments?!"

Inspector Rafalkes did not answer right away. Inspector Rafalkes sat up straight in the armchair, slowly leaning his face toward Shimen's. The courteous little smile flowed over his full cheeks like oil.

"Forgive me for the question, Panie Shifris, but are you a socialist?"

Shimen turned red. He didn't understand what the Inspector meant by that, nor by the fact that in the meantime he held out a hand to him, "If you'll permit me . . . If so, then we're comrades."

Shimen defended himself, "Oh . . . I don't belong to any party."

"That's no matter," the inspector assured him. "The point is the idea."

A scruffy boy came into the bank, "Someone's calling, a nobleman's calling."

Rafalkes went over to the window and leaned out. Below a motor was running. Someone's bass voice could be heard.

"Coming, coming!" the inspector yelled down.

"Come on," he said to Shimen, "I will introduce you to the representative."

They walked down the front steps. People were standing around a freshly waxed car and idly gawking at the distinguished guests. Seated in the car was Representative Wojdisławski himself whom Shimen recognized from his photograph. Inspector Rafalkes introduced him. The representative held out a substantial hand, offering it to Shimen with companionable ease.

"Get in," the representative said in a strong bass voice. "Well, this one will finally point out the lovely Godlbozhits girls."

The Inspector laughed. Shimen climbed into the car, sitting down next to the representative. He noticed that the representative's meticulously trimmed beard didn't match his roguish eyes.

"And where are your girls?" the representative demanded.

"Girls?" Shimen pretended not to understand. "The area around here is interesting."

"Young man," said the representative, slowing the car. "I've known Godlbozhits since before you even existed. So tell me, how do you live here during the winter?"

"Another life," Shimen sighed. "We vegetate."

They drove slowly uphill. A narrow lane that the car could barely make its way through, so as not to cut any swathes out of the fields. On both sides there were young, green shoots on the freshly ploughed earth, like the first silken hairs on a baby's soft little head. A bit further on stood a tall stone fence, a church, noble headstones, iron wreaths of wealthy, respectable burghers, peasants' oak crosses and, lower down, little birch crosses of those who fell in battle. Some kind of cemetery.

And now they were finally at the top of the mountain. The Representative hastily turned the wheel, the car spun around facing the city and came to a stop.

All three got out of the car, admiring the shtetl stretching out below them.

"Beautiful," said the representative.

"Magnificent," the inspector corrected.

Shimen stood beside an oak and said nothing. The sun was setting and pouring gold over the hills facing them. All around was empty, not a person to be seen. Valleys and hills, green and greener still. Far off in the distance a windmill was lazily spinning. To the left by the stream blossoming orchards embraced the shtetl in a semicircle: red roofs and silver roofs, golden straw and green moss. Tiny little people were bustling about comically like ants in the middle of the market-place, clambering around the well. A car came driving up, and the porters besieged it, running around, carrying bags. Everything took place so quietly, as if in pantomime. How beautiful it was!

It had been years since Shimen had been here on the mountain, even though all told it wasn't even a kilometer from the shtetl. How stuck to his chair must a Godlbozhits bookkeeper be to be too lazy for a bit of a climb and to look at himself from one story up. One keeps digging and scraping deeper inside oneself.

Zosia . . . The beloved name unconsciously resurfaced in his heart. Even to be together here one more time, one more time she could lay her head against his chest and say whether it was worth it to suffer such doubts, when here it was so beautiful all by itself . . . so lovely . . .

"Dreamer," she would laugh sadly. She had bound her fate to hard-ened people; hands, so bony, like that Vilner's, so broken, eaten away by acids like the tanners'; such tormented, bloodless faces like the bak-ers' . . . Zosia! Zo-o-o . . .

The car honked. The other ones were already inside, and he, he was coming . . .

"Godlbozhits dreamer," the representative laughed expansively in a sonorous bass.

Embarrassed, Shimen got in. They drove downhill, slowly.

"So how many families, would you say, are there in this shtetl?" the representative asked.

Shimen answered, "Several hundred, maybe a thousand, but it's no life. So, for example, I . . ."

"Do you have political parties, organizations?"

"There is a Zionist one, but I, for example, don't belong to any party. Of course, I do have certain sympathies."

The representative kept interrupting him, "And how do the Jews here occupy themselves?"

"They trade, but all the business isn't worth a penny. So, for example, take an uncle of mine . . ."

"And how does the youth here occupy itself?"

"Better not to ask. They idle about; what else is there for the Jewish youth to do? No office will hire them."

"And you, what's your employment?"

"A bookkeeper."

"How much do you earn?"

"A hundred fifty a month."

"Very good, very good."

"By local standards," interjected Inspector Rafalkes, "it's definitely good. What does a family here need to have? Food is cheap."

Shimen nearly cried out: "And you, Rafalkes? People know very well you've got a salary of two thousand, and an expense allowance, and first-class train travel besides. Why is that not enough? Why are you responsible for all the banks and give nothing back?" But instead he slowly added, "But what's the use when there are no jobs? The bank is no more, and there are no more jobs in Godlbozhits. I think, gentlemen, perhaps you know something?"

Rafalkes jumped as if he'd been burned, "Oh, what are you talking about? Today in Warsaw there is a crisis, a surplus of bookkeepers."

"Have a seat, if you please," said the representative.

And a moment later he added, "Incidentally, if you happen to be in Warsaw . . ."

The representative didn't finish his sentence, and Shimen hadn't managed to grasp that thread. They were already in the shtetl. The car stopped right in front of the pharmacy and the representative jumped out.

"You'll see, I've got hold of . . ." the representative winked an eye. He airily hopped down off the runningboard and danced into the pharmacy. Shimen noted with disappointment how short he was, the merry Representative, with legs that were warped into a bow.

Shimen saw the representative's roguish eyes flirting with Bebele Rabinovitsh. And Bebele laughing back with her wide mouth. And the pharmacist standing to the side with a fawning smile.

"Perhaps the Herr Master would be so good as to give the miss an hour's liberty?"

"With the utmost delight," the pharmacist's face flooded with satisfaction, "with the utmost delight."

"And no one needs to ask me?" Bebele held her head proudly aloft, laughing.

"Ah!" The representative drew his crooked legs together in a ridiculous way, and bowed, half serious and half in jest. "Forgive me, would not the mademoiselle be amenable to taking a walk with us? The whole car is at your disposal, honored fräulein."

Bebele grew serious, angry even.

"A little too late, and not successful, Herr Representative . . ."

"Oh! What proud girls you've got, Herr Master." The Representative took out a silver cigar case, inlaid with gold. "Please, perhaps the mademoiselle smokes? Please, Herr Master . . ."

The pharmacist bounded over, taking a cigarette. Bebele had flushed pink, considering something stubbornly, assessing a prescription. The representative bowed deeply, and took his leave; the pharmacist accompanied him like a spoiled child, imploring him, bowing obsequiously and not knowing how to please his important guest.

Shimen slid deeper down into his seat. So at least no one could see him. Bebele might yet think that he had inflicted that arrogant suitor on her.

People again gathered around the car. Several Jews in Sabbath kapotes pushed their way through and graciously lifted their little round hats.

"A delegation to the Herr Representative from the local Jewish community, from the local business community, from the local tradesmen's community."

The Herr Representative held the car wheel with one hand and the other was in his trouser pocket.

"By all means, let them, the Jews of Godlbozhits, write a memo to the minister; obviously, to the real minister. I, for my part, will certainly . . . intervene . . ."

The delegation bowed nearly in half, "The Herr Representative is so obliging."

The little round hats lifted high and graciously in parting.

Suddenly a crowd had formed in a corner of the street. Representative Wojdisławski didn't consider it for very long. He started up the car and was at the wheel.

Moshke Abishes was standing in front of a flour store, yelling angrily in through the open door, "That's the burghers for you! Who didn't know his dad, the cooper! He scraped the moldy greenery from the staves and gobbled it down. Got to be a well-off person!"

A thin shopkeeper woman, totally covered in flour and slathered with herring juice, yelled back, "Something's got you going, Moshkele? Won't go scratching your pockets for money, eh?! The chief sent you packing, eh?! Leah Stänglmeier's not going to pretend to make any crêpe de Chine clothes for my blood, eh?!"

"Khanele Snotter! Maybe you'd like a piece of bread with your snot?!"

Her husband, all white with flour, and with angry eyes, came out of the shop to drag his wife back in, shouting, "Shut your mouth already, mute Khane! You're making a scene. Why'd'you have to stand there arguing with that informer?!"

And to Moshke, wagging a finger, "You won't shoot yourself, Moshkele Thief, like the secretary did! You won't get any community coffers! You'll still die violently, like your dad did!"

"Who is this Moshke?" the representative asked Shimen.

"He had been president of the community. But he abused the office, stole, and now he's out."

"And what's he doing now?"

"An informer, a vile youth."

"And his father, what was he?"

"A horse thief."

"So why didn't he work out as president?"

Shimen looked the representative right in the eye. There was something he couldn't quite figure out: was the representative being serious or making a joke when he said that?

✦ 31 ✦

How Balaam the Wicked Drove Khaykl to Curse, and Surprisingly Began to Pray

When the old police commander left and made his tearful good-byes to everyone, Godlbozhits expressed its sympathy to his face, and behind his back lifted its eyes to heaven: "Such a swift and speedy end, such a calamity, dear father in heaven, for Moshkele Thief and Khaykele Bastard!"

And even though the severely overworked shopkeeper men and women of Godlbozhits knew from experience that one mustn't ask for a new king, that each new ruler of the city proved to be worse than the last, their desire with regard to Moshkele Thief and Khaykele Bastard was nevertheless sincere, from the bottom of their hearts. And again, as for the old boorish police commander, let him also take some punishment. He knew too much about them, the old commander did, knew what was cooking in everyone's pot, stuck his nose into every hole, through every gap in a door that was open till seven o'clock in the evening, into every false lid of a writing desk where a flimsy box of homemade cigarettes lay hidden.

More than anyone it was two Jewish shopkeeper women who celebrated and clapped their hands for joy. Here's who they were: the broadly built Khane-Dine, a herring-and-flour-woman with a disheveled wig on her head and large, malevolent eyes, a Jewess who prayed piously and still more piously cursed from early in the morning till late at night. And the other was her neighbor in the butter store across the way, the heartsore and heartstealing Pesele with the little eyes worn out from crying. These two goody-goodies shared a weight for their

395

scales that was stealthily added when someone came in to buy butter, and they shared a brother-in-law with long *tsitsis* and long *peyes*—a grain merchant who swore by his head and by his beard and peyes that in all of Godlbozhits one couldn't find a single grain merchant who didn't cheat left, right, and center on weighing the grain—not one single grain merchant, that is, of course, except for him, the God-fearing Jew.

Still, there were also some who mentioned the old boorish police commander favorably. It did sometimes happen, for example, that after paying the peasant woman for a large piece of butter and after cutting it in half you'd find a whole mess of grated potato inside. Oh, how the old commander would break out his whip!

So if the relationship of the shopkeepers to the old commander was a significant one, depending on the time, conditions, and the people involved to whom he displayed his power, Moshke Abishes and Khaykl the sexton's son were undeniably at their wits' end, like orphans, over losing their livelihood.

In the course of many years these two men had been the middle-men between the shopkeepers and craftsmen on the one hand and the authorities, embodied by the dismissed police commander, on the other. True, the people of Godlbozhits asserted that they had no use for these middlemen, and perhaps once in a while they really did honestly believe that, but now a whole city was simultaneously asserting that they had no use for the rabbi while still going running to him with lawsuits, for the sale of leavening during Passover, for answers to questions about whether some food was kosher. Go believe people who don't even believe themselves.

Meantime the city's new police commander had arrived and the two community providers started circling him and sniffing like dogs. A thin man, polished, in bookish glasses, who held himself stiffly—go figure what that all meant.

Moshke went to visit the nobleman at his home. He removed his hat while still in the foyer, and cautiously opened the door.

The commander came out to see him in the kitchen.

"At home I don't do work; I take care of everything at the office. Well . . . right into my home they'll come creeping to me, these Yids."

So Moshke Abishes went right to the middle of the marketplace and announced the news, "Jews . . . we won't soon be rid of him, we're done for. As I live I've never seen such an anti-Semite."

Meantime, a sackful of illicit hares, shot out of season, had been confiscated from a village Jew. So this time Khaykl went; he'd know what to do. He took a twenty-zloty note, stuck it in an envelope, and handed the commander the "request."

When the commander opened the envelope he threw it back, shouting, "Take it away! Get out! I'm shutting the door!"

So Moshke went and sent home to the commander's wife a soft, fat hare, a few partridges, and a couple hundred eggs. The commander ate the fine food and, it seems, didn't grasp their meaning. The morning after the feast he saw no one and, what's more, let no one in to see him.

Moshke Abishes was not surprised. He was certain that in his life he had known far more incorruptible people who had eventually taken, and taken in such style! Regretting the earlier lean years . . . Moshke had already lived a lifetime between Russian bureaucrats, Austrian gendarmes, and Polish policemen, and it was his opinion that they all took: some sooner, others later.

But Khaykl didn't have much faith in the business qualifications of the new police commander. Khaykl was falling to pieces; he might as well put back on the armband and go running after the summertime visitors: "This house, *proszę jaśnie Panna*,[1] is two thousand thirty years old; and here lived, proszę jaśnie Panna, that King Sobieski who slayed the dragon; that is a kind of beast with a hundred legs that breathes fire . . ."

Concerning the new police commander, people learned that it was not for nothing that he held himself so stiffly. It turned out that he came from a distinguished lineage, a family of judges and prosecutors,

---

1. *proszę jaśnie Panna* (Polish): the honorable miss.

and that the deputy prosecutor Galewski, who came to summer in Godlbozhits and had his own villa there, was a first cousin of his. Still it turned out that commander Galewski was not so much an anti-Semite as a mortal enemy of unioneers and strikers, and his anti-Semitism sprang from the fact that he identified socialists and unions with Jews.

And therefore it was the job of the authoritative elements in Jewish Godlbozhits to persuade him of his error. It's quite true, that is, regrettably, that there were strikers among the Jews, but the vast majority of Godlbozhits Jewry, etc.

The opportunity to clarify the situation came quite quickly. One morning the commander summoned the rabbi and the head of the community and asked them:

Were they at least aware, these leaders of the Jews of Godlbozhits, of all of the strikes that their co-religionists were calling and of all of the rebellions they were inciting?

Were they prepared to hand over the names of those Jews who were the chief agitators among the workers?

What assurances could they give, these leaders of the Jews of Godlbozhits, that all of these abhorrent crimes would not be repeated?

The rabbi and the head of the community answered, trembling with fear:

First, they were the spiritual leaders of the Jews of Godlbozhits, so with regard to political matters they didn't know what to say.

Secondly, if the people in Godlbozhits found out that they were coming here and talking, that might, Heaven protect us, set those people off, or even, may it not happen, they might be killed.

Thirdly, they can vouch for all of Godlbozhits's bourgeoisie that God forbid they should do such a thing.

Fourth, the nobleman ought not think that honest people have done this. The local unioneers are of the most abject kind, people of the lowest class: cobblers, tailors, bakers, tannery workers, rascals.

Fifth, what did he want from them, the honorable Herr? Oughtn't the nobleman rather go there to their union . . . oughtn't he . . .

Sixth . . .

But the nobleman didn't want to hear the sixth. He had had enough. He thanked them, the spiritual leaders of Godlbozhits Jewry, for their information, and that very day ordered an audit be conducted of the union's books, and then a thorough inspection of the union.

As a result of the review the union's books and documents were sealed and sent on to the supervisory authority. Particularly special attention was paid to conducting a check of those present during a report meeting, and it turned out that more than half of those present did not possess any union identification. Among those the majority were juveniles and even school children.

The executive committee of the union defended the presence of the school youths by saying they were waiting for the lectures of their "evening courses." Obviously this justification was weak and, moreover, wouldn't it certainly be worthwhile to know what was being taught there in these "evening courses"? The history of socialism, historical materialism, and, once again, class struggle in history.

The school inspector took an interest in the matter. He brought to the attention of the director of the grade school that children of school age were not permitted to belong to any organizations and associations other than the school organizations and intramural sports clubs. The director of the school immediately sent home the children guilty of having attended the "evening courses" in the union, and ordered them to come with their parents. Instead of going to see the school director the parents—overworked poor people—went to the leaders of the union:

It's quite true, their children have benefitted greatly from the evening courses in the union, and above all they wanted to know a Yiddish word, but after all, one had to know how to write and speak a little Polish; without that these days you couldn't do a thing.

With no other option they resigned from the "evening courses" for schoolchildren as well as from a wide array of cultural activities that the supervisory authority had prohibited. "This was a trade union," it was explained from above, "and if the union were to undertake affairs other than its professional ones it would be closed immediately."

With that warning the union was returned its sealed books and documents and went back to organizing its activities. But in the meantime the city's burghers and breadwinners had developed an appetite. "But now is the time to close the union once and for all," people said to one another. "If not now, then who knows when there'll be another opportunity."

And unable to find any support for their demand from the authorities, they decided to take care of the matter on their own. First of all, at a meeting of property owners it was unanimously decided that no one would rent any apartment to members of the union, and then the landlord of the building where the union was located should begin court proceedings to evict the union. "Now," one of the property owners joked, "the union would have to decide whether to build their own building or to move into city hall."

The eviction was not so easy to achieve. The building the union occupied was under tenancy protection and the union hired a lawyer for the case. But the landlord hired a better lawyer and demonstrated that the union prevented him from getting any sleep, and additionally that the tenants made a racket in their frequent meetings till late at night. The upshot was that the court approved the eviction.

The union appealed that verdict and that time, too, it lost the case. The bailiff then showed up right away and with the help of foreign men brought in especially for the purpose (in Godlbozhits not a single porter could be found to do the work) removed several tables, chairs, and bookcases out into the street, just as the passion of the members rose to self-sacrificial heights. Each one of them suddenly felt as though he personally was being thrown out into the street. That was how the union was extracted from its cramped pair of rooms and dragged into the large marketplace of Godlbozhits. All you could hear anywhere was union this and union that.

Around the homeless union there started to gather admirers and hangers-on. The bookkeeper at the sawmill, thanks to the strike that the workers had pursued there, had won a 20 percent wage increase, an eight-hour workday, and a month's vacation. Shmuel Zaydman, the pharmacy clerk, had won still more—he had won the sympathy of his old love, Bebele Rabinovitsh.

Here's what happened: When Shmuel learned that the bank had gone bankrupt and that his own bit of money, his savings from so many years of toil, was suddenly lost, at first he wanted to commit suicide; then, when he remembered the blue tongue of the pharmacy clerk girl, hanging before his eyes from the lamp hook, he right on the spot repented of such an ugly death and prepared himself to take poison.

That kind of a suicide by poison would admittedly have been tragic, but entirely natural and in keeping with the worldview of a little person who constantly worked his way up and suddenly fell, breaking his neck. But for Shmuel and his catastrophe a miracle occurred, like the lightning that cures a paralytic in an instant.

Instead of committing suicide, he went to Bebele.

"You know, Bebele, I am convinced that from honest labor you cannot become a wealthy man; I am convinced that those bandits will always find a way to deprive you of your hard-earned penny."

And Bebele, who already knew all about Shmuel's failure at the bank, pretended not to hear.

"You know," she said tenderly, "I like the soft collar on you better than the stiff one."

And he explained further, "So, for example, I squandered my entire youth, not eating, scrimping, you'll pardon my mentioning it, to wash a shirt, guarding my money like an eye in my skull. Heard that Meierbach had gone bankrupt—gave it to the pharmacist; heard murmurs against the pharmacist—insured myself at the bank. And now what? My labor's again fallen into the hands of the bloodsuckers."

"Don't worry, Shmuel, you'll make more money," Bebele consoled him.

"I don't want any more money! I don't need any more money!"

He spoke heatedly and stubbornly, like a little child, as though someone were arguing with him.

But soon he added, embarrassed, "You know, Bebele, I would like to do something for this situation."

"Do what?"

"I don't know. I want to give something for the unemployed."

"You can do it through me."

He took out his wallet, withdrew a few banknotes, and then shook out the purse.

"Here, Bebele, that's everything."

"That's too much for you, Shmuel, really, you can't be left without a penny."

"And 'they' have more?" said Shmuel deliberately. "Please, Bebele, take it. Tomorrow I'll get my salary for half the month."

Bebele put the money in her purse. She thought for a while and said, "If you'd like, you can accompany me to the factory yard, I'm bringing them sweets. But maybe you're afraid?"

Shmuel turned red.

"No, no! I'm not afraid. Why shouldn't one need to . . ."

Bebele started grinding a medicinal paste in a stone mortar and pestle. All of a sudden she dropped the pestle, grabbed Shmuel's hand, and looked warmly into his eyes.

"You must absolutely not wear stiff collars. Ok? And you mustn't smear your hair with grease . . . I don't like it."

"Fine, Bebele."

"I've thought about it and you won't go to the factory with me. You don't need to draw too much attention."

"If you say so, Bebele."

"And I'll tell Nosn about you."

"Nosn doesn't like me; I've disappointed him once already."

"He'll like you soon enough, I will . . ."

"Thank you, Bebele."

Such were the miracles that took place in Godlbozhits in those days. People were drawn in from all sides. From one side there were unsteady intellectuals, erstwhile Zionists, and from the other side raw youths, even underworld characters, whom the struggle had drawn out and impressed, even before they understood its significance. All arranged by Khaykl. He truly did everything he possibly could to display his loyalty. Even Yoyne Roytman, who hadn't had a conflict with the union for a long time, people said, had become quite an admirer of the union. And the miracles people told about his brother Hertske; that one, people said, was an ardent socialist and could even speak to an assembly.

In the narrow circle of the committee a question was discussed: Whether to accept the individual assistance from everyone who was prepared to give it, allowing an ever-growing number of adjuncts glom on to a healthy core till it develops into an impressive ball; or to discourage fellow travelers, sympathizers, enthusiasts from now on, and let all activities be conducted only by the strictly trustworthy?

Khaykl himself was an entire topic of discussion. On the one hand this was his positive, risky work, performed with passion and self-sacrifice, and on the other hand his traitorous, politically unaware, middleman's nature. The local comrades knew his deeds from before, and were of the opinion: "Renounce him, distance yourself from him—neither your honey nor your poison"; the ombudsman, who hadn't been there long, spoke short and sharp: "Harness to the wagon even the devil himself; keep an eye on him, check up on him."

So Khaykl stayed.

With diligence and skill he carried out all of the tasks assigned to him and earned back the trust of a goodly portion of comrades. At the same time, however, he also made his name heard about town, associating himself with all of the actions of the union, particularly the successful and victorious ones. The intense daily activities were anonymous and Khaykl was easily able to spread the idea that everything revolved around him, that everything was carried out according to his orders, that he knew all and ruled all.

And in case that was not enough, in case he thought that he was still insufficiently important, he went back to his old tricks of threats and finger-pointing. When the union sent off a set of demands somewhere, Khaykl straightaway pursued it with his own hand and convinced people he was in charge. If only someone might think, God forbid, that he, Khaykl, wasn't the top man on the totem pole.

But just as often as he bustled about everywhere for the sake of the Jews of the shtetl, he disguised himself and hid from the security

authorities. He removed his cap obsequiously before the police commander and sometimes brought something to his attention. That is, he
was the burgher most utterly loyal to the authorities.

And as for the police commander, why did he need to go looking?
Didn't all those wealthy Jews, shopkeepers, know who the rebels were
in the shtetl? Of course they knew, but so what? They didn't want to
betray their co-religionists, and if so, he'd deal with them.

He started coming to the marketplace more often, making surprise visits to shops and writing reports:

For keeping the shop open one minute after seven in the evening;
for not hanging the license in a prominent place; for lacking a price
list for the merchandise; for not keeping the bread under a glass case;
for not hanging out the national flag on a holiday; for not closing the
door during a Christian funeral procession . . .

He notified the shopkeepers:

He would pester them however long it took until there was a spittoon, and over the spittoon a sign reading *Spit in the Spittoon*; and the
sign should be behind a glass case.

Naturally you could never find those three things together in a
Godlbozhits shop. The mind of a busy, preoccupied shopkeeper never
turned to such nonsense. If the spittoon were there, then the sign was
missing, and if the sign was there, then the glass case was missing. For
not carrying out precisely the order of the thin commander there was
truly no end of misery for the Godlbozhits shopkeepers. But Jewish
shopkeepers had a God in heaven and believed that it wasn't the thin
constable who was their God, just the opposite, their God would tire
out the thin constable.

But the commander didn't tire. He just kept doing the little thing
of writing reports; and then came time to pay the penalty, and again
little things: ten zlotys, twenty zlotys, fifty zlotys.

And money is of course something else altogether. For money a
Godlbozhits shopkeeper would do anything in the world, including
abiding by sanitary regulations.

So there came a day when all of the spittoons in all of the shops
in Godlbozhits were spick-and-span, and above them, demanding

Attention! hung signs behind shiny glass, like the buttons of a soldier on parade.

But the commander discovered fresh sins among the Godlbozhits Jews. So, for example, selling in a shop behind closed doors after seven o'clock in the evening. They might take in a few pennies, but they'd pay a stiff penalty of tens of zlotys.

The commander did what he did—he wrote reports.

And a report is money, crude money; and in order to make money a Godlbozhits shopkeeper would do anything in the world, even close his shop early. But as soon as that hardship was gotten rid of, the commander would devise some new annoyance. Meantime they grew lazy about the spittoons so the commander reawakened them to it, and issued new decrees: You have to set up basins of water with towels and soap in every shop; you have to wear a white apron. What wasn't there to torment a shopkeeper?

And that might have lasted who knows how long. Jewish shopkeepers were accustomed to all kinds of situations, and when a Jew grows accustomed to misfortunes they start looking to him like pleasures. But all of a sudden the thin commander got the itch to pick a fight with the pharmacist. Well, the pharmacist showed him he wasn't just some little Jew.

Here's what happened: The lame pharmacy clerk Szledziński, who during the strike worked maybe two days for the Jewish pharmacist, had, after having been dismissed from his post, begun drinking worse than usual. He could be found regularly lying in the gutter, and in the intervals he made scenes in front of the pharmacy, threatening to inform on the pharmacist, to send him in chains to hard labor in Siberia. At first these scenes made a terrible impression on the pharmacist, especially the idea of being informed upon, but gradually he grew accustomed to it; it was like the barking of a dog.

But one time someone noticed how the lame pharmacy clerk, lying in his customary position in the gutter, had white foam around his mouth. They alerted the police and a doctor: "Poisoned." He was immediately brought to the hospital and resuscitated. "Where did you get the poison?" "From the Jewish pharmacist." It was obvious this was nothing but a slanderous accusation, but in the meantime the rescued suicide it seems had whispered something else, so an inspection of the pharmacy was made and, according to the instructions of the half-drunk, lame pharmacy clerk, a small jar of fine white crystals was removed. In vain the pharmacist claimed that the little jar contained harmless medicine. The commander cited the expertise of the pharmacy clerk and noted that "the rest was for the health inspector to decide."

For the shtetl's anti-Semites led by the Christian pharmacist it was a cause for celebration: Some big shot! The fact was soon written up in the *Great Poland Catholic*, and that paper printed a front-page headline in bold print:

A Band of Cocaine Smugglers Uncovered, The Jewish Pharmacist of Godlbozhits Its Ringleader

By contrast the Jewish pharmacist had gone red as a beet from the story. His old stomach malady returned with renewed vigor and he felt stabbing pains like knives in his insides. Herr Isidore ran back and forth across the room like a wild animal, holding his head with one hand and his belly with the other, bellowing with pain.

Until at last an idea occurred to him.

"Khaykl! Get Khaykl over here right away!"

Khaykl the sexton's son came.

"What's to be done about him?" the pharmacist grimaced with pain.

"About whom?" Khaykl feigned ignorance.

"About the commander."

"There's nothing else for it," Khaykl determined. "He must be gotten rid of."

But the pharmacist didn't have such grand plans. No, that's not what he meant. What he meant was, even if it cost a hundred, two hundred, three hundred, and if it were necessary even more, as long as a retraction was sent straightaway to the *Great Poland Catholic*. The whole city would send a repudiation, signed by the municipal authorities and all of the upstanding burghers. He wasn't very well going to be ruined for nothing. It was a blood libel pure and simple, and all because he was a Jew.

At that moment Iser Meierbach came into the pharmacy. He had come about a private matter, when he encountered the pharmacy couple in an agitated state. The pharmacist was running back and forth across the shop and from time to time clapping his hands together despondently, sitting down on a chair, while his wife, well, she was afflicted with constant spasms.

"What has happened?!"

Khaykl told Meierbach the story of the inspection and the article in the paper, and Meierbach, instead of giving some advice and calmly easing the pharmacist's grief, set upon the pharmacist with sharp words:

"What do you have against him, the wimp! No matter that he's as excitable as a woman, just go say something to him. Is that it?! Galewski is everything? There's no one bigger than him? Were I in your place, foolish man, I might as well tell you, pharmacist, that I would have gone myself to see the Inspector so that he could ascertain right away what's what and accuse the paper of libel himself. And then Galewski himself might yet be out as the local police commander as a result."

Meierbach put the foolish pharmacist, like a wooden golem, into a taxi and rode along with him to Warsaw. On the way back the pharmacist didn't need to be put into a car. He had revived and his courage plucked up, laughing and slobbering, "To the top! Right to the top you should go!"

The Inspector from Warsaw had indeed ascertained that the confiscated little jar contained not poison but fine little crystals of the antiperspirant *salifirin*. Moreover, the inspector added, the pharmacy was in point of fact required to stock cocaine, which it could, however, only dispense with the prescription of a doctor.

"Now," the pharmacist boasted, "I will show him, that thin constable, that I'm not some puny shopkeeper with a spittoon. I'll show him, that anti-Semite!"

"He must be gotten rid of," he argued to the shopkeepers. He only wanted from them some money to cover the expenses. The cheap shopkeepers had taken precautions in advance.

"Money? Who has money these days? Otherwise mightn't a worse dog come? Well, we've already seen such things, 'one mustn't ask for a new king.'"

Fortunately, however, the pharmacist had taken charge of the matter, and along with him came other Jews who were used to working without pay for the public good, lending their hands and their wallets for the sake of the community.

Moshke Abishes went from shop to shop, swearing, cursing, imploring, crying, threatening, and squeezing out money for the expenses. Khaykl appeared where he was needed and no more than glanced with his two criminal eyes: one glance and the shopkeeper would start shaking like a leaf, they would hurry off to their writing desk, to their apron pockets, they would cry and pay.

At first the pharmacist himself should have gone to the prosecutor to detail all the woes that police commander Galewski had inflicted on the Godlbozhits shopkeepers. But once his initial anger had subsided he thought better of it: "It's better to send a memo." A long memo was sent by mail, a petition to the prosecutor, in which were listed all of the troubles and oppressions which the new ruler of the city had perpetrated against the Jews of Godlbozhits, and Khaykl once again went in personal to accuse the thin commander of whatever came into his head. Khaykl, as was well known, was personally acquainted with all of the great noblemen, with the prosecutor and with the judge; he was known by all of the ministers and all of the directors, all of the writers and all of the artists; he was written about in all the books and in all the newspapers.

Deputy Prosecutor Galewski greeted him like an intimate, "Ah, *Panie* Khaykl! How are things in our dear Godlbozhits?"

Instead of an answer Khaykl removed from the inside pocket of his coat a copy of the memo and handed it to the prosecutor.

Prosecutor Galewski took a look at the paper, stretched out in his armchair and yawned.

"Is it so? Is it that you've already sent us this document?"

Khaykl nodded, *"Tak, proszę jaśnie Pana."*[2]

The prosecutor hastily leaned toward the desk. He looked through the stack of papers in front of him and, pulling one out, he began to read it aloud from somewhere in the middle:

"Since the constable Galewski has been senior police officer in the city mischief has significantly dissipated. No proprietor has a right to his property, no businessman to his business. Everywhere the trade union rules omnipotently. When it, the union, wishes, people work, and when it wishes, they strike. 'The appetite grows with eating,' and today in Godlbozhits no one can freely choose a person for work in a shop or factory. For all of this one is dependent upon the benevolence of the leaders of the union, and senior police officer Galewski . . ."

"My cousin," interjected the prosecutor with bitter irony, "instead of undertaking to sweep away evil, busies himself with tormenting and harassing the merchants, with a hail of reports on spittoons that are either too small or too large, for licenses that are crookedly hung."

"It is a fact that two unknown individuals, whom police commander Galewski might have been able to find by expending a modicum of effort, entered the rear door of the pharmacy like thieves, fired a revolver and nearly killed the pharmacist, his wife, and a small child. So, have the police found the terrorists? No. Police commander Galewski sleeps and these acts of terror and violence increase daily, taking on fearful forms. Police commander Galewski . . ."

"Again, Galewski," the prosecutor spat. He leaned toward the desk, hastily grabbing the telephone receiver:

"Hallo . . . Pan Wojciechowicz? . . . *Tak, tak* . . . We spoke yesterday . . . From Godlbozhits . . . Ah, *nie* . . . A trustworthy person . . . On my responsibility . . . A thoroughly honest person . . . Right away . . . I'll send him to you . . . His family? Pan, Pan . . . Khaykl . . ."

2. *Tak, proszę jaśnie Pana* (Polish): yes, honorable sir.

"Szameszson," Khaykl helped.[3]

"Szameszson, *tak*, Szameszson . . ." Deputy prosecutor Galewski put down the receiver, scribbled something on a piece of paper, and handed it to Khaykl.

"So go to this address. Right away. And this paper, and also bring the memo with you."

Khaykl went to the indicated address. Wide stairs led up to the first floor. A long hallway. Little rooms. Many numbered little rooms. Number seventeen. He knocked.

"Enter!" was heard from within.

Without any boldness Khaykl opened the door and closed it gently behind him. A little room completely filled with cupboards and stacks of paper. At the desk sat a solidly built gentleman with a crooked mouth and two piercing little eyes.

"Ah, you are the Herr Szameszson. Please, sit, Herr Szameszson." He took from Khaykl the offered paper, the crooked mouth grimaced amiably, the little eyes piercing.

Khaykl sat. The crooked mouth squinted one eye, and with the other very quickly scanned the paper lying in front of him on the desk, underlining with a red pencil, once, again.

"Ah, so. So your name is Szameszson? And what, pray tell, is your occupation, Herr Szameszson?"

"Me?" Khaykl was momentarily confused, stammering, but soon thrust out his chest heroically, "Me? Everything, *proszę jaśnie Pana*. All the judges know me, and all the prosecutors, and all the doctors, and all the artists, and all the directors."

"A well-connected, that is, a reliable person . . ." the crooked mouth grimaced cheerfully and with affected interest.

"*Proszę jaśnie Pana* . . . In Godlbozhits there are such houses that are maybe two thousand years old, and I can give all of their histories,

3. *Szameszson*: Khaykl is known among the Godlbozhits Jews as the sexton's (*shames*) son; here Khaykl creates an ersatz patronymic surname from that moniker.

as well as the history of King Sobieski, who with his sword slew the dragon, a beast that breathes fire . . ."

"A connoisseur, that is, of antiquities," the crooked mouth said with interest.

"Ask whom you will, *Panie mecenasiu*,[4] ask whom you will among the *jaśnie Panowie*:[5] when people come to Godlbozhits for the summer, they come first to Khaykl, to me. Well, all the summer visitors just adore me. For me, well, they go gaga for me . . ."

"A tour guide for the summer visitors, that is."

Khaykl took offence, "With all due respect to *jaśnie Pan mecenas*. By us a tour guide is, well, one who provides, well, I wouldn't like to say what . . . I am, *proszę jaśnie Pana*. I am one who provides information, I am."

From the inside pocket of his coat he took out a small packet of papers. He searched, rummaged, pawed through them and removed one with a large round seal, laying it down on the desk.

"Here, *proszę jaśnie Pana*, is the certificate from the municipal authority."

"I beg the Herr Information Provider's pardon," the crooked mouth became serious, one eye squinting entirely shut, and the other trained with all its piercing intensity on Khaykl, "but might the Herr Information Provider be able to provide me with a few pieces of information?"

"About what, *proszę jaśnie Pana*?"

"About a girl. A little Jewess."

"If I know her, *proszę Pana mecenasia* . . ."

"You know her. You certainly know her. After all, she's from Godlbozhits."

"Who is it?"

"One by the name of Zosia; Zosia Lerner, they call her."

"No longer in Godlbozhits, she left."

4. *Panie mecenasiu* (Polish): Mr. Attorney.
5. *jaśnie Panowie* (Polish): the honorable gentlemen.

"Not far. She's somewhere near Godlbozhits. I know it precisely. For shame, Panie Szameszson," the crooked mouth said cheerfully, "that you, an information provider, know less than I do."

Khaykl waved his hand with disdain, "Big deal, if it was at least a girl, as I understand it. You call that a girl?! As tall as this desk. I know artistes from the cabarets, real beauts . . ."

"Ah!" the crooked mouth gave a start. "And you know Nosn Shifris?"

The piercing eye followed every movement on Khaykl's face; Khaykl hesitated.

"I know him," he said.

Now the crooked mouth got up from his chair, went over to a cupboard, opened a door, pulled out a small drawer and removed a file.

"And Enzl Buterbrot, do you know him? And Moyshe . . . Moyshe Shusterman, do you know him?"

Khaykl nodded.

"And now," the crooked mouth moved his chair closer to Khaykl's, "would you perhaps by any chance know the names of those who fired shots in the pharmacy? Perhaps . . ."

"How should I know that?" said Khaykl, already agitated.

"Please, you are getting upset, Panie Szameszson. That is not seemly. I am asking you because you are an information provider. What? Is that not so?"

Khaykl was silent, lowered his head. The crooked mouth opened a silver cigarette case.

"Please, help yourself."

He lit a match himself, lit a cigarette, took a deep drag, and held the smoke in his mouth for a long time.

"Ah! By and by. It interests me . . . whether by any chance you know who organized the strike in the bakeries that left Godlbozhits without bread for five days?"

Khaykl spoke softly, "No, I don't know."

"And perhaps you remember the strike at Meierbach's factory? Perhaps you know who led it? Maybe you are familiar with who ordered the machines to be destroyed?"

Khaykl was trembling.

"Me? How would I?"

"There's nothing to be upset about, Panie Szameszson. Please, you've declared yourself to be an information provider, so I have thought to find out from you about a few trifles that are of interest to me."

"Certainly I am an information provider," Khaykl regained his composure. "A true information provider for the greatest noblemen, but I have nothing to do with that scum."

"And how much, Panie Szameszson, if I might know, do you make from your information providing to these greatest noblemen?"

"I used to earn nicely, but today—little, very little. The noblemen have become poor, the whole world is poor."

"But how little, how much roughly?"

"It's not worth mentioning. Sometimes ten, sometimes fifteen zlotys a week."

"And how might you be disposed, Panie Szameszson . . . But please, don't be offended . . . How might you answer if I were to offer you a permanent position?"

"I don't understand. What does the *Pana mecenas* mean?"

"I mean, a secure position, not counting bonuses for each piece of information."

"A . . . nark?" said Khaykl frightened.

"An information provider," the crooked mouth grimaced.

"Not that."

"Really? Think it over . . ."

"I've already thought it over."

"No, just think. Consider it well. No one ought refuse to do his civic duty. You, Herr Szemeszson, I hope, are a loyal citizen; you, Herr Szemeszson, are an official information provider, acknowledged, as you yourself have said, by the municipal authority. I expect you to help the administration in its concern for peace and order. I hope to see you here often."

He held out to him a long hand.

"Good-bye, Herr Szameszson."

→ 32 ←

The Forty-Year-Old Man

Yoyne Roytman turned forty years old. According to all modern psychologists that is, without exception, a critical period in a person's life. A matronly, eminent lady at that age will fall in love suddenly and passionately with a young and desperate hazard player; an aristocrat, a father with grown daughters, an exemplary husband and a respected attorney, will allow himself to be drawn into a love affair with a syphilitic cabaret singer; while others at that age, those who formerly transacted great business deals, start going bankrupt, likening it to becoming wealthy men. As for Yoyne Roytman, he was on the threshold of his fifth decade. After a difficult struggle for survival and having climbed his way up he now fell victim to a small youthful passion.

Having begun as a small lad as the whipping boy of a coachman, he quickly earned a reputation as the greatest specialist in noblemen's saddle horses in Abele Babisker's band of thieves. Then he abandoned this risky profession and became a coachman of his own and little by little did some business in the horse market with a combination of stolen and purchased horses. Just when cars took over—first as a conductor for the Meierbachs and then as the owner of a bus—he turned respectable, started putting some zlotys together, bought his wife a plush coat, fell in love with Leah "Stänglmeier," shouted louder than the cantor during the priestly benediction, outbid in the synagogue for the recitation of Jonah, and was chosen to become a member of the community council.

Until the crisis suddenly arose and it all evaporated. He even had two buses already, but both were repossessed for delinquent payments.

The tax office was suffocating him with taxes, and now, as if out of spite, his passengers were being snatched away.

Twice already today he drove empty to the train station and back. Now it was getting to be toward evening. It was a shame to have to burn the lamp. Yoyne stretched out on his seat inside the bus and waited for the train to arrive.

The driver sat at the wheel, yawning. Yoyne unburdened his heart.

"They should all burn up, those cars, till not even a memory is left. I swear, I'll douse them with gasoline and light them myself. Then won't the bailiff have to come and take them away?"

The driver had heard but didn't turn around. Maybe he believed Yoyne's threat, and maybe not. At any rate, he just sat indifferently behind the wheel, yawning with everything he had. That's drivers for you: the boss could rack his brains trying to figure out where to scrounge up enough for the tax installment and he could keep driving back and forth completely empty just as long as he fiddled about at the wheel, driving wherever and regularly taking home his pay.

The approaching train could be heard. Yoyne went out through the door of the bus, stuck his hands into his trouser pockets, and looked with resignation at the empty platform. The rakish visor of his cap hung loosely down over his eyes like the lower lip of an exhausted horse; now they'd have to schlepp on.

Suddenly he jumped up from his spot, Yoyne did. Coming down the station steps was a single passenger with a very large, imposing belly and a small leather satchel in his hand. The satchel was taken cordially by Yoyne's capable yet none too refined hands. The engine made a growl; Yoyne turned over the starter. "Ah, good evening to you, Panie Meierbach! An unexpected guest."

Iser Meierbach rested his short, fat fingers on his soft knees. His strained, imposing belly spilled over with pleasure, and his grinning, wide face injected into the conversation a pair of satisfied, cunning little eyes.

"Didn't you recognize me, Yoyne? Ha-ha-ha! Fine times! So what did you think? That when one leaves shitty Godlbozhits one suddenly becomes a different person, one goes about dressed like a human being, associates with people. Eh? Yoyne . . ."

"Of course," Yoyne agreed, "and when did you leave the factory again, Panie Meierbach? It might cause a bit of a to do."

"The factory you say, eh?" The laugh lines smoothed out on the industrialist's face, which flushed with red blood, the swollen, cunning little eyes spun round with their stinging side up. "Ah, would that it had burned down, the factory, ten years ago, along with all of Godlbozhits! Ah, it should have gone up in flames so that no trace remained! So, Nosn Garber's going to be my breadwinner, my provider!"

"You're not going to work at all?"

"Do I need to work? Let the Belgian horses with their big heads do the work. To work and not make any money? Let Nosn Garber work for all he's worth!"

Yoyne said fawningly, "But you produced such a nice piece of leather, Panie Meierbach, aye, now that was leather. Merchants demanded it, delighted over it, suffered apoplectic fits for it."

"Do I need leather?! Dunderhead! I really thought you were clever, Yoyne. I need leather? I have no need for leather! I need money! Money! Do you understand? And the Warsaw cartel of leather-factory owners is giving me money for not working."

"I don't understand: for not working?"

"Dolt! What don't you understand?" The red tension on the industrialist's face dissipated, and he spoke earnestly and calmly. "Come, let me explain: it's in their interest that a piece of Meierbach leather not find its way to market, it's in their business interest."

The bus shook, swaying like a rocking chair. Just then the industrialist observed, "What's this? You've got no passengers, Yoyne?"

"Don't ask, Panie Meierbach, every day fewer passengers and more taxes." Yoyne took out a bundle of papers from his pocket. "You see? This is just what's from the tax office and the regional council, not the municipal authority."

"And every day it's like that? But still, what's become of all the passengers?"

"Everyone goes in the big cars from the Warsaw company. Why should they drive with me to the train station, wait, spend their time there when here one could just as easily drive like noblemen to Warsaw, and cheaply to boot."

"Incredible, the big cars are already going to Godlbozhits?"

"And further on, to Prashnik, and further still, to Chelm."

"And Jews are employed on the buses?"

"My brother Hertske is a conductor on the one that goes through Godlbozhits."

"It seems he himself had a car?"

"Wrecked it, easily done."

"And so what's the news in Godlbozhits?"

"What should it be? Nothing, Panie Meierbach. There was a big demonstration in Godlbozhits on May first, Jews and Christians together, they carried banners and sang songs."

"Really? They were being incited," the industrialist said half angry and half sad. "It makes no difference to me, but I tell you, Yoyne, that all the miseries come from these guys. How long was I able to manage with my peasants in the factory before Nosn Shifris and his gang started meddling."

Yoyne shook his head.

"Quite so, Panie Meierbach. It's not good. And what's the result, that the factory's closed and they have nothing? That they wander around idly, starving to death, that's better?"

The bus drove into the city and stopped. Curious onlookers gathered around the bus, peering inside, and went away disappointed. It was nothing new.

Iser Meierbach extracted himself through the narrow bus door, nearly pulling it off its hinges, and went down the steps. Maybe ten porters rushed over to take his satchel, arguing amongst themselves over it. Iser Meierbach stood to the side, smiling good-naturedly as one of them said, "Believe you me, I'd like everyone to earn some money; but on the other hand, can't I carry this light satchel all myself? But never mind, Meierbach likes people to make a little money off him."

Yoyne ordered the driver to pull into the garage. He was ready to go home and eat his cold supper, while in the meantime a long bus with richly illuminated and curtained little windows had quietly and discreetly slipped into the marketplace. This was the bus from the company. Blind Hertske jumped elegantly down from the bus; from a strap hung a leather purse like the train conductors wear. He saw Yoyne and invited him, "Come, Yoyne, let's get a bite to eat."

They went into the restaurant of Leybish Shmuel-Arn, whom people called "Dead Cat." Hertske ordered beer.

"I talked to the director about you," Hertske said. "I presented the idea to him. If you'll be respectable, behave yourself, it's yours to have. But it's a firm. They like their conductors to be strong young men."

Yoyne drank his beer in silence.

"Well, why so silent?" Hertske asked. "With your bus do you make more than two hundred zlotys a month? But as long as you don't feel like making money on the side you can live and let live."

"What do you mean?"

"I mean, it's a firm with all the bells and whistles. If they catch you at the littlest infraction then it's 'scram, beat it!'"

Yoyne was silent.

"So, what do you think? What'll I tell the director?"

Yoyne was silent.

"So is it yes or no?" asked Hertske encouragingly.

Yoyne stood up, ready to leave.

"What can I say. You're my brother. I can't do without a penny on the side, can't do without a bit of 'offcut'."

The bus's horn sounded, honking out over the dark marketplace like a slaughtered gander. Hertske got up, paid at the buffet, and once again put down his brother who was already standing in the doorway, "You want to be and always will be a total failure!"

Yoyne stood like someone who'd been whipped. "Now is finally precisely the right time to go home and eat my cold supper," he thought, but soon reconsidered. To pluck up his courage he jingled the few coins in his trouser pocket and went over to the buffet.

"Now listen here! Don't doze, Dead Cat! Just make with a tin of sprats and a small bottle of brandy. Right away. And some bread, and herring, and a half kilo of kishke, just the lean part, with pepper. Another bottle. And add three bottles of beer. Another fifteen groschen. What can one get for fifteen groschen? So add three cigarettes."

He loaded it all in his pockets and went off to Leahle.

"Just listen, Leahle, put away the washtub with Moshke's dirty underwear and come here to me. I'm screwed, totally screwed. Tomorrow the bailiff's selling off the bus. But just remember what I'm telling you: Yoyne's still not dead."

Leahle washed her hands with a filthy dishrag. Apart from the washtub with the dirty laundry, two beds, a table, and several broken stools, there was nothing in the house. No trace of the erstwhile restaurant. He had laid waste to it all, Moshke had. That hubby of hers! And now he was wandering around the room, piously girded with a shawl, strolling up and down, reciting his evening prayers aloud and imitating Abele Babisker's mischievous antics. "Why did I need such an old Jew for a husband," Leahle said abruptly. "Would it please me if I were still today a young woman?"

She unpacked the bag that Yoyne had brought home and sliced the bread and the herring. Moshke kept ranging around the room, pacing back and forth, counting the Omer, spitting, reciting a chapter of Psalms.

It annoyed Yoyne, "So tell me, fidgety Hasid, maybe you could sit down already?"

Moshke washed his hands, holding them piously aloft: "*Se'u yedeichem kodesh*,"[1] wiped them well with the towel, once, twice, said grace, and while singing lifted a piece of bread to his mouth.

"Give him some," Yoyne said to Leahle, "let him start with the sprats; he obviously won't eat any kishke, that holy saint."

Moshke took a glass and tasted a drop. "Lechayim! Lechayim, friends!" Then he dunked a piece of bread into the brandy and

---

1. "Lift up your hands in the Sanctuary" (Psalm 134:2).

sanctimoniously emptied the glass into his wide-open mouth. His sunken cheeks blossomed, his extinguished eyes lit up.

"Let them both suffer a disaster, the rabbi and Stänglmeier together! I'll show them all! Young and old alike! My name's Moshke!"

He pulled himself closer to his wife, caressed her bare arm.

Leah jumped, let out a shriek, "What're you pinching me for, you old fool?!"

Moshke knocked back another glass.

"I'm pinching? If it's true let me be stricken! If it's true . . . Me?"

He suddenly doubled over. Yoyne stood over him.

"How many times have I told you not to pinch? How many times?!"

Leahle stuck herself in between them.

"Leave him alone, Yoyne, you've stunned him so he's hardly alive."

"A toothless dog," Yoyne couldn't be calmed.

And meantime Moshke had tossed back another glass, wiped up with his finger the last little bits of sprat in the tin, and tipped out the foam from the bottom of the beer glass.

"Go to bed!" ordered Yoyne. "Go, Leahle, make him up the cot in the kitchen."

Leahle went into the other room and soon came back. Moshke could hardly hold himself up on his feet to recite his evening prayers.

"So, go on already, shattered Hasid!" Yoyne hurried him along. "You've already said your prayers."

"*And thou shalt love the Lord thy God with all thy heart, and with all . . . with all . . .*"

With two fingers Yoyne grabbed him by the undercollar and pushed him with his knee through the door to the next room. Leahle laughed till tears came. Through the wall they could hear Moshke's drunken whines. The lamp on the table smoked from too little kerosene. Yoyne kept unspooling the wick.

"Come here, Leahle, do you love me?"

Moshke appeared in the doorway. Undressed, in a shirt, he stood and trembled.

"It's cold," he whined.

Leahle burst out laughing, "Just look at him! Maybe warm him up a little? Nurse him? Give him a nipple? Just a nip . . . Ha-ha-ha! . . ."

Moshke could hardly hold himself up on his narrow feet, scratching himself.

"Co-o-old . . ."

"Maybe put him in another bed?" Leah asked Yoyne.

"Like hell! He'll show you soon enough, the pig. Guzzled the whole container of sprats."

And to Moshke, "Are you going or not?! Do I have to apply some pressure?"

Moshke made as if to stand up.

"So . . . If I spit, you'll run!"

Moshke went back into the kitchen. On the way he lost his yarmulke so he piously covered his bare head with his hand.

Yoyne was apoplectic.

"Bloated Hasid, *yop yevo mat*!"[2]

And when Leahle finally lay down undressed in bed Moshke's whines could again be heard coming from the kitchen, "Leahle . . . Leahle . . ."

Yoyne was in the middle of taking off his boot.

"Don't answer him," he said.

A moment later, from the other side of the door, "Leahle, I'm not feeling so good, Leahle . . ."

Leahle sat up in bed, listening.

Moshke again appeared in the doorway. His head was wobbling back and forth.

"Go to bed, I'm telling you," Yoyne yelled tense and wrathful. "To hell with you!"

Moshke scratched himself, casting his head back and forth, smacking his lips.

"Maybe just a drop of berry juice . . . Not well . . . Maybe just a bit of cherry brandy . . ."

2. *yop yevo mat* (Russian): screw his mother.

At that very moment a dark object flew across the table, breaking and extinguishing the lamp. The sound of broken glass. Without a groan Moshke slumped down in the doorway, and again there was silence.

Leahle slipped out of bed like a cat, went over to the door, nearly falling over the man lying there.

"Yoyne, what a disaster's befallen me! Yoyne, you've killed my husband!"

Yoyne calmly drew up the slack straps of his trousers, and, hopping on one boot, came over to take a look.

A groan. Moshke sighed and tried to get up leaning on Leahle's arm. Yoyne felt around in the darkness for his other cast-off boot and looked for his jacket.

"You're leaving?" Leahle asked.

"What's it to you?"

"You're just leaving me like this?"

Yoyne turned to her briskly, "Go to bed with that old stinker, it'll be very cozy for you."

Yoyne unchained the door and went outside. He patted his trouser pocket and while leaning on the fence pulled out a little flask. With his palm he popped out the stopper, spat, and tipped back the flask into his wide-open mouth: *glug, glug, glug!* A shake of his head like a wet dog just out of the water.

"Bah, absolutely necessary!"

His heart grew more cheerful.

"Hup! Hup! I . . . I! Ne-ce-ssa-ry!"

He walked across the marketplace. The streetlights were still lit but it was too gloomy. Shadows covered the path. A patrol left the city hall building. The thin constable approached him, "Don't make any scenes, Yoyne, go on to bed."

Yoyne grabbed the thin policeman by the arm, wanting to kiss him, his hot breath fogging his glasses. The thin commander grew angry, "Either go home, or go to jail!"

"To jail? Of course, Y-y . . . Yoyne wants jail, Y-y . . . Yoyne loves living in jail . . . Bah, ne-ce-ssa-ry! A-a-a . . . I . . . Let the constable take him to jail . . . won't do it himself . . . drank too mu-u-uch, dru-unk . . . Ba-ah, necessary!"

So the thin constable accommodated him and took him away, but in the doorway of the jailhouse Yoyne turned stubborn: He wasn't going in on his own; he wanted to sit with the Pan constable.

They stood in the open doorway. The policeman tried to push Yoyne in by force. Yoyne held him by his silver embossed pocket flaps, by his thin little neck.

Together . . . he wasn't going on his own.

The policeman grabbed hold of his revolver.

"Let go, or I'll shoot!"

So Yoyne released him slowly enough that the thin constable could somersault behind him, and his pince-nez fell with a crash onto the asphalt. Yoyne jumped over him and ran into the police station.

He wanted to go over the brick wall into the street, so he ran over to the wall, clawed his way up with his nails, with his knees, tried to pull himself up and jumped right back down with a shredded bloody hand: the top of the wall was strewn with glass from broken bottles.

He was already half sober. Behind him he caught the sound of a bell. Aha! He was calling for the guard. Yoyne understood his predicament; he scurried to the walls and nearly fell over something.

It was a ladder. The ladder led up to the roof. Not giving it a moment's thought he went up, crept along a tin gutter, and scrambled up a tile roof till he reached a corner. A wooden building. Tenons from protruding joists in the corner led conveniently down like stairs.

Now he was in the synagogue courtyard. Was it real, or was he imagining it? In one of the low, semicircular, and barred little windows there was a sudden flash. Perhaps the moon was being reflected in the synagogue windows? But the moon was behind the clouds.

He passed by the little windows. Another light! Darkness. A fear beset him.

"Ghosts . . ."

He wanted to up and run away, but he felt as though he were nailed to the spot. His heart started pounding. "Running away would be worse still," he thought. "'That' would chase you and catch you from behind."

He crept over to the nail-riddled door of the synagogue. A push—the door wasn't locked. So he hastily opened the door. Darkness, an abyss, he couldn't see any stairs down. Suddenly a circle of light, like a large matzah, cut across the Eastern wall. It sparkled, flashed, and disappeared. Everything went dark again.

His ears started ringing. He didn't close the door, trying to remember, but not turning his back. His hands held forward, his eyes burying themselves into the darkness, his breath held—ready.

All of a sudden he saw a light. A memorial candle illuminated the middle of the synagogue, the lectern. And by the lectern—shadows in white *kitl*s.[3] He distinctly heard the voice of a Torah reader, "Let him be called, Yoyne ben Menakhem-Mendl Ha-Kohen, *maftir*!"

Terrified, he remembered that when the dead call one to the Torah, one must go; otherwise, one won't live out the year. Moyshe-Borukh the water carrier sometimes passed by at night carrying two full buckets of water, and from the synagogue would come the call for him to come to the Torah. He would go and make the blessing; the dead would drink the water from the buckets and let him go in peace.

Feeling his way with his hands he moved forward. Ever more clearly and distinctly he saw the lectern with the Torah scroll, and the dead with their faces covered, and draped in *kitl*s and tallises.

Suddenly the moon shone through the window right up onto the lectern. The shadows disappeared. There was no one around him. Alone he stood by the lectern. In the place of the Torah scroll, on the sill there was a rolled up, crumpled tablecloth.

He held onto the lectern and looked around. His eyes stopped at the ark across from him. The ark was open, and in front of it—he was not mistaken, he saw it clearly—a ghost standing in a white *kitl*, standing and not moving.

Yoyne steeled himself, plucked up his courage. He let out his held breath, "Are you a ghost, or aren't you?!"

---

3. A *kitl* is a white outer tunic worn by pious Jews on certain holidays; it can also refer to a shroud.

An echo resounded from every corner, which buzzed momentarily in his ears and again—silence.

The white shadow by the open ark didn't move from its spot. Yoyne collected himself, "Dead is dead!"

He slowly descended the stairs to the lectern, keeping his eyes constantly on the ark. Maybe he was imagining it? No, it was so clear: a white ghost. Yoyne walked on by measured steps, hands balled into fists, teeth clenched. Here he was at last by the porch leading up to the ark. The white ghost stood at the open ark, its hands leaning on the doors. Yoyne lifted a foot—one step. Suddenly the ghost let go the doors of the ark and went down in the opposite direction—one step. Yoyne went up—another step; the ghost down—another step. Yoyne was above—the ghost below. Yoyne started following in the footsteps of the white shadow, going cautiously as the ghost walked by measured steps in the direction of the door. It seemed to him, to Yoyne, that he could just stretch out his hand and catch hold of him. But his hand didn't stretch out, it was stiff, and the ghost walked on slowly, step by step, forward.

But on reaching the synagogue's vestibule the ghost suddenly started to march forward with stiff, booted strides. As for Yoyne, it was as though he were awakened from a daze. His feet bore him and his hands itched.

"Stop, ghost! A spirit!"

The ghost made tracks.

"Stop, you son-of-a-bitch!" On the threshold the ghost got tangled in its white wrappings and fell. In one bound Yoyne was next to him, falling on him like a wild beast, grabbing him by the throat and starting to strangle him. A pair of dark-sleeved arms tore loose from under the white wrappings, searching for Yoyne's neck. Yoyne felt sharp nails biting into his hands, tearing, scratching, burning. He was howling with pain, with murderous burning rage.

But he didn't let his victim go.

⇘ 33 ⇙

Run Away!

Shimen Shifris found himself unexpectedly at the center of partisan work. He hadn't gone looking for it, nor had anyone spent much energy propagandizing him, but it so happened that a short time after getting drawn into the work he was already preparing lectures by his own hand, leading study groups, and speaking to crowds. And, as people observed, he spoke quite well and persuasively. He did not, in fact, belong to the committee, but there was hardly any important action about which he wasn't informed nor his opinion sought.

Once he heard behind his back, "Shimen Shifris is embarrassed about his romantic escapade."

Another time he was simply allowed to hear, "If Fayvele Shpilman's bank still existed and Shimen Shifris were again the principal bookkeeper, he still wouldn't be one of us."

True, he, Shimen, didn't deny that Zosia Lerner had exerted a powerful influence on him in that direction, and he also admitted that unemployment and need had driven him, the self-satisfied bookkeeper, onto the right path. He merely asked whether, even though he had come to the movement by a different path, an indirect one, he was therefore less of a socialist than the others? And he, Shimen Shifris, asked: Why did the comrades have so little sympathy for his feelings? Why were they so . . . indelicate?

He remembered it was the very beginning of the month of May. After a long, hard winter that had cooped them all up everyone was drawn to the green outdoors. The two rooms of the union had suddenly become cramped and stuffy. So people wanted to go on May

Day picnics. In a clearing in the green woods it couldn't be worse than in that stuffy room with the low ceiling.

The group sat in a circle on an empty hill amongst the pine trees. The needles pricked them, leaving marks on their hands and knees. But no one felt it; they were all paying rapt attention to the speaker. Leaning on a tree stood Zosia, with a peasant's floral kerchief on her head, speaking to the group. She spoke about the May First holiday during which hundreds of millions of workers' hearts beat strongly and as one. Everything was expressed in simple and understandable words. But still, Shimen confessed to himself that not long ago such words had stopped speaking to his heart, no longer penetrating his mind. For the first time after many months of bitterness he felt rejuvenated, and didn't know why—was it because of the green of May outside or what was in his heart.

After Zosia a comrade spoke, but he didn't speak for long. The youthful group couldn't sit still in one place for long, nor was it reasonable to weary them with lectures. So they were dismissed and groups scattered over the forest, laughing, chatting, joking, cracking pumpkin seeds, taking out bundles of food, devouring a feast, and filling the forest with talking and gaiety.

Down the road came a dog, a shepherd, and stopped to rub its hindquarters on a tree. "Where there's a dog there's a man," said Zosia, as if a fitting aphorism on its own, and she evaded Shimen's question about what she was thinking about by asking another question, "Look, Shimen, am I not like that little dog, that shepherd?"

"In what way?"

"Here, for example, my retroussé nose."

"You are like," Shimen said gently and with affection, "a village lass."

Down the road came a peasant with a leather bag slung over his shoulder and a gnarled walking stick in his hand. The mailman, the village mayor of Karczówka—they knew him very well.

The peasant extended his greetings, "Good morning! Ho, ho! On a May Day picnic! And what kind of interesting newspaper is this?"

Someone had handed him a humor rag called *The Yellow Fly*. He turned his head, delighted by the illustrations, but one could clearly see it wasn't this he was thinking about. Then he took his leave and strode off, his dog behind him.

Gradually the group started to disperse. Pairs and small groups had formed on their own. Shimen and Zosia went off to the furthest end.

"So, Shimen, do you like the work?"

"Yes," Shimen said definitively.

"Then I would advise you to look for a job, first and foremost a job."

"Are you really saying that?"

"How childish you are. One must earn a living to survive, you especially need to."

"Well, fine," he said somewhat irritated. "But I won't get any work here."

"People are looking elsewhere, some are trying Warsaw. You've rather given up, Shimen . . ."

"Oh! Those Warsaw people. They promise you one thing, but do something that isn't what they promised."

"If you won't do it yourself, no one is going to do it for you."

"But I do have a promise after all," Shimen said bitterly. "Tyko-ciński promised me, Eyges promised me, and even Representative Wojdisławski gave me the nod."

"That can't ever hurt," said Zosia. "Patronage comes in handy these days."

"Spoken like a petty bourgeoise, Zosia."

"Me . . . a petty bourgeoise? No matter, Shimen, I'm capable of many things, you've got nothing to worry about me."

They had nearly begun to quarrel. By the evening they had made up. But the idyll didn't last long. At dawn a comrade arrived, a Christian, and took Zosia away with him. She almost forgot to leave Shimen her contact information, in Rogów. He'd get more information later. Wojciech Makuch.

<hr />

For three days he wandered about aimlessly, sleeping till noon, yawning, idling like a roast on a rotisserie. On the fourth day, late in the evening, he was summoned. At the meeting there were the strange comrade—the Christian—Khaykl, Zalmen, Simkhele, and a few others. The stranger delivered greetings in passing from Zosia, cordial greetings, then right away moved on to the matter at hand:

"Tomorrow is the day of the hunger march. A banner with a suitable slogan needs to be hung in a prominent place. The content should be *Free to Work*."

"Where should it be hung?"

"In a prominent place, probably by the city hall."

"They won't allow that."

"So by the post office."

"Out of the question."

"So where then?"

"On the synagogue," said Khaykl.

"Good," said the Christian.

"I don't think so," said Shimen.

"Why?"

"That's what they say, it's always the Jews."

"You talk like a Zionist," the stranger said.

"Like a nationalist," echoed Khaykl.

"And you, Khaykl, want to provoke a pogrom against the Jews," said Shimen, unable to restrain himself.

"How do you get out?" the Christian asked.

"The way he left," Khaykl repeated.

"Then I won't participate," Shimen declared. "I don't want any part of it."

Khaykl stood up.

"We can do well without the bourgeois elements. Comrades! Who's in?"

Shimen left the deliberations and went straight home. His landlady was already asleep. Quietly, gently he knocked and didn't have to wait long. The chain on the door popped off.

"On the table there's a candle and matches," he heard the landlady's voice from the dark corner.

Shimen reproached himself for making the old lady get out of bed and come let him in.

As it turned out the poor landlady had been very good to him, very decent. On the table was a meager supper: bread, butter, and a piece of herring.

"Take a glass of tea," came the landlady's voice. "It's not so hot anymore."

Shimen went to the kitchen. The baking tins were already cold, but on top of a chafing dish had been carefully stacked a pile of old, washed out rags to hold some heat. From under that heap of rags Shimen took out a boiling teapot.

"Landlady, are you sleeping?"

The old woman didn't answer. Surely she was already asleep, weary from a whole day of toil, vigilantly waiting for her tenant.

Shimen tiptoed to the table. He thought with gratitude about how good people could be. Here this old, childless widow, who lived off of mending underwear and knitting sweaters, had already extended him three months credit on his room and board. Had she been a mother she would certainly already have had an ailing liver and a hole in her heart, but she, this unfamiliar woman, she didn't need to weep for anyone with her rheumy eyes. Did this feeling, therefore, bid her work over hard to feed an unfamiliar person? What kind of satisfaction was it she that derived from this Shimen Shifris whom she strove to get to tell his woes, to show him a hospitable face, full of the finest, kindly smiling wrinkles?

He finished the meal quickly and went straight off to bed. On the bedspread lay a newspaper—the newspaper that came regularly even though he hadn't paid the subscription in three months. Under the newspaper was a postcard from one of his acquaintances in Warsaw whom he had asked to remind Tykociński of the position he had promised. Yes, Tykociński was quite busy with an exhibition that he was readying; he promised to speak with Eyges; Eyges promised to speak with the representative. At any rate, he needed to be in Warsaw, at once. "Don't think that you're the only one Representative Wojdisławski has in mind."

He took a quick look at the newspaper. The first page reported a visit by Representative Wojdisławski to Godlbozhits:

"In April our shtetl received a visit by the Herr Representative Wojdisławski accompanied by Herr Editor Eyges, who spent almost a whole day investigating the condition of the local business and artisan communities. The Herr Representative conferred with the representatives of the commercial organizations and even personally visited some of the stores and workshops, jovially discussing things, as is his wont, with each one. That evening a banquet was held in honor of the esteemed guests. The Herr Representative displayed a good deal of interest in the needs of the merchants and craftsmen, promising to intercede . . ."

Terribly weary Shimen put the newspaper down. He was seized by nausea and disgust, bitterness spilling into his heart. He snatched the postcard from the table and ripped it to pieces. The best thing would be not to know them, those eminent people: the representatives, editors, painters; the pharmacists, Meierbachs, Fayveles. Better to run away somewhere far off where one might never meet all of those ignoble souls, where there might only be such old ladies with rheumy eyes who mend underwear and feed you like a mother; and such girls like Zosia Lerner.

He suddenly recalled a note from the day before that he already knew by heart:

Dear one, behave well. Have you had any news? When are you coming to Warsaw? I love my people, but I long for you—Zenia.

Tears flowed from his eyes. He was simultaneously overjoyed and jealous of those people whom she loved. Before his eyes stood the strange comrade, the goy with the fanatical expression on his face . . .

Calming down a little, he began to take stock of his excited emotions. Where would they lead him? He lay in bed; the lights were out and all around it was absolutely dark and quiet. From the street came the hoarse cries of a drunk. A police whistle sounded, interrupting his thoughts and keeping him from getting to sleep. And how would it be? So he would go to Warsaw, get a job—maybe a good job, under the representative's patronage—he would rise higher and higher. Then he would write to Zosia: "Come to Warsaw, I'm earning good money, we'll live a refined, cultured life."

That unimportant postcard from his acquaintance in Warsaw all of a sudden began to take on some importance. How unartful was he, Shimen, to think that everyone was just standing there ready and waiting for him to deign to come and accept a job. For a position in life one must fight with one's elbows; when they throw you out the door you've got to crawl back in through the window.

Nearly calmed he fell asleep promising himself that tomorrow he would muster himself and go to Warsaw. He had to have gotten to sleep very late because when he opened his eyes it seemed he had hardly closed them.

His landlady was standing over him, terrified.

"Just get up," she said, "there's quite a commotion in the marketplace, the synagogue's been robbed."

"Who, thieves?"

Shimen hastily sat up and broke into the yawn of someone who hadn't slept well. It still seemed to be quite early, and he could have done with a little more sleep, but his curiosity overcame him. In a hurry he resolutely roused himself and, turning up the collar of his jacket, flew out into the street.

Outside still had the look of early morning. Apart from one shop, a teahouse, all of the rest were shut. But in the street stood dense clumps of people. Some spoke and the others pricked up their ears.

Shimen approached one of the groups of people.

"What's happened?" he asked, curious.

No one answered. They shrugged their shoulders, heedless of his question, but from their grave faces he understood that something important had happened.

"Did someone rob the synagogue?" Shimen asked again.

An unwashed young man covered in feathers ran into him.

"Just look how posh he calls it—'rob.' Robbers don't defile Torah scrolls, robbers don't murder people."

He, Shimen, didn't understand, but the tone of that brash young man called for him to be careful. Vexation was written on everyone's face, full of suspicion and contempt for those who either didn't understand or played dumb.

Cautiously Shimen began to ask around, and here's what he learned:

At dawn, when the sexton went to open the synagogue, he found not far from the doorway a dead body—Moshke Abishes. He was completely blue; it seems he had been strangled. The synagogue was unlocked, the ark wide open. All told two Torah crowns, a fescue, and the old Torah cover embroidered with pearls had been taken. One Torah scroll had been thrown down on the ground and another was ripped up and covered with blood. In the doorway they found a discarded bed sheet. It seems that the thieves were prepared to take more but they'd had a scare.

But that was not all:

At the same time the street sweeper noticed a red banner hanging from the synagogue roof. The police set up a tall ladder and took down the banner. The banner was embroidered with white lettering—the kind of broad, white lettering one can only get from little Yosele's shop.

"Today?"

"Today we obviously know that Khantshe, who works in Yosele's shop, is a communist, so the police picked her up for questioning and they're going to demand she give up her accomplices."

"What accomplices?"

"The ones who stole the Torah crowns, who ripped up the Torah scroll and killed Moshke Abishes."

"How could Khantshe be reduced to thievery?"

The thin, poorly shaven cobbler who was filling Shimen in waved him off and smiled disparagingly at Shimen's naivety.

"You, lunkhead! So you also believe that thieves would rip up a Torah scroll?"

Along with other curious people Shimen went to take a look at the synagogue. But they were only permitted as far as the synagogue's vestibule. There lay the murdered man, covered with a bloody sheet. A policeman stood guard and didn't permit either the face of the dead man to be uncovered or the threshold of the synagogue to be crossed. "There will be an inquest," said the policeman sternly.

In front of the synagogue people were heatedly discussing Moshke's death. Old Jews told miracles about his father, Abele Babisker, the horse thief. That Abele would omit not one single Psalm nor one midnight vigil. Moshke took after his father in praying word for word, in observing the midnight vigil, and in getting up at dawn to pray.

Sallow Moyshe remarked kindly, "When all is said and done, he wasn't a bad young man, Moshke. Of course, if he'd had a mind to, he might have lived. But people warmed up to him, I'll have you know, quicker than to the finest rich man."

The Talmud-Torah teacher was listening attentively, crumpling half his beard in his hand and looking at the clump of hair, when he started talking as if to a reasonable person, "Met such an unhappy end . . . you know? Abele Babisker also, it shouldn't be wished on any Jew, died a violent death."

"Really . . ."

Jews shook their heads and smacked their lips, spitting, "A corpse, Lord help us."

"And right on his way to observe the midnight vigil he had to meet such a death," said a Psalm reciter regretfully.[1]

"But isn't it written," refuted the Talmud-Torah teacher, snatching half of his beard into his mouth, "but isn't it written: *shluchei mitzvah eino nizukin?*"[2]

"There's probably something else besides," answered an unassuming voice.

Some sage interrupted him, "How else could it be? He went into the synagogue, probably recognized one of the thieves, and, well, he killed him. How else could it be?"

"He, on the other hand, is already finished," another echoed him. "If you're such a wise man, then prove it, tell me: who are the thieves?"

---

1. Psalm reciters were people paid to recite Psalms to intercede for the benefit of those departed or for the sick.

2. "No harm will befall those on their way to perform a mitzvah" (Tractate Pesachim 8b).

"That's for me to know," the sage assured him.

Shimen already knew almost everything, and understood nothing. All of a sudden he realized that he was wandering around the marketplace without a collar like some shoemaker's lad. So he left the group and went home to recover his composure. In the marketplace there were still thick clumps of people standing around debating, but the shopkeepers were already opening their shops—"A living's a living, and Cain's not Abel."

Shimen washed, smartened up, and was once again ready to head out into the street, not waiting for breakfast. But in the meantime his landlady had come in and held him up: First of all, he should eat something, a well-fed man is something else entirely; and secondly, he shouldn't just roam about the street. The police, they say, are on the hunt, making arrests. It's better to stay at home.

Shimen was spurred on by a fresh curiosity: Who were they arresting? He was instantly at the door, ready to race back out into the street. In the doorway he ran into Khaykl. Khaykl rushed in, in a state of agitation.

"Listen, Shimen, best not to show yourself in the street."

"What's happened?"

"They're arresting the whole group."

"Who?"

"Zalmen they've already taken, Enzl's taken, Moyshe too; Nosn—by a stroke of luck he happens to be in the village."

Shimen blanched.

"What's going on here?"

"Don't ask questions." Khaykl dragged Shimen into a corner. "We have to see about rescuing Zosia. Do you know where she is?"

Shimen trembled momentarily.

"I know."

"Well then, there's no time to waste. She's got to disappear. The police are looking for her. Don't worry about me, I'll manage. But they've had her under surveillance for a while, she's been in prison after all."

Shimen stood as if paralyzed.

"Why are you standing there like a clay golem?" Khaykl said hurriedly. "Every minute might be too late. So go, get her onto the train and away you go! No rooster'll crow . . ."

"Here? At the station, in Godlbozhits?"

"You're right," said Khaykl, "it's risky. They might still be waiting for her."

"Where then?"

"I know . . . better one station earlier: Klemantów."

Shimen left the house. He went by a circuitous route, via River Street. Right beyond the city he got onto the road leading to Rogów. He looked around constantly. No one could be seen in the fields. On both sides of the road the corn had turned golden. Another week or two and the harvest would begin and it would be teeming with people. Meantime, however, it was good that no one was about.

He had reached the top of the mountain and started down the other side. All of a sudden he heard panting behind him. He looked back. At the top of the mountain stood a small, brown dog with pointy ears, panting with its tongue hanging out. The dog looked around everywhere and finding himself face to face with Shimen he ran down toward him swift as an arrow; entwining himself around Shimen's feet without barking, he sniffed and sniffed, and, not detecting anything, ran back up the mountain. "Where there's a dog there's a man," Shimen remembered the old saying, and not giving it any more thought went on his way. Not much time had passed when from afar he spied the first straw-roofed huts of Rogów.

But right there near the village the little brown dog with the pointy ears and an upturned nose caught up to him again. This time there was also a person very close by.

A peasant with a large leather bag slung by a strap over his shoulder approached, coming right up to Shimen.

"Good morning, Pan Cashier," the peasant said, drawing closer and contentedly twirling up the ends of his mustache.

"Do you know me?" Shimen asked with surprise.

"Of course I know you. Who doesn't know the Pan Cashbox Clerk? Ho, ho! Who don't I know in Godlbozhits?"

"What are you carrying there in your bag?" Shimen asked.

"Just the mail, *proszę Pana*, the mail for the whole township of Karczówka."

"Who pays you for that? The post office?"

"You're kidding! The post office is going to pay? The peasants pay, the township pays."

"Do you know where Wojciech Makuch lives?"

"Wojciech Makuch? Of course I know. I'm going to see him right now."

"Are you stopping in Rogów? Aren't you going right to the township?"

"Soon, *proszę Pana*, you'll soon understand everything. I'm carrying the mail right to the township in Karczówka, and from there the village mayors take it and deliver it to all of the surrounding villages. But Wojciech Makuch is 'basically' a regular Joe, a good friend; he gets all the newspapers and letters, 'basically' the peasant newspapers, and he wants none of our peasant-and-worker-unity to make it to the township. There they'd ask right away: Where from? And why? The secretary would open and read all the letters. Makuch is a clever peasant, common sense in his head; he asks me, and I bring them to him right from the post office."

They had come to Makuch's hut. The mailman went inside. Shimen stayed outside. Soon a young peasant came out in a hempen shirt with white linen cuffs. In one hand he was holding a whetstone, and in the other a scythe. Eyes and hair—black, gypsy-like. His face—triangular.

"Are you Makuch?"

"I am."

Shimen told him his name and asked about Zosia. The peasant didn't answer and unceremoniously turned his back on him. He went over to the open barn, attached the sharpened scythe to a narrow box like a trough, and started to cut hay; the straw yielded itself bit by bit and was reaped by this primitive form of chaff cutting.

Shimen stood at sixes and sevens, uncomprehending, and started to consider whether he hadn't been hoodwinked. He made up his mind and followed the peasant to the barn.

The peasant interrupted his work and asked sternly, "What're you going to say? Who are you?"

"I've already told you."

"Are you a child or are you a man? Why do you babble so much, and why have you come with 'him'?"

"The . . . the mailman?" Shimen asked.

"An impostor."

Makuch put down the scythe and softened.

"I," he said, "I know them well, how to deal with them, to deceive them. Listen, go right on over the ditch, find your way back onto the road into town, and turn at the glade of hornbeams. Perhaps you know Jan Materek?"

"Yes, I know him," said Shimen, "the mason."

"Yes, the mason. You can stay with him while you wait for us to come."

"When will you come?"

"That I don't know. Possibly first thing in the evening. It depends. But you must wait and be ready. See to it that Materek prepares a cart."

Shimen took his leave and went off in the indicated direction. It was maybe an hour that he wandered about, lost in the forest, and just when he was close to the hornbeam glade he started to be plagued by fears. The glade of hornbeams was close to the city and what if someone was following him? What if the mason was off at work somewhere? To whom could he turn?

Luckily he found Materek in front of his door. The mason was using an axe to chop the little twigs off a log. His wife was in the field. Materek calmed him down. Everything would be perfectly alright.

That evening Zosia came. She arrived alone; she didn't need an escort. Shimen wouldn't have recognized her: she was sunburned and looked like a peasant girl.

Materek hurried them. The cart was ready, but it wasn't a question of the cart. There wasn't a train waiting, and it would certainly be at least ten o'clock before they would arrive at the station in Klemantów.

They got up into the waiting cart. The well-fed horses gave the cart a tug; the driver didn't need to use the whip, he had merely to smack his lips and they got the urge to run. Shimen and Zosia sat in the middle of the cart on a bed of hay and nearly fell down every time the horses gave the cart a jerk.

In front of them, off in the far distance, stood a dark-blue forest, and over the forest the fiery red half circle of the sun. The other half of the fiery circle had dipped behind the treetops, which turned molten, their canopies catching fire. The silent, pensive travelers gazed at the flaming dusk, at the mirage of little red and pink clouds that swirled, took shape, spread out, and dissolved. The fiery circle kept sinking, diving, shining till it finally disappeared.

"The sun has set," Shimen said quietly, as though to himself.

Zosia leaned her head on his shoulder.

"I'm tired," she whispered.

"Wait, I'll make it more comfortable for you. There, now put your head down."

She stretched out, her head on his knees.

"Is that good, child?" he asked.

"Good."

"Have you really not slept a whole night?"

"No."

"Why?"

"I spoke at a meeting."

"And during the day?"

"Worked."

"In the village?"

"In the orchard."

"What did you do in the orchard?"

"Picked apples, earned two zlotys."

"How can that be?"

"One has to eat."

Shimen got angry.

"Well, doesn't the party give you any kind of support?"

"How well you've got it all figured out. And if there's no money?"

For a moment he didn't know what to say, and then, "Zosia . . ."

"I."

"Are you asleep?"

"Yes . . . No."

He leaned over toward her face. Her eyelids were closed, her lips half open.

"Child . . ."

A cool wind had begun to blow. With his body and his coat he shielded her from the wind, holding the sleeping girl tightly in his arms. If only the cart wouldn't shake so.

"Hey, driver! A little slower."

The driver obediently turned the cart off the road and drove on the side, next to the field. Now they were moving slowly, but calmly and quietly.

It was fully night. All around everything was in shadow. Overhead in the sky the white disc of the moon floated indifferently. Shimen remembered himself as a child at his mother's lap and his mother telling him, "The princess stamped her little foot: Bring me the heart of the little bird that flies under the clouds, the moon will at least be mine."

The little one awoke.

"Was I asleep long?"

"Not even an hour, child; lay back down, you're exhausted."

"No, Shimen, I don't want to sleep anymore. Where are we?"

"We'll be to the train quite soon."

"Not so far then?"

"Maybe three or four kilometers."

"So, am I really going?"

"That's what you want."

"I must."

"And that's it? Is that all?"

"Little fool, I shall write letters, such letters . . . When I can . . . Will you come to me in Vilne?"

Shimen was taken by surprise.

"You're going to Vilne, not to Warsaw?"

"I'm going to stop in Warsaw," she said. "I have only money enough to get to Warsaw. But you'll come to see me in Vilne . . . right?"

"To Vilne—no. I'll go to Warsaw."

"Why don't you like Vilne?"

"And why do you want Vilne?"

"They need me there; I know Belorussian well."

Shimen was silent.

"Why are you silent, Shimen."

He didn't answer.

"Tell me the truth, Shimen. Are you jealous? Of Grisha?"

He looked right into her eyes.

"Yes. That's what I am."

"Go on! I hate that!" She pushed him away, burying her face in her hands.

After a minute she nestled back up to him, throwing her little hands about his neck.

"Come now, Shimen."

"What, Zenia?"

"I love you, little boy. I want to be with you."

"Do you want to get married?"

"Marriage: no. Just to live with you."

"But one must after all, otherwise, a child . . ."

"A child . . ."

"Just like you."

"Just like you, just like me. Half and half."

"The same retroussé little nose."

"Such long fingers."

"Do you want that?"

"Yes, but that's all."

Shimen laughed.

"Why so suddenly?"

"Otherwise I'm not so sure of myself," she said seriously.

"What do you mean?"

"Maybe . . . if I were dependent upon you, weak . . . Otherwise my mind works clearly. I want to be independent; I am drawn to work."

"I would work for both," he said determinedly.

"And me?"

"You would have a child, raise it."

"And you would earn money."

"Of course I would."

"Hubby dear, give me some money."

"You're hurting me, Zosia."

"Fine, little bear, bear of mine. I won't anymore. Hit me!"

"Why?"

"I'm bad."

"You are good."

"You are good, you . . ."

"Zenia . . . Golden . . ."

Suddenly the cart bounced and was up on the hard, resonant gravel.

"Oh! We've made it to the station, to Klemantów," the driver informed them. "The train's not here yet."

But soon thereafter a noise was heard from far off, like before a storm. The train was approaching, pounding, banging, panting, yielding its last breath.

"Is the train leaving right away?" Shimen asked a passing conductor.

"Ho, ho! Still plenty of time. They've got to attach cars, take on water; there's still time."

Shimen and Zosia went into the station. Dusty lamps cast shadows on an ill-rested crowd. There was a line standing in front of the ticket window.

"We've got to stop and buy a ticket," said Zosia.

"I'll do it."

He left her to wait while he went to get in line. A Jewish woman struggled to push her way in. A noblewoman with an old-fashioned chignon and a black cloche on top of her head argued with her, cursing at full force. A policeman intervened, restoring order. A small cart on iron wheels rode past the train station cutting the line of people in two. A gang of porters swarmed the cart, making a din and a racket as though it were carrying who knows what kind of heavy cargo. Meantime the line had been thrown into confusion; but it only took a moment to recompose itself, and once that was done Shimen ended up one of the last people in line.

The line moved forward slowly. Everyone's attention was intently fixed on the little barred window from which a hand ejected tickets and scooped up money. Shimen counted out the silver, the nickel. The extended hand scraped it down off the counter, a bang on the machine, and a ticket popped out.

All of a sudden Shimen sensed an emptiness around him. He looked around. Everyone was scrambling in the direction of the platform exit, jostling, standing on their toes.

With the ticket in his hand Shimen left the ticket window, scanning around for Zosia whom he had lost in the rush of people, inquiring of the person who was standing furthest from the crowd, "What's happened?"

"Some lady pickpocket," he answered, "caught red-handed."

The crowd started leaving through the outside door. Shimen pushed on through from behind. Suddenly he heard: "Undercover agents . . ."

His heart failed him, he nearly shrieked from terror. And on he went, pushing his way forward, scanning: Zosia . . . Zosia . . . Nothing.

He struggled further into the crush of people, getting squeezed into the open door. Now he was finally outside. The crowd dispersed across the platform. Some got into the train cars. Some walked further on up the platform, standing there gaping. A policeman was holding back the crowd, urging them back and not letting them through.

All at once Shimen caught sight right there: Two short, leather jackets behind, and Zosia in front.

For a moment Shimen stood in a daze, his legs paralyzed, but soon he was running forward. Like a moth to a flame he headed on, seeing nothing around him.

The policeman blocked his path.

"Where'd'ya think you're going?"

He wanted to say something, Shimen did; he opened his mouth and emitted some incomprehensible words. Powerless, he turned his head this way and that, looking for help.

"Khaykl!"

An angel from heaven descended. From a door to the second-class waiting area in the station emerged Khaykl. He hesitated a moment,

then came over to Shimen and made a sign for him to be quiet. Shimen
followed him obediently.

They went into a shadowy corner.

"Why are you yelling? Why are you making such a racket?"
Khaykl scolded him.

"But Zosia?!"

"Young man, are you going to help? Do you want to get stuck in
the middle yourself?"

"But Zosia, they've arrested her."

Khaykl brought his whiskers right up to Shimen's face.

"I advise you, Panie Shifris . . . Don't go yelling, just leave, while
there's time."

Shimen's eyes bulged, his breath caught. Something became terribly clear to him. He took a few steps back.

"You . . . provocateur!"

<hr/>

"Hey! You, big shot! Intellectual!" These last of Khaykl's words Shimen heard behind him. His mind was working with perfect clarity:
Leaving Zosia alone—how could he? Follow to the police station?
They'd likely arrest him too and hold him for weeks till he could prove
his innocence.

Home! a judicious voice exhorted within him. Home, and think the
whole situation over, vouch for Zosia, prove Khaykl's frame-up with
the red banner on the synagogue roof, courageously uncover all of his
duplicity.

He ran to the bus station. The Warsaw bus, the one that goes
through Godlbozhits, was brightly lit, its motor running noisily and
the conductor calling the latecomers; he couldn't wait a minute longer.

He had already taken hold of the door handle, one foot on the step.
One moment more and he'd be racing home to his comrades in need.

But all of a sudden a fear gripped him, a gloom. Godlbozhits stood
before his eyes: a dark night in Godlbozhits, and he, Shimen Shifris,
an out-of-work bookkeeper, a sentimental man without a penny to his
name, who had abandoned a beloved girl in her distress and himself

returned to live at the expense of a poor widow. And what would he tell Nosn when he saw him? "I've just taken good care of Zosia Lerner, the Zosia Lerner who was entrusted to me, my Zosia . . . out of every danger . . . in a safe place . . ." And what greetings would he send to her comrades in the city? How would he be able to look them in the face?

"Run away! Run away!" resounded hollowly in the heart of the once solid bookkeeper.

"Ru-un a-way!" echoed a mind accustomed to calculating.

Steam started coming from under the wheels of the stationary train. A trainman with a long hammer struck the final blows over the wheels. The locomotive started panting arduously. A conductor shone a lamp, calling out, "The train to Warsaw—all aboard!"

Shimen opened his clenched hand—a warm and crumpled piece of cardboard—Zosia's ticket to Warsaw.

He didn't know when and how he found himself on the steps of a train car. A conductor with a lamp in his hand came toward him shining the light in his eyes.

"Hey you, eh? Do you want to fall under the wheels?"

And not waiting for an answer he pushed Shimen into the car, shutting the door.

A whistle pierced the air.

"Departing!"

→ 34 ←

You Had, Boor, a Golden Horn

Those arrested were led off to prison in Warsaw. The press was informed in a prominent place: "A criminal cell was liquidated, 'reds' murdered an old sexton, robbed a synagogue and defiled Torah scrolls . . ."

During a discussion evening in the "Democratic Intellectuals' Club," a question was floated: ought one consider thieves and murderers as political opponents.

In the synagogue anxious and learned Jews interpreted the verse: "*Ha-ba lehargekha hashkem ve-hargo*"[1]—meaning I've forgiven you a debt of money, meaning I've forgiven you everything, but one still risks one's life with them . . .

In a meeting of the city council a councilman from the national-civic bloc interpellated the mayor: "Does the Herr Mayor know what kind of criminal activities the councilmen from the 'sixes' are conducting in the city? In that connection, can one still consider their mandate valid?"

The leaders of the democratic parties started to revise their liberal traditions in their struggle with their opponents on the left. Pot-bellied sympathizers of the strikers in '05 gazed with open-eyed astonishment at the past and smacked their fattened lips: "Ah, we were once socialists, revolutionaries."

---

1. "If someone comes to kill you, preempt it and kill him first" (Tractate Sanhedrin 72a).

446

Investigating magistrate Taucher conducted the investigation energetically. The thin police commander Galewski was ostensibly obedient, but he was not a willing helper. The thin constable hated magistrate Taucher, the converted Jew from Galicia, for his religious name, Albert-Maria; for his Semitic shofar nose that stretched from the middle of his brow down over his lips; for his clever, sly eyes; and for the pious way he crossed himself at the littlest opportunity, with his hands at his heart: "Ah Jesus Maria!"

But service is service, and constable Galewski went to the investigation to testify.

The Semitic shofar nose was searching through the reports, asking in a friendly, informal voice, "Has the Herr Commander found any evidence of murder?"

"No, Herr Magistrate."

"Was the murdered man's wife questioned?"

"Yes."

"And?"

"Nothing. She knows nothing. She said he often used to go to the synagogue at midnight to observe the midnight vigil."

"And what is your opinion, Herr Commander? I mean, who are the murderers? I mean . . . communists?"

"Of course they're communists."

"On what do you base that opinion?"

"Well, how shall I put it. The Jews, they have their own ways of reckoning."

Magistrate Taucher's nose whistled sinisterly, his cunning eyes piercing.

"Did you know the murdered man personally?"

"I knew him, but never wanted anything to do with him."

"Why so?"

"Because he was a loathsome Jew. Tried to buy me with a bribe."

"What do you mean 'tried'?"

"Wanted to pay, counted it out."

The shofar nose stood over the paper, whistling cheerfully.

"A fool gives, and a wise man takes."

Constable Galewski stood up straight, his chest thrust forward.

"Herr Magistrate, I inform you. Senior police officer Galewski does not take bribes . . ."

Magistrate Taucher crossed his hands over his heart, chirping piously, "Jesus-Maria! But that's only a folk saying. You are very anxious, Herr Commander."

The thin constable stood in the same position, holding himself stone-still, keeping his head perfectly motionless.

"Following orders, Herr Magistrate!"

The nose whistled with displeasure, "Well, good, good. So you can tell me: Have you found out whether the victim spent time in the company of those arrested? Was he in their society?"

"Just the opposite. According to my information, those arrested had reason to hate the murdered man."

"Why do you think so?"

"The victim was a Jewish informer for the municipal authorities, for the tax office, and . . ."

"And . . ."

"For the police."

"Interesting. Was he, therefore, in contact with the police?"

"In my time, no; it was earlier, during the last police commander's time."

"Did he refuse to serve you by providing information?"

"No. I threw him out on his ear."

The shofar nose was earnestly surprised.

"Why is that?!"

"He . . . He wanted to buy me off."

The nose shook his head regretfully.

"Buy you off."

"Tried," the policeman said spiritedly. "One could buy me off for a drink of brandy, one could *try* to buy me off."

"Buy you off," the shofar nose repeated with parodic liveliness. "Well, that's sufficient, Herr Commander, sign your name."

That was a reprimand.

Another time his cousin, the deputy prosecutor, summoned him to Warsaw.

Deputy Prosecutor Galewski was a handsome, slim man with large, effusive eyes, and a pleasant, sonorous voice. Prosecutor Galewski loved the theater and cabaret, oratory and such like.

He summoned his cousin, "the big commander of little Godlbozhits," in order to speak with him both officially, as a prosecutor, and unofficially, as a cousin. Here's how it went:

He needed to know, police commander Galewski did, that such cases do not happen every day in Godlbozhits, that such a complicated story of a political murder in a little shtetl was rare, and it was an extraordinary opportunity for such a senior police officer to display his talents, to get ahead and advance himself. It's now or never! Only a fool or a layabout would fail to exploit such a golden opportunity. "So, what'll it be, my little commander? Do you want to stay forever with your reports on stinking garbage heaps and dirty spittoons?"

The thin police commander stood straight, head aloft, and looked right at the mouth of his high-ranking cousin. The prosecutor, like a slender rider to his obedient horse, tickled his sensitive belly gently with his spurs: "A political case for a policeman is like a war for a soldier. It's a small task to catch a pickpocket and stick him in the clink; but it's a point of honor for a policeman to catch the organized enemy of the state, the enemy who is often as intelligent as a born government minister, and as bold as a heroic fighter. The effort is worthwhile and the pay is good."

And as they said their good-byes the prosecutor reminded his cousin, "Remember, don't miss the opportunity. You have a golden horn in your hand . . . Do you recall Wyspiański? *You have a hat with feathers on your head* . . . Remember, don't lose it!"[2]

---

2. From *"Wesele"* (*The Wedding*; 1901), a play by Stanisław Wyspiański—*"Miałeś, chamie, złoty róg"* (act 3, scene 35): "You had a golden horn, peasant, / you had a hat with a feather: / the gale blew the hat from your head. . . . Now you're left with

So commander Galewski went home to Godlbozhits and promptly forgot the beautiful oration of his cousin. He got home at eight o'clock in the evening and still found half of the shops open. While he was away the shopowners had been playing fast and loose, reckoning that they were rid of him for a couple of days.

So he got off the bus and straightaway set to writing reports. Having entered a grocery store and found them selling tar grease for a train car he looked behind the counter and found it full of rubbish. So with his boot he swept aside the trash and uncovered a small container of saccharine (for such a discovery the sugar monopoly paid a hefty premium). And so he set to writing reports on all of this, writing and gathering evidence. It took him a whole day and then another day to boot.

Police commander Galewski completely forgot the great political case that was to be for him exactly like a glorious war for a soldier. He hounded the petty shopkeepers, poked around in the day's petty events, and bartered away for pennies the gold coin, the golden horn.

By chance, luck favored him. The enchanted hen came flying into his home and laid her golden eggs.

It was on account of a row between two disheveled Jewish wives: Leah "Stänglmeier" and her neighbor Beyle-Yite, a relatively innocuous woman whose voice, though, should be sealed up!

Leahle, it seemed, wasn't mourning so intensely for her tragically deceased husband if the very day after the end of sitting shivah she set to washing a load of laundry and hanging it out so as to wreak utter havoc on her neighbor's poverty. Beyle-Yite had her own line on the roof on which she hung out her bit of laundry to dry, when the beautiful Leah came and threw down the still wet wash, crumpling it up, making a mess of it, and then hanging out her own flashy pongee blouses, blouses that she should hang, dear Lord, by her hair! Beyle-Yite argued, "Is it your line? May you be strangled and suffocated!"

---

just the cord" (Stanisław Wyspiański, *The Wedding*, trans. Gerard T. Kapolka [Ann Arbor, MI: Ardis, 1990], 193).

"Of course it's mine," said Leah, "So who else's would it be, yours, mangy Beyle-Yitee?!" So Beyle-Yite said, "You whore! Who're you calling mangy?!" Leahle answered, "And who steals fish in her wash-tub in the market?" Beyle-Yite grabbed her adversary by the hair, "You slut! You think people don't know who strangled Moshke?" Leahle turned as white as chalk, grabbed Beyle-Yite by the throat, threw her down, and started choking her.

A crowd gathered: men, women, and children. Yells came from all around: "Come on, break them up!" But no one went near them, and the two women scratched each other's faces, biting each other with their teeth and taking out whole chunks. Soon neither face was recognizable.

A fit policeman came running up, pushed the crowd back, and sep-arated the wild women. He stood in between them and, holding one woman in his right hand and the other in his left, led them off to jail.

The crowd ran after them as if witnessing some marvelous feat; children squealed, making a racket, women scolded, and young whip-persnappers made crude comments, having great fun at the whole scene. Leahle walked on the policeman's right side with a flushed, scratched up face, her eyes lowered, too ashamed to lift her head. She was likely already regretting the whole affair. But Beyle-Yite was as restless as the Sambatyon, flapping her hands and her lips, scream-ing, "She thought she'd strangle me just like she did Moshke! As I'm a mother to my children I myself heard how she gave him one over the head with a weight! She along with Yoyne! Such a whore! Such a slut!"

It all resulted in an investigation. Yoyne was also brought in for questioning. The police commander didn't look Yoyne in the eye when he spoke, rather he spoke into a sheet of paper in front of him:

"Roytman is your name?"

"Roytman, *tak jest*, Panie Commander."[3]

"Age?"

"Two score; that is, forty, *proszę Pana komendanta*."

"What were you doing that night in the victim's house?"

---

3. *tak jest* (Polish): yes it is.

"I'm in love, *proszę Pana* . . ."

"And she?"

"Leahle? She loves me too."

"While the victim was alive?"

"Who asked about him?"

"And what was he? Nothing?"

"Thank God, they let him sleep in the kitchen."

"Tell me how it happened."

Yoyne explained:

"Leahle was already in bed; I was in the middle of taking off my boots; he was sleeping in the kitchen on a cot. Then he comes in naked, scratching himself and wanting to get into bed. So I say: 'Hell's bells!' He just keeps standing there. So I take a boot and give him one in the head. Then he pretends to be dead. So I go to poke him with a finger and he gets up. But I still wanted to give him a whack and he was already up on his feet."

The police commander ordered Yoyne put in jail, and he also arrested the two women, then he himself went off with his report to the district commander. The district commander was not at home, so he had to come back later. The constable had no patience to wait so he went off himself to the investigating magistrate.

"Something important in a matter of murder," he informed him, wound as tight as a string.

Magistrate Taucher read the report, scratching a finger in his nose, and said casually, "Important? This women's talk? Well, leave it be, Herr Commander."

The casualness of the shofar nose, who was setting about scratching with his finger with evident pleasure, infuriated the thin commander.

"I inform you. Senior police officer Galewski informs you that he has discovered the murderers!"

Magistrate Taucher was not impressed, his attacking finger did not stop boring into his nose.

"Well, go on, then. The murderers have already been discovered for a long time."

The thin commander gave a start and went off to Warsaw to see the prosecutor.

He didn't meet his cousin, Prosecutor Galewski, either at home or at the office.

"Later, this evening," an acquaintance of his, the law clerk Maciejewicz, informed him, "the prosecutor would be in."

The thin constable waited patiently, idling like a roast on a rotisserie, pacing the long corridor back and forth. Quite late, the electric lights still aglow, the prosecutor arrived.

"What's happened?" he asked.

"It's about the murder."

"What murder?"

"The . . . in Godlbozhits."

"Well, don't you know the way to the district commander's? You should be ashamed. You, a senior police officer."

The thin constable was silent, standing erect like a telegraph pole, keeping silent.

"What's all this actually about?" the prosecutor asked.

"I have discovered the murderers."

"Ah, so!" Prosecutor Galewski cheered up, his effusive eyes were large and shining like searchlights. "Splendid! You've discovered the murderers! Ah, wonderful! Wonderful! You've done this yourself?"

"Myself, Herr Prosecutor."

"Perhaps . . . Has anyone helped you?"

"All on my own, Herr Prosecutor."

Prosecutor Galewski slipped his hands in his trouser pockets, looked to the side, and spoke in the solemn tones of a voice on opening night, "Perhaps . . . Someone discovered them earlier?"

"Impossible, Herr Prosecutor!"

"Perhaps . . . They have themselves confessed?"

The thin constable thrust forth his narrow chest and blinked.

"There is a report, Herr Prosecutor!"

"A report? A report you say!? On emptying slop buckets? On filthy spittoons?" Prosecutor Galewski walked back and forth across his office, laughing maliciously, laughing artificially, laughter filled with actorly irony.

Suddenly he halted his walking around his office. He sat down astride the corner of his desk, crossing his hands over his heart, his eyes sparkling, clenching his lips with disgust. He declaimed:

You had, boor, a golden horn,
You had, boor, a hat with feathers;
The hat from your head the wind carried away,
The horn sounds in the forest,
Now you're left with . . . the string.

the string!"

Frightened, forgetting to salute, constable Galewski left the prosecutor's office. Either he or his cousin had lost his mind, that's what the thin constable thought as he ran along the corridor, not hearing the call coming from behind him.

Just as he was descending the stairs the voice caught up to him and he turned around. It was his acquaintance, law clerk Maciejewicz, the recorder.

"I heard everything," said Maciejewicz while shaking his hand. "Our prosecutor is a little . . . a strange one; good, but strange."

Constable Galewski complained, "And what have I done to deserve this? Because I discovered the murderers?"

"What do you mean—'discovered'? After all, they themselves confessed . . ."

"Who confessed?"

"Well, the ones who were arrested . . . the communists . . ."

"The . . . communists?"

"Obviously, well yes, confessed . . ."

"How so?"

———

Police commander Galewski stood for a moment perplexed. That meant he had led the investigation down a blind alley. And the quarreling women? And Yoyne Roytman's statement?

But all of a sudden he felt a personal pain. A great injustice had befallen him. He remembered his cousin's words and perceived in them an insult, a great insult.

Like a beaten child he complained to Maciejewicz. Maciejewicz commiserated with him, "Yes, yes, a tough job, police service; no matter how much effort you make it's never enough, no matter how much effort you make."

"Besides," Maciejewicz went on, "Herr, friend, you mustn't get too worked up over it, better have something to eat. As it is I'm parched. I really wanted to suggest: let's go to dinner."

"But you know I don't drink, on principle," said the constable.

"Whatever; this time you'll do it as a favor to me. After all, you wouldn't want to insult me, right? I would be quite insulted. And you, you haven't had a very good day today. This will make you feel better, you'll spill the worm. Bah! A tough job, police service?"

"Ah," the commander groaned. "When one can't catch a break . . ."

"Now just leave it alone. Better let's talk about happy things. You know why I've held you up? Soon one of your little Jews from Godlbozhits will be along, a good chap! Certainly you know him, Khaykl Szameszson. Has he got Jewish women! Oh, has he got Jewish women! I tell you, real little brunettes, with smoldering eyes. Here he is now!"

Khaykl arrived. He was wearing a new leather jacket. Galewski offered him his hand tepidly.

"Is the Herr Commander coming too?"

"Yes," Maciejewicz answered for him.

Soon all three were sitting in a tavern drinking. Constable Galewski drank more than the others, silently knocking back one glass after another, his eyes swimming in brandy, and he never uttered a word. A melancholy of sorts was gnawing at him, eating his heart. Suddenly, for no apparent reason, he got up from his seat, took a drunken step forward, a step back, and bellowed like a slaughtered ox:

"To insult me! Why?! Wh-y?!"

→ 35 ←

Justice

The whitewashed walls of the Godlbozhits courthouse offered a modest greeting. The "hall" was hardly wider and only a little longer than a peasant's hut. The ceiling hung low on the walls' shoulders with massive pine rafters, netted with dust and cobwebs, breathing with old, moth-eaten acts and even older justice.

The table—the "green" judge's bench—was made of yellow-painted boards, planed down, covered with a kind of a frayed cloth, which bore every bizarre shade of green, stained with ink and soiled by the sweaty peasants' paws of the assessors, the aldermen.

The honest, sober aldermen were seated upon fixed carpenter's benches. The task of signing their names was like rolling heavy logs; beads of sweat like kidney beans stood out on the wrinkled, furrowed brows, on the blood-filled, greasy necks of wealthy peasants. Assessors.

The judge was a quiet, washed-out, emaciated thing in a black, old-fashioned morning coat. He rose, ordered the crucifix kissed, and "in the name of the Republic" hurriedly enumerated sentences of two days, two weeks, three months.

From time to time there was a sentence of six months. Some embittered peasant spoke ill of the government and the magistrate had passed judgment. Then—it was said—the emaciated old judge took out a white kerchief and spent some time blowing his nose; or perhaps he was crying into it. He, the little old man in the dark, threadbare morning coat, went on to condole with those nearby that that was the first time he'd had occasion to mete out such a harsh punishment. Perhaps he had a soft heart, that old judge, or perhaps he was no jurist (one of the last prewar magistrates). At any rate, after the verdict the

456

defense attorney whispered in the defendant's ear: "Six months, that's a lot for him! Maybe he can no longer count?" The defendant laughed at the joke, and about a month later the old judge retired.

How surprised, therefore, the low, whitewashed walls became when one beautiful day they observed a great ado, a preparation, a polishing of the floor, a clearing away of the cobwebs. The little, stooped bailiff ran hither and thither on mincing, twisty little steps, like a poisoned mouse, spreading a new, green cloth over the table, wiping the silver crucifix with his sleeve, testing the rusty bell, placing next to the table three borrowed arm chairs, and in front of them two lecterns.

"All rise! Court is in session."

One after another the three judges entered in their black robes with green trim. The first to sit at the table was the fat Herr with the gold-rimmed glasses, after him the other two judges on either side.

The yellow, poorly planed table gave a groan; the presiding judge cleared his throat and, coughing, looked around through his gold-rimmed glasses at the people in the hall. The packed house lowered, shrunk, and sat down.

Among the clear, fluid words of the indictment that the presiding judge beat into the green tablecloth with his chilly, cold-rattled voice, two were caught distinctly, flying up to the ceiling and resounding with a terrifying echo over the low, white walls:

"Article such and such . . . fifteen years in prison . . ."

"*La boga*," a peasant let out a pent-up groan of terror.[1] The presiding judge interrupted his reading for a moment and with stern malice in his gaping eye looked over his gold-rimmed glasses. Advocate Dobosz smiled encouragingly at the defendant. His smile said: "Just be brave, have no fear," and the prosecutor caught the smile, digesting it with satisfaction, and relayed it by confidently ironic lips, by radiant, effusive eyes up to the judges' bench: "Advocate Dobosz is defending—that itself is the best indictment."

---

1. *la boga* (Polish): Good God.

Advocate Dobosz was a slender, blond young man with mild facial features. If he'd had a beard he would have looked like Christ, but his eyes spoiled it all with his steel eye-reflectors. A kind person, with a sensitive heart, defendants loved him, but that didn't mean success. There was seldom a political trial in which Advocate Dobosz acted for the defense that didn't result in prison time.

And nevertheless, knowing this, defendants still asked for Advocate Dobosz, no one but Comrade Dobosz for the defense.

Earlier it would have been someone else: the famous Advocate Miller, the man of phlegmatic speech and iron reasoning, the famous winner of political cases.

It cost a treasure of gold. People scraped and scrabbled it together, friends gave their last penny, their pay, overtime—and once again it came up a little short. Mountains of small change were converted to banknotes, to dollars, brought to the famous advocate with the phlegmatic speech and the iron reasoning. He honestly and forthrightly conceded, "I have undertaken to defend the accused. Of general political matters I will not speak."

"Why, Herr Advocate?"

"It is of no significance to the case, that is empty show."

"But, Herr Advocate . . ."

"But what? We—let us be candid with one another—I have undertaken to defend your accused, but not to be a spokesman for your political beliefs before the court."

"And if one of those arrested should die in prison, is that also nothing?"

"What has that to do with the case? Is it not enough for people to die in freedom?"

"But, Herr Advocate . . ."

"But what? How strange you are. What would you say?"

"She was healthy; there are witnesses."

"What witnesses? Galloping consumption is no subject for witnesses; that's under the authority of the report of the prison hospital, the prison doctor."

"And where did the consumption come from?"

Advocate Miller stood up.

"Well, please. Well, be so good," the phlegmatic speech trembled lightly like a tapped tuning fork. "Am I then a doctor? Am I a medical man? Please, please . . . I am an advocate, I know how to undertake a defense, logically, to plead with appropriate argumentation, but not how to obstruct the court, not—empty show."

But those arrested would dig in their heels.

"You say Miller? Fine, let it be Miller. But Comrade Dobosz must also be there. A certainty of prison? It is easier to bear the hard years of prison if Comrade Dobosz is for the defense."

<hr />

The leather jacket swore on the Bible. The leather jacket testified:

He himself had worked for a spell in the union, thinking it was a trade union like all of the unions. It turns out, he was convinced, it was a criminal cell. They received money from abroad. Nosn Shifris had a steady salary . . .

"He's lying!" someone protested from the dock.

Two healthy policeman's hands pushed the disrupter back down; the presiding judge warned that he would punish, severely punish. And Comrade Dobosz's mild smile encouraged.

"The accused Shifris," the leather jacket continued with his tongue whetted in the big city, "ostensibly transported peddler's wares and notions to the village, but in truth he was never in need of resorting to such a wretched livelihood. The salary that he received from 'there' was enough for everything. He lived well, eating, drinking, and doing the easy work of inciting the peasants against the government, the laborers against the lords; conducted a wide-ranging criminal agitation in the village, arranging meetings during which their 'den mother' Zosia Lerner gave her incendiary criminal speeches."

There was a stir in the hall. One of the judges leaned over to the presiding judge, asking something quietly, and the presiding judge declared aloud, "Zosia Lerner, otherwise known as Regina Bojman . . . was active under false papers, real name unknown . . . died in the prison hospital from galloping consumption . . ."

Then the witness went on to talk about the rest of the defendants. He knew them all, often having conflicts with them over the tactics of the trade union. He, the witness, was always in favor of limiting themselves to purely professional matters, of coming to a peaceful settlement with the employers, whereas the defendants were always constantly inciting the workers to illegal demonstrations.

He began to repeat himself, the witness did, getting tangled up in his own flood of words till what he had to say stopped interesting anyone, even the judges, and the presiding judge declared, "This testimony is over; the defense may begin questioning."

Advocate Dobosz trained on the witness his steel eye reflectors.

"How long has the witness been in Godlbozhits?"

The leather jacket looked arrogantly right into his eyes.

"A year, more than a year . . . a year and a half."

"And how was the witness employed, when in Godlbozhits?"

"A merchant, a broker . . . various things."

"And how is the witness now employed?"

The presiding judge interrupted, "The witness has the right not to answer the question."

The defense: "And how was the witness occupied at that time?"

The presiding judge: "I do not allow the question; it is irrelevant to the matter."

The defense: "Perhaps the witness can then say from what he makes a living? A person must after all live off of something?

The witness: "Trade . . . various things."

"Trade? Trade in what? In textiles?"

"No."

"In shoes?"

"No.

"In food."

"No."

"Perhaps as a partner in a business?"

"No."

"Perhaps an agent for an insurance company?"

"No."

"Perhaps . . . a procurer for older gentlemen? Perhaps a pimp?!"

The presiding judge gave a start, banged on the table in a fit of coughing: "Impermissible! I shall punish!"

The tension in the defense attorney's steel eye reflectors subsided, his stern eyes turned mild, submissive. This calmed the presiding judge a bit.

But for the defense attorney it was merely a respite, a pause, in which to load his two ocular batteries with new tension.

He took out of the file on the lectern a piece of paper with an official seal, stating calmly, "I ask the high court to admit into evidence this judgment of the Crown Court in Warsaw. There it states that Khaykl Szameszson, on the seventeenth of September, therefore eight months ago, was sentenced to a month of mandatory imprisonment for being a broker of prostitution . . ."

The hall erupted. The presiding judge quickly snatched up the paper, hiding it under the pile of files. The judges on either side hardly had time, over his elbows, to catch a glimpse of the letterhead of the Crown Court.

And with that he rested, Advocate Dobosz did. He had no further questions.

———•—•———

After the closing statements of the defendants the court adjourned for its deliberations. The deliberations lasted a long time. Early on everyone had been tense, concentrating their attention in the direction of the door where the judges were sitting and deliberating, but later that tension subsided. The hall suddenly grew dark; a storm had started up outside, threatening through the window. The defendants lowered their weary heads into their hands and were lost in thought.

But suddenly the hoarse voice of the little bailiff interrupted their thoughts: "All rise! Court is in session."

And then the presiding judge spent a long time wiping his gold-rimmed glasses with a soft white cloth, set them on his nose and over his ears, and read, quietly, the formulaic beginning of the verdict, the names of the judges.

And then more loudly:

"Nosn Shifris, a tanner; for belonging to an illegal party and conducting illegal agitation in city and village—six years in prison.

"Enzl Buterbrot, a baker; Zalmen Mosman, a bootmaker; Moyshe Shusterman, a cobbler; for belonging to an illegal party and conducting illegal agitation in city and village—four and a half years in prison.

"Simkhe Tishelman, a painter's apprentice; for belonging to an illegal party—three years in prison."

And so on with names, professions, numbers . . . for belonging to an illegal party.

"The court has taken into account the lower cultural station of the defendants. An appeal of the verdict is in effect."

Editor Eyges, who had been in attendance till the end of the court proceedings, immediately cabled the verdict to his paper, *The Jewish Courier*, under a sensational headline:

TWENTY-SIX AND A HALF YEARS IN PRISON
IN THE GODLBOZHITS TRIAL

⇨ 36 ⇦

What the Sighted Did Not See
and What the Blind Hertske Did

The downpour had just subsided. The marketplace was empty and glistened with puddles of rainwater in the anemic light of the electric streetlamps. From a side street a long richly illuminated bus slipped into the empty market, its little windows curtained like a boudoir. It circled around, reversed, and came to a stop.

The conductor, the blind Hertske, exited, leaving the door open behind him. He searched quickly through the tickets in his leather purse and asked the approaching porter, "Hey, no passengers to Warsaw?"

The porter shook the last few raindrops from the glossy visor of his cap, and answered, "It seems the dark-haired writer's going."

"Eyges?"

"The devil knows him, whatever his name is there."

"You can find him in the hotel," Hertske said, "he likes his beer."

"Well then . . . I'm off! He can give you the disease and stomach troubles."

"What are you talking about?" said Hertske, astonished. "Yoyne said . . ."

The porter interrupted him, "Forget it! He was once a beggar, went about without any shoes, loved to give a drink of brandy. Today he is Panie Editor! You could die for a penny of his . . ."

The driver pressed the horn. Like a severe asthmatic attack, or like a slaughtered gander, a sound tore through the empty marketplace and died away.

463

Descending from the hotel on the mountain came a man with a wrinkled fedora, a wide traveling coat, and a black shovel-like beard. He walked completely within the area covered by the headlights. He approached and got in.

The door to the bus was still open. From within the padded-leather seats, the gleaming nickel bars advertised, inviting the empty marketplace: "Just drive with the buses from the Warsaw company; they're comfortable, cheap, convenient."

One more passenger got in: a leather jacket. Including the writer there were now two passengers boarding in Godlbozhits, and two travelling through, from Prashnik or further still.

Those two—a young man with a substantial, bespectacled nose, and a girl with a stylish little hat on her head—were carrying on an interesting conversation amongst themselves.

"Do you know what they call Godlbozhits?" the bespectacled nose said. "They call Godlbozhits nothing other than 'union city.' Without their union no one would dare hire or give anyone a job either in a factory or in a store."

"My dad wouldn't let himself say who he'd hired in his store," the stylish little hat protested.

"What do you mean? Not in Godlbozhits," the bespectacled nose assured her.

"So what can they do, my dad doesn't want it? Oh! Don't you know my dad? Dad is stubborn. How he can dig his heels in!"

The bespectacled nose shook his head back and forth skeptically, unconvinced about her stubborn dad.

"The Godlbozhits 'boys' . . . they can give you a bang from a revolver in the middle of the room!" he tried to take the little red hat by surprise.

"Had dad sent for the police," the little red hat was not at all surprised, "they'd have been put in prison, and there they would have stayed."

The bespectacled nose assured her, "Well, I wouldn't envy your dad that. And when they are imprisoned, do you think, what, there wouldn't soon be others in their place? And had their whole leadership been imprisoned a year ago others would have taken their place right away."

At that the stylish little hat completely gave in, asking politely, "You are from Godlbozhits?"

"From near Godlbozhits," boasted the bespectacled nose.

Blind Hertske got in, looked around with his good eye, evaluating the passengers. He glanced at the baggage; everything in order. Then he sat down in the very back, taking out something to chew on.

The leather jacket who was sitting near him asked, "Are we going to stay here long? Can I still get off for a moment?"

And the passenger in the wrinkled fedora who was sitting in the front behind the driver turned his head toward the rear and sent over the back of the seat a bit of his shovel-like beard.

"Perhaps we can go already?"

"Seven minutes," Hertske answered and chewed his dried snacks indifferently.

The leather jacket stood up, went over to the luggage net, and tried to pull out a suitcase.

A man's coat fell off of the suitcase.

"Ah, excuse me," said the leather jacket, "is this your coat?"

The bespectacled nose answered politely, "Don't worry about it."

With his hand the leather jacket brushed off the new coat he had just picked up, smoothed it out, and lay it back on top of the suitcase.

"Will you be gone long?" Hertske asked.

"Two minutes," said the jacket, already at the door.

He got off, then lingered. A broad-shouldered policeman had approached and stuck his nose in, asking, "What's all this then? So few people?"

And just like that he had gotten on board, the broad-shouldered policeman had, looking into the ceiling, in the lamp, at the passengers; he walked over to the luggage net and smiled widely as if embarrassed.

"Whose is that suitcase?" he asked the bespectacled nose.

"Some gentleman in a leather jacket."

"And the coat?"

"Mine."

The policeman lifted the coat up, looking underneath it.

A few papers, leaflets, fluttered down from the luggage.

The policeman picked one of them up.

"And so what's this?"

No one answered.

So he, the policeman, slowly took down the coat, unfolded it . . .

Ho, ho! A full bag you've got!

Blind Hertske stopped chewing, a piece sticking in his throat. The black shovel-like beard turned around, looking, watching, observing. The stylish little hat moved over, separating herself from the bespectacled nose, pushing herself into a corner.

And the broad-shouldered policeman encouraged the bespectacled nose, "Your pamphlets? Who gave them to you?"

The nose was mute with surprise, stammering, "Panie Officer! Me? How? Me?"

And right away he became more animated, grabbing for his trouser pocket.

"Me? I am a Zionist-Revisionist."

He took out a briefcase, opened it wide with trembling hands, searching, searching, then drawing out a cardboard card.

"Here is my identification card, Panie Officer."

"And do you have a passport?" the policeman asked.

The bespectacled nose handed him his passport.

"Come with me," he said curtly.

The bespectacled nose sat as though nailed down.

"Take your coat and come! Quickly!"

The bespectacled nose stood up as though he had a pain in his back. He wanted to say something, stammered, but nothing came out. The policeman let him by, hastily gathered up the fallen leaflets, and followed him out.

He slammed the door of the bus after him, but someone soon pried it back open from outside. The leather jacket entered and asked, frightened, "What's happened? Arrested?!"

No one answered. Blind Hertske felt his trouser pocket, cinching the belt around his belly.

"What's happened?!" the leather jacket asked again with desperation.

No one answered. Then he slammed the door, running into the street.

Blind Hertske, his right hand in his trouser pocket, hurriedly opened the door with his left hand, pursuing him.

The driver cleaned the windshield, amplifying the light from the headlights. The two remaining passengers leaned toward the driver, watching with goggling eyes the brightly lit exterior.

They saw people running from all around, whispering, speaking surreptitiously.

They noticed the leather jacket pushing his way into the crowd, his neck stretched out forward, snooping around, and after him, step by step, the conductor.

The driver once again amplified the light from the headlights so the group was illuminated. People pushed, the circle grew tighter; and the leather jacket kept pushing boldly, with his elbows, making his way into the middle.

The conductor followed him.

Suddenly there was a bang. One, and then another! Shots! The crowd scattered in a panic. Who shot?! Where was the shot?! The leather jacket teetered, his feet wobbling like a drunkard's, and he fell.

The crowd scattered. Apart from the leather jacket two others remained in the field of vision: the policeman and the bespectacled nose.

The door of the bus opened wide. The passengers looked around: the conductor.

"Take off!" commanded blind Hertske.

The driver bent over, pushed the pedal; the machine made a growl and moved.

✤ 37 ✦

The Reporter Is Scrupulous
and the Editor Is Moral

The clock said quarter to nine. Shimen Shifris snatched the bag with the roll from his pocket and went down into the street. Now they'd surely have to wait fifteen minutes for the streetcar; that was always just his luck. The upshot was he was going to be late again to the office.

His luck served him well this time. Just as he left the gate a streetcar approached. He still had time to run to the stop and climb on board.

The benches inside the streetcar were all occupied. Some of the passengers were reading newspapers, others were looking seriously, grimly in front of them.

"What kind of a deathly earnestness has come over them?" Shimen was pleased with himself, that he could so easily head down his stairs and catch a streetcar right away. He went out onto the stairs to the where engine-operator stood. He was in a cheerful mood: the streets looked festive, washed; the air was brisk, fragrant; the houses were covered in shadow, like little elderly women who squint their eyes to help against the abundantly delightful sun.

"And what about his brother with the six years in prison?" He drove away that evil thought as with sticks. Why should he be tormented with evil thoughts? Why should he punish himself? Why should he be gnawed away at like rust? Could he help it?

"*Today! Moment! Today! Moment! Je-ew-ish Cou-ri-er!*"[1]

---

1. *Haynt* (Today) and *Moment* (Moment) were two of the most important Yiddish newspapers of interwar Warsaw.

A ragamuffin with a sack of newspapers under his arm was running after the streetcar, screaming at the top of his lungs: "Terrible train catastrophe with human casualties! Sensational trial! Another horrifying murder in Godlbozhits!"

Shimen made a sign with his hand; the little boy hopped onto the streetcar and asked, "*Today? Moment?*"

"*Courier.*"

Shimen took the paper and scanned the headlines:

TERRIBLE TRAIN CATASTROPHE WITH HUMAN CASUALTIES

Paris. 14. The suburban train number . . .

He'd get to that one later . . .

THE GERER REBBE GOES TO THE LAND OF ISRAEL

Shimen scanned further:

BRIDE BITES OFF GROOM'S NOSE
THE PANNA SALA FROM SMOCZA STREET . . .

"Such a thing couldn't happen in a month of Sundays," Shimen smiled and turned to the second page of the newspaper:

HORRIFYING FRATRICIDE
ONE WORKER MURDERS THE OTHER

[¶] We were telephoned from Godlbozhits. Yesterday at 8:30 in the evening, while the worker Khaykl Szameszson was calmly walking in the street, a gang of unknown persons approached him. One of them shot him twice from behind and left Szameszson dead on the spot. The murderer fled. As we were informed by a reliable source the murder was carried out by one Simkhele Tishelman, a painter worker, known by the nickname "Revolution"—a well-known cutthroat in Godlbozhits. Given as a reason for the murder was the fact that the victim was against the use of terror in the various economic actions of the trade union. (For more on the murder read the editorial in today's issue.)

Shimen pulled out the middlemost pages of the newspaper and folded them in half. Within a decorative border, in fancy letters:

Villain, Why Have You Slain Your Comrade?
by D. Eyges

Elsewhere in our paper today the reader will find a notice concerning a new horrifying murder in Godlbozhits. This time both the victim and the murderer are members of a trade union. The murder, as may be seen in the notice, arose from ideological differences between the murderer and his victim.

The writer of these lines has struggled for years in speech and writing for extensive democracy on the Jewish street; the writer of these lines is known for his sympathies for the Jewish working masses. Daily the newspapers bring news of demoralization, treason, and provocation in the ranks of the professional labor movement. All of these facts are known to the writer of these lines, and if he has been silent till now, it was a feeling of responsibility and great concern for the fate of the working masses that dictated this silence. Now, however, one can no longer be silent! Innocent blood cries out! Something terrible, horrifying has happened! The face burns with shame, the heart bleeds with pain, the pen refuses to write. What has become of those beautiful dreams of liberty and fraternity? What have you done with the immaculate ideal called socialism?! Blood! Worker blood flows. It is not the hand of the Czarist executioner that has spilled that blood. Oh, no! One brother murders the other!

The engine operator turned the handle roughly. At first the streetcar seemed to stall but soon gave a lurch forward, howling like a gale.

Shimen looked around: "A new world . . ." Again he missed his station by a stop. He swiftly put aside his newspaper, ready to jump off the streetcar, irritated—always the same thing—he gets lost God knows where in his ideas and then has to head part of the way back.

THE END
1934

Leyb Rashkin (pen name of Shol Fridman; 1903/4–39) was born in Kazimierz Dolny, where he was the manager of a cooperative bank as well as several hardware stores. He began writing stories in the 1930s and his only novel, *The People of Godlbozhits*, was published in 1936. The novel is a fictionalized version of his hometown, mordantly depicting and analyzing the social and political stratification and struggles surrounding the decline of the shtetl in the interwar period. *The People of Godlbozhits* was awarded a literary prize by the Polish Jewish PEN club. Rashkin was killed at the outbreak of the Second World War as he tried to escape to the Soviet Union.

Jordan Finkin is a librarian at the Klau Library of the Hebrew Union College in Cincinnati. A specialist in modern Jewish literature and Hebrew and Yiddish poetry, he is the author of several books, numerous scholarly essays, and articles. His most recent book, *An Inch or Two of Time: Time and Space in Jewish Modernisms*, explores the metaphorical intersections of time and space in Jewish modernism. A book on the Yiddish poet Leyb Naydus is forthcoming.